Enter the unexp[...]
darkness an[...]
Discover the brilliantly [...]

John Gideon

Kindred

*The hypnotic and shocking novel that
redefines the word "vampire."*

An ordinary man discovers the nature of evil in the jungles
of Vietnam—and unwittingly inherits its darkest gift. Now,
home in America, he learns the terrible truth about what he
has become. And soon, he will come face-to-face with others
of his own kind . . .

Golden Eyes

*The spellbinding story of an ancient vampire—
and the town that surrendered to his will.*

The good people of Oldenburg, Oregon, were fascinated by
the reconstruction of an ancestral mansion in their town, trans-
ported from Europe stone by stone. And they were irresistibly
drawn to the strange man who built it. A man who unleashed
the darkest passions in their souls . . .

Greely's Cove

*John Gideon's smash debut novel—
an epic masterwork of small town terror.*

The first miracle in Greely's Cove was a joyful one—the
sudden cure of a young autistic boy. The other miracles were
different, stranger, and darker. Now every man and woman in
Greely's Cove is terrified by evidence of human sacrifice . . .
and resurrection.

Titles by John Gideon

KINDRED
GOLDEN EYES
GREELY'S COVE

KINDRED

JOHN GIDEON

JOVE BOOKS, NEW YORK

KINDRED

A Jove Book / published by arrangement with
the author

PRINTING HISTORY
Jove edition / April 1996

The Putnam Berkley World Wide Web site address is
http://www.berkley.com

ISBN: 0-515-11724-2

A JOVE BOOK®
Jove Books are published by The Berkley Publishing Group,
200 Madison Avenue, New York, New York 10016.
JOVE and the "J" design are trademarks
belonging to Jove Publications, Inc.

PRINTED IN THE UNITED STATES OF AMERICA

10 9 8 7 6 5 4 3 2 1

For Pooski,

Who rode her bicycle down to the sea,
And lingered in the sand to talk with me.

Prologue

May 1992

DURING THE LAST seventeen minutes of his young life, Ron Payne got laid. A hundred heartbeats after the final jolt of orgasm, he ran his fingers along the backbone of the undulant creature stretched next to him, savoring the satin feel of her skin and the sweet smell of sex, never dreaming that he had so little time left.

"Want a toot, babe?" he asked. He felt compelled to play the host now that they'd gotten to know each other.

"I don't do drugs. I'll take a smoke, though, as long as you're up."

With exactly fifteen minutes left to live, Ron Payne shook a Camel filter from the pack on the bedside table, lit it, and gave it to her. "Don't set the bed on fire, okay? I don't have renter's insurance yet."

The woman sighed and gazed through the floor-to-ceiling window at the lights of the city below, her cigarette glowing orange in the dark. "Ronnie, I can't tell you how good I feel right now. This is what we were both made for, don't you think?" Her accent was Southern honey—golden sweet and slow.

"It's what we were made for," he answered, grinning in the dark.

Within a mere month, Ron Payne's life had come together like the knitting of a broken bone, bringing him money, respect, a shiny future. This woman, too, had become his, willowy and dusky, her eyes exotically mismatched. An hour earlier she'd literally materialized in his living room while he'd been in the shower, having gotten in without benefit of a key— the kind of miracle that only happened to guys who wrote letters to *Penthouse*.

He'd seen her around the clubs during the past few months, always alone, always mysterious, and he'd fantasized over her more than once, imagining with great precision the exact moves he'd made only moments ago in this very bed. *Amazing what a little fame and money can do for a man—right, pard?*

Down on the streets of Portland he'd been just another grungy metal man with tattoos and wild rock-and-roll hair, someone to avoid, someone to protect your teenage daughters from. Only weeks ago he'd lived as a squatter in the basement of the warehouse where his band had practiced, in a musty room with concrete-block walls and paint cans for furniture. But that sojourn into purgatory was behind him now, all part of an irrelevant past. Up here the air was sweet, and the stars burned clean.

God, is it good to have money, or what?

Ron Payne, twenty-four, was the lead singer of Demon Beef, a "particularly corrosive" heavy-metal band, in the words of a local underground newspaper writer. For the past six years he and his cohorts had made the rounds of every sleazy venue in Portland, Oregon, rocking and rolling their hearts out for a slim percentage of the gate and all the bar food they could cram into their faces. Ron had lost count of the apartments from which he'd been evicted for nonpayment of rent, not to mention the meals he'd missed. He'd lost count of the drummers, keyboard players, and rhythm guitarists who'd come and gone, not to mention the rapacious scumbags who'd called themselves managers. He'd lost count of the girl-friends who'd given up on him and walked away, leaving him to endure his restless nights alone.

Over the years Demon Beef had gathered a following among Portland's metallic rock hounds, and Ron had become a minor local celebrity—reputation-rich but cash-poor. A year ago the band had started playing regularly at Satyricon, a rock-and-roll club in northwest Portland, where an executive of Kaleidoscope Records eventually heard them. The rest was fairy-tale stuff, right out of a small-time rocker's wet dream. The executive had offered them a chance to cut a demo at Kaleidoscope's studio in L.A. The tape had turned out good (*damn* good, in fact) and had brought an offer of a recording contract. Kaleidoscope had then bought two dozen of Ron's songs for sheet music and had booked Demon Beef on a national concert tour as the opening act for Megadeth, one of the heaviest heavy-metal groups in the land.

Demon Beef was now big news in town. A week ago the *Portland Oregonian* had run a long feature on the band in its Arts and Entertainment section, replete with color photos, a tribute to local boys made good. THEY'RE DOING THE DEVIL'S BIDDING! read the tongue-in-cheek headline, a play on the group's Satanist themes and visuals. The piece had included a color close-up of Ron in full snakeskin makeup, snarling into the camera like a thing possessed. "That ought to generate some letters from the religious right," he'd quipped to the photographer.

Since receiving his first hit of money only a month ago, Ron had leased a used Porsche, rented this showy apartment in fashionable Washington Park, and scored more cocaine than he could use in a year. He'd bought two new guitars, a Fender Stratocaster for the stage and a Marten acoustic to write songs on. He felt as if he had everything he would ever need.

"Tell you what, babe. I'm going to do my nose, and then I'm coming back to bed to let you do my hose."

The woman laughed softly. "I guess that sort of thing comes naturally to you songwriters."

"Hey, I'm just getting warmed up. Stay put, okay? And don't set the bed on fire."

"You've already told me that." She pulled his hand to her lips and kissed his palm. Ron shuddered with delight: he had no inkling that his life would end in a mere six minutes.

Wearing only a pair of leather wristbands studded with pure silver rivets, he padded into the bathroom, where he switched on a light and pulled a Glad freezer bag from a drawer. He poured a mound of white powder onto the marble countertop. With practiced ease he used a shiny straight razor to pulverize the lumps, then channeled the powder into four straight lines.

"Want to know something, babe?" he asked, his voice bouncing harshly off the bathroom tiles. "This success trip scares me a little. My music is pretty angry, right? When you get beyond all the shit about demons and devils, I'm talking about the world like it really is, and there's a lot to be pissed off about out there. But I'm not *out there* anymore—I'm in here where it's clean and warm and comfortable. I'm a little worried about staying pissed off.''

He fetched a small chrome tube from the drawer and bent low, holding the tube in one nostril. He sucked up a line of cocaine, took a few deep breaths, and moved on to the next. After doing this one, he stood upright a moment. A stirring reached his ears from the bedroom, leading him to believe that the dark woman was moving around on the bed, making herself ready for him.

''You needn't worry about losing your anger,'' he heard her say in a voice husky and low. ''I'm willing to bet that it outlasts you.'' The coke ignited a chilly fire in Ron's nasal passages, which he enhanced by breathing hugely. He had less than four minutes now.

''I don't know about that, babe. It was easy when I spent every fuckin' minute wondering where my next meal was coming from.'' He sucked up the remaining two lines, the last cocaine he would ever do. The cold fire exploded again, producing sparks behind his eyelids. After massaging his gums with the last stray grains of the drug, he killed the light and padded into the bedroom. His eyes took a moment to readjust to the gloom, and he was momentarily blind. A breeze licked his naked skin, telling him that the woman had opened the sliding-glass doors that led to the deck.

''What's the matter, babe, did you get a sudden case of the hots?'' He chuckled to himself as her sprawling image gradually took shape in the dark, and his dick started to get hard again. He lay down beside her, but she made no move to welcome him. She lay as silent as a Nordstrom mannequin, except for her breathing, which seemed weirdly guttural.

Ron endured a sudden, irrational thrill that clawed its way to the front of his mind and hung there like a big ugly spider. He'd felt nothing like it since he was a little kid, when some tiny sound had stirred him awake in the dead of night, leaving him trembling under the sheets.

She's changed.

His hard-on withered, and his throat constricted. He reached for her tentatively and found her skin slick with slime. Her eyes stared at him with an eldritch light behind them—one eye warm with bloody fire and the other with glacial ice. She sat up suddenly, a lunatic shape that might have escaped from one of Ron Payne's songs.

"There's magic in your anger, Ron," she rasped, "but it's not enough for me. I'm sorry."

Unlike the images in his screaming music, this thing had breath. It breathed rage. Ron stared stupidly at her, his mouth dry as cotton, his jaw working and yawning. The final few seconds of his life ticked away as moonlight glinted off her teeth, as something sliced through the dark with a faint hiss. He felt it pass over his throat, and suddenly his windpipe was clogged with blood.

Part One:

The Man With the Deep Blue Shadow

One

i

THOUGH THE BLAST occurred at least a thousand meters away, it rattled Lieutenant Lewis Kindred to his core. A dark speck caught his eye, rocketing up through a geyser of gray smoke. "What the fuck . . . ?" His stomach did a slow flop. "Is it incoming or what?"

"Engine block," muttered Specialist-4 Jesse Burton, the most seasoned .50-caliber gunner in the platoon, his marble-hard eyes following the speck as it fell to earth. "Some poor motherfucker ran over a mine or something."

Lewis keyed his radio headset and ordered the platoon to halt. His four squad leaders relayed the order, and the ten armored personnel carriers, or "tracks" as the men of the scout platoon called them, growled to a stop. He switched frequencies and called the battalion tactical operations center, which lay in a laager some ten kilometers from this noxious, tangled corner of Vietnam: "Main Rancho Four Zero, this is Tango. I'm approximately five hundred meters north of Charlie Papa Five. I've just observed an explosion about one klick to my west, lots of debris in the air. Looks like someone hit a mine or a booby-trapped artillery round. . . ."

"That was no mine," muttered Lewis's driver, PFC Danny Legler, a squat lad who spoke with the ponderous, common-sensical monotone of the rural Nebraskan that he was, "and it sure as hell was no artillery round. That was at least a god-damned five-hundred-pound bomb." He clucked and wagged his large blond head.

"Leg, what the fuck do you know about five-hundred-pound bombs?" demanded Specialist T. J. Skane, the M-60 machine gunner, a lanky black kid from L.A. "You wouldn't know one if it crawled up and licked your dick."

"Cut the man some slack," said Jesse, standing now in the cupola of the track to get a better view. Tall and bull-shouldered, he wore a fragment of an olive-drab T-shirt tight around his head, a "do-rag," which was de rigueur among young black GIs in Vietnam. Beneath his flak jacket he was bare-chested but for his dog tags and a plastic peace symbol on a chain. "The gooks can handle any fuckin' thing we throw at 'em, man. Charlie finds a dud five-hundred-pounder out in the bush somewhere, and presto, it ends up buried in some fuckin' road, converted into a fuckin' mine."

He turned to the fifth man on the track, a boyish little soldier with high cheekbones and severe almond eyes. Tran Van Hai was a "Kit Carson," a former Vietcong who had joined the American side. "Ain't that right, No Bick? Fuckin' NVA don't sweat no little old five-hundred-pounder, do they?"

Hai apparently knew little English, and he usually responded to questions with a phrase that to American ears sounded like "no bick." In the hybrid lingo that Americans and Vietnamese used on one another, it meant simply, "I don't understand," but Lewis's men suspected he understood much more than he let on. T. J. Skane had pinned No Bick on him as a nickname.

"So how about it, Hai? Did your old homeboys bury a five-hundred-pounder in the road and booby-trap it?"

"No bick," said the little man, avoiding Jesse's eyes.

"Why bother askin' him?" ventured Skane, grinning savagely around his granny glasses. "He'll just sit there like a frozen jar of piss and say 'No bick' until his hair falls out and his ass drops off." Danny Legler guffawed when he heard this. He thought T. J. Skane was the funniest man on God's green earth.

Lewis adjusted his headset so that one earphone rested atop his steel helmet, leaving one ear uncovered. After listening to a short radio message, he nodded unenthusiastically toward the gray mushroom in the western sky. "The Old Man wants us to go over there and check it out."

"Why doesn't that surprise me?" grumbled Jesse.

Lewis unbuckled his seat belt, stood, and made circles with his hand above his head, signaling his squad leaders that he wanted a meeting. They dismounted and gathered at the rear

of his track for a confab that lasted a mere two minutes, long
enough for Lewis to tell his NCOs to approach the blast site
in a disciplined tactical formation. Sergeant Marino's squad
would take the left flank, Sergeant Hillman's the right. The
platoon sergeant, a profane old lifer named Markowski, would
lead the two remaining squads in the center.

"Maintain strict fire discipline and stay alert," said Lewis,
wrapping up. "That device, whatever it was, could've been
command-detonated, which means the bad guys might still be
in the area. And make sure your people are wearing shirts, flak
jackets, and steel pots, for Christ's sake. The Old Man's gonna
be in a chopper overhead, and I don't want to get my ass
chewed because somebody's out of uniform."

The "Old Man," which was what the troopers of the 2nd
Battalion of the 22nd Mechanized Infantry Brigade called their
forty-year-old commanding officer, was notorious for his temper, and nothing could set him off faster than the sight of a
GI without a shirt or helmet.

ii

Lieutenant Kindred's scout platoon rumbled westward out
of the Ho Bo Woods, leaving behind a wasteland. Since 1965,
the Americans had saturated the area with the defoliant Agent
Orange, pounded it with B-52s and artillery, and bulldozed it
repeatedly in a futile effort to deprive the enemy of their bunkers and tunnels. By 1970, the once lush jungle had become
dusty and desolate, a riot of dead and broken tree trunks, useless to anyone but the enemy, ironically, who found the revised
terrain easier to negotiate and suitable as a staging area for
guerrilla attacks on Saigon and its environs.

Belching black diesel fumes, Lewis Kindred's tracks
emerged into an open area sectioned into orchards of nut trees
and gardens of manioc, sweet potato, and peanuts. Though the
monsoons had ceased in early September, a month ago, the
twenty-ton fighting vehicles left wet ruts in the red laterite soil.

The soldiers rode atop the vehicles, sitting on ammo crates and flak jackets, or, as in Lewis's case, actual passenger seats cannibalized from wrecked trucks or downed helicopters. To ride inside a track meant certain death if it hit a mine or took a rocket-propelled grenade, so even the drivers sat topside and used extensions made of metal tubing to work the throttles.

Lewis pointed his platoon northwest toward the column of gray smoke rising from a dirt road. Behind the cloud reared an extinct volcano that Westerners knew as Black Virgin Mountain, a hazy purple mound against the warm morning sky. Many old folks among the Vietnamese believed that the Black Virgin, whom they called Nui Ba Den, was a sleeping goddess who would someday awaken to unleash destruction upon the land. Gazing now at her war-scarred face, Lewis felt a premonition squirm like a snake in his gut.

A light observation helicopter, or "loach," orbited overhead as the platoon approached the mysterious blast site. In it was Lieutenant Colonel Gilbert Golightly, the commanding officer of "Triple Deuce," as the 2nd of the 22nd was known. Over the radio he tried to describe what he saw on the ground below, what Lewis and his platoon would find when they arrived.

But the scene around the crater defied words.

iii

At a distance of two hundred meters from the blast site they found twisted shards of metal, engine parts, and ragged chunks of human bodies. As they drew closer, the grisly wreckage became denser and more ghastly. The explosion had showered the land with bits of clothing, luggage, watches, eyeglasses, jewelry, arms, legs, heads.

The crater, which was easily thirty feet across and six feet deep, lay a quarter mile outside an unnamed hamlet, where a dirt road passed between a stand of bamboo and a rice paddy. The demolished frame of a civilian bus hunkered near the rim of the crater, a skeleton with its sides blown outward, its roof shredded. The scene was eerily silent, except for the furious buzzing of flies that had attacked in legions to feast on the atrocity.

Lewis deployed his platoon in a tight defensive circle and ordered the men to dismount, leaving one man on each track for security. The scouts approached the bus on foot, taking great care where they stepped, their weapons ready. Jesse Burton stayed close on Lewis's heels, for Jesse was his RTO whenever they dismounted—"radio telephone operator" in the acronymic language of the army. Using the radio strapped to Jesse's back, Lewis stayed in touch with his men in the tracks and with the Old Man in the chopper overhead.

"Main Rancho Six, this is Tango," he said into the radio handset while stepping carefully over a fragment of an old woman. "The vehicle looks like a civilian bus, one of those old Isuzus you see everywhere. Apparently it hit some kind of high-explosive device, equivalent to three hundred, maybe four hundred pounds of C-4, judging from the crater and the damage. There don't appear . . ."

He gagged as his eyes alighted on the remains of a young woman. Her body was gone below her rib cage, though her yellow *ao dai*, the traditional full-length tunic worn by young Vietnamese women, was mostly intact. Her pretty face appeared unharmed except for the gray neutrality that signified the fleeing of life. Death, Lewis had learned during his six months in Vietnam, leaves the human face void of emotion, as blank as a round of cheese.

". . . to be any survivors."

"Tango, this is Rancho Six. Can you estimate the number of casualties?"

Lewis's stomach roiled. The bus, he figured, could have carried thirty passengers by Western standards; by Vietnamese standards at least three times that many. "I estimate ninety dead," he heard himself say.

Colonel Golightly informed him that a company of "Little People" was en route from the town of Trung Lap, just a few miles to the south. "Little People" was American code for

ARVN (pronounced "Arvin"), which stood for Army of the Republic of Vietnam. Their job would be to clean up the mess, and—while they were at it, maybe—to mourn their butchered friends and neighbors. Many of the ARVNs from Trung Lap likely had relatives among the dead.

"I want you and your men to un-ass the area as soon as the Little People get there," continued Golightly. "They're liable to be tetchy when they see what's waiting for them, and the last thing we need is some kind of incident with our allies. Then I want you to conduct a sweep of the hamlet to your north. I'll bet you a case of George Dickle that the guys who did this are hiding up there, and we better find 'em before they do it again. Got a good copy?"

"This is Tango. Good copy."

iv

Lewis Kindred had arrived in Vietnam barely six months earlier, a newly graduated philosophy major from the University of Oregon. Beyond his next-to-worthless sheepskin he owned little but the distinction of being a next-to-perfect poker player, a status that he'd pursued ardently since early boyhood. He'd landed in the war zone just in time to participate in the U.S. Army's "incursion" into Cambodia, where he'd received his baptism of fire.

After Cambodia, Triple Deuce received assignments in the notorious Michelin rubber plantation, which lay in the shadow of Black Virgin Mountain; in the Boi Loi Woods and the Ho Bo Woods; in the infamous Iron Triangle; on "VC Island" south of Saigon; and finally, back in the Ho Bos again. Lewis had seen his share of corpses during the first half of his tour, and he'd seen enough suffering, destruction, and accidental casualties to last three lifetimes.

But *this* was by far the worst he'd ever seen—anywhere, anytime.

"Careful where you step, L.T.," warned Jesse Burton,

grabbing his arm. The nickname was simply the abbreviation for lieutenant. Lewis glanced down and saw a severed arm so filthy with red mud that he'd almost failed to recognize it for what it was. The dead fist gripped the handle of a wicker cage, into which the owner had crammed four or five live ducks, a common way to transport fowl in Vietnam. Incredibly, several birds were still breathing and quacking loudly, having somehow survived a blast that had killed every human being on the crowded bus.

Suddenly Tran Van Hai darted in front of Lewis and snatched up the cage. He wrenched the dead arm off the handle and tossed it away as if it was so much garbage. "Numbah one chop-chop," he said, holding up the cage and grinning into Lewis's face. "Numbah one, okay?"

Good food, yes, in the pidgin English of Vietnam. *Numbah one* meant "good," just as *numbah ten* meant "bad." *Chop-chop* meant "food." The Vietnamese wasted nothing, left no potential victual to spoil, not even a clutch of ducks gripped in the fist of a dead man.

Lewis glared back at No Bick, loathing him ferociously for stealing ducks from a dead man, for being practical and opportunistic in the midst of unspeakable carnage. He loathed him for the madness that raged throughout this painfully beautiful land, as if No Bick was responsible for it all.

"Let him be, L.T.," soothed Jesse Burton, his grip tightening on Lewis's arm. "He's just doin' what he's doin', same as you, same as me." Lewis's anger drained out of him, and for a harrowing moment he feared that he might break down and cry like a two-year-old.

The afternoon was well under way before four trucks arrived, bearing the company of ARVN from Trung Lap, all wearing grim faces and carrying their M-16 rifles tensely with their fingers on the triggers. The air around the crater was now gaggy with death. As the ARVNs piled out and started poking through the carnage, the American scout platoon saddled up and headed north for the hamlet, grateful to leave the tension and the stench behind.

"It won't piss me off if I never see anything like *that* again," said Danny Legler in his slow, midwestern way. "Anyhoo, nobody back home would believe me if I told them about it."

"Fuck it," replied T. J. Skane, lighting a Kool. "Don't mean nothin', man." Which was GI slang for *Don't think about it*.

Lewis reported to the Triple Deuce tactical operations center that his men had found no coaxial wire leading away from the crater, so the explosive device had not been command-detonated. Still, the Old Man suspected the presence of enemy in the hamlet, and ordered a thorough "cordon and search." Triple Deuce's Alpha and Bravo companies had established blocking positions north, east, and west of the hamlet, ensuring that the bad guys couldn't escape when Lewis and his men went in after them.

V

A cruel sun beat down upon the citizens of the hamlet, about three dozen strong, all of them women, children, and old people, since draft-age males either served in the South Vietnamese military, fought on the side of the Vietcong, or hid out to evade conscription whenever allied units were in the neighborhood. The people squatted in a tight bunch around a stone well, cowering under the guns of the Triple Deuce scout platoon. Lewis ordered his medics to give them water every half hour.

"Main Rancho Six, this is Tango," he said into the handset of Jesse Burton's radio. "We've searched all the hooches and found nothing incriminating. We've questioned the villagers, and nobody admits to knowing anything about the mine in the road. All their IDs check out, and they all have nice tans. Over." Someone with a tan obviously hadn't been holing up in a tunnel during the daylight hours, which meant that he probably was not an NVA soldier or a member of an active

Vietcong unit. Lewis felt that his platoon was wasting time here, and his tone of voice said as much.

Colonel Gilbert Golightly answered from the shade of the headquarters tent in the tactical operations center, between sips of ice-cold Mountain Dew. "Tango, this is Six. Somebody's not being square with you, son. No way in hell the bad guys could bury that much explosive in the road without being seen by somebody in the hamlet. My guess is there's a squad of NVA hiding in a bunker somewhere nearby, and the folks in that hamlet know where they are. You stand your ground, y'hear? I'm sending you an India Papa Whiskey."

India Papa Whiskey stood for "interrogator of prisoners of war," a man trained by the U.S. Army to extract information from uncooperative captives. The 25th Infantry Division, the parent element of Triple Deuce, teamed its IPWs with specially selected ARVN interpreters. On a moment's notice the IPW teams went by chopper from the sprawling division base camp in Cu Chi to wherever they were needed.

Lewis felt his gut twist, because he'd seen them at work before—several times in Cambodia and again near the city of Dau Tieng, which lay on the edge of the Michelin rubber plantation. In his mind, IPWs were out-and-out sadists. They had informal license to commit acts that the Geneva Convention didn't allow, presumably under the pretext of "exigent need" or "tactical emergency." In Cambodia he'd watched an IPW dislocate the elbow of an NVA soldier who'd refused to reveal where his unit had cached its food and ammo, then break both the man's eardrums by firing a .45-caliber pistol mere inches from his head—this without ceremony, first the right ear, then the left. The same beast had permanently crippled another prisoner, a boy no older than sixteen, by pulverizing his kneecaps with a crowbar.

Torturing enemy soldiers was an ugly business in and of itself, but uglier in Lewis's mind was the mistreatment of civilians. U.S. Army units frequently "detained" civilian Vietnamese encountered during reconnaissance-in-force operations. Such detainees sometimes knew about enemy activity in the area but were understandably reluctant to share information with the foreign devils who had just plowed through their houses and gardens with tanks and armored personnel carriers. Lewis strongly believed that turning loose an IPW on civilians, as often happened—on helpless old mama-sans and papa-sans, and at times even on children—was unconscionable. But what could he do, if the Old Man was bent on sending an IPW? A lowly lieutenant couldn't tell a light colonel to take his IPW team and stuff it sideways up his ass, not if he wanted to stay out of Leavenworth.

"Sit tight," he told his men through grinding teeth. "There's an IPW inbound." A smattering of *yeows* went up from the platoon, the kind that Lewis figured you might hear at a cockfight.

vi

A helicopter settled to earth at the edge of the hamlet, whipping up dust on the road and scattering ripples across the nearby rice paddy. An American soldier and an ARVN jumped out and jogged toward Lewis, their fatigues flapping in the rotor wash. The helicopter ascended again, dipped its nose, and thundered away.

"Sergeant Gamaliel Cartee reports," said the American, saluting smartly. "Sir, I understand you need someone who knows how to ask questions. That's my specialty." A striking man, Cartee was as young as twenty or as old as thirty-five, as tall as Lewis but hard looking in a rangy, sinewy way. His accent was thick southern syrup. He was apparently racially mixed, for he had the features of an African and the complexion of a Greek or an Arab. His tailored fatigues were crisply laundered and his boots spit-shined, as if he'd moments ago stepped out of a recruiting poster.

Though he wore reflective aviator-type sunglasses, something potent poured from his eyes that Lewis found unsettling. *You're still freaked-out from this morning*, Lewis told himself, fighting down crazy notions. He pulled himself together and briefed Cartee concerning the suspicions of his battalion commander, that someone among the huddled civilians knew where to find the bastards who'd planted the monster mine in the road.

"But you don't agree with the Old Man, do you, Lieutenant?" offered Cartee, grinning. "You're thinking they're all innocent civilians, right? I'm surprised that anyone who's spent more than a week in this stink hole could believe there's such a thing as innocence anymore."

"It doesn't matter what I think, Sergeant," answered Lewis, taken aback by the remark. "What do you say we get to work and do our jobs, okay?"

Cartee removed his sunglasses, which he handed to his ARVN interpreter. "Yes, sir. There's no worse crime than waste of time, the old ones say." With the glasses no longer hiding Cartee's eyes, Lewis saw that the right one was a stony blue and the left one a deep, somber brown. He'd known more than one person with different-colored eyes, but he'd never before found the effect so unnerving. As Cartee walked toward the knot of civilians, Lewis saw something that his brain rejected, a spectacle so illogical that it failed to register more than superficially: Cartee's shadow, cast by a blazing afternoon sun on the clay-paved apron around the village well, was a deep, almost iridescent *blue*. It had a grainy texture that seemed somehow alive, like an inky swarm of microscopic insects. Lewis looked away from it and stared instead at Nui Ba Den, the forlorn Black Virgin Mountain, telling himself that he'd not seen anything out of the ordinary. The premonition he'd endured earlier squirmed again.

Jesse Burton's low voice tugged him back to reality. "That's one strange motherfuckin' dude, L.T. If you want to know the truth, that's maybe the strangest motherfuckin' dude I ever saw in my life."

vii

Gamaliel Cartee began by addressing the civilians as a group—in Vietnamese, which came as a shock to Lewis. Americans who could speak more than a few words of real Vietnamese were rare as hen's teeth in Vietnam, and until today, he'd never met one. He wondered why Cartee even bothered to bring along the ARVN interpreter.

"What's he saying?" he asked the interpreter, a spidery sergeant in tiger-striped camouflaged fatigues. The man pursed his lips and shook his head as if brushing off a boy who'd stuck his nose into the business of grown men. "I asked you a question, Sergeant, and I'll get an answer, damn it! What's he saying?"

Suddenly Tran Van Hai, his own Kit Carson, was at his side, whispering urgently, his stare fixed on Cartee. "He tells the people they must keep silent, because he wants the pleasure of beating the truth out of them. He tells them he will give them such pain that their dead ancestors will cry out from their graves."

"Jesus, I hope this isn't his idea of winning their hearts and minds." Lewis glared at Cartee, then turned back to Hai again, his mouth dropping open in shock. He'd never heard his Kit Carson string together so many words of English—good English at that, only mildly accented. All this time, it seemed, No Bick had only pretended to *no bick*.

"Sergeant Cartee means merely to frighten them, sir," offered the interpreter, glaring a dagger at Hai, the former Vietcong. "They are much more willing to cooperate if they are afraid. They understand nothing so well as they understand fear."

Cartee waded into the squatting mass of civilians, his voice rising to a shriek, the liquid syllables of the language rolling over his white teeth like lava over stones. The people cowered before him, bowed their heads, and pressed their palms together in front of their eyes, an Oriental gesture of respect and supplication.

Cartee selected one of them, a spindly old woman with a walnut face and silver hair knotted at the back of her head. Like nearly all the others she wore loose trousers of black silk, a white shirt with long fitted sleeves, and a conical hat that hung down her back on a string. Her lips were stained red and her teeth black from chewing betel nut, a mild stimulant favored by many elderly Vietnamese. Cartee's fist closed around her shirt and lifted her upward as if she weighed nothing. Another flood of words flowed from him, harsher now, more threatening. The old woman groped ineffectually at his forearm and issued a low moan, while Cartee's other fist closed around the knot of gray hair and pulled her head back, causing obvious pain.

"*Yeoww!*" screamed someone among the spectators of the scout platoon. "Don't take no shit from that old mama-san, Sarge! Break her fuckin' neck if you need to!"

"She is the elder of this village," whispered No Bick, his face dark with hatred. "She will tell him nothing. She will die before giving in to him."

Lewis's fingernails bore deep into the skin of his fisted palms. He watched Cartee slap the old woman across the face twice, three times; heard her gurgling screams, heard the cries of the huddled civilians. One among them, a young woman whom No Bick identified as the old woman's granddaughter, leaped up and flew at Cartee with her hands spread into claws. Cartee whirled smoothly and slammed a fist into her face, and she went hard to the ground, where she lay sobbing, bleeding. More approving yells went up from the crowd of GIs.

"He demands the names of those who placed the explosive in the road," No Bick translated. "He commands her to show him where their tunnels are." But the old woman only wailed pitifully and raised her pressed-together palms to her forehead, begging mercy.

Cartee appeared cool and unruffled. *This is just another day at the office to him*, thought Lewis, his rage mounting. *He's enjoying this, the cocksucker!*

Cartee beckoned to the interpreter, who jumped to his aid

with a length of cord, and they tied the old mama-san's hands behind her back. Cartee snatched up the young woman from the ground by her hair. They dragged both women to a nearby ditch, which carried brown river water to the surrounding rice paddies. Cartee then announced his intentions to the mama-san loudly enough for all to hear, and No Bick translated for Lewis: unless she gave him the information he wanted, he would kill her granddaughter slowly and painfully. He promised that the old woman would hear the girl's dying screams in her sleep until the end of time.

"He ain't really gonna do that, is he, L.T.?" asked Jesse Burton, having overheard No Bick's translation.

"I think he's just trying to scare them," Lewis answered lamely.

Cartee asked for an empty sandbag, and Lewis's own platoon sergeant, Frank Markowski, fetched one from his track. "I've seen this trick before," Markowski announced to the crowd. "This is gonna be good!" Bumptious laughter went up.

Cartee launched a spit-shined boot into the young woman's chest, where it landed with a thud, and the girl drew herself into a ball, gagged, and gasped for air on the muddy bank of the ditch. He hoisted her by the hair again, and Markowski, grinning with his bad teeth around the butt of a Pall Mall, forced the sandbag over her head. Cartee cinched the bag tight at her throat and thrust her down toward the brown water.

The old mama-san filled the hot afternoon with her wails, and Lewis needed no translation of the words she hurled at the American. The granddaughter fought back as her head neared the water, flailed and kicked and grabbed fistfuls of Cartee's fatigues, but the man was like granite. Her head slipped below the surface of the water, held firmly by Cartee's hand at the back of her neck, and her screams died amid a flurry of bubbles.

A full minute dragged by, during which Lewis groped for images of sanity from his past life, where no mines destroyed busloads of people and no handsome monsters like Gamaliel Cartee tortured young girls. It was a life of *American Band-*

stand with Dick Clark, poker in the friendly card rooms of downtown Portland, and matinee movies with his fiancée, Twyla. It was a life of laughter and pizza and deciding whether to attend graduate school. At this moment the quiet world of Portland, Oregon, the City of Roses, seemed so inaccessible as to have been mythical, like the lost city of Atlantis.

Somewhere on a distant rice paddy a water buffalo bellowed. A dog barked. A GI's cassette player poured out the Beatles' "Come Together." Gamaliel Cartee jerked the girl's head out of the water, and the fans cheered. The girl gulped for air, but the wet sandbag clung to her mouth and nostrils, letting in only enough to tease her burning lungs.

T. J. Skane, looking fragile under his bulbous Afro, turned away from the spectacle and retreated toward Lewis's track. "Fuck me," he breathed. "This shit's no good, man."

Danny Legler followed close on his heels, like a little blond mongrel with its tail between its legs. "Don't mean nothin'," he murmured helplessly.

Cartee shouted more threats, more evil promises, and his fans clapped him on while the old woman moaned and wailed, her voice hoarse, her red-stained mouth contorted into a tragic yawn. As Cartee repositioned himself to renew the torment of the girl, his shadow fell across her body, a shadow that seemed implausibly deep and blue, full of wriggling strands of ink. The girl shivered, as if a blanket of ice crystals had fallen over her shoulders.

Am I the only one who sees this? Lewis asked himself. *Doesn't anyone else understand what's happening . . . ?*

He happened to catch Jesse Burton's eyes, and their stares locked together. *Jesse knows*, said a voice in Lewis's head. *He sees it, too!*

Cartee pushed the girl beneath the water again, and he shrieked like a demon, the whites of his eyes showing wholly around the mismatched irises. Then he jerked her upward again and dug his knee into the small of her back, as if to garrote her with the tie string of the sandbag. He glanced at the old mama-san, whom his interpreter held tightly, and hurled another stream of words at her.

"He tells her that he will break the girl's back," translated No Bick, and Lewis thought he could hear vertebrae popping. "She must immediately tell him where the NVA are, he says, because the girl cannot endure much more."

"Man, this shit's got to cease," hissed Jesse Burton.

"You're right," said Lewis, his voice thick. He chucked aside his steel helmet and strode toward the bank of the ditch, teeth grinding, fists balled tight. He no longer cared whether he incurred the wrath of the Old Man or even whether he was about to jeopardize the success of a combat mission. He could not stand by quietly and watch the commission of an atrocity.

As a student of philosophy, he knew the hopelessness of trying to define concepts like truth, good, and evil, and he'd set himself against the absolutists who claimed monopolies on such definitions. But now he felt as if he'd found a genuine absolute—right here in a dusty little hamlet just north of the town of Trung Lap, the Republic of Vietnam, maybe the last place on earth where a philosopher would expect to find absolute *evil*. There it stood, wearing the uniform of the U.S. Army, a man who had one blue eye and one brown. A man who cast a deep blue shadow.

"That'll be enough, Cartee!" Lewis thundered. "Let the girl go, and stand at ease!"

The platoon sergeant, Markowski, strode forward and caught hold of Lewis's arm. "You better back down, sir," he said, his nostrils flaring and the Pall Mall bouncing on his lower lip. "This man is executin' an order given to him by the commander of this battalion. Now, if you don't have the intestinal fortitude—"

"Take your hand off me, Sergeant Markowski, or I'll have you standing in front of a summary court-martial."

"You're making a big mistake, sir. The man's just doin' his duty!"

"I said take your hand off me!" Frank Markowski's hand fell away, and the war-ragged old veteran stepped back, scowling. A chorus of boos went up from the spectators.

Gamaliel Cartee had not released the young woman, who still struggled and choked in his death grip, while the grandmother hung limp in the arms of the interpreter. Cartee himself gazed at Lewis expectantly, smiling just enough to show the tips of his ivory teeth, his mismatched eyes twinkling.

"You heard my order, Sergeant. Release that girl."

"You're wrong to direct your anger at *me*, Lieutenant Kindred," Cartee replied, grinning now. "*I'm* not the problem."

Lewis unholstered his service .45, pulled back the slide to chamber a round, and leveled it at Cartee's forehead. "Let her go, or I'll blow your fucking head off, I swear."

"Do you want to know who to be angry with?" asked Cartee. "Be angry with yourself, because that's where the problem is. You've gone to war, Lieutenant Kindred, and you've killed people. You'll kill again before you're finished. You'll tell yourself it's your duty, and you may even believe that, but if you really think—"

"You have two seconds, Cartee. If you don't shut your fucking mouth and let go of that girl, you're dead."

Sergeant Frank Markowski piped up again, his face purpling. "Lieutenant, you're committing an assault against a noncommissioned officer who's acting in the line of duty! According to the Uniform Code of Military Justice, I can relieve you of your command to keep you from—"

"Don't quote the UCMJ to me, you shit-brained old lifer! Sergeant Cartee has committed blatant violations of the Geneva Convention, which I've sworn to uphold as a commissioned officer, and you're a fucking accomplice, as far as I'm concerned. I could blow you both away and probably get a medal."

Smirking, Cartee let go of the girl, and she sank to her knees. The ARVN interpreter loosed the hands of the old woman, who twisted away from him. She went to her granddaughter, tore off the sopping sandbag, and cradled the girl's head in her arms. Lewis shouted for his favorite medic, a brawny Wyoming cowboy named Scott Sanders, who instantly showed up at his side with a first-aid rucksack.

"Make sure they're both okay, Doc," he instructed, "and give them something for the pain. If either of them is hurt bad, we'll dust them off to the 12th Evac." *Dust-off* meant evacuation by helicopter to the 12th Evacuation Hospital in Cu Chi.

"You got it, L.T." The young medic started toward the huddled women, but turned back briefly to Lewis. "Nice goin', sir. You did right." Lewis wanted to thank him, wanted to shake his hand. He glanced briefly around at his men, seeking out the friendly faces—Jesse Burton's, T. J. Skane's, Danny Legler's—while avoiding the others, chief among them the beetle-browed face of Sergeant First Class Frank Markowski.

Two

i

NOTHING MUCH CAME of the incident north of Trung Lap, at least not at first. Sergeant Cartee returned to his headquarters unit in Cu Chi, seemingly unruffled and bearing no grudges, which Lewis found hard to comprehend, given that he'd come close to blowing the bastard's head off. The Triple Deuce scouts went back to conducting routine reconnaissance-in-force operations in and around the Ho Bo Woods, where they located no NVA and engaged in no firefights, found no mines or booby traps, and suffered no casualties.

Lewis would have put the incident with Cartee behind him, if, a few days later, Sergeant First Class Frank Markowski hadn't complained to Triple Deuce's command sergeant major about his "no-guts" platoon leader and hinted that he might bring a formal charge against Lewis for assaulting an NCO with a deadly weapon. The command sergeant major relayed the complaint to the Old Man, who called Lewis to his track one evening for an informal chat.

Colonel Golightly smoked a pipeful of rancid-smelling tobacco and delivered a "GI issue" lecture on the moral dilemma that confronts every officer—how to avoid becoming a killer and a thug while carrying out warfare. Warfare is basically an honorable pursuit, he insisted, one worthy of officers, gentlemen, and lesser humans, notwithstanding that it occasionally demands bending the rules of decency. A good officer does this, said the colonel, only in accordance with something called the "law of war," and though he may regret doing so, he will never let civilian notions of morality interfere with his mission. He will suffer no pangs of guilt or sleepless nights, quite simply because he understands that any outrage he's forced to commit is honorable within the context of warfare. Golightly advised Lewis to forget about rightness and wrongness, and concern himself instead with honor.

The lecture, short and neat as it was, merely hardened a conclusion that Lewis had reached months earlier: only killers and thugs go to war.

ii

A week later the scout platoon rolled into Cu Chi Base Camp for a three-day stand-down, which gave the scouts a chance to pull maintenance on the tracks, drink some beer, and get their laundry done. Located on Highway 1 about twenty miles northwest of downtown Saigon, the camp was a veritable city. It had movie theaters, USO nightclubs, restaurants, swimming pools, bars, barbershops, tennis courts, baseball diamonds, gyms, massage parlors, a PX, and even a bowling alley. Unfortunately it was severely lacking in the one comfort that GIs longed for above all else—round-eyed girls.

Because it housed the headquarters of the 25th Infantry Division, Cu Chi Base Camp enjoyed heavy security. The Americans could move around unarmed inside the perimeter with little worry about snipers, booby traps, or mines, thanks to a two-story fortified berm that surrounded the complex. Still, the enemy occasionally lobbed in a mortar round or a 122-millimeter rocket just to keep them honest, and occasionally a REMF, or rear-echelon motherfucker, went home in a body bag.

Lewis welcomed the chance to sleep indoors on a mattress with actual sheets, but even so, he never slept soundly in Cu Chi: too many helicopters coming and going at all hours—surveillance ships, gunships, troop ships, dust-offs, cargo carriers, and couriers. The air was always astir with the *whup-whup* of rotor blades, and he'd come to think of the base camp as a massive hive, the choppers as bees.

After getting his men safely settled in the Triple Deuce battalion area, he staked out a bunk in the company-grade officers' hooch, which boasted a dayroom with a pool table, dartboards, and a television set. He took a leisurely shower, dressed in freshly laundered fatigues, and ambled by the Headquarters Company orderly room to pick up his mail. En route back to his bunk he paused in the dayroom to catch the evening news on AFVN, the Armed Forces Vietnam Network, which operated the only English-language television station in the region. The station ran all the latest American network sitcoms and action shows, and like its counterpart on the radio, served as a little slice of home for war-weary soldiers, sailors, and airmen.

An air-force sergeant with a sober broadcast voice read an item that made Lewis feel slightly ill:

"A spokesman for the Criminal Investigation Division reports no leads yet concerning the grisly serial murders that have occurred during the past four months in and around the Saigon area. Army Major Vernon Karsten says that U.S. Military Police have formed a joint task force with the Saigon District Security Police to investigate the murders of twelve young women . . ."

The very idea that serial murder could occur here seemed absurd to Lewis. Serial murder seemed so gut-wrenchingly Western, so unworthy of the inscrutably subtle Southeast Asians. *I'll bet it's a GI,* he thought.

". . . and CID investigators are at a loss to explain the brutality of the crimes. One investigator described a murder scene as looking as if some kind of animal had attacked the victim. . . ."

Lewis left the dayroom, shaking his head, and went to his bunk to read his mail. A letter had arrived from his fiancée, Twyla, and it improved his mood even before he cracked the envelope. She hadn't written in over two weeks, which would have unnerved him if he'd not known that she'd just started graduate school at Portland State University. Her schedule, he figured, was a heavy one, and he didn't begrudge her some time to settle into a new routine. As was his custom, he saved Twyla's letter for last, opening first a letter from his maiden aunt Juliet, who owned an apartment building in Portland. He didn't get far into it, for Aunt Juliet was a flaming born-again Christian whose letters were mostly sermons peppered with scriptural quotes.

More exciting was the one from his mother, which promised a "CARE package" full of home-baked butterscotch cookies within the coming week. She also shared some important family news with him: his younger brother, Ken, had taken a job on a drilling rig in the Gulf of Mexico, leaving his mother alone in the big family house near Laurelhurst Park in southeast Portland. Reading between the lines, Lewis surmised that she was desperately lonely. His father had died of cancer only two years earlier, and though his mother had many friends, and was active in her church and garden club, she missed having family around, missed having someone to look after. *She can live with Twyla and me after we're married*, Lewis resolved right then and there. *She can help with the kids we're going to have.*

Which brought him to the last letter, Twyla's. He held the envelope to his nose and inhaled, expecting the usual rush of

Chanel No. 5. He'd given her a bottle of the costly stuff for her birthday more than a year ago, and she'd taken to scenting her letters with it after he'd gone into the army. This one, however, lacked any trace of Chanel No. 5.

He suffered an attack of paranoia as he turned the envelope over in his hands. Twyla's neat cursive handwriting seemed neater than usual. Too, the return address was new, closer to Portland State, but Lewis himself had written to her and urged her to find an apartment closer in, so this was nothing to worry about, surely. He tore the envelope open. Carefully. Slowly. Took out the single page, unfolded it.

> *Dear Lewis,*
> *I've been dreading telling you this, and I've been searching for the right words, because I didn't want to hurt you. . . .*

Ah, yes—a Dear John. The bane of every GI who has ever slogged through a combat zone. Lewis barely skimmed the body of even handwriting, his eyes snatching up only the operative words, devouring them, then racing on in a rush to get this nightmare over with.

> *. . . someone I met at a party in August . . .*
> *. . . can't help it, but I love him . . .*

An ache developed somewhere near his solar plexus and spread throughout his chest. He felt numb.

> *. . . no one you know . . .*
> *. . . moved in together . . .*

He set the letter aside and stared through the screened window of the officers' hooch, through which he could see the trailing edge of a tangerine sun slipping behind the berm of Cu Chi Base Camp. The sky looked angry, as he supposed he himself should be. He braved a final glance at the evil thing on his bunk.

. . . sent the engagement ring to your mother's house . . .

A helicopter thundered across the bunker line of the base camp, spraying for mosquitoes, and Lewis glanced up at it. Within the few seconds that he followed it with his eyes, the sun slipped completely away, leaving only the angry redness behind.

The numbness gradually left him, and the sky darkened to purple velvet. Night devoured Vietnam. Lewis didn't cry, though he was alone in the hooch and could have done it without shaming himself. Hell, he *wanted* to cry, even felt as though he should, but he felt drained of whatever it took to muster tears.

He dug through his duffel bag and found the spare shaving kit he'd bought at the PX when he first arrived in Vietnam, in which he'd kept all the letters Twyla had written to him since then. Among them was a photo portrait taken during her senior year at the University of Oregon, the most recent one he owned. He took a moment to study the heart-shaped face inside the brass frame, the intelligent blue eyes, and the straight golden hair. That she'd thrown aside the vow she'd made—the promise to be true, to keep him uppermost in her mind and heart—pained him acutely.

"Taxi girls" were a dime a dozen in Vietnam, lithe and willowy beauties, many of them, and for the equivalent of five dollars Lewis could easily have relieved himself of his ever-present sexual itch. He could have done so a hundred times, in fact, but he'd never been seriously tempted. The mere thought of Twyla had been enough to see him through the tough spots, along with the assurance that she would be there for him when he came home from this hellhole.

He zippered the portrait and the letters into the shaving kit, then left the hooch, carrying the kit under his arm. He followed a cement walk to an asphalt road and turned toward the Triple Deuce motor pool, which was a cluster of Quonset-type garages near the base-camp perimeter. Here the air stank sharply of Vietnam, a mixture of petroleum fumes, mildew, and burning shit. The army handled the product of its temporary latrines in a most direct, if not environmentally sound, manner— burned it with kerosene. The worst duty a GI could pull was the "shit detail," which involved dragging the brimming barrels out of the latrines, pouring in the kerosene, and setting them afire.

Lewis strode past a row of latrines and circled around behind them, taking care to stay on the walkway made of perforated steel planking lest he blunder into putrid, ankle-deep mud. He approached a flaming barrel, which was a fifty-five-gallon drum cut off to fit under the toilet seat of a latrine. Ghastly orange-and-green flames licked its inner edges. The stench was overpowering.

Without stopping to think further about it, he lobbed the shaving kit into the barrel, where it thudded softly into the molten excrement. A swarm of sparks rose into the night as the leather kit caught fire. In mere seconds Twyla's portrait and perfumed letters burned to nothingness.

iii

The game was well under way when Lewis arrived in the motor pool. The players squatted on ammo boxes or sat in folding chairs around a low metal table in the center of the aluminum building—black guys, white guys, a Hispanic or two, even Tran Van Hai, the Kit Carson. Half a dozen spectators loitered on the periphery, smoking and joking, trading small talk about the "world," which was anywhere outside Southeast Asia.

As Lewis approached, one of the players glanced up, saw him, and shouted a *'Ten-hutt!*, but Lewis quickly replied, "Carry on, carry on," which spared the enlisted men from leaping to attention. A lightbulb hung on a cord from the ceiling, shrouded in a metal shade that directed a conical blast of light onto the table. Nearby stood a garbage can full of beer and ice. The garage smelled tartly of diesel oil, beer, sweat, and cigarette smoke. From somebody's tape player issued the voluptuous voice of Aretha Franklin.

"What's happenin', L.T.?" asked T. J. Skane, keeping his eyes fixed on his cards. "You slummin' tonight, or did you clean out all the officers already, and you're lookin' for a new game?" A wide-tooth comb with a long handle protruded from his 'fro.

"Hell, those college boys know better than to play cards with the L.T.," said Scott Sanders, the good-natured medic from Wyoming. "They ain't as dumb as they look, y'know." The men all laughed. Most had heard how good Lewis was at poker, and several had experienced his prowess firsthand.

"I'm looking for a low-stakes game," Lewis replied with a sad smile. "I don't intend to clean anyone out." This brought another round of chuckles.

Most of the seven or eight sitting players were members of his scout platoon, among them Skane and Sanders, as well as Jesse Burton and Danny Legler. Several others were REMFs who worked in the motor pool. Lewis had not yet seen the face of the man who sat with his back to him, the one who hadn't bothered to turn around and acknowledge his presence.

"I'm gettin' the fuck out of here," said Jesse, slapping down his cards. "I'm down my last paycheck and most of my next one."

The man whose face Lewis had not yet seen turned around and grinned, his eyes glittering blue and brown. "Why don't you join our game, Lieutenant?" he drawled in his syrupy New Orleans accent. "I can let bygones be bygones if you can. We promise not to rat on you for fraternizing with us degenerate enlisted types—as long as your money's green, that is."

Lewis's mouth went dry and his voice caught like a fish bone in his throat.

"L.T., I need to talk to you a minute," said Jesse, moving toward him around the table. "It's a personal problem, okay?"

"Save me a seat," said Lewis to the group, then turned to follow Jesse out. They talked under a yard light that was under siege by hordes of anopheles mosquitoes.

"You don't want to get into a card game with that moth-erfucker," Jesse warned. "He plays poker like most dudes breathe. Now, I know you're good—"

"I can handle myself in a card game, Jess."

"I know that, sir, but—"

"Don't sir me when no one's around, damn it. How many times do I need to tell you that?"

"Would you *please* fuckin' listen? You're good at poker, maybe the best I ever saw before tonight, and I'm from the South Side of Chicago, man. I've *seen* some good poker play-ers in my life, hear what I'm sayin'? But this motherfucker is like nothin' I've ever seen. He knows what cards you're hol-din' in the hole, like he's got X-ray eyes or something. And he's lucky like nobody has a right to be. He's lost maybe two hands so far, and we've been playin' a good hour. He's al-ready—"

"How much are you down?"

"Never mind that, man. What I'm worried about is—"

"How much are you down, damn it?"

"Six hundred and change—so fuckin' what? Cartee is some kind of machine. He won't walk out of here until he's wiped out every swingin' dick in that game."

"Hang tough. I'm going to get your money back for you."

Lewis turned and strode back toward the Quonset, but Jesse grabbed his arm. Under the glare of the yard light his black face shone with sweat. "It's not the money, L.T. It's—it's—"

"It's what?"

"I don't know. It's something else. You feel it, too, I know. Cartee isn't . . . *right*. My old granmama would've said he ain't a natural child."

Something cold tickled the base of Lewis's spine, and he hoped it was merely sweat running down the crack of his ass. "You're talking like a little kid, Jess. This is the grown-ups' world, and there's no such thing as the bogeyman here."

"Say what you want, but you've seen it, too—I know you have. You saw it when Cartee was beating the bejesus out of that little girl out by the Ho Bos. You saw his *shadow*. . . .''

Lewis pulled free of Jesse's grip. ''I don't want to hear any more of this. Stick around, and I'll get your money back for you. You can buy me a beer later to show your gratitude.''

iv

At the age of five Lewis Kindred learned the game of five-card draw from his father, Lyle Kindred, a beer-swilling, cigar-chomping civil engineer who'd built bridges on five continents and had played poker on six. At the age of ten Lewis knew the rules of a dozen poker games, but his favorite was seven-card stud, because it required much betting and allowed for massive bluffing. In the same way some kids become passionate about baseball, tennis, or chess, and go on to devote major shares of their lives to those passions, Lewis became passionate about poker. By the time he reached high school he could hold his own in games with seasoned adults, and by the age of eighteen he was competitive with most professionals.

''That kid is the most natural poker player I've ever seen in my life,'' Lyle Kindred had often bragged to his buddies. ''He figures odds like a computer. I swear he could bluff a honey bear off a beehive.''

Having reached his early twenties and having played ten times as much poker as most people play in a lifetime, Lewis understood the game on a level that few even know exists. He knew that winning requires much more than luck, that the laws of mathematics distribute good cards and bad cards with remarkable evenness. To win, a player must not only figure the odds of getting the best possible hand, but also calculate the probability of taking the pot with that hand. Lewis appreciated that winning at poker takes *courage,* which separates the great players from the mediocre. A winner has the guts to back his good hands with his hard-earned cash.

Like all strong players he played conservatively, avoiding dramatic showdowns over big pots, never sandbagging his opponents to stimulate betting, never raising or calling too often. He quietly kept track of his position in the betting order and memorized the cards that showed in every hand. As the game went on he analyzed the betting and bluffing patterns of everyone at the table. After losing a hand, he put the loss behind him, knowing that no player wins every hand, no matter how good he is. He seldom put his trust in mere luck, and he almost never left money on the table.

Gamaliel Cartee welcomed him to the game with the offer of a beer, but Lewis never drank anything stronger than Pepsi when he played poker. Neither did he smoke or eat. From the moment he sat down, his mouth elongated into an amiable little smile that he would maintain until the very end of the game, come hell or high water, win or lose. It was his game face, his poker mask.

"Dealer's choice, Lieutenant," said Cartee, lighting the biggest green cigar that Lewis had ever seen. "Dollar ante, maximum bet of ten, jacks or better to open."

"Don't call me lieutenant tonight," said Lewis through his poker smile. "Everybody's a sir in a card game, all right?"

"That's egalitarian of you. What should we call you—Lewis or Lew?"

"Call me anything you want, as long as you do it with a smile."

V

They played on a table covered with an olive-drab army blanket, using the brightly colored "Military Payment Certificates"—MPC—with which Uncle Sam paid the troops in Vietnam. The government printed the stuff and used it in place of greenbacks in order to keep the latter from falling into the hands of civilians and ultimately those of the enemy, who needed hard currency for buying weapons. GIs, of course, referred to MPC as "Monopoly money."

During the next hour players dropped out like flies, casualties of Gamaliel Cartee's murderous betting strategy. Lewis detected what most others at the table did not—that Cartee often faked a weak hand to entice bettors. Too, he occasionally folded to let someone else win a hand, even though he held stronger cards, just to keep people in the game and enhance his chances of cleaning them out. Nearly every hand quickly became a big one, and Cartee won far more than his share. Lewis won enough hands to stay afloat, keeping his thin smile in place, trading "card talk" with the others while hiding his knowledge of what was happening.

"This is gettin' too rich for my blood," drawled Scott Sanders, sounding like a refugee from a John Wayne Western. He tossed in his cards and herded his lanky frame away from the table. "I've never seen anybody so lucky in my whole life."

Gamaliel made a show of thanking him graciously and promised that next time things could be different. "Every dog has his day," he said, smiling around his green cigar.

"Ain't gonna be no next time for this dog," muttered the cowboy.

Now only Danny Legler and T. J. Skane were left, in addition to Gamaliel and Lewis. Most of the spectators had wandered off to bars or movies. While Gamaliel dealt the next hand of seven-card stud, Lewis scrutinized his every movement, trying not to be conspicuous about it. If Gamaliel was cheating, he was the best cheat Lewis had ever seen, bar none. If he was *not* cheating, then his luck was nothing short of unholy.

Leg was the next to go. He shook his corn-colored mop of hair and declared that Mama Legler hadn't raised any dummies. T. J. Skane managed to last another three hands before slapping down his hole cards and getting to his feet. "Ain't no fuckin' justice," he griped, eyeing the mountain of MPC in front of Gamaliel. By this time Lewis, too, was substantially down.

"Justice has nothing to do with poker, brother," replied Gamaliel. "It doesn't matter whether you're a good man or a bad one, you win if you hold the right cards."

"No way I'm your brother," said Skane, shambling off with exaggerated soul. Several other blacks went with him, as did Leg, leaving but two spectators—Jesse Burton and Tran Van Hai.

Gamaliel took a long moment to relight his cigar, then stared at Lewis with his mismatched eyes. "Just you and me now, Lewis. We've separated the sheep from the goats, it seems."

Jesse moved close to the table and clapped a hand on Lewis's shoulder. "Time to pack it in—right, L.T.? Everybody has a bad night now and then."

"Let's not try to make his mind up for him," protested Gamaliel, fanning the deck of cards expertly with long, snaky fingers. "The lieutenant—I mean *Lewis*—is a big boy now, and he's perfectly capable of making his own decisions. Isn't that right, Lewis?"

Like all strong players, Lewis knew exactly how much money he had left, so he didn't need to count it—thirty-nine dollars, which meant he was down more than a hundred. Jesse was right: even the best player has a bad night occasionally. A prudent man resists the impulse to throw good money after bad, but Lewis could not bring himself simply to give in to Gamaliel Cartee.

Suddenly he suffered a mental snapshot of the bloody scene on the road north of Trung Lap, the pieces of human bodies littering the countryside like the leavings of some unfathomable carnivore. He saw the hamlet where Cartee had terrorized a spindly old woman and nearly killed an innocent young girl. He heard again the words of the AFVN announcer, describing the handiwork of a serial murderer who had struck a dozen times in and around Saigon.

"I know what you're thinking," said Gamaliel, tobacco smoke curling from the corners of his mouth. "No man can possibly be as lucky as I am. You suspect I'm cheating."

"I haven't seen you cheat, and I know what to look for. I'm not exactly new at this."

"I know. I recognize that you're a great poker player, Lewis, much better than I am, believe it or not. You understand odds and bluffing. You've got card sense, I think it's called. I don't.''

"So you're saying you're just lucky, huh?"

"Not at all. What I lack in skills and knowledge, I make up for with this." His hand slipped into a pocket of his fatigue jacket and brought out a globe of brilliant red crystal, which he placed on the table next to his mound of MPC. Lewis stared wide-eyed at the object, for its innards swarmed with stuff that looked like protoplasm. Slightly larger than a golf ball and perfectly spherical, it thudded onto the army blanket as if it was much heavier than it looked.

"Motherfucker," breathed Jesse. "What in the hell is it?"

"Exactly what it appears to be, just like me," answered Cartee, exhaling cigar smoke.

"And what in the hell is *that*?"

"Call it a gemstone or an orb. Call it a good-luck charm. It doesn't really matter what you call it, I suppose. All that matters is what you *do* with it."

Lewis's smile shrank. The impression of movement inside the gem disturbed him.

"There's nothing to be afraid of," soothed Gamaliel, prodding the thing with a long finger. "We're only playing poker here."

Lewis felt an eyelid flutter, felt a muscle in his cheek start to twitch. "What do you want from me?" he managed to ask.

"A game, that's all. It's what we're here for, isn't it—a small diversion from the cruelties of the real world? Since we're the only two left, let's lift the betting limit and make things interesting."

"I don't have that kind of money with me."

"No problem. You're an officer and a gentlemen, so I trust you. If you lose, you can owe me. I have almost nineteen hundred dollars on the table, but let's start with an ante of say, ten dollars. We can cut for the deal."

"Don't do it, L.T.," pleaded Jesse. "Let's get out of here, okay? You don't need this shit, man. You don't want to *owe* this cocksucker—"

"Shut up, Jesse," Lewis hissed. He cut the cards and came up with a deuce. "Deal, Cartee. I'm in for ten."

"Then it's five-card draw," said Gamaliel, grinning wickedly around his cigar. "We've played enough stud poker tonight, I think. I'm in the mood for something more pure, aren't you?" Lewis didn't protest. Given his small cash reserve, he needed a game that didn't require at least four rounds of betting with every hand.

Gamaliel dealt five cards each to himself and Lewis, facedown. Lewis drew the deuce of clubs, three of hearts, four of diamonds, five of hearts, and jack of spades—a potential "double-ended" straight, meaning that he needed either a six or an ace to complete a strong hand. He bet ten dollars, knowing that in order to get that hand he must overcome five-to-one odds to draw either of those cards. Under normal circumstances he never would have trusted in pure luck, but these didn't seem like normal circumstances.

Gamaliel saw the bet and called instead of raising, apparently in deference to Lewis's shallow finances. Lewis discarded the jack and, lo, drew the precious six he needed, giving him a six-high straight. Gamaliel, too, drew one card, but his handsome face gave no inkling whether it was a good card or a bad one.

"The bet's to me," intoned Gamaliel, laying aside the rest of the deck. "I'll bet eighteen hundred and thirty-one dollars, which is everything I have on the table. As I said earlier, your credit's good."

Lewis checked his hand again and felt a bolt of anticipation. The odds were finally with him. He'd gotten his card to complete the straight, which was a mind-boggling achievement in a game of five-card draw, one-on-one. The chances of Gamaliel beating this hand were mathematically remote. "If my credit's good, I'll see you and call," he answered, feeling a droplet of sweat crawl down his neck.

Gamaliel leaned back from the table and puffed on his cigar, fouling the air. He knitted his long-fingered hands on his stomach. "Let's engage in an experiment before we show our cards, Lewis. It's a simple one, and it requires absolutely no effort on your part. I'll guarantee that you'll find it entertaining.''

"What kind of experiment?"

"It has to do with tasting power and the possibilities it offers. Not everyone gets a chance like this—only a privileged few. Are you game?"

"I don't like mixing poker with parlor tricks."

"This isn't a trick, I assure you. All you need to do is put your cards down and wait. I'll do the rest."

Lewis was wary. Something about the proposition smelled vaguely Faustian. A taste of *power*? Suddenly it all seemed overly theatrical and downright funny. Gamaliel Cartee was obviously some sort of performing prestidigitator, and the red orb was a prop. Lewis had heard about sleight-of-hand artists who could cheat at cards so smoothly that not even the most experienced players could catch on, and Gamaliel was clearly one of these. Casinos routinely barred Gamaliel's kind. Lewis felt like a country bumpkin who'd lost his wad to a big-city cardsharp. The boy-wonder poker player, it seemed—the kid who could bluff a honey bear off a beehive—had met his match not in Las Vegas or Paradise Island or Monte Carlo, but in a dingy motor pool in South Vietnam!

He felt a smile tug his face, felt a laugh grow in his gut. A giggle squirted out between his lips, and suddenly he could contain himself no longer. He laughed long and loud, slapping the table with his hand and stomping the floor with a boot. He hadn't laughed like this in months, maybe years. Gamaliel watched him for a time, perplexed, but then he, too, started to laugh. Soon the pair of them were roaring like drunken lodge brothers. The hilarity halted abruptly, however, when Lewis caught sight of Jesse Burton, who stood like a black pillar outside the cone of light, his face grave. Deeper in the shadows stood No Bick, a sharp-eyed wraith. Lewis turned back to Cartee, who immediately fell silent.

"About the experiment," said Gamaliel, flicking the ash of his cigar into an empty beer can. "You know that if you turn down this opportunity, you'll never forgive yourself. You have the curiosity of a cat, Lewis, just as I do.''

Lewis sat silent a long moment, staring at the orb. ''I'll agree to it under one condition: you don't touch the cards.''

''Agreed. I have absolutely no need to touch the cards—not in the physical sense, anyway. Now please take one last look at your hand and place it facedown on the table in front of you.'' Which Lewis did. He expected to be nearly two thousand dollars richer very shortly, as long as Cartee kept his hands in plain view.

''The experiment begins,'' said Gamaliel. He picked up the orb and placed it on Lewis's side of the table, next to the facedown cards. ''The bauble is now yours to keep, Lewis. I hope you enjoy it. I have no doubt that you'll make good use of it in the years ahead, as I have. But—I believe you called, didn't you?'' He turned over his hand, card by card, and Lewis developed an immediate, blinding case of nausea. Gamaliel had drawn one card to complete a full house, jacks over nines, a phenomenal display of luck, considering that a lowly pair of deuces was statistically good enough to win more than half the hands in a one-on-one game of draw. The feat dwarfed Lewis's taking one card to fill a straight.

With his tongue feeling large and cottony, Lewis croaked his concession. He put his palms on the table and tried to stand, but his legs felt leaden. His vision went fuzzy. His own stupidity appalled him: he'd stayed in a game with someone he knew to be a sleight-of-hand artist and a cheat. Now he had the devil to pay.

''You may wish to check your hand,'' said Gamaliel. ''With so much money in the pot, it would be a shame to make a mistake.''

''I know what my hand is.''

''Yes, but I don't.''

''I'm under no obligation to show a losing hand,'' Lewis retorted bitterly, which was true according to the rules of poker. A good player never displays a losing hand, never reveals anything about his betting and bluffing strategies, even in defeat. "I'll pay you tomorrow, after the post American Express Bank opens. I assume you can be reached through division headquarters."

"Let's not get ahead of ourselves—you agreed to the experiment, remember? You even accepted my gift." Gamaliel gestured toward the orb that sat in its place near Lewis's hand, still emitting its toxic red light. Lewis glanced quickly at the thing and ground his teeth. He hadn't considered it a gift and didn't plan to accept it even now. He doubted whether it had any material value, not that it mattered.

Jesse moved close and whispered, "Can we *please* get the fuck out of here now? Haven't you done enough damage for one night?"

"I didn't take you for a man who would go back on his word," drawled Gamaliel. "I assumed that someone like you, an officer and an expert poker player, would care about his honor. Apparently I underestimated you."

Lewis didn't care about any officers' code of honor, but he *did* care about his honor as a poker player. His father had instilled in him the belief that a dishonest man has no business at a poker table, because poker is an honest game and true aficionados are honorable to the core. He *had* agreed to the experiment, which meant that Gamaliel was entitled to see his cards. Besides, he would never again play poker with this man, so what did it matter if he showed his hand?

Lewis turned the cards over all together and involuntarily sucked a deep breath when he saw them: four sixes and a stray five. He looked up at Gamaliel, then at Jesse, then at the bloody red orb, his mouth working soundlessly. The room seemed to tilt.

"Well, shut my mouth!" exclaimed Gamaliel, letting the Louisiana syrup flow freely. "I do believe that you've been trying to sandbag me, Lieutenant Kindred. You've been trying to set me up for a big old double-or-nothing bet, haven't you? Oldest trick in the book, and I must say, you're good at it— *damned* good, in fact! I'm sad to say that I've reached my limit for one night, so you'll need to find yourself another pigeon.'' He pushed his mound of MPC to Lewis's side of the table. ''Thank you for the game and for your participation in the experiment. It's been a stimulating evening, to say the least. Now, if you gentlemen will excuse me . . .''

''Wait!'' said Lewis hoarsely. He snatched up the orb and held it toward Gamaliel. It was heavy and disturbingly warm, as if it contained newly taken blood. He intensely disliked the feel of it. ''This belongs to you.''

''*Au contraire*, my friend. I gave it to you in return for your participation in the experiment. It's yours to keep.''

''No. I never accepted it.''

Gamaliel took a long moment to extinguish his cigar butt, exercising care not to let any ashes fall onto the army blanket. ''You surprise me, Lewis. You've seen what this little bauble can do. In the hands of someone like you—well, you can just imagine the possibilities. All you have to do is *accept*.''

''I don't accept! I don't want anything from you! I hope to God I never lay eyes on you again, Cartee, and you'd better hope the same about me.''

A long, turbulent silence followed, during which Lewis heard neither the background *whup-whup* of helicopter blades nor the thudding of his own heart. He glared defiantly at Gamaliel, as if to blink first would be to surrender. Finally Gamaliel rose from the table and placed his bush hat squarely on his head. He straightened his fatigue jacket and smoothed out the wrinkles. He took the orb in his hand and tossed it a few times in the air before slipping it into his pocket.

''Good night, Lewis. Good night, Jesse and Sergeant Hai.'' He turned and swaggered slowly toward the door, and for one fraction of a second his shadow fell across the table. Lewis was certain that it made a sound as it slid across the army blanket, a soft rustling, like living skin on fabric. Gamaliel halted a moment, spoke again. ''I knew you would be here tonight, Lewis. That's why I came—to have a game with *you*, not with these other poor fools. And I'm glad I did, too, despite the outcome. We'll play again sometime—if not poker, then another game—and maybe things will be different.'' He slipped out the door, and the night swallowed him.

Three

i

BECAUSE THE HOME base of the 25th Infantry Division was in Hawaii, the main recreation area in Cu Chi Base Camp was known as Waikiki East. The restaurant there had torches for light, potted palms for atmosphere, and locally hired waitresses dressed in muumuus and leis. The food, however, was Chinese, since Hawaiian cuisine was beyond the range of locally hired cooks. Whatever its pretensions, the place was pure Vietnam, right down to the stooped mama-sans who bused the tables and the skinny boot-shine boys who accosted every customer who came through the door.

Jesse felt like celebrating, and he badgered Lewis into joining him there for dinner. Between bites of pot-sticker he said, "I feel like I just walked through a trip wire, but the booby trap didn't go off. It's like I got a new lease on life. That Cartee is one dangerous son-of-a-bitch, L.T. Don't ask me how I know this—I just know."

Lewis nodded, but kept quiet while Jesse sipped his fifth Pabst Blue Ribbon. He wanted to talk about Gamaliel's shadow, but he couldn't bring himself to broach the subject, not even with a bellyful of beer.

"You got my money back for me," Jesse went on, "and here I am, wearing a clean uniform and pushin' Chinese chow into my face, drinking beer like there's no tomorrow—I gotta say it, man, I feel good!" He laughed deeply, his bull shoulders lurching, but then he became serious and put down his chopsticks. "I'm grateful to you, L.T. It looks strange, a soul brother gettin' tight with a white lieutenant, but I don't give a fuck what anybody thinks. You've been straight with me. I want you to know I appreciate it."

Lewis grinned sloppily. He hadn't drunk this much beer since his freshman year in college. "I can't take any credit for getting your money back, Jess. It was all part of Cartee's trick to get me to take that big red marble." He leaned on his elbows and massaged his eyeballs through closed lids. "I've never seen anybody cheat that well, not in all my years of playing poker. The way that son-of-a-bitch handles cards, he should be on the stage."

"Why do you suppose he was so all-fired determined to give that thing to you, anyway?"

"I don't have a fucking clue."

Jesse paid for dinner, and they retired to the bar to listen to a Vietnamese band render a passable version of the Jefferson Airplane's "White Rabbit." Lewis wondered briefly if the Kewpie-doll singer understood the lyrics she was singing, then decided that it didn't matter—in Vietnam live music was live music. He stared absently across a torch-lit patio full of GIs dressed in baggy jungle fatigues, crammed cheek by jowl around tables laden with beer bottles. Cigarette smoke blanketed the area like a tropical fog. Without knowing exactly why, Lewis felt as sorry for them as he felt for himself.

"Something's eatin' at you, L.T., and I don't think it has anything to do with Cartee," said Jesse, lighting a Kool. "I don't doubt he rattled you as bad as he rattled me, but I think there's something else, too."

Lewis felt drunker than he wanted to be and wished he was in his bunk, alone in the dark. Despite the beery fog in his head, the painful reality of Twyla's betrayal came to him again and again, like the tide on a dark shore. His face must have displayed the pain.

"You okay, L.T.?"

"Yeah, I'm okay—I guess. I . . . uh . . . was just thinking. I've told you about Twyla, haven't I? She's my fiancée, or at least she *was*."

"Right. I've heard you talk about her."

"Sent me a Dear John. Got it this afternoon."

Jesse shook his head, studied his newly polished jungle boots, and eventually hissed a *motherfucker*! To the troops in Vietnam only two things topped a Dear John on the scale of personal catastrophe—getting wounded and getting killed.

"She steppin' out with Jody?" asked Jesse, referring to the

mythical thief of women's affections after their men had gone off to battle. The army's marching songs were full of references to the loathsome Jody, who was rich, handsome, and for some reason immune to the draft. Lewis nodded and bluntly summarized the Dear John. He recounted matter-of-factly how he'd thrown his stash of Twyla's letters into a shit-burner out by the motor pool, along with her picture. Jesse listened sympathetically, nodding as if he'd heard many such stories. When it was over, he said, "Didn't waste any fuckin' time doin' it, did you? Throwin' her letters and pictures into a barrel of burning shit seems pretty final, not to mention symbolic, if you get my drift."

"I wanted to insult her, and I wished like hell she could've been there to see me do it. But afterward I felt—empty. All I wanted to do was play cards, because the world gets real small and manageable when I play cards." He drank deeply of his beer, lowered his eyes, tried not to be dizzy. "Trouble is, a poker game doesn't last forever."

Jesse crushed out his Kool and lit a fresh one. "Let me ask you a question, L.T. Could you ever forgive the bitch for this? Could you take her back if she apologized and promised to be true till the day she died?"

"I could forgive her, maybe, but take her back? I don't think so. I'd always wonder if I could trust her. Whenever we were apart, I'd imagine her in the sack with some graduate student, or some professor, or some goddamn pizza delivery boy. And I don't think I could ever forget what it was like, sitting on the bunk tonight, reading that letter."

"I hear you, man. Now, I'm gonna suggest something, and don't say no until you've thought about it. You need some *therapy*, and I'm not talkin' about mind-altering substances. I'm talkin' about pussy, which I know from personal experience is the best damn therapy for just about anything that's hurtin' a man. You gotta do the one thing that proves you can make a new start, L.T.—you gotta put the boots to some strange."

"Get serious. This is Vietnam, remember?"

"I *am* serious. I'm gonna take you to a place in Cu Chi City—it's called Mama Dao's—where a dude can get himself a first-rate blow-bath and a steam job. The girls are pretty, they got tight asses, and in the immortal words of Jimi Hendrix, they're *experienced*, hear what I'm sayin'? It'll make a new man out of you, I swear."

"I know the place you're talking about. It's outside the wire, for Christ's sake."

"Of *course* it's outside the wire. They couldn't run a place like that inside the base camp—what's wrong with you, college boy? Now listen up, 'cause this is important. For a few bucks the MPs on the east gate will let us out, and all we gotta do is double-time a couple hundred meters right into Main Street Cu Chi. Mama Dao's is only a block this side of the big ARVN compound. We slip inside, get our bananas peeled, have ourselves a relaxing bath and massage, and slip back into the base camp before sunup. Nobody's the wiser."

Lewis laughed and raised the predictable objections. But then he imagined himself going along with the scheme, slipping into the city of Cu Chi with Jesse, finding himself a lean little whore with long, satiny hair and strong, knowing hands. He saw himself submitting to her ministrations, tasting her lips, feeling her fingers on him. Suddenly he had a hard-on, right there at the bar in Waikiki East. He knew then that Jesse was right, that throwing Twyla's letters into the shit-burner hadn't been enough.

"I can't believe I'm about to say this, Jess"—it was the beer talking, he knew, but he couldn't help it, not when his dick was doing his thinking for him—"but you better lend me one of your shirts and some rank insignia. It might cause a stir at the gate, a lieutenant sneaking out of the base camp to visit a cathouse."

ii

Unfortunately for Lewis he began to sober up just as he and Jesse reached the halfway point between the final strand of concertina wire around Cu Chi Base Camp and the city. With the cold stars above him and the black of night pressing in, the safety of the bunker line and the berm far behind and prospects of court-martial ahead, he became violently sick. He staggered to the side of the road and, in the language of the U.S. Army, blew chow.

Jesse held on to him, kept him from fumbling into the puddle of his own puke. Lewis was sober as a Puritan deacon now, and dehydrated. And scared. Despite the humid warmth of the tropical night, he shook like a newborn lamb.

They made their way over the potholed asphalt road to the outskirts of Cu Chi, past a jumble of huts built of flattened American beer cans, testaments to the fact that Vietnamese could find good uses for just about anything the U.S. Army threw away. They halted briefly at an ARVN roadblock manned by a trio of soldiers with QC on their helmets, which was the abbreviation for the Vietnamese equivalent of "Military Police." The senior QC gave them the once-over before waving them on with a grin and a wink. He knew exactly what they were up to.

Farther on stood shops and stalls, secured for the night with barred gates of wrought iron. Lewis caught glimpses of people peering out through the bars, saw their cigarettes flare in the dark, heard their singsongy voices as they chatted among themselves. Closer to the heart of the town he saw more people on the streets, papa-sans and mama-sans, kids, ARVN soldiers. The lights were brighter here, the buildings more substantial. Commercial signs covered virtually every square inch of wall space, hawking Coca-Cola, Marlboros, Michelin tires, San Miguel beer, and a hundred other products in Vietnamese, English, and French. A banner strung over the street bore the likeness of President Nguyen Van Thieu. A moped zipped past, carrying three scrawny young men. Dogs barked and babies cried. Vietnamese music drifted on the evening air, mingling with the soft light of colored lanterns and the smells of oily cooking.

Jesse led him into the main marketplace, beyond which lay

an ARVN compound with tall watchtowers and a heavily fortified bunker line. During the daylight hours this market teemed with townspeople and farmers who carried on a brisk commerce in everything from American-made flashlight batteries to roasted monkeys. Seeing it deserted gave Lewis a chill.

They stopped at a two-story building fronting a narrow side street, flanked by lush tamarind trees. Shrapnel had pocked the pink stucco walls here and there, marks of the Tet offensive of 1968 when the VC rocketed the hell out of the city, but otherwise the building was in good repair. A wide balcony overlooked a courtyard, where the management had strung colored-paper lanterns between the pillars. Bougainvillea grew in a leafy riot along the walk, and someone inside was playing the Carpenters' "We've Only Just Begun" on a stereo.

"Welcome to Mama Dao's, L.T.," said Jesse, patting Lewis on the shoulder. "I'm gonna get you inside and make sure the good mama-san fixes you up with somebody real nice. Then you're on your own, my man."

iii

The girl was exactly as Lewis had fantasized, lean but not skinny, tall for a Vietnamese and raven-haired, maybe nineteen. Her huge almond eyes bore a faint hint of European blood, suggesting a French colonialist in her family's past. She wore an elaborately embroidered *ao dai* of powder blue and, beneath it, white bell bottoms and a New York Yankees T-shirt that some grateful soldier had given her.

Her name was Thuy Thanh, but she instructed him to call her simply Thanh, and she laughed sweetly as she talked, making Lewis feel as if he was the greatest joy she'd yet found in life. "You gee-eye beaucoup horny, yeah? You want boom-boom one hour, fie dollah MPC. You want boom-boom all night, only twenny-fie dollah MPC, okay?"

Yes, he *was* one very horny GI, having sobered up; and he

probably *could* boom-boom all night. The fee was just fine. He thought Thuy Thanh was the most beautiful creature he'd ever seen, and he would have given all he owned for a night with her. He dug into his wallet and handed a wad of MPC to Mama Dao, who was a chunky mama-san well under five feet tall with huge brass hoops through her earlobes. She took his money with a grin blackened by decades of chewing betel nut, and made a production of linking Thanh's hand with his.

Thanh led him up a flight of narrow stairs to a small, candlelit room that stank of incense and marijuana. A low bed lay against an interior wall, and French doors opened onto a shallow balcony with a filigreed railing, beyond which stars twinkled like gems. On a low mahogany table was a clutter of religious appurtenances—a small jade Buddha, colored candles, punky sticks of incense, and framed photos of dead relatives. Thanh undressed him, carefully folding his clothing and stacking each item on a bamboo mat next to the table. She then pulled him into a standing position, wrapped him in a clean Turkish towel, and giggled at the lump that his hard-on made beneath it.

She steered him down the hall to the steam room, which was little more than a closet with a bench in it. She deposited him on the bench and ordered him to stay put. The room was excruciatingly hot and pungent with some biting spice. Before long, he was thoroughly soaked with sweat, and his stinging eyes ran like faucets. He felt as if he was sweating out the evil humors he'd poured into himself at Waikiki East, along with a multitude of worries and anxieties. This was good. He felt mentally sharp and acutely sober.

Fifteen long minutes later Thanh reappeared, having changed into a flowered two-piece bathing suit. She shepherded him to a tiled room with an ancient bathtub in it. Following her orders, Lewis lowered himself carefully into the soapy water.

Somewhere a stereo played a Byrds album, and his mind drifted in a fog of purely physical sensation, where no worries of the past or the future could intrude. Thanh gave him tea and sugary little rice cakes, scrubbed his back raw, lathered his hair, rinsed him thoroughly, dried him. She then led him back to the bedroom.

Silhouetted against a fulgent moon that had risen behind the tamarinds, she slipped out of her swimsuit and stood a moment at the foot of the bed, letting Lewis survey her. He did so slowly, hungrily, marveling at her satiny skin, her graceful limbs, her beautiful little breasts, and the mound of dark silk between her legs. He marveled, too, at her smile, the warmth in her flawless face, the way the candlelight burnished her skin and made her look like something off the cover of a fantasy novel.

He now appreciated fully the addictive effect of the Orient on countless Westerners over the centuries—not just because of women like Thuy Thanh, who could make a man feel like a potentate for the price of a good bottle of wine, but because of the culture that produced such women; a culture that ignored deadlines, bureaucratic decrees, and other Western devices inimical to true human nature. If not for this insane war, he felt he could live out his life in a place like Cu Chi city, probably with a woman like Thanh, and become intoxicated with merely being alive. He could see himself basking forever in the coppery sunlight of this land, drinking in the fragrant colors of the landscape, reveling in the velvety nights. He could see himself growing fat on the zesty food and fathering a platoon of exquisite Amerasian kids. Unburdened of the demands of modern Western life, he would read philosophy and bloat his intellect on the idealism of Kant and the pragmatism of Nietzsche; maybe synthesize the two with the Asian mysteries that he yearned to unravel, and emerge as the great philosopher of the twentieth century. The thought made him smile.

Thanh lay down on him suddenly, covered his mouth with hers, and thrust her tongue deep. So much for philosophy. The touch of her breasts against his chest nearly catapulted him to orgasm, but he somehow managed to hold back the flood. He rolled her over and went to work on her nipples with his tongue, making her moan softly. His cock was between her legs now, and she was already driving her groin against it, seeking it. Her fingers found it and pressed it into service, taking only the tip at first, but urging it deeper with every thrust. Ten such thrusts, and he was wholly inside her, engulfed in her heat. With practiced pelvic muscles she held his cock and coaxed it, squeezed it, twisted it this way and that. She sighed and moaned, nipped at his earlobes with her tongue, and dug her fingernails into his buttocks as she pulled him ever tighter and deeper. Their bellies made kissing sounds as they slapped together and pulled apart.

Suddenly his orgasm exploded like a grenade launcher, and Thanh yelped as she rode him out, grinding against him until finding completion herself. Afterward they lay together a long while, their sweaty skin cooling in a breeze that whispered through the open window. Only one of the candles remained alive, the others having burned themselves into shapeless piles of wax.

"You gee-eye make me come," she whispered in the near dark, touching his cheek. "I not come with other gee-eye, but you make me come, okay?"

"I'll bet you say that to all the boys."

"No, I not say it before. You good boom-boom, okay? You make me come. You gee-eye numbah one."

"You, too, Thanh." He kissed her face and gently smoothed her long black hair. "I've never known anyone like you."

He wasn't lying. He and Twyla had slept together countless times, children of the Western sexual revolution that they were, but Lewis had never felt with Twyla or anyone else the sheer sexual exhilaration, the total immersion and release, that Thuy Thanh had given him. The fact that he'd paid for the girl's services didn't matter in the least. He wondered whether he would feel this good in the morning, when the afterglow had worn off.

Sometime later he detected a flicker through closed eyelids, as if something bright had passed near his face. He reached for Thanh, but found only a tangle of damp sheets. He assumed she'd gotten up to go to the bathroom, that she would soon return, since he'd paid for a whole night with her. A glance at his watch told him that it was only minutes past one in the morning.

He became conscious of the *silence*—a silence that deadened the chirping of crickets in the foliage beyond the balcony and the *whup-whup* of helicopters landing and taking off from the nearby base camp. He raised himself on his elbows. Something was wrong, but he couldn't fathom what it was.

A red glow caught his eye as the door opened slowly and threw a wedge of bloody light over the bed. Lewis watched in amazement as the source of the glow came into view, and suddenly his heart began to thunder like a kettledrum. A sphere of red crystal hung in the air over the threshold, unsupported by anything visible, glowering like a crimson eye and casting its rays over the bed and walls, over Lewis himself. It was slightly larger than a golf ball. It moved lightly from side to side and up and down, as if riding a languid wave over an invisible tropical ocean. If it wasn't the same gemstone that Gamaliel Cartee had tried to give him earlier in the evening, it was identical to it.

For what seemed an eternity Lewis stared at the thing, disbelieving, blinking to purge what he hoped was a hallucination. He tried to swallow, but found that he had no spit. His scalp prickled as his brain flipped through a list of possibilities. Invisible wires? Mirrors? A projected image? He rose from the bed and approached the orb, but it moved deeper into the black corridor as if it feared his touch. He took another step toward the door, and it floated down the corridor to his right, bouncing lightly along on invisible currents.

No lights shone under the doors of the other rooms, which seemed terribly wrong, because Mama Dao's whores and their johns should have been coming and going, so to speak, until dawn. Too, a light should have burned over the staircase at the end of the corridor, but the staircase was as dark as a mine shaft. The whorehouse had plunged into a coma, seemingly.

Leaning through the door into the corridor, Lewis saw the

orb halt near a room two doors away, and something made him wonder if that was the room Jesse was in. Apparently the object was waiting for him to follow, and he decided to oblige. Some real-world explanation lay behind all this, he was sure, and he decided that he must find it. He stepped into the corridor, naked, feeling as vulnerable as he'd ever felt in his life.

He approached the orb slowly, cautiously, and wondered whether it would let him close enough to detect the thin wire that surely must hold it. The orb did not retreat from him, but only bobbed lightly on its invisible wave. Sweat beaded Lewis's forehead, and he felt the splintery old floorboards bite the soles of his feet, heard the wood creak under his weight. Gooseflesh rose.

When he'd drawn to within an arm's length of the orb, he heard sounds from the room next to which the thing had halted—breathy, greasy sounds; the sounds of sex, he thought, and maybe something more. . . .

He reached for the orb, and it didn't flee. His outstretched fingers moved to within an inch of it, but he stopped himself, for his heart was trying to climb into his throat. The image of Gamaliel Cartee loomed vivid in his mind, tall in the hot sun of a nameless hamlet near the Ho Bo Woods, casting a shadow swarming with microscopic vermin, just as the interior of this bauble swarmed with life. Somehow Lewis forced his hand to close around the thing, and the orb surrendered itself, warm and heavy, feeling just as it had felt earlier in the evening when Gamaliel had tried to give it to him. He found no wires attached to it and no threads, saw no tracks along the floor or on the ceiling through which a stage magician or a trickster could have guided the device. The damned thing had indeed levitated, a reality that gave Lewis a sick feeling in the back of his skull.

He turned toward the door. The sounds of passion in the room beyond it were becoming stronger, more violent. He tasted an unreasoning fear that filled his gullet and threatened to choke him. He labored to shape words, tried to call out, but his vocal cords balked. "J-Jesse?"

He tried again, harder this time. "Jesse, are you in there?" Near-total darkness engulfed the corridor, since Lewis held the only source of light clenched tightly in his fist. A few crazy beams of crimson escaped between his fingers, enough to show him that the door of the room was slowly swinging open. The greasy sounds became louder still, and moonlight spilled through the balcony of the room into the corridor.

"Jesse, for Christ's sake, are you . . . ?"

Now the door stood open wide. Blood was everywhere, spilled over the floor, slung in great inky dollops across the walls—flowing from the body of Thuy Thanh, who crouched on the low bed as something took her doggy-style from behind, something that didn't look human.

Whatever this was, or *whoever* he was, he hunkered over the poor little whore like some freakish canine, his monstrous cock plunging in and out of her like a piston, literally splitting her up the middle and scattering strings of blood in all directions. His hands had long, gnarly nails that had left parallel tracks of red across the girl's skin. While fucking Thanh to death, the thing tore strips of meat from her neck with his teeth and bolted them down like a wolf. Incomprehensibly, the girl appeared to verge on orgasm, even as the thing bit into her again and again.

Lewis stood stone still, his eyes unblinking, his senses overloaded, until at last Thanh shuddered and slumped forward into the swamp of blood that had pooled on the bed. The beast pulled out of her, sated, turned his face toward Lewis, and grinned with a mouthful of dazzling teeth, all pointed like a crocodile's. His brow was a bony exaggeration, his nose flared. His jaw was almost doglike. He wore camouflaged jungle fatigues that were soggy with the girl's blood, sewn with the rank insignia of a sergeant. His atrocious cock stood out from his body like a medieval instrument of torture, throbbing and glistening in the moonlight, dripping blood.

Lewis caught the glint of the beast's mismatched eyes—the right one blue, the left one brown. *No question about who this is, is there, Lewis old boy? Not anymore! Did you have any doubt . . . ?* Light glinted behind those eyes, almost as though Gamaliel had a candle inside his skull. Lewis sucked a huge lungful of air and screamed his revulsion until his throat cracked and his lungs burned.

Through lips and teeth ill-suited to speech, Gamaliel whispered, "I knew you would come, Lewis. I knew you'd be here, just like I knew you would show up last night in the motor pool to play poker. You'd be surprised how much I know about you."

Lewis reared back like a pitcher on the mound and hurled the orb with all his might at Gamaliel's head. The thing flew as straight and true as a major-league fastball, but halted abruptly a mere foot from Gamaliel's face—arrested by some invisible force. Gamaliel grinned and plucked the object out of the air, held it a moment in his clawed hand as if to taste the glittery red ghosts of light it cast. Then he stared again at Lewis with those cold-hot eyes, probing him, reading him, maybe even *loving* him, and Lewis could endure no more. He doubled over and retched, but little more than acid came out.

Gamaliel turned away and leaped nimbly through the open French door, perched a moment on the railing of the balcony like a huge dark bird, and cocked a talon toward Lewis. Through blurry tears Lewis imagined that he saw his face shifting, rippling, returning to its normal shape and features, but he couldn't be sure of this. A heartbeat later Gamaliel plunged into the night as though he could fly, and perhaps he *could* fly, for Lewis heard no crash in the courtyard below, only the songs of insects and the faraway whipping of helicopter rotors.

Kneeling in the corridor outside the room, shaking so badly he could hardly breathe, Lewis covered his face with his hands and cried. He didn't hear the approach of Jesse Burton behind him, and he scarcely felt Jesse's hand on his shoulder.

Four

i

THROUGHOUT THE FOLLOWING day and most of the next, Lieutenant Lewis Kindred went about his chores as if nothing extraordinary had happened. He attended briefings by the brigade operations officer and conducted perfunctory inspections of his platoon. He drafted morning reports, disposition forms, and requisitions of new equipment. He approved and denied requests for leaves. In short, he did everything that a scout platoon leader would do during stand-down and astounded himself that he could carry on in so normal a fashion, having seen what he'd seen at Mama Dao's.

On the final afternoon of the stand-down he used the land line in the Headquarters Company orderly room to call division headquarters and ask whether a particular IPW, one Sergeant Gamaliel Cartee, would be available to participate in combat operations during the coming weeks. Most assuredly, answered the grouchy warrant officer who'd answered the phone—all IPW teams were available for duty anywhere within the 25th Division's area of operation, including Sergeant Cartee. Lewis hung up before the man could ask who was calling and why.

Specialist-4 Jesse Burton had assumed a low profile since the episode at Mama Dao's, which Lewis found understandable. On the final night of the stand-down Lewis found him in the enlisted men's dayroom, sitting zombie-eyed in front of a TV set, chain-smoking Kools. The news was on, and the anchorman read an update on the latest serial murder in the vicinity of Saigon, the thirteenth such killing. The victim was a young prostitute in Cu Chi city, a part-time student.

Lewis lowered himself into a frayed armchair and listened in silence, trying in vain not to conjure images of Thuy Thanh's wonderful face, made *un*-wonderful by Cartee. A sudden ache in his chest took his breath away. "We need to talk," he said finally.

Jesse didn't look up, but poked absently through a pile of magazines on the coffee table in front of him. "So talk."

"Not here. Too many ears."

"Somewhere else, then. What the fuck do I care?"

They went out into the dark and walked toward the bunker line of the base camp, past the Triple Deuce motor pool into the 2nd of the 34th Armored's tank park. Helicopters thundered overhead with typical regularity, like worker bees attending the hive, even in darkness. Parachute flares popped near the distant horizon, accompanied by the faint *chunk* of grenades and the *crump* of mortar fire, indicating encounters between the enemy and Allied ambush patrols. Red tracers arced silently into the night, barely coming into view over the edges of the berm. Men were dying out there, Lewis knew. While he and Jesse ambled casually along the bunker line, others were suffering shattered limbs, sucking chest wounds, and ruined dreams.

"This should be private enough, don't you think?" asked Jesse, propping a jungle boot against the road wheel of a parked tank. He lit a fresh Kool, and the flame from his Zippo glared briefly in his marble-hard eyes. "So what do you want to talk about?"

"You know."

"What's there to say, man? I mean, there's nothing we can actually *do*, right? We can't go to the MPs—you said yourself that nobody would believe you about seein' Cartee doin' what he was doin' to that girl. There's nothin' we can accomplish, except maybe gettin' your ass court-martialed and me busted. Isn't that what we decided?"

Yes, that was what they'd decided, while running in blind panic from Mama Dao's cathouse, pulling on their clothes as they stumbled toward the base-camp gate, chased by the screams of a whore who'd found Thuy Thanh's body. They'd barely slipped into the safety of the berm when the sirens of QCs' Jeeps erupted in the city, the sounds of cops called to the scene of the crime.

"We were damn fortunate to un-ass that place without gettin' ourselves arrested," Jesse went on. "Hell, we might even have been suspects in the murder. If you ask me, the best thing we can do is let sleeping dogs be."

"We can't do that, and you know it."

"Why the hell not?"

"Because Gamaliel is *evil*, that's why. We've both seen it. We've both felt it."

"Of course he's evil. He's a fuckin' GI, right? We're *all* evil, man. I mean, think about it. We're over here in this stinking little country, shootin' the shit out of everything that moves, knocking down people's houses, breakin' heads, and splatterin' little yellow dudes all over the landscape—and for what? For Nguyen Van Thieu and his fat generals? Hell, half his people are dealin' smack to the U.S. Army. The other half are runnin' whores, or stealin' from the government and salting it away in Switzerland. If you ask me, it's evil to kill for these motherfuckers."

"I won't argue with that. But Gamaliel's different from the rest of us, Jesse. I wish you could've seen his face when he was . . . when he was with Thanh. He wasn't even human."

"Come *on*, L.T. He's a trickster, that's all—a performer. He should be on the stage. You said so yourself."

"What he did to Thanh was no trick. I'm telling you he was some kind of animal, the kind you had nightmares about when you were a little kid. You saw what Thanh looked like when he was finished with her. He's a *monster*, Jess. I've never believed in things like this, but I know what I saw. I can't just walk away from it, and neither can you."

Jesse disagreed. He pointed out with dry logic that fighting men left Vietnam daily by the planeloads after putting in their tours. Every one of them, he was willing to bet, left a piece of himself in this smelly, rat-infested purgatory. Every one of them had suffered a day or a night or a moment that he wished to God he could take back, a snapshot in time that couldn't have happened anywhere but Vietnam, during which he'd sunk to something less than human. But in the end, every swingin' dick managed to walk away without looking back, just as Jesse himself intended to walk away when his time came. "When I get back to the world, the air's going to smell sweet, man, not like burning shit," he declared. "I'm goin' to a *good* place, man. Vietnam won't even exist for me."

"Don't be so sure about that. As long as Gamaliel exists, so will this filthy little war. There'll never be a good place, Jess—not while he's alive. Not for you and me."

"How can you be so fuckin' sure of that? What makes you the fuckin' authority, huh, college boy?"

Lewis rested his forehead against the cool hull of the tank and wondered whether he was about to taste his friend's knuckles. He breathed in smoke from Jesse's cigarette, his eyes clamped tight. A mosquito stung his cheek, but he didn't care. "He tried to give the red ball to *me*, remember? I think that's important somehow."

"And why would you think that?"

"I don't know. I just do." He opened his eyes. "Remember when he left the motor pool—after I made him take it back? He turned around and said he'd *known* I would show up to play cards that night. He said he'd come to have a game with *me*, not with all you other poor fools."

"He was fuckin' with your mind, that's all."

"But later at Mama Dao's he said the same thing. After he'd"—Lewis took a slow breath—". . . after he'd killed Thanh, he looked at me with those . . . those weird fucking eyes of his, and said that he'd known I would be there, too, at Mama Dao's, just like he'd known that I would show up in the motor pool to play poker. 'You'd be surprised how much I know about you,' he said, and it was like he was inside my head, Jesse, like he'd singled me out from everybody else in order to . . ."

A helicopter flew over low, a Cobra gunship outbound for some firefight deep within the seamless night of Vietnam. Lewis let its thunder fade before speaking again. "He has *plans* for me. I don't know what they are, but I know I can't wait around to find out. You can understand that, can't you?"

Jesse sucked deeply from his Kool, blew the smoke out

slowly, harshly, and kept quiet a long time. Finally: "So what do you want to do about him?"

Lewis reached under his fatigue jacket and pulled a blunt semiautomatic pistol from his belt, a Chinese-made K-54 that he'd taken from a captured NVA captain several months earlier. It had unusual pearl-handled grips that marked it as a source of pride to its original owner. Moonlight gleamed off its oily surfaces as he held it up in front of Jesse. "There's only one thing we *can* do, I think."

"Jesus," the black man breathed, his eyes round and wide. "You don't need to say any more—I know where this is goin' . . ."

ii

Lewis got the opportunity he needed six days later on the southern edge of the Michelin rubber plantation, near the town of Dau Tieng in the shadow of Black Virgin Mountain. Colonel Golightly had sent the scout platoon on a mission to recon an overgrown area that had once been a string of hamlets, where plantation workers had lived before the U.S. Army decided to move them out in order to cut off their support of local Vietcong units. According to intelligence reports, the NVA had since dug tunnels and built bunkers where houses once stood, and now used the area to stage attacks on Dau Tieng and the surrounding communities.

A pale rain fell as the tracks crawled forward through the low brush, their engines growling and belching back smoke as they ground down wild banana trees and pepper bushes, their crews clinging to the topsides as they jolted and bucked over clumps of bamboo and remnants of old walls. Black Virgin Mountain loomed close in the mist like a remembered dream, and Lewis found himself gazing at her time and again, getting lost in fantasies about eruptions of lava and ash. *Do it!* he implored the goddess under his breath. *Do it, and make all this unnecessary.*

Noon. The scouts circled the tracks in a comparatively flat area and broke for chow. "This is supposed to be the fuckin' dry season, man," groused T. J. Skane, tearing open a rain-soggy box of C rations. "And it ain't supposed to be cold in Vietnam. It's supposed to be *hot*. This place is so fucked up that even the weather don't know how to act." Danny Legler laughed so hard at this he almost feel off the track.

Lewis noticed that No Bick wasn't eating, that he was behaving as if he was on sentry duty. He sat rigidly on an ammo box with his rifle at the ready, his slitted eyes scanning the dark wall of rubber trees in the distance. Since the episode with Gamaliel Cartee in the hamlet north of Trung Lap, Lewis hadn't heard the Kit Carson utter more than two consecutive words of English, even though all the scouts knew by now that Hai spoke English better than most Americans. The nickname that T. J. Skane had given him still stuck—"No Bick"—and nearly everyone in the platoon called him that. If Hai took any offense to this he didn't show it.

He senses something out there, Lewis said to himself, studying the small man's austere face. *He knows how the bad guys think, because he's been one of them. And he's scared. . . .*

Lewis set aside his cold can of "Beef with Spiced Sauces," one of the less appetizing entrées in a case of C rats, and moved next to No Bick, who acknowledged him with a faint nod. "What is it, Sergeant Hai?" he asked simply. "I've got to know."

No Bick gazed silently at the rubber trees as if Lewis didn't exist, his eyes sweeping slowly from side to side, water dripping off his bush hat. "*No bick,*" he replied flatly, as if this would make Lewis go away.

"Give me a break, Hai. I've heard you speak the King's English like an Oxford don, remember? This no-bick routine doesn't pack it for me." Hai's expression hardened, became decidedly defiant. It reminded Lewis of the faces painted on targets at the firing ranges at Fort Knox, caricatures of the villainous Vietcong—a wily and bloodthirsty enemy who needed killing. "Okay," said Lewis, holding back his anger, "have it your way. But if you see or hear something I should know about, my door is always open."

He moved back to his own spot, where Jesse Burton was engrossed in the chore of eating pound cake from a small green can with a plastic spoon. Their eyes met, and each knew that the other was asking himself, *Is this the day?*

Lewis hoped ardently that this *was* the day, but he'd begun to wonder if it would ever come, if the right combination of circumstances was too much to hope for. He needed the proper tactical conditions and a suitable detainee. If he was to do the deed and get away with it, he needed a situation that would make believable the story that he and Jesse would tell. *What are the odds,* he wondered with his poker player's brain, *that it will all come together? Ten to one? A hundred to one?*

Half an hour later the platoon was under way again, sweeping close to the boundary of the plantation. Soon the scouts were near enough to make out the spiraling grooves cut into the bark of the trees, from which oozed white, rubbery sap that dripped into shallow bowls hanging from pegs driven into the trunks. The rain relented around two o'clock and the sun broke through, generating a steamy mist that lay heavy on the land. Lewis halted the platoon briefly so that Leg could take a snapshot of a web strung between two rubber trees, in the center of which sat the most ferocious-looking spider any of them had ever seen—a red-and-black monster the size of a grown man's two fists. Raindrops in the web reflected the sunlight like diamonds suspended in space.

"There!" shouted Jesse, standing up in the cupola, pointing ahead. "We've got movement, gentlemen!" Lewis unbuckled his seat belt and craned to see what he was pointing at. A hundred meters to their front stood a makeshift hooch nestled in the ground fog, one built mostly of thatched elephant grass. A man stood near it, casually eating a banana, apparently fearless of the approaching Americans and their thundering war machines. He wore a faded Hawaiian sport short, dirty blue trousers, and a ragged conical hat. His right arm, Lewis noticed with a cringe, ended just above the elbow.

"Yeah, it's movement, all right," he said sarcastically. "This guy's a real menace." But he was thinking, *The odds just improved . . . !*

Over Lewis's headset came the gravelly voice of the platoon sergeant, Frank Markowski, reporting that he, too, had seen the man. "This guy's no little kid," said Markowski, "and he's sure as hell no old papa-san, so he must be fair game. I recommend we recon by fire. Over."

Lewis nixed that idea, which he was certain only reinforced Markowski's conviction that he was a spineless puke and unworthy of leadership. He then ordered the platoon to halt and instructed his squad leaders to form a tactical perimeter not closer than a hundred meters from the hooch. Jesse, who also wore a headset that was plugged into the track's radios, overheard the transmission, and cast a knowing look at Lewis. *This is it, isn't it?* said his eyes. Lewis ignored him and told Markowski that he wanted a meeting with the squad leaders at his tailgate as soon as the perimeter was secure.

"Okay gentlemen, listen up," he told the gathered sergeants. "Jesse and I'll interrogate the guy in the hooch. He's obviously an ARVN vet who's been wounded and discharged, but he may know something about the NVA activity around here. Sergeant Hillman, I want you to take six men on foot and set up a listening post a hundred meters west of that hooch. Sergeant Marino, I want you to do the same a hundred meters east of it. Make sure you each take at least one M-60 machine gun, and bring radios so you can stay in contact with me. The rest of you stay here with Sergeant Markowski, and keep your eyes open. Be ready to move out when I give the order, and maintain fire discipline. Also, make sure every swinging dick is wearing a steel pot and a flak jacket. Got a good copy?"

They all had good copies.

iii

Lewis called battalion headquarters on the radio and advised Colonel Golightly of his situation, saying that he was about to detain and question a civilian, to which the Triple Deuce commander gave his blessing. The two foot patrols left the perimeter as Lewis had ordered, and a few minutes later he and Jesse set out on foot for the hooch, where the civilian stood as if he was waiting for them, unruffled, sunning himself.

The twenty-minute "interrogation" took place inside the hooch, while Jesse stood guard in the doorway, his PRC-77 radio strapped to his back and his M-16 locked and loaded. The one-armed detainee's identification card verified what Lewis suspected—he was an ARVN veteran who had lost his arm in combat. Through sign language and pidgin English Lewis learned that the man was destitute, having lost his family to the war, along with his home and most of his friends. He now lived by poaching rubber sap from the plantation and selling it in nearby Dau Tieng, earning barely enough in combination with his veteran's pension to subsist alone in this dilapidated shack. Lewis felt intensely sorry for him and wished there was something he could do for him.

The sun now blazed hotly, and inside the hooch the air was dank and smelly. Flies buzzed and bit, mosquitoes stung. The ARVN veteran incessantly scratched the stump of his severed arm with his fingernails, causing Lewis's own skin to tingle and itch.

"Okay, it's been long enough," said Lewis, glancing at his watch. "Time to call the Old Man."

"Sure you want to go through with this?" asked Jesse.

"We've talked about it a hundred times. We don't have a choice, remember?"

The big black man clamped his teeth together, causing the muscles in his jaw to ripple. "I remember." He unhooked the radio handset from his chest strap and handed it over, avoiding Lewis's eyes.

"Main Rancho Six, this is Tango . . ." Lewis prayed his voice wouldn't quiver. "I think this situation calls for an India Papa Whiskey. I have a feeling that this detainee knows more than he's letting on. . . ." He told the lie smoothly and even embellished it, but at length he got to the crux of the matter—

the fact that he wanted not just *any* IPW. He wanted Sergeant
Gamaliel Cartee, whose name he spelled out in code, the accepted radio procedure in Vietnam. Golightly, who by now
was orbiting high above the Michelin rubber plantation in a
loach, said he would be delighted to send an IPW, but he
wondered whether sending *that* particular man was a good
idea, considering his history with the scout platoon.

Lewis was ready with an answer, having crafted it to appeal
to Golightly's soldierly sensibilities. "This is Tango. Sir, I
want a chance to make things right with the man, to show him
that there're no hard feelings on my part. I think we both
deserve a chance to prove we can work together like professionals. When it comes right down to it, we're both in the
same army, and despite whatever differences he and I've had,
he's the best damn India Papa Whiskey I've ever seen. Over."

There. He'd spat it all out, but he feared that it had sounded
canned and out of character. Golightly was no dummy, and he
undoubtedly knew that you can wash a pig but you can't teach
it to make doilies. When the colonel keyed his radio, however,
he was chuckling merrily, much to Lewis's relief. Golightly
promised he would do all he could to bring *that* particular IPW
on station.

Lewis lowered the handset and took several deep breaths in
an effort to bring his pulse back to normal. *Okay, what are
the odds that I'll actually get Cartee? One in three? One in
five?* The enormity of what he was doing had just begun to
sink in, and the ease with which he was doing it was scary.

The Vietnamese veteran squatted in a dark corner of the
hooch, his mouth twitching with worry now, for he'd seen how
Americans often handled detainees, having been a soldier himself, and he clearly knew the term *India Papa Whiskey*. Lewis
tried to smile at him, tried to assure him that he wouldn't be
harmed, but the worried furrows didn't leave the man's brow.

Jesse's radio crackled, and he answered it. "It's Skane," he
muttered, holding the handset toward Lewis. "Something
about No Bick starting to talk."

Lewis took the handset. "This is Tango. What's going on? Over."

Skane answered from the cupola of Lewis's track, which was parked the length of a football field from the hooch. "That *dinky-dau* Kit Carson of yours has started to talk a blue streak, man, and he's usin' good English, you dig? Says we're parked near a big bunker complex, probably the headquarters of a regimental-size NVA unit. I say again—*regimental* size November Victor Alpha. Ain't that a bitch? Over."

Lewis remembered the tension he'd seen in No Bick's face earlier in the day. The fact that the Kit Carson had decided to break his near-legendary silence was cause for worry, as was the possibility that he was working for the other side. The little man's sudden decision to start behaving like a real Kit Carson might have been a trick to mislead the scouts about what was really here—a cache of NVA weapons, possibly, or an underground hospital, or any of a dozen other things that a spy wouldn't want the Americans to find. Lewis keyed the radio, called the platoon sergeant, and asked whether he had monitored the transmission from Skane.

"This is Delta," answered Markowski. "That's affirmative. Seems to me we should get ready to un-ass this location. I don't like to think about what might happen if there's a regimental-size unit of November Victor Alpha out here, do you? Over."

"This is Tango. Don't go off half-cocked, Delta—it might be a trick. Stand fast for now, but stay alert. If you see any movement, call me before you fire. I say again, call me before you fire. Got a good copy?"

"This is Delta, roger that. We're standing fast and staying alert. We're also wearin' our steel pots and flak jackets. Out." The sneer in Markowski's voice was damn near palpable.

Twenty minutes later Lewis detected the faraway throb of rotor blades, which grew steadily louder until the sound was directly overhead. Jesse went outside to "pop smoke" for the chopper pilot, which meant tossing a colored smoke grenade into a clear area to mark a suitable landing spot. The big slick

touched down only for a moment, scattering miniature tornadoes of bright yellow smoke in all directions, barely long
enough to disgorge two men—a Vietnamese and a tall American who was neither white nor black and yet was both.

Lewis watched from the doorway of the hooch, squinting to
see through the swirling veils of yellow. Not until the helicopter rose again was he able to confirm that the tall man was
indeed Gamaliel Cartee, immaculate as always, his creases like
razors and his boots like mirrors in the hot sun. The spidery
ARVN interpreter trailed him like a dutiful manservant.

Jesse slipped back into the hooch. "We've still got time to
change our minds," he whispered.

"No way."

The radio crackled again. "Markowski wants to know what
the fuck is going on," said Jesse. "Wants to know why you're
not setting up security on all sides of the hooch. What should
I tell him?"

"Tell him to mind his own business."

"Lewis, I can't do that. He's the fuckin' platoon sergeant.
Besides, he's got a legitimate point—we're hamburger if
there's big NVA unit out here."

"Tell him whatever you think sounds good, but make sure
he stays his distance. Now go do your thing, like we planned."

Jesse puffed his cheeks and blew out air, then spoke briefly
to Markowski on the radio. He turned to head out the door,
but held up a moment. "What we're gettin' ready to do—it's
right, isn't it?" he asked. "I mean, we're not becoming like
him, are we?" He motioned with his head toward the approaching IPW.

"What we're doing is good," Lewis answered softly.

Jesse intercepted the IPW team and told them that the lieutenant wanted only Cartee in the hooch with the detainee.
"Hey, this detainee's one spooky gook, man," he lied. "He
used to be an ARVN, but we think he's workin' the other side
of the street now. The L.T.'s afraid that if he sees an ARVN
uniform he's gonna clam up, hear what I'm sayin'?" Smiling
his most disarming smile, he offered the ARVN interpreter a

cigarette, and the two of them put their feet against a stump and lit up.

Cartee apparently swallowed the line and walked on toward the hooch alone. Lewis backed away from the door as he came near, having glimpsed his shadow, which rustled faintly as it swarmed over the ground like a stampeding horde of lice. For a moment Lewis plunged into pure panic, the kind a mouse must feel when cornered by a toothy cat. He forced himself to concentrate on what he must do, step-by-step, one small action at a time. The panic evaporated as suddenly as it came.

He took a glove from the side pocket of his fatigue shirt and pushed his right hand into it. Then he took the pearl-handled Chinese pistol from his belt, chambered a round, and hid it behind him in the small of his back.

Cartee ducked his head to pass through the door, straightened to his full height, and grinned ruthlessly at Lewis, who stood against the far wall of the cramped hooch, the ARVN veteran squatting at his feet. Saluting crisply, he said, "Sergeant Cartee reports, sir. Nice to see you again. Played any poker lately?"

Lewis felt the heat of anger build inside him, like lava inside a volcano. He remembered Thuy Thanh as he knew he would remember her all his life, not as an exquisite young woman, but the gory victim of the monster who now stood before him. The northern slope of Black Virgin Mountain was visible through the open door of the hooch, behind Cartee, and Lewis mouthed a silent prayer to the goddess: *Do it! Erupt now, or I will!*

"With all due respect, sir, you don't look at all well," drawled Cartee. "You haven't been forgetting to take your malaria pills, have you?"

Lewis couldn't speak. His mouth and throat had gone completely dry, which was fine, because he didn't have any idea what to say to someone just before blowing his head off.

"Well, you're a big boy now, aren't you, Lewis? You can take care of yourself, I'm sure. You take *all* the proper precautions, don't you? Like brushing your teeth after every meal and using foot powder to prevent jungle rot. I'll bet you wear rubbers when you're with whores to keep from getting the clap, don't you? Is that what you do, Lewis, when you go to Mama Dao's—wear a rubber? I don't use rubbers myself, because I don't worry about things like the clap, but I can certainly sympathize with people who do." His mismatched eyes glittered like jewels. "I'll bet you take other precautions as well. You're probably wearing a glove on the hand you plan to kill me with, aren't you? That way, you won't leave any fingerprints. This assumes, of course, that the Criminal Investigation Division will actually check for fingerprints, which they won't. Better to be safe than sorry, though, isn't that right, Lewis?"

Lewis brought the pistol from behind his back and pointed it squarely at Cartee's forehead. "*Ong!*" he said to the Vietnamese squatting at his feet, which meant *man* or *sir*. It was what Vietnamese men called each other. "You *di-di mau*, okay? Take off now. Go!" He gestured north, indicating the rubber plantation, and used a hand signal to advise the man to stay low, to keep his head down. "You're number-one good guy. You're no VC, no NVA, you *bick*? You *di-di mau*."

The man cowered even lower on the clay floor of the hooch, pressing his one hand against his stump in an awkward simulation of the Southeast Asian gesture of respect and supplication. He probably feared that he would be gunned down while trying to "escape," which was not unheard of in the annals of dead detainees. The more Lewis hissed at him to *di-di mau*, the more he cowered and scraped.

Cartee found all this amusing and laughed wickedly. "Lewis, Lewis. Can't you see that the miserable wretch has no intention of cooperating with you? You may as well get used to the idea that you'll need to kill us both. You sure as hell can't shoot me and leave him as a witness."

Lewis's lower lip trembled. "What *are* you?" he demanded hoarsely. "What in the name of God *are* you?"

"Invoking the name of God now, are we? That surprises me—an educated man like yourself, a naturalistic philosopher, and a confirmed humanist. I thought God doesn't exist for people like you.''

Lewis's eyes began to tear, and beads of sweat skittered down the sides of his face. He knew he could kill Cartee easily, but he wasn't about to harm the innocent man at his feet. The question now was whether he was ready to spend the rest of his life in federal prison, or maybe even face a firing squad for doing the world the service of exterminating Gamaliel Cartee. He wondered what the odds were that the ARVN vet would testify against him, if the U.S. Army's Criminal Investigation Division sought him out and questioned him.

''What's this?'' asked Cartee, taking a step nearer, his mismatched eyes flashing. ''Is your anger fading? Don't let it fade, Lewis, please. Anger is *magic*. It's *power*. Don't dilute it with reason. It smells so delicious when it's pure, like yours was a moment ago.''

Lewis again urged the ARVN veteran to *di-di mau*, but the man was paralyzed with fear. Lewis's right hand started to shake, the one holding the pistol. He steadied it with his left, gripping the wrist tightly.

''Really, Lewis, you're beginning to disappoint me. You call me all the way out here from Cu Chi, promising me a detainee to play with, and I haven't been here two minutes before you pull a gun on me. You tease me with all that sweet-smelling anger, and just when I'm starting to think, Hey, this is getting interesting, you start shaking like you've got malaria, and your anger goes limp. What's going on, Lewis? Are you losing your conviction, or are you just losing your nerve?''

Lewis shouted at the Vietnamese veteran to *di-di mau*, not caring whether Cartee's interpreter heard him. But the vet curled into a fetal ball, shut his eyes tight, and shivered.

Gamaliel made disgusted clicking sounds with his tongue and shook his head. ''I swear that in all my years I've never seen a more sickening display than this. I've severely underestimated you, I'm afraid. You've got no balls at all. I suppose I have no choice but to help you along. . . .'' Gamaliel drew his own pistol, a clubby service .45, clicked off the safety, and leveled it at the head of the ARVN veteran. Lewis's eyes widened as Gamaliel took precise aim. Fire exploded from the barrel, and Lewis felt a blast of heat on his face. Loud laughter issued from Gamaliel and hung in the air like the stink of rotting meat. Lewis stared down at the twitching body of the veteran, and saw the man's brain spilling onto the hard clay floor, watched dark blood spread like a plague. Lewis's own boots had bits of the man's scalp stuck to them.

Anger like Lewis had never known filled him. Through hot tears he sighted on Gamaliel's face and squeezed the trigger of the Chinese-made K-54. The pistol bucked and spat fire. The bullet hit Gamaliel just below his left eye, the brown one, and he went down gracelessly, as if he was a marionette and someone had cut his strings. He lay on the floor of the hooch, squirting a stream of blood through the hole in his face with every failing heartbeat, until the heart stopped.

Lewis watched himself move as if detached, a disembodied spirit observing a body on autopilot. He went to the rear wall of the hooch and kicked a hole in the thatched elephant grass. He took a hand grenade from his webbed pistol belt, pulled the pin, and rolled the grenade through the hole. Footfalls came from beyond the door, and shouts—Jesse and the interpreter rushing to investigate, having heard the shouting and the pistol shots. Now he heard the pop of the grenade's fuse, and he threw himself to the floor, mindless of the lake of blood there.

The grenade exploded with a bone-crunching *chunk!* Shrapnel whistled overhead through the thatched walls of the hooch. Lewis fired into the ceiling with the K-54 again and again and again until the clip was empty. Scrambling to his feet, he snatched up his own M-16 rifle and fired a burst through the far wall, punching a score of holes that admitted shafts of sunlight. He rushed out of the hooch, his fatigues gooey with blood, none of it his own, and saw Jesse toss a grenade into the brush, then another. Both men hit the dirt, and the explosions showered them with clods and twigs.

"Where's the interpreter?" yelled Lewis, wiping dirt from his eyes.

"He's un-assing the area," answered Jesse. He pointed to the ARVN, who ran toward the circled tracks as if a demon was on his heels. "The man thinks this is the real thing! He likes to beat up old mama-sans, but he wants nothing to do with the fuckin' NVA!"

Lewis laughed, and laughing felt good. The interpreter's cowardice made things tidier. The worst was behind him, he was certain, and he felt liberated, cleansed. He glanced at Nui Ba Den and imagined that the goddess, too, was laughing, despite the fact that a U.S. artillery battery occupied her summit. He locked a fresh magazine into his rifle and peppered a grove of bamboo, celebrating. "Come on—let's make this look good!"

"And sound good, too!" Jesse joined him in spraying the brush harmlessly with rifle fire. They filled the sky with their ricocheting tracers.

"We were in a firefight, okay?—just like we talked about," shouted Lewis over the noise. He wanted to make certain one last time that their stories meshed. "We'll say we were probed by a squad of NVA, and one of them fired into the hooch. They killed Sergeant Cartee—"

"He's actually dead? You really put smoke on him?"

Lewis beamed from ear to ear, and let fly another burst of ammo into the brush. "I put a round through his head, Jess. I watched his heart stop beating. This blood all over me—it's mostly Gamaliel's!" His cheeks darkened a shade, but his grin did not. "The detainee didn't make it, I'm afraid. Gamaliel blew him away, the murdering cocksucker. He blew him away just to give me some pain."

Jesse grimaced, but loaded another magazine and resumed firing. Together they did an excellent job of simulating an encounter with a nonexistent unit of the NVA. After another full minute of noise and fury, which approximated the average length of a firefight in Vietnam, Lewis flipped the pearl-handled pistol into the brush, hoping that it would never be found, but not really caring. No one could prove it was his. He tossed aside the glove he'd worn, which, as Gamaliel had pointed out, had probably been a needless precaution against fingerprints. "Let's get our asses out of here," he said to Jesse.

iv

Never in his life had Lewis run this hard, his legs pumping like pistons as he dashed through the shimmering heat. He vaulted low shrubs, dodged clumps of bamboo, and crashed through an ocean of elephant grass, loving the sting of sweat in his eyes and the tang of adrenaline in his veins. He ran as if he really had something to run from, heading for the dark green shape ahead—his armored personnel carrier. He could see T. J. Skane standing tall in the cupola, a hand shading his eyes as he tried to make out something of the "firefight" that had erupted in the hooch to his front. Leg sat atop the driver's hatch, his hands on the laterals, ready to spin the vehicle and speed away, if the order came. *Where in the hell is Hai?* Lewis wondered.

A dozen strides later the other nine tracks came into view, circled like a wagon train under threat of Indian attack, their crews standing on the topsides and craning in the direction from which they'd heard explosions and small-arms fire. Gamaliel Cartee's interpreter had scrambled atop Sergeant Markowski's track, and was gesturing frantically toward the hooch, no doubt trying to tell the platoon sergeant that the lieutenant and his own boss, Sergeant Cartee, had blundered into an NVA ambush.

When Lewis and Jesse had only twenty strides left to go, the afternoon suddenly crackled with a sound that reminded Lewis of a hundred flamenco dancers shaking their castanets with no attention to rhythm or time signature. He had heard the damnable sound many times before, and as always it nearly stopped his heart—incoming small-arms fire. Green tracers laced the sky and kicked up chunks of earth around him. Green was the color of tracer rounds that the NVA used, in contrast to the red that spewed from Americans' guns. The Triple

Deuce scout platoon was under attack by an element of the
North Vietnamese Army.

A whoosh of blue fire nearly blinded him, and the concus-
sion of the resulting explosion knocked him onto his back. A
rocket-propelled grenade had slammed into Lewis's track, and
even before he comprehended this, the vehicle's fuel tank exploded, sending arcing trails of fire and smoke high above him.
He rolled to his chest and pulled himself onto his hands and
knees, braving an onslaught of enemy rifle fire. He saw T. J.
Skane on the ground, having been blown off the vehicle, whirling and writhing, a human torch. His flesh burned away as
Lewis watched.

Jesse dashed toward the fiery hull, screaming for Danny
Legler, but the vehicle was an inferno now, and its load of
ammo began to cook off. A case of hand grenades exploded,
hurling a blizzard of shrapnel outward. Jesse fell back on the
ground and covered his head with his hands.

T. J. finally lay still but for an occasional twitch, and Lewis
started to go to him, but Jesse grabbed a fistful of his shirt and
forced him down. Lewis twisted out of his grip. "We can't
just leave him!" he screamed. He bolted away and immediately tripped over what was left of Legler—a mere torso and
a head of dirty blond hair hidden in the tall elephant grass.
Lewis's knees buckled. His eyes flooded and his throat seized
up. He went down beside the body and searched madly for
arms and legs, but found none.

The guns of the scout platoon erupted on all sides, firing in
many directions—heavy machine guns and light machine
guns, M-79 grenade launchers, M-16s, light antitank weapons,
and hand grenades—a mind-shattering display of firepower.
But the enemy was apparently well dug in, and the deadly fire
response didn't stop them from launching a barrage of mortar
rounds at the scouts. The earth shook with the detonation of
every incoming round.

Lewis came to his tactical senses and snatched the handset
of the radio off Jesse's shoulder strap. He called "Delta," the
platoon sergeant, and asked for a "sitrep."

"This is Delta!" shouted Frank Markowski into the radio, his voice high and tight with the near panic of combat. "I thought you'd gotten blown away, Tango! Welcome to the fuckin' Vietnam War, you no-nuts little puke. Here's a sitrep for you—we're getting hit by a regimental-size element of November Victor Alpha, and we're getting the shit kicked out of us! Unless you can think of something better to do, I'm going to take our people and execute a controlled retrograde movement so's maybe we can get our shit together before we all get fuckin' killed . . . !"

Lewis saw GIs running past him, low to the ground, hugging the brush and trying to dodge green tracers. He recognized Sergeant Hillman, and remembered the foot patrols he'd sent out earlier.

"Negative, negative!" he shouted into the handset. "Don't leave until we've recovered the foot patrols . . . !"

Scott Sanders, the amiable cowboy medic from Wyoming, followed close behind Hillman. Blood covered his hands and forearms, either his own or that of someone whom the squad had been forced to leave behind. Sanders happened to see Lewis and Jesse, and he halted suddenly, turned, and jumped into the brush alongside them.

"Thought you were a goner, L.T.!" he shouted above the clatter of battle. "Where you bleedin' from?"

Lewis glanced down at his own fatigues, filthy with the blood of Gamaliel and the one-armed ARVN veteran. He tried to explain the situation to Sanders, whose young face seemed so earnest, but a bullet fired by an NVA soldier ripped through Sanders's rib cage and blew his heart out through his back. The cowboy's face went instantly slack and his forehead thudded onto Lewis's shoulder.

Lewis and Jesse ran, knowing they could do nothing for Sanders, knowing that if they stayed in that spot another thirty seconds, they, too, would die. Lewis tasted tears in the corners of his mouth. All around him lay dead and wounded GIs, or pieces of them among the chunks of aluminum armor that only minutes earlier had been tracks. Lewis recognized many of the bloody faces, and shouted their names as he ran. They were dead or maimed, he knew, because of *him*, because of his insane obsession with killing Gamaliel Cartee. If he'd kept his head on straight, he would have paid attention to his tactical responsibilities, and would have called for gunships and artillery support before halting his platoon near the suspected location of so many NVA.

But he'd not kept his head on straight.

Something made him turn toward Nui Ba Den—a voice in his head? He would wonder about this for many years afterward, whether a voice had called his name.

Lewis . . .

He saw the volcano wearing her misty cloak, holding a rainbow as a queen might hold a scepter. "You didn't do this, did you?" he asked, waving a hand to indicate the chaos all around him.

Lewis . . .

Movement to his left: he saw Tran Van Hai scurry through the brush, whether chasing the enemy or fleeing to the enemy's welcoming arms, Lewis could not know. Suddenly Hai came to a dead halt and stared straight at him. Lewis felt the fury in the little man's eyes, and he wondered if it was hatred, or . . .

The eruption cut off his stream of thought, and as he slipped away he assumed it was the work of the Black Virgin, that she had finally tired of the madness and had decided to put an end to it.

V

When he opened his eyes he felt terribly cold, as if his legs were submerged in ice water. A shape came slowly into focus, metamorphosing into a soft face clothed in a surgical mask. It had clear brown eyes that were unmistakably feminine. And kind. And *warm*. He yearned to reach up and touch that face, to steal a bit of the warmth from those eyes and wrap himself in it.

"Lieutenant Kindred, can you hear me?" the nurse asked. Her question barely penetrated a twanging in his ears, the result of having stood too close to an exploding volcano. Lewis managed to nod. His body felt leaden. *Morphine. They've given me morphine....*

"You're in the 12th Evacuation Hospital in Cu Chi. You've had surgery, and you're in the recovery room. Do you remember what happened to you?"

"I—I think so." His tongue felt as if it belonged to someone else. Probably the effects of the general anesthetic, he figured. "What about Jesse—Specialist Burton? And Sergeant Hillman? And . . ."

Another face came into view, which he recognized instantly despite the surgical mask it wore. It belonged to Lieutenant Colonel Gilbert Golightly. "Take it easy, son," said the colonel, placing a hammy hand on his chest. "You're going to make it. Feeling okay?"

Again Lewis managed to nod, though he felt far from okay. The ringing in his ears was driving him crazy, and he felt like a stranger in his own body. "What about Jesse and—"

"Your country owes you a man-sized debt of gratitude, Lewis, and I want you to know that I'm proud of having soldiered with you." He reached into a pocket of his starched jungle fatigues and took out a pair of medals, which he proceeded to pin to Lewis's blanket. "This one's the Purple Heart, which is probably the greatest honor a soldier can receive—it shows he bled for America. There's nothing better a man can do for his country than bleed for it—I believe that with all my heart. And this one is the Silver Star with Oak Leaves and *V* for Valor—"

"Fuck you and your medals!" Lewis spat. His legs were so very cold, and his left arm felt like a block of stone. He sensed a boulder of pain hovering precariously over him, held by mere threads of morphine. He couldn't abide Golightly's military drivel just now, not when there were things he needed to know. "What about Jesse? Is he okay? Can you tell me that much?"

"Specialist Burton was only lightly wounded," answered

Golightly, his eyes brimming. "He carried you from the field on his back, Lewis, after you were . . . *wounded* by that mortar round . . ."

So it was a mortar round, was it?—and not the Black Virgin after all. Too bad.

". . . I'm recommending him for the Congressional Medal of Honor. I've seen uncommon valor in my time, but never anything like his."

"What about the others—Hillman, Marino? Markowski and—"

"Sergeant Markowski took an AK-47 round through his head. I'm told he didn't suffer. As for Hillman and Marino . . ." The colonel said no more, but only bowed his head.

Lewis clenched his eyes for a moment and suffered an insane mix of emotion—numbed relief that Jesse had survived in one piece, laced with fiery grief over the others who hadn't. He wanted to cry, laugh, scream. And something in the colonel's eyes frightened the living hell out of him.

"One thing more," said Golightly, his voice hitching. "Two men are missing in action, and we're afraid they're prisoners of war—Sergeant Tran Van Hai, your Kit Carson, and Sergeant Gamaliel Cartee. I want you to know, Lewis, that I'm proud as hell of the way you treated Sergeant Cartee. It showed me the kind of soldier you are, the kind of man you are, and I'm . . ."

Lewis turned his head away. He knew now what he saw in Golightly's eyes: *Pity.*

Mustering every ounce of will, he reached down to touch his leg, struggling to make his right hand cooperate against the deadening spell of morphine. He expected to find the skin there as cold as ice, because his feet actually ached, they were so cold. Panic scurried through him as he pawed and groped with his unwilling hand, finding no legs at all, not even knees—only heavily bandaged stumps. But still his feet felt so cold, which was lunacy. *How can you have cold feet when you don't even have legs?* He didn't realize just yet that he was screaming, that the nurse was trying to hold him down, that

Colonel Golightly was yelling for a doctor to bring more morphine . . . more morphine. . . .

vi

How long he floated in an ocean of featureless gray, he
didn't know: hours or days, perhaps—as long as it took for
someone in authority to decide that it was time for Lewis Kindred to wake up and face the music. He regained consciousness in stages as the morphine wore off, crossing a region of
dreams that many years later he would insist were more than
dreams.

Somewhere in that region, amid swirling clouds and whispering mists, he'd talked with his father, two years dead of
cancer, and had tried to make him understand why he'd had
no choice but to kill Gamaliel. His father had listened sympathetically, rubbing his high, narrow forehead with the tip of
his index finger, a mannerism that Lewis himself had inherited.
*Just remember that nobody ever figures the odds right all the
time*, his father had said. *When you figure 'em wrong, you live
with the consequences. There's no way to get the shit back
into the horse, once it's on the ground. . . .*

When he finally burst into full consciousness, the first thing
he saw was an expanse of corrugated aluminum that curved
over his bed like a canopy. He lay in a bed with crisp white
sheets. A chrome IV rack towered over him, holding a clear
plastic pouch full of something yellow. The ringing in his ears
had subsided to a jangling dissonance. Other beds lay in a row
to his right, maybe eight or ten of them, all holding men heavily bandaged like himself. Now and then someone coughed or
groaned.

His feet and ankles itched maddeningly, but he couldn't
have scratched them, even if he could have moved his arms.
His legs weren't there. He thought of the ARVN veteran in
the hooch near the Michelin plantation, who had endlessly
scratched the stump of his arm.

Doctors and nurses quietly came and went, tending the patients. Underlying the clean hospital smell was the unmistakable reek of Vietnam, and he knew now that he was still in the 12th Evac in Cu Chi, where he would probably stay until he was strong enough for transport back to the world. Then he could launch a new career selling pencils from a wheelchair.

Maybe I'll get a platform with casters, and push myself along the sidewalks with a block of rubber strapped to my fist. I'll put plastic caps on my stumps and wear a sign around my neck, with scrawly handwriting: HELP A VET, AND MAY GOD BLESS. . . .

A fragment of a dream crossed his consciousness, in which he saw No Bick staring at him in the moments before the mortar round exploded, boring holes in him with those rat-shrewd eyes. For a few moments after the explosion, Lewis floated above his own body like an angel, surveying the grisly scene while the 174th Regiment of the North Vietnamese Army decimated the Triple Deuce scout platoon. He watched No Bick crawl close, a rodent on the prowl, then skitter away, having snatched up one of Lewis's severed legs.

Numbah-one chop-chop, okay . . . ? The notion that the Kit Carson had stolen the leg to eat it was beyond sanity, and Lewis knew this, but he couldn't make it go away. Some rural Vietnamese ate dogs; others ate monkeys. Still others ate unborn chicks still in the eggs and drank coffee made of beans vomited up by weasels. Nowhere in Vietnam, though, did people eat people, and Lewis had absolutely no reason to think that Tran Van Hai, an educated man, would make off with an American lieutenant's leg to make a meal of it.

But Hai isn't like other men, Lewis had tried to tell his dead father. Hai was the kind who let himself be called No Bick even though he spoke immaculate English. The kind who stole ducks from a dead man. The kind who let his commanding officer circle the tracks on the doorstep of an NVA regimental tunnel complex, withholding any warning until it was too late. The long and the short of it was that Hai was still a VC, an unrehabilitated enemy soldier who saw the advantage of playing dumb. Sneaky, duplicitous, untrustworthy.

And the little bastard had run off with one of Lewis's legs.

vii

The window of the recovery room faced the Black Virgin, but Lewis couldn't see much of her, thanks to the high berm that enclosed the base camp. Actually he didn't care to look at her anymore, because he'd lost all faith in her. She'd failed him, left him a hopeless cripple, even though he'd declared himself her ally.

He watched helicopters crisscross the sky, listened to the engines of tanks and tracks, heard occasional shouts from GIs as they passed by the 12th Evac. The world was carrying on without him, and the realization staggered him, brought tears that he couldn't hold back.

He must have napped briefly, but only briefly, because the sun still hung like a red orb above the berm when he opened his eyes to discover a man silhouetted against the window, dark and tall, whose features he couldn't quite see. "Jesse, is that you?" he croaked. "How in the holy hell did you get them to let you in here?"

The man stepped toward the bed, casting a deep blue shadow onto the white sheets that covered the hillocks of Lewis's stumps. A shadow that rustled as it moved. "I didn't have any trouble getting in," the man replied in a deep southern voice. "But then I seldom have trouble going where I want to go."

Lewis nearly swallowed his tongue. The visitor's cheek was crusty with dried blood. Beneath the left eye, the brown one, was a small round hole with ragged edges, a bullet wound. Lewis could smell the gore that still clung to the visitor's camouflaged fatigues.

This wasn't Jesse.

The man, or whatever it was, ran a long finger over the

medical chart that hung on the foot of Lewis's bed. "You
certainly managed to get yourself messed up, didn't you,
Lewis? It says here you've lost both legs above the knees.
You've suffered a shattered ulna in your left arm, a perforated
spleen, fractured vertebrae in your lower lumbar region, and
assorted lacerations over your entire body. Sounds to me like
you're about to become one of the world's experts on scar
tissue."

"How . . . how did you . . . ?" Lewis's mind balked at the
hellish truth standing at the foot of his bed, and for a moment
he let himself believe that he was dreaming. This couldn't be
Gamaliel Cartee. He'd watched Gamaliel's heart stop beating,
for the love of Christ. He'd watched the geyser of blood subside to a mere trickle through a bullet hole in the man's face.

Someone at the far end of the room coughed, and Lewis
knew that this was no dream. He remembered Colonel Golightly's revelation that two men were missing in action, Tran
Van Hai and Cartee. Could this mean . . . ?

"I won't keep you awake long, Lewis. I know how very
tired you must be. I just wanted to drop by and give you my
regards." Gamaliel came around the side of the bed and leaned
close, affording Lewis a clear view of his ruined face. The
blue and brown eyes glittered, despite the sickly yellow where
white should have been. His breath made Lewis want to vomit.
"To show that there aren't any hard feelings, I want to give
you this."

Lewis felt something pressing into his right hand, something
hard and round and disturbingly warm. He lacked the strength
at the moment to hoist it up to look at it, but he knew what it
was. The orb.

"No need to protest, Lewis. I want you to have it. You need
it now. You've *earned* it."

Earned it? The idea was ghastly.

"Good-bye, Lewis, and take care of yourself. I look forward
to seeing you again, though I'm not sure when that will be."

He touched Lewis's cheek with a long, blood-crusty finger, a touch that was lifeless and cold. The touch of a dead man. Lewis felt his gorge rise, forced it down, and clamped his eyes tight. He heard footsteps fading, and when he opened his eyes again, Gamaliel Cartee was gone.

For madness as a blessing—'tis denied me.

—Lord Byron,
Manfred: A Dramatic Poem

Part Two:
Dream Creature

Five

i

On September 12, 1992, the crowd was shoulder to shoulder at the Rockaway Lounge in downtown Portland, Oregon. An untidy mix of American subcultures gyrated, thrashed, stomped, and slammed in time to the cannonading music of the new Demon Beef. There were punks with neon-colored hairdos and safety pins through their ears, hard rockers with riveted leather straps around their necks, and Gothics who looked like anemic spiders in their white skin and black clothes. There were skinheads with bristly scalps and Nazi jewelry. There were grungies wearing ultra-baggy shorts and layers of deliberately ruined shirts. There were modern-day hippies in tie-dyed jeans, preppies in rugby shirts, and denizens of subcultures that pundits had not yet named.

Seventeen-year-old Josh Nickerson wore the uniform of grunge, replete with a frayed flannel shirt and a battered Minnesota Twins baseball cap worn backward. His choice of footwear, however, gave him away as something less than a dedicated follower—costly Nikes that qualified as anything but grungy.

He was tall, lean, and auburn-haired, almost a redhead—a little gawky in the baggy clothes but smooth in his movements. And sure of himself in a way that made him seem older than he was. His green eyes snapped with a restless intelligence as he scanned the crowd, poking his stare into every dark booth and corner, searching.

Not everyone at the Rockaway Lounge that night was a disciple of Demon Beef, but everyone there had at least one thing in common: curiosity. This was the band's first public appearance since the sensationally gruesome murder of its lead singer, Ron Payne, four months earlier. With his passing, Demon Beef's liftoff to stardom had abruptly belly-flopped, but the surviving members of the band had enrolled a new front man and had doggedly set out in quest of the big time once again. Portland's rock-and-roll faithful had turned out in droves to catch the band's new act.

The final song of the set ended with an eye-popping barrage of colored laser beams, shredding guitar riffs, and a molten scream from the throat of the group's new singer, Glenn Felix. The applause was polite but not frantic—only a smattering of *yeows* and an occasional *woof!-woof!* As the musicians plodded off the stage through a fog produced by smoke machines, Josh Nickerson and his companion drifted with the crowd toward the front exit.

"It's not the same without Ron," he muttered. "They're just another band now. When they lost Ron, they lost their soul."

"I don't know how you can stand this kind of music," said Nicole Tran with a cute sneer. "It's nothing but screams and ear-splitting guitars. I think you're regressing, Nickster."

"I'm here for professional reasons, you know that—not because I'm into death metal. If you hate it so much, why did you come along?"

"I like to watch you when you're stalking."

"I didn't come here to stalk anyone."

"Oh, right."

"I'm here to do research, Nicki. That's all."

They sidled past a pair of no-neck bouncers and slipped outside. The cool night air felt good on Josh's face, and he drank deeply of it, grateful to breathe without the sting of cigarette smoke. He took a moment to scan the crowd that still poured from the Rockaway Lounge into the street. Apparently many others felt as Josh did: without Payne, the band no longer had a soul. The crowd was voting with its feet.

"See, you're doing it," said Nicole.

"Doing what?"

"Stalking."

"I'm *not* stalking anyone. How many times do I have to tell you?"

"She has big snoobs, doesn't she?"

Josh tried to hold back a grin, but couldn't. Nicole had been doing this kind of thing since they were little kids. He didn't doubt that she knew him better than his own sister did, and sometimes he wondered if Nicole could actually read his mind. "It's not what you're thinking," he allowed. "She's part of the story I'm working on, I swear. She's some sort of Demon Beef groupie, or at least she was before Ron Payne got killed. I was sure she would be here tonight."

Nicole grinned slyly, keeping her lewd suspicions to herself.

They walked north on Fourth Avenue toward the lot where they'd parked his old Escort. High above the sleek office towers of downtown Portland, stars peered feebly through a haze of urban light pollution, and the night air tingled with autumn. The streets were chaotic with traffic, this being a Saturday night—carloads of teenagers, mostly, cruising and trolling, their stereos thudding with rap music.

"So tell me how this babe with the big snoobs figures into the story," pressed Nicole.

"I don't want to get into it right now—it's too complicated. You can read all about it when *Rolling Stone* prints it."

Nicole laughed, but not derisively. She was Josh's strongest supporter in his bid for a career in investigative reporting. She'd seen the pieces he'd written for his high-school newspaper and had found them compelling and gritty, well researched, passionate. Josh Nickerson was nothing if not passionate. Nicole had remarked, though, that his writing seemed over the heads of most high-schoolers, that his targeted audience simply didn't appreciate him. She'd suggested that he undertake a freelance project, something entirely of his own choosing, and that he submit it to magazines.

He'd taken the suggestion seriously and had hit on the idea of covering the flight to stardom of the hometown rock band Demon Beef. The subject matter was close to his heart, for he'd been a devotee of heavy metal as a young boy (before his musical tastes had "matured," he was fond of telling people). He knew rock and roll, the inside terms, the jargon. The story of Demon Beef was right up his alley.

He'd talked to the group's manager, attended rehearsals, and interviewed each of the musicians, including Ron Payne himself, as well as the sound and light guys, the agent and the publicist, even the roadies. The group had allowed him backstage during several local gigs, and he'd become friendly with many of the people involved with the band. He'd taken reams of notes and had begun cobbling together the beginnings of a feature story when catastrophe struck.

Someone killed Ron Payne mere weeks before the band was to embark on a national tour. Not just *killed*—ripped him to pieces, devoured parts of his body, left him looking as if wolves had set upon him. The Portland Police Bureau withheld the bulk of the grisly details, but the news media gleaned enough to convey the savagery of the crime, and the good people of Portland lapped up the coverage like good chowder.

All this had happened last spring, when Josh and Nicole were finishing their junior year in high school. Feeling crushed and defeated, Josh had toyed with abandoning his project. But Nicole had argued that the story of Demon Beef was still worth pursuing, even if the band didn't manage another serious shot at stardom. The police hadn't found Ron Payne's killer or even a clue about the motive, according to the news coverage. Whether or not Demon Beef ever achieved stardom, the tragic story of Ron Payne was a juicy one, an unsolved mystery that a good writer could turn into gold. Nothing captures a reader's attention faster or holds it longer than an unsolved mystery, she'd said.

All this was true, Josh agreed. A good writer would find a story in the impact of Ron Payne's murder on the lives of those who had known him and depended on him. A good writer would explore the ins and outs of the mystery and relate the theories offered by those close to the victim, then lay out a theory of his own. The tale of Demon Beef was a mother lode waiting to be mined, no question about it.

He'd never told Nicole this, or anyone else, either, but he knew something about the murder that the police and the news media did not know, and he was sure that this knowledge gave him an edge, an exclusive angle that would make his version of the story an unqualified hit. But he needed to develop it, uncover more details. He needed to find a certain tall woman.

ii

"Come on, babe, you can do it . . . make me proud now. Come *on*, babe . . ." The old Escort's starter groaned and wheezed, but refused to turn over. It issued a final groan and gave up entirely. Josh thumped the steering wheel with the heel of his hand. "I swear to God this car hates me."

"Stop feeling sorry for yourself," scolded Nicole. "It's not the car's fault that you didn't buy a new battery."

"Who has money for stuff like that? I'm a struggling writer, remember? I finance all my own investigating."

"You know perfectly well that your father would buy you anything you asked for. If you were to say the word, you'd find a brand-new Miata in your driveway, and your car troubles would be over."

"And you know perfectly well, Nicole," he answered, parroting her preachy tone, "that I cannot accept gifts from that sanctimonious hypocrite. It's bad enough that I let him pay my tuition at Gavin Dell, which I do only because my mom insists on it. Enough said, okay?"

A central feature of Josh's life was his resentment of his father, Gregory Nickerson, who was a senior underwriting executive of Northwest Columbia Mutual Insurance Company, a nationally ranked firm with home offices in Portland. Greg had divorced Josh's mother a decade earlier, having found a pretty young secretary who was eager to play house with an important officer of a big corporation. Eventually he'd jettisoned the secretary as easily as he'd jettisoned the mother of his children.

"Why don't we walk?" suggested Nicole. "The exercise will do us good."

"You're up for hiking twenty-five blocks, most of it uphill? I think I'm having a seizure."

"We're young and strong, and we're not exactly pressed

for time. Come on, get out. The sooner we start, the sooner we'll get there.''

They strolled three blocks west to Broadway, the main thoroughfare that ran through the heart of downtown Portland, then turned south. From here the street ascended a gentle hill to the campus of Portland State University, taking them past trendy storefronts and restaurants, the lobbies of corporate office centers, theaters, hotels and the Portland Center for the Performing Arts. The street swarmed with Saturday-nighters both young and old, moviegoers and symphony patrons, barhoppers and plain old sightseers. The mood of the crowd was festive.

Josh's mood improved as they walked. He and Nicole conversed with an easy familiarity that comes only with long years of friendship. Theirs had begun more than a decade earlier, when they were both in the first grade. Immediately after her divorce, Josh's mother had moved her brood into a venerable old Colonial Revival apartment building in Gander Ridge, a woody hillside on the southern fringe of the southwest business district. The Tran family lived in a house down the block.

Josh soon became best friends with Nicole, who was then an elfin tomboy with lively Asian eyes. They became known throughout the neighborhood as the ''Dynamic Duo of Gander Ridge,'' for one was seldom seen without the other. Though they attended different schools, they spent most of their spare hours biking or skateboarding, going to movies, watching TV, or playing video games—always together. Josh called her ''Nicki,'' and she called him ''Nickster.'' Their friendship had never developed into a boy-girl thing. Josh now had a girlfriend named Laurel, a classmate at Gavin Dell whom he'd dated more or less steadily during his junior year. Nicole had never dated, but her willowy Asian looks had lately begun to attract glances from males of all ages.

They strolled past Pioneer Courthouse Square, which teemed with people, most of them high-schoolers who strutted the costumes of their respective subcultures while listening to rap music played brutally loud on boom boxes. The night was alive with honking horns, laughter, squealing tires. A pair of mounted policeman rode around the edge of the square on their glossy brown horses, wearing Smokey the Bear hats and looking bored.

As Josh and Nicole crossed Salmon Street two blocks south of the square, an Old Cutlass with faded yellow paint and cheap chrome wheels turned abruptly off Broadway and nearly ran them down. Josh grabbed Nicole and hauled her back to the curb just in time, having seen the car approach from the corner of his eye. He was about to give the finger to the driver when the car halted with a shriek of rubber. The passenger door burst open, and a tall teenage boy jumped out, scowling malevolently.

"Why don't you watch where you're going, you fuckin' gook lover?" the boy screamed at Josh. "What's the matter—ain't white babes good enough for you? Or are you so hard up for pussy that you've got to hit on gooks?"

The guy's thin face was a mass of pimples, and he wore a camouflaged military-surplus field jacket over a black T-shirt. His hair was shaved almost to the scalp. He sported a chrome Nazi swastika on the pocket flap of his field jacket. Josh thought, *This guy's a skinhead with a capital* S. . . .

Unlike their comparatively harmless imitators for whom neo-Nazi gear was little more than a fashion statement, real Nazi skinheads carried lethal toys—guns, knives, aluminum baseball bats, and God knew what else. They cruised the streets in search of excuses to use those toys. Like the sight of a racially mixed couple.

"So, what are you—deaf—you race-mixing shitbag?" The skinhead pounded the top of the Olds with a fist, and immediately his cohorts inside the car began pounding back. The effect was that of stampeding horses. "I want to know why you're out with a gook cunt instead of an honest white girl—and I want to know *now*!"

"Don't say anything to them," whispered Nicole. "Let's turn around and go the other way, okay?"

"I can't let him get away with calling you that."

The driver was out of the car now, a fireplug of a man who

looked twenty, maybe twenty-two. "Hey, the man asked you a question, gook lover . . ." His square jaw was blue with stubble, like his scalp, and he wore a brown leather jacket, faded jeans, and spit-shined Doc Marten boots that reached to mid-calf. "You deaf or something? You *better* be deaf, because if you're givin' us attitude, you're going to be one sorry motherfuckin' gook lover." He started toward them, and Nicole pulled furiously on Josh's sleeve, urging him away.

Suddenly horns started honking. The skinheads were tying up traffic. A police siren whooped, and red and blue beacons flashed. Josh's heart leaped with relief as a unit of Portland's finest pulled around the queue of cars and halted behind the Cutlass, upon which Pimples and Fireplug plunged back into their car. As they roared away, Fireplug shouted something obscene through the driver's window, but Josh didn't catch it. The police car gunned away in pursuit.

Nicole exhaled a long puff of air, her eyes huge with excitement, and for a giddy moment Josh thought she was the most beautiful thing he'd ever seen. "You okay?" he asked.

"I think so, yeah. I hope to God the cops put those jerks in jail before they hurt somebody."

"Never happen. Unless they've got drugs or open beer in the car, they'll only get a lecture."

iii

They cut over to Thirteenth Street, which bordered I-405, a busy freeway that skirted the west-side business district. Turning south again, they headed up the hill toward Gander Ridge. It was not yet 11:00 P.M., so traffic was still heavy. A stream of cars whooshed past them on the one-way street, bound for the on-ramp of the freeway.

"It's been a long time since anything like that has happened to me," said Nicole. "I can't even remember the last time someone called me a gook."

Nicole's father and mother had come to America from Vietnam in 1976, when Nicole was an infant. They'd been "boat people," refugees from a cruel new order that aimed to "re-educate," imprison, or kill anyone who had supported the old one. They'd arrived in Portland with little more than the clothes on their backs and a determination to build decent lives for themselves. Mr. Tran had worked with a city road crew by day and a janitorial service by night. Within five years he owned the janitorial service, and had built it into a thriving business. Within the next five years he'd tripled his revenues and had become a moderately wealthy man, a walking illustration of the American dream.

"Face it," replied Josh. "There's no shortage of cretins in this world. They'll never quit hating, because hating is so much more convenient than loving. In order to love someone, you need to know him, right? And that takes effort, and maybe even some brains."

"Sounds like you've been talking to Lewis again."

"Why is it whenever I say something halfway smart, you think it's something I've gotten from Lewis?" He feigned being insulted, then laughed and punched Nicole lightly on the arm. "But you're right, that was something Lewis said. I think he was on his third bottle of Beck's, and he was starting to wax eloquent."

Lewis Kindred, a veteran of the same war that drove Nicole's family from their homeland, was a middle-aged double amputee who lived in the apartment immediately below the Nickersons'. He was also the nephew of Miss Juliet Kindred, who owned the building. If someone had asked Josh to name his best friend, he could not have chosen between Nicole Tran, who was like a sister, and Lewis Kindred, who was like a big brother or an uncle.

"Oh God," breathed Nicole. "It's them, isn't it?" An old yellow Cutlass cruised past on Thirteenth, headed up the hill, its smoked-glass windows obscuring the faces of its occupants. Approaching the next corner, its driver signaled left, slowed to a crawl, then tromped the accelerator and took the corner on two wheels.

"It's them, all right. They must've seen us."

"I can't believe this! Over a million people in this city, and we meet those Neanderthals twice in the same night. Do you think they'll come after us?"

"We better not take any chances." He steered her into the parking lot of an apartment building, and they cut through it to an alley. Josh figured that once he and Nicole reached the campus of Portland State University, which was now less than a block away, they could elude the skinheads among the campus buildings and make their way safely to Gander Ridge.

Suddenly they heard the roar of a big V-8. Josh whirled and saw the yellow Cutlass approaching from behind, having rounded the block and turned into the alley. Its headlights caught them straight-on, casting his and Nicole's shadows huge against the brick wall of the building behind them.

"This way!" he shouted. They darted to their left, hoping to cut between the buildings to Twelfth Street, forcing the skinheads to get out of their car in order to follow or give up the chase. But two figures stood in the way, one of whom Josh recognized as Pimples. "Shit! They must've let two guys out on Twelfth . . . !"

Nicole caught his sleeve and pulled him around toward the opposite direction, and he gathered himself for an all-out sprint back toward Thirteenth Street, but two other figures blocked the way, both carrying metal baseball bats. Josh's testicles constricted as he realized that the skinheads had deployed men on his and Nicole's flanks to cut off their escape.

The Cutlass skidded to a halt scarcely ten feet from Josh and Nicole. The engine shut down and the headlights went black, leaving purple splotches on Josh's field of vision. The driver's door opened and Fireplug stepped out, an ugly smile twisting his mouth. His jaw rippled as he chewed what must have been a fist-sized wad of tobacco.

"Well, if this ain't a happy little coincidence," he said in a voice that seemed too small and high to belong to someone as blocky as he was. "We were just talking about you guys, y' know? Talking about how nice it would be to meet up with you again. I mean, its's not every day you catch some chicken-shit little white man walkin' the street with a mud woman. It's sort of frustrating to get all primed to beat the dude's head in, only to have the fuckin' cops show up and give you a lecture about tying up traffic. But I don't see any cops around now. Do you see any cops, chickenshit?''

Josh's mind worked furiously while Nicole clung to him, her face pale. *There are five of them, and one of me. I have a brick wall at my back, one of them in front, two on each side. God, what I wouldn't give for a baseball bat or a tire iron, or a . . .*

Or a gun. For the first time in his young life, Josh Nickerson actually wished for a gun, something big and deadly, designed specifically for combat. Lacking one, he needed to rely on his wits. And his mouth. ''Hey, are you dudes *good*, or what?'' he said to Fireplug, forcing a smile. ''I should've known better than to think we could outrun you. You guys are pros, right?''

Fireplug spat on the ground. Pimples walked slowly forward from Josh and Nicole's right, flanked by a black-jacketed young man who wore his bleached-yellow hair like Adolf Hitler's. ''Save your breath, gook lover. You can't talk your way out of this. You just stumbled into the worst fuckin' night of your life.''

''Nickster, what are we going to do?'' hissed Nicole, press-ing her cheek against his shoulder. It seemed too crazy to be true—a pair of young friends out walking, bothering no one, and for some incomprehensible reason thugs attack them with crowbars and bats. But it *wasn't* too crazy to be true: several years earlier, skinheads had bludgeoned to death a young black student from East Africa in the parking lot of an apartment building in northwest Portland. This was reality, crazy or not, in the handsome, liberal-minded city of Portland, Oregon.

''I'm expressing my admiration, that's all,'' Josh managed to say, still holding the smile that Lewis Kindred had taught him to use while playing poker. ''Hey, could you dudes use a beer or something?''

Fireplug spat a brown stream of tobacco juice onto Nicole's

bright green pullover. "You think we would drink with filth like you?" He slipped a set of brass knuckles on his right hand, and flexed his stubby fingers. "You think we'd dirty ourselves by drinking with some chickenshit who sticks his dick into a mud woman?"

Josh felt himself go dizzy with rage and terror. "I was only thinking that you might be thirsty. . . ." His voice cracked, and he knew now that he had no choice but to fight. Maybe he could wrench a bat away from one of the attackers, he thought, then do enough damage with it to drive the others off. Maybe . . .

"You're trying to bribe us, ain't you, chickenshit?" said Pimples, now only an arm's length away. "You're trying to bribe us with *beer*!" The others laughed and whooped and spat on the ground. "For your information, gooklover, we're real Americans, and we don't take bribes."

"Know what I think?" asked Fireplug. "I think he's a Jew. First thing a Jew tries to do when he's in trouble is bribe somebody. Jews are a lot like slopes that way. What we've got here, troops, is a double bonus—a dirty slope-headed mud woman and a slimy Jew. We've got our work cut out for us."

All five started forward, converging on Josh and Nicole like wolves on a pair of frightened deer. The blond Hitler raised his aluminum baseball bat, Fireplug drew back his brass-knuckled fist, Pimples wound up for a swing with a tire iron. Josh launched himself straight at Fireplug, screaming like a banshee, meaning to rip the animal's throat out if he could. Suddenly the roar of an engine rolled over them, and the alley lit up under the glare of headlights. The sound and light distracted Fireplug, and his brass-knuckled fist missed Josh's head, glancing off his shoulder. But Josh's fist didn't miss— he drove it hard into Fireplug's larynx, and Fireplug went down, choking, clutching his throat with both hands. Nicole screamed and ducked under the roundhouse swing of Pimple's tire iron, then darted into the shadows.

Josh leaped over the writhing form of Fireplug and whirled on the other attackers, who seemed confused in the noontide

glare of the headlights. He saw a blur of white—a woman, tall
and dark-skinned, wearing a white minidress that barely covered her torso. Moving like a panther, she waded into the knot
of skinheads, caught the blond Hitler by the hair, and hurled
him against a wall, where he impacted with a thud and slid
down beside a Dumpster. She caught Pimple's tire iron in
midswing, wrenched it from him, and broke his arm loudly,
causing him to vomit all over himself. He hit the ground unconscious and lay motionless in a pond of his own filth.

The woman moved so quickly that Josh's eyes couldn't
quite fix upon her, so smoothly that her body seemed to shift
and flow. Her strength was nothing short of supernatural. She
went after the remaining two thugs and caught them by the
collars of their leather jackets. She smashed their heads together and they collapsed in a heap of knees and elbows and
stubbly scalps. Fireplug got back to his feet, pulled a blunt
pistol from a shoulder holster inside his jacket, and assumed
a shooter's crouch, leveling the weapon at the woman. Josh
kicked him in the side of the head, putting every ounce of his
weight into it. Fireplug went sprawling, but he held on to the
gun and struggled upright again. Suddenly Nicole flew out of
the shadows, waving a baseball bat that one of the skinheads
had dropped, and brought it down hard on Fireplug's bristly
skull, making a crack that sounded like a base hit. He buckled
to the asphalt facefirst, and lay twitching like a dog having a
bad dream.

Silence now, warm and heavy. The traffic on I-405 and
Twelfth Street seemed distant and inconsequential. Nicole
pressed herself into Josh's arms, and he held her as she sobbed,
liking the feel of her cheek against his chest. He became conscious of his own heartbeat, his own breathing. He was thankful beyond words to be alive and in one piece.

The woman in the white dress examined each of the senseless, bloodied skinheads, kicking away their weapons lest they
wake up and decide to renew the fight. Then she stood in front
of Josh, her arms folded across her ample breasts. She might
have been twenty, thirty, or any age in between. She was ra-

cially mixed—neither white nor black. Her face was long and strong, her lips full, her wide nose gracefully curved and flared. Her rusty hair tumbled to her shoulders in intricate dreadlocks. Most striking, however, were her eyes, which were deeply set and huge—eyes that captured light and tossed it back into the world like finely honed gems. They were mismatched, which only heightened her exotic appeal: the right one was a frosty blue, while the left was the color of warm brown earth.

iv

She was the woman Josh had hoped to see tonight at the Rockaway Lounge. She'd been an admirer of Demon Beef, of Ron Payne in particular, perhaps *more* than an admirer. Josh had never before gotten close enough to taste the magic of her eyes.

She'd attended all the band's rehearsals and gigs, lingering alone in the shadows near the stage, staring intently at Payne with an expression full of something that Josh had assumed was lust. Josh had admired her from a distance, imagining how it would be to insinuate himself between those deliciously long legs. And he'd encountered her on the night of Ron Payne's murder.

He'd needed to talk to her, to ask her why she'd been in Payne's apartment that night. He'd searched for her throughout the summer, contacting people who'd been close to Payne and Demon Beef, asking who she was and where she lived. But no one had been able to give him any answers. He'd figured that she would likely show up for tonight's gig at the Rockaway, but she'd disappointed him. Josh had considered the evening a waste of time.

Until now.

Did he dare ask her *now*?

"I want to thank you," he said lamely, his voice shaking.

"I don't know how you did it. . . ." He glanced around at the broken and bruised skinheads.

Nicole had collected herself by now, and was no longer blubbering against Josh's chest. "No kidding, thanks for helping us," she said, wiping moisture from her eye.

"Don't thank me," said the woman. "You would've done the same for me, I'm sure." Her accent was Southern with a hint of Caribbean.

"How did you happen to come by?" Josh asked. "This alley isn't exactly on the beaten track."

"Long story—too long to tell you tonight, I'm afraid. Perhaps another time." She looked each of them up and down with narrowed eyes. "Is either of you hurt?" They both shook their heads. "I'm sorry that the pig spit tobacco on you, Nicki."

"How do you know my name?"

"Everyone knows the Dynamic Duo of Gander Ridge. If I were you, I would be more picky about who I hang with from now on." She smiled whitely.

"I don't think we've ever been introduced," said Josh, offering his hand. "My name is—"

"I know who you are, Josh. I'll admit that it's no coincidence that I'm here. I've been looking for you. I was hoping that you might do something for me."

"Do something for you?" He stared at her blankly. "I—uh—you bet. I'd be happy to do anything. . . ."

"We'll do anything you ask," put in Nicole.

"Good." The woman turned and strode to the open door of her car, a black Jaguar convertible. Josh noticed for the first time that she was barefoot. She'd kicked off her stiletto heels while jumping out. As she slid in behind the driver's seat, Josh watched the parting of her long brown legs. Her minidress rode high up on her thighs, and he saw that she was without underwear. He felt himself go hard and looked away.

She retrieved something from the glove box and returned. She held it out to him, a sphere of bright red crystal about the size of a billiard ball. The thing caught the glare of the headlights and produced a thousand shards that flitted and darted with every movement of her hand, almost like living things. Josh glanced at Nicole, who stood transfixed, the rays from the orb dancing across her face.

"What's inside it?" she breathed, venturing to touch it with a finger.

"I can't honestly say I know," replied the woman. "Someone gave it to me a long time ago, but it wasn't mine to keep. He made me swear that I would eventually return it to its rightful owner."

"And who's that?" asked Josh.

"A mutual friend of yours and mine, I think. His name is Lewis Kindred."

Josh shook his head, incredulous. "*You* know Lewis?"

"In a sense, yes." She caught Josh's right hand and pressed the orb into it. The weight and the warmth of the thing struck him immediately—a disquieting warmth that made him think of sinking his hand into the guts of a freshly killed animal. He wanted to pull away, but the power of the woman's blue-brown stare held him. "Give it to Lewis as soon as possible," she urged. "Tell him that all good things come to him who waits."

"Should I tell him who it's from—I mean, who you are? He'll want to know."

She leaned against the graceful fender of the Jag and slipped her shoes on her feet. "My name is Millie. You can tell him that. You can also tell him that Millie would greatly enjoy playing poker with him."

"If you're a friend of his, why don't you give it to him yourself?"

Millie stood up straight, walked slowly back to Josh, and laid her palm against his cheek. "You're a curious young thing, aren't you? So full of questions, so passionate. You're capable of great anger, aren't you, Josh?"

"I guess so."

"That's good. *Very* good, in fact. Never try to hold your anger in. Always let it out. Let it grow. Let it become strong and hard. *Use* your anger, and great things will happen for you."

He felt an icy spot between his shoulder blades, though

Millie's touch was as warm as the orb in his hand, and exciting. He felt as if his life had changed from the moment she touched his face. Something major was happening to him, but he didn't know what it was.

"You still haven't told me why you can't give him this—this *thing*—yourself? Why do you need me?"

Millie lost her smile, and her mismatched eyes became hard. "I'm afraid that he wouldn't accept it directly from me. But from *you* . . ." She caressed his cheek again, and he just managed to keep himself from reaching out to touch her breasts. Something in her expression told him that she wouldn't stop him if he did. ". . . Lewis trusts you."

She walked back to the car, her heels popping on the pavement, her buttocks rolling smoothly inside the white minidress. Before getting in, she advised Josh and Nicole not to loiter too much longer. Then she grinned a good-bye and whooshed off in a smear of gleaming black metal.

Watching her taillights disappear down the alley, Josh could not suppress the notion that Millie had planned everything that had happened tonight.

Six

i

THE APARTMENT BUILDING in which Josh Nickerson lived stood on a wooded hillside named Gander Ridge, in a cul-de-sac called Gander Circle. Built in 1892 by a prominent Portland judge named James Sloan, the grand old Colonial Revival house overlooked Portland State University and the downtown business district. Painted white and surrounded by monumental

New England elms, the house had a look of four-square sturdiness. Tall Georgian columns flanked the front entrance, and a terrace swept across the front to open porches on either end. Massive chimneys rose high above the roof, and dormers jutted out from the third story, where the present owner, Miss Juliet Kindred, had her quarters.

The Nickersons' apartment occupied half the second floor. From the window of his room on the east end of the house, Josh could look across Gander Ridge to Goose Hollow, the home of Civic Stadium, where the Triple-A Portland Beavers played baseball, and where a spectacular fireworks display occurred every Fourth of July. Farther east, the gleaming towers of the central city seemed almost close enough to touch, as did the Fremont Bridge, a colossus of arching girders that spanned the Willamette River. Josh could look eastward and see a forested mound named Mount Tabor, which stood like an island in southeast Portland's urban sea. On the far horizon loomed majestic Mount Hood, an extinct volcano that wore a coat of snow in winter and served as a playground for Portland-area skiers, climbers, and trekkers. On clear days he could gaze north across the wide Columbia River, beyond the city of Vancouver, and deep into Washington State, where Mount St. Helens hunkered in uneasy quiescence, blunt-topped now after literally blowing her lid on May 18, 1980, when she rained gray death over the Pacific Northwest.

Miss Juliet Kindred, the seventy-two-year-old owner and landlady of Sloan House, had two passions: evangelical Christianity and gardening. When not doing volunteer work for various causes of the religious right, she labored in the gardens around the mansion, where she grew roses and giant trillium, western azaleas that bloomed in the early summer, and Pacific rhododendrons with big, bold leaves and lavish trusses of purple flowers. Every fall she harvested Oregon grape along the rear walls of the mansion and made preserves, which she distributed to her renters in Kerr jars with hand-lettered Bible verses on the labels.

The Nickersons' apartment had three small bedrooms and

two baths, a kitchen, a dining area, and a living room that opened onto a railed deck, where they sometimes ate their meals and spent warm summer evenings. At night a breeze usually whispered across Gander Ridge, rustling the foliage and clearing out the haze of rush-hour pollution. Josh often spent hours in a stretch out here, sprawled in a reclining patio chair with the headphones of his Sony Discman on his head, a book in his lap and the breeze in his face—fighting his restlessness with visions of places far away from Portland, Oregon.

His room was small and cluttered, a "wasteland," his mother called it. The cleaning lady who came once a week refused to enter it, apparently fearful of what she might encounter amid the mounds of books, fast-food wrappers, and dirty clothing. A small wooden desk stood against one wall, on which sat his computer. A year ago he'd bought a metal filing cabinet, in which he kept his "background" files—items from books or periodicals that he thought he might need someday for one yet-to-be-written story or another, cataloged by subject. Shelves lined another wall, crammed with reference books, almanacs, and how-to books on writing and research. There were tomes on past obsessions: the Civil War, photography, remote-control model airplanes, classical Rome, others. Within the past year he'd taken down the poster-size photos of his heroes on the Portland Trail Blazers and replaced them with travel posters that showed dreamy views of London, Hong Kong, the delta of the Amazon, the canals of Venice, places he hoped to visit someday on assignment as a journalist.

ii

On Sunday, September 13, 1992, Josh got up around 10:15 and herded himself into the shower, drowsy and bleary-eyed after an uneasy sleep. He'd dreamed repeatedly of Millie and her mismatched eyes, how she'd handled the skinheads, and afterward, the way she'd stroked his cheek. Inevitably the dream had taken another direction, in which she'd stroked more than his cheek. He'd awakened barely in time to grab a fistful of Kleenex from the stand next to his bed. Even after *that* he'd not slept well, for his brain had refused to shut down, and had hummed with questions about who Millie really was, her connection to Lewis Kindred, Ron Payne, and Josh himself.

After showering, he ambled into the kitchen. His mother had attached a note to the refrigerator with a magnet in the shape of a duck, telling him that she and Kendra had gone to church, that they planned to grab brunch at Papa Haydn's and return around one.

After poking around in a bowl of Wheaties, Josh went back to his room, unable to put off any longer a task that he didn't look forward to doing. The baggy shorts he'd worn the previous day hung on a bedpost at the foot of his bed, and he poked his hand into one of the pockets. He pulled out the orb and held it up to the morning light. The interior of the thing swarmed with texture. Was it his imagination, he wondered, or was the orb warmer than it should be? He pocketed it hurriedly.

He unlocked his cabinet and found a file jacket, labeled "Demon Beef" and "Ron Payne," respectively. From the inner folder he pulled four envelopes he'd received in the mail over the past summer, together with the newspaper clippings they'd contained, each from a newspaper in a different city. One had come from the South, another from the Midwest, a third from the East and a fourth from the West Coast. The envelopes bore no return addresses, so he had no idea who had sent them. The stories concerned murders that were startlingly similar to that of Ron Payne. Shuffling through the clippings, biting his lower lip, and rereading each for the hundredth time, he debated with himself about whether to keep these little horrors a secret any longer.

iii

Josh knocked on Lewis Kindred's door, then pushed through it as he usually did, needing no invitation. Inside, a television set was on, providing the background din that Lewis liked when he was working. A freelance "desktop publisher," Lewis designed and edited newsletters, brochures, and manuals for small corporations and businesses throughout the Portland area, using a Macintosh computer to generate graphics and typesetting. Combined with his veteran's pension and his weekly poker winnings, his business income gave him a decent living. He kept his studio here in his apartment, and often worked on weekends, as he was apparently doing today.

"It's me," Josh called out to Lewis. "Want anything from the kitchen?"

"I'm in the studio. Get us a couple of Diet-Rites, why don't you? Make mine a red raspberry."

The apartment lay immediately below the Nickersons', but it had two bedrooms instead of three, one of which served as the studio. Mount Hood was visible from the living room window, a fact that would have added substantially to the rent if Lewis weren't the landlady's nephew. The furnishings were of high quality—leather furniture, oak miniblinds and cabinets, plain earth tones in the upholstery and rugs. Lewis abided no figurines or knickknacks, but he kept a veritable jungle of potted plants, the most prominent of which was a ficus tree that was much too large for the living room. The apartment contained nothing that a man couldn't reach while sitting in a wheelchair. Bookcases and shelving lay low to the floor. The closets had been customized to accommodate someone who couldn't stand, as had the bathroom. Even the kitchen sported the "low look," which enabled him to cook for himself.

He looked up from the computer screen when Josh came into his study. "It's about time you joined the world of the living. I thought we had a breakfast date at nine."

"Sorry," said Josh, handing over a Diet-Rite and flopping

into an easy chair. "I didn't get up until after ten. I was late getting in last night."

"You missed a truly awesome batch of blueberry-and-banana pancakes. I hope she was worth it, whoever she was." He winked and backed his wheelchair away from the computer in order to face Josh.

"It wasn't that kind of date. I was working."

"Your Demon Beef story?"

Josh nodded, then looked away. "Something weird happened last night, Lewis."

"Weird as in silly or weird as in scary?"

"Weird as in I wouldn't've believed it if I hadn't seen it myself. I'm not sure I believe it now, except Nicki was with me, and she saw it, too."

Lewis leaned forward in his wheelchair, his gray eyes curious. He had a long, narrow face and a naturally drooping mouth that had a tendency to look sad. His hair had gone pewter-colored, prematurely so for a man in his midforties, but it was still thick and lustrous, combed straight back from his high forehead. Josh's mother had often said that Lewis Kindred would be a "striking" man if he were—well, if he had both legs and two normal arms. Shrapnel from the same mortar round that crippled him had left scattered pits of scar tissue along his jaw and above one eye, giving him a disreputable look that many women thought sexy.

"Try me," Lewis said. "I know weird when I hear it. In fact, I'm an expert on weird, as all my past girlfriends can testify."

"There's something I haven't told you about the Demon Beef thing. I probably should have told you a long time ago." Josh pulled the bundle of envelopes out of the waistband of his jeans and flipped them into Lewis's lap. "These came in the mail, addressed to me. They arrived a month or so apart. The postmarks are from the cities where the newspapers are—"

"I can see that. Give me a minute, okay?" Lewis took his horn-rim reading glasses from the computer table and started reading the articles, his brow wrinkling. Josh got up and wan-

dered around the study, absently fingering the edges of the
books on the shelves—thick volumes by scholars like James,
Nietzsche, Wittgenstein, Foucault, Quine, Kuhn, Sellars, Der-
rida, Rorty, Scheffler. Stuffed among them were Xeroxed copies of articles and monographs that claimed insights into such
burning issues as the reconciliation of postmodern antifoun-
dationalism with scientific humanism, things that only dyed-
in-the-wool philosophy buffs like Lewis Kindred could
appreciate.

Josh was no dummy. He was an A student at a tough school,
someone who several of his teachers considered "gifted." But
when he'd tried to read this stuff, he'd run smack-dab into
terms like *incommensurable, ontological* and *epistemological*,
and had ground to a halt. The issues of philosophy, it seemed,
lay submerged in tortured syntax and five-dollar words.

He stared at a grouping of framed photographs above a low
bookcase. One was the wedding picture of Lewis's parents,
Lyle and Bonnie Kindred, a handsome couple standing at the
altar of a church, surrounded by flowers. Next to it was a
portrait of Lewis's younger brother, Ken, square-jawed and
bright-eyed like Lewis—a high-school-yearbook picture. Josh
glanced over at his friend and felt a stab of sadness: the three
faces in the pictures belonged to dead people. Lewis's father
had died of cancer before either of the boys reached adulthood.
His mother had died of a stroke five years after Lewis returned
from Vietnam. An oil-rig fire off the coast of Scotland had
taken Ken's life in 1987, leaving him without family, except
for his maiden aunt Juliet.

Lewis cleared his throat and looked up at Josh, having finished the last article. "What do you make of all this?" he
asked.

"I was going to ask you the same thing."

"You're telling me that these clippings have something to
do with whatever it is you saw last night?"

"I'm not sure, but I think so. Do you think there's a possibility that all these murders are—connected somehow?"

"That's hard to say. According to the *Atlanta Constitution*, a man died in Athens, Georgia, in much the same way Ron Payne did, if you can believe the reporter. He was a night watchman, it says. Cops thought he'd been mauled by a big dog at first, but they later came to suspect some kind of cult involvement.'' Lewis grinned. ''Have you noticed that whenever something really bloody happens, somebody always suspects cult involvement?''

''He was killed about a month after Payne was killed,'' said Josh, not smiling.

''So he was. And next came''—Lewis squinted to read the date on a clipping—''the dentist in Des Moines, Iowa, according to the *Des Moines Register*. Same kind of deal, except this guy wasn't attacked in an alley. The police think he picked up some babe in a bar and went to a hotel with her.''

''But they don't think a woman could've done *that* to him.''

''No. They don't.'' Lewis's face went ashen, as if a bad memory had flared up inside his head. ''And then there was the guy in Burlington, Vermont. Sales manager of a Toyota dealership, divorced, lived alone in his condo.''

''They found him in his hot tub, torn to pieces. 'Massive tissue loss,' the coroner said, like some kind of animal had eaten parts of him.''

''And last, the windsurfing instructor from Lake Tahoe, found dead in his car outside Sacramento. The physical condition of the body was more or less like the others, judging from this story in the *Sacramento Bee*.''

''That one came in the mail just last week.''

Lewis stared a long moment at the control console of his motorized wheelchair. When he looked up again, his normal color had returned. ''We've got two big questions here, it seems to me,'' he said. ''The first is whether these murders are related, like you said earlier. The second is why someone would go to the trouble of clipping these stories and mailing them to you, of all people.''

Josh sprawled into the armchair again. ''I've been asking myself the same two questions ever since the first envelope came. But there's more to this thing, Lewis. I was at Ron

Payne's apartment on the night he was killed."

"You were *what*?"

"Hey, don't have an infarction, man—no way I was hangin' with him or anything. In fact, I wasn't actually inside the place."

"Then where were you—*actually*?"

"I was parked in the lot, kind of like staking the place out. I'd heard this rumor that some major-league rockers were in town—people from a big-time black-metal band, right? The rumor was that they were planning to meet at Ron Payne's place and do some partying. If it was true, I wanted to be there to document the meeting. This might've been the kind of the thing that could be significant in the future, especially if De-mon Beef ever hit it big. Groups break up and merge all the time, you know, and if Ron Payne ever ended up playing with some combination of those guys, I wanted to be the one who wrote a story about an early meeting."

"Sounds reasonable. I guess."

"Anyway, the rumor turned out not to be true. If any heavy-metal stars were in Portland that night, they didn't come to see Ron Payne."

"But someone else did come to see him, unless I miss my guess."

"Yeah. The only trouble is . . ." Josh shook his head, as if he himself didn't like what he was about to say. "Okay, this doesn't seem logical, but here it goes. At eight-thirty I fol-lowed Ron from the Rockaway to his apartment up in Wash-ington Park. Nothing happened for the next two hours or so. Ron shut off the lights and the place stayed dark. At about ten-thirty I started to get a sore butt, because my ride doesn't have the most comfortable seats in the world, you know? It was pretty clear that the rumor about big-time guys had been a crock. Then I saw somebody come out to the deck of Payne's apartment, so I dug out my binoculars to see who it was."

"Wait a minute. This was at ten-thirty? It must've been dark as hell."

"It was dark, yes, but not *that* dark. There were yard lights around the apartment building.''

"So who did you see?''

"A babe—a *major* babe. She walked out of Ron Payne's bedroom onto the deck and just stood there awhile, like she was having a cigarette or something.''

"Who was she?''

"I recognized her, but I didn't know her name at the time. She was a groupie I'd seen around the clubs. I saw her at all the Demon Beef gigs, always right up near the stage, always giving the dreamy eyes to Ron. She's world-class gorgeous, man—half-black and half-white, I think. Wears really cool dreadlocks and minidresses that don't leave much to the imagination.''

"I don't see anything weird about a groupie ending up in a rock singer's apartment.''

"I'm not finished yet. After I watched her for a minute or so, she moved over to the far side of the deck, where I couldn't see her. I thought that she'd probably gone back inside, but then, before I knew what was happening, she walked around the side of the building on the ground—didn't even come out of the front entrance.''

"Probably went out the back door.''

"No way. There wasn't time. I'm talking maybe six or seven seconds here. And get this: Ron Payne's apartment was on the *third floor*.''

"Are you trying to tell me she rappelled off the deck or maybe parachuted down to the ground?''

"I don't know how she got down. All I know is that she got down, and she walked within two feet of my car on her way out. She looked right at me, but I just sat there like a dweeb with my mouth hanging open. I watched her in my mirror, and she . . .'' The vision came back to him momentarily, of Millie's buttocks rolling inside the tight dress as she walked.

"I'm still listening.''

"She disappeared before I was able to get my head together

and go after her. I mean, I didn't know anything had happened to Ron—''

''You still don't know that this woman had anything to do with the murder. Maybe it hadn't even happened yet. Did you see any blood on her?''

''No, I didn't. Anyway, I wanted to ask her if she'd heard the rumor about heavy-metal stars. I felt like I halfway knew her, because I'd seen her around the band so many times, and I figured it was time to introduce myself. So I went after her, but when I pulled out of the lot onto the main road, she was . . . *gone*.''

''What do you mean? She was on foot, wasn't she?''

''She was on foot,'' Josh confirmed. ''She must've parked her car somewhere away from the lot, maybe along the main road, but I hadn't noticed any cars parked out there when I drove in. It was like she'd vanished into thin air.''

Lewis leaned back in his wheelchair, took another long swig of Diet-Rite, and offered the opinion that nothing Josh had told him qualified as Weird with a capital *W*. He was concerned, though, over the fact that Josh hadn't told the police what he'd seen that night. The groupie might not be responsible for Ron Payne's death, but she might have information that the police would find useful. Lewis urged him to take what he knew to the cops.

''No way,'' Josh answered. ''If the cops ask me what I saw, I'll tell them, but until they ask me, this information belongs to me. It's my exclusive angle, Lewis. If the babe knows anything, I want her to give it to me before anybody else. That's why I've spent all summer looking for her.''

''So who do you think sent you the newspaper clippings?''

''Probably someone who knows I was outside Ron Payne's apartment that night.''

''Like the black-white woman, maybe.''

''I guess it could be someone else, if she told someone she saw me.''

''Or she might know who the killer is, and she might be

trying to tip you off to some of his other crimes by sending you those clippings.''

Josh's green eyes brightened. ''Hey, I like that! She wants to remain anonymous, right? She doesn't want to get involved directly, because she's worried about becoming a suspect. Or she's scared that the killer might try to silence her.''

Lewis wrinkled his nose as if something smelled bad. ''Blind speculation. Face it: we don't have any idea who's sending you those clippings, or why. The postmarks came from the cities where the murders happened, remember? It might be the killer himself.'' He crushed his empty soda can with his good hand—wadded it up as if it was a paper cup— and hooked it into a wastebasket on the far side of the room. When a man has only one good hand, that hand becomes very strong. ''I still think you ought to take this thing to the cops. You ought to call them right now and tell them everything you've told me. For all we know, Payne's killer might be watching you. He might be playing with you, testing you, seeing how far he can push you. God only knows what makes a maniac like that tick, or what he might do next.''

Josh studied the carpet between his sneakers. Outside, a cloud bank moved over the sun, and the room darkened a shade. ''I haven't told you what happened last night.''

''No, you haven't. Tell me now.''

Josh related what had happened in the alley downtown. He described how Millie had waded into the gang of Nazi skinheads, saving Josh and Nicole from a brutal beating or worse. He described the woman herself in great detail—her long legs, her full breasts, her mismatched eyes of warm brown and frosty blue. Then he dug into the pocket of his jeans and took out the orb.

That was when Lewis Kindred became violently sick.

iv

He wouldn't touch the thing.

He drew back as if someone had sprayed ammonia in his

face. He begged Josh to put it away, to get it out of sight.
Then he made for the bathroom as fast as his wheelchair could
go and got there barely in time to spew the contents of his gut
into the toilet bowl. He continued retching for nearly ten
minutes behind the locked door, as if trying to vomit out a
gutful of poisonous memories.

Josh thumped frantically on the bathroom door. "Lewis,
should I call an ambulance? Are you okay? Is there anything
I can do? Lewis, *answer* me, damn it!"

Finally Lewis came out, feeling shaky as a newborn lamb,
his mouth tasting sour. His phantom feet itched like crazy, and
he wanted nothing more than to roll up his cuffs and scratch
the hell out of his stumps with his fingernails. But he only did
this when he was alone.

"I suppose you're wondering what the hell that was all
about," he said. Josh had made tea, and he handed Lewis a
cup. The warmth felt good against his cold palm.

"I've never seen you like this before, Lew. It . . . *scared*
me."

"It scared me, too. A little." He put on his poker smile and
tried to hide behind it. "When you showed me that—that
thing, I got a blast of memories, that's all. It reminded me of
Vietnam, and—and some things that happened there." His
gaze wandered to a near wall, where a framed photograph
showed a knot of GIs sitting on a mound of sandbags under a
hot Vietnamese sky. Josh's gaze followed his and alighted on
the picture. Lewis had told him the names of the grinning men
so often that Josh felt like they were friends of his.

T. J. Skane, the baddest of the bad dudes from East L.A.

Danny Legler, the chunky little Nebraskan with corn silk
for hair.

Scott Sanders, the Wyoming cowboy.

And Jesse Burton, the streetwise brother from South
Chicago.

Sitting in the midst of them, his fingers spread into a V that
meant "peace" in those days, was none other than Lieutenant
Lewis Kindred, the grinning kid who played poker like most

folks breathe. In the picture he was tall and tan and unscarred. He had two good legs and a pair of strong arms.

"That's not all it was, Lewis. It took more than a blast of memories to do that to you."

"You think you know me pretty well, don't you, Joshua?"

"We've been hangin' together a long time, man. I know it takes more than a blast of memories to make you spaz out like that. There's something you need to tell me, isn't there? You know something about the red ball, and I need to know it, too."

"I suppose you won't leave until I spit it all out."

"That's a fact—I won't."

Lewis took a deep breath to steady himself, to order his thoughts. He drained his cup and asked for a refill. Then he leaned back in the wheelchair, holding the warm cup against his chest, and told Josh the story of Gamaliel Cartee.

V

". . . so you've been hangin' out with a murderer all these years, my man—either that or a crazy man. I've been willing to let myself think that I imagined all the business about killing Cartee."

"That wouldn't be so hard to understand. I've read that combat does strange things to your head. Plus, you got wounded pretty bad."

Lewis laughed. *Pretty bad*, yeah. Bad enough, he supposed, to rob him of his sanity for a time. He knew now that after coming home from Vietnam, he'd endured all the various phases that Elisabeth Kübler-Ross had described in her book *On Death and Dying*. Denial. Rage and anger. Bargaining. Depression. Acceptance. Lewis had tasted them all in grieving for the man he'd once been. In the end, he'd forced himself to believe that nothing he remembered about Gamaliel Cartee had been real, that it had all been the product of a psychotic dream induced by physical trauma and massive doses of pain-killing drugs.

"What did you do with the orb he gave you when he came to see you in the 12th Evac?" Josh asked.

Lewis recalled that he still had the thing when he arrived at the Portland Veterans Affairs Medical Center after Vietnam. Perched near the crest of scenic Marquam Hill in southwest Portland, the VAMC was a toilworn facility that seemed more like a prison than a hospital—dingy, drafty in winter, stiflingly hot in summer. Lewis had hated the place. He'd yearned desperately to go home with his mother, who'd visited him every day while he was there. But the doctors had insisted on keeping him at VAMC for the full six-month program of physical therapy and recovery.

"I kept the orb in a drawer next to my bed," he said, the recollections flowing back, "and I sometimes took it out and looked at it. I never liked the feel of it."

"I know what you mean."

"I played some cards with the other patients, penny-ante games, nothing big. I didn't want to add to any of these guys' problems by cleaning them out. Then one day they brought in a guy from New York, only lightly wounded, a loud talker who claimed he couldn't be beaten in poker. He organized a big game among the patients. . . ." His voice trailed off as he tried to establish whether he was remembering a dream or an actual event. The recollections swirled inside his head, making him dizzy.

"What did you do?"

"I asked for a seat at the table. Then I took the orb with me to the game, and"—Lewis wanted to believe that this hadn't really happened—". . . and I played cards. I could feel the thing in my pocket while I was playing, warm and *alive*. Sometimes I even thought I could feel it move."

"It was like you were repeating the experiment you did with Gamaliel Cartee in the motor pool at Cu Chi, right?"

Yes. And the outcome had been the same. Lewis couldn't lose a hand without consciously trying to do so, not with the orb in his pocket. He'd silenced the loudmouth, and he'd tasted some small justice in that, but he'd also cleaned out everyone else at the table. "What I did made me sick. These were wounded GIs, none of them rich. Some of them were like me, missing arms and legs. One guy had lost the hearing in both ears and the sight in one eye. I had no business taking these guys' money, but that's what I did. I took it and I didn't give it back, almost as if the orb wouldn't let me do anything else."

"What happened then?"

Again Lewis struggled with the boundary between fact and fantasy. Had he actually bribed an ambulance driver to take him to the Sellwood Bridge in the wee hours of the morning, or had he dreamed it? Had he really reared back and pitched the orb into the black waters of the river, watching it arc downward like a red neon streak on black velvet? He saw the replay in his brain so clearly that it might have happened yesterday. "Until you pulled it out of your pocket a few minutes ago, I'd hardly even thought about the thing since then," he added, almost whispering. "It was all part of another time. I'd assumed that I was free of it."

Josh patted his friend's arm. "I'm sorry, man."

"You had no way of knowing."

"I'll find Millie and make her take the orb back. I'll tell her you don't want it."

"If I were you, I'd throw it in the river."

"She said you were a friend of hers, that you and she go way back together. She wanted me to tell you something—" He looked away, remembering. "*All good things come to him who waits.* That's what she said."

"I've never known anyone named Millie. She's no friend of mine, I can say that for sure. I was serious when I advised you to throw that thing in the river, Josh. Promise me that's what you'll do. Promise me you'll do it today."

"What should I tell her when she asks me if I've given it to you?"

"Tell her the truth. Say I made you do it. Then tell her you never want to see her again."

Seven

i

NICOLE TRAN PHONED shortly after dinner that night, tearing Josh away from his homework and firing questions at him. Had he given the orb to Lewis, as the woman in the alley had instructed? Were Lewis and the woman really friends? Did he say who she was or where she'd come from?

"I can't really talk about it now," Josh replied. "I'll fill you in next time we get together, okay?"

Couldn't he at least say whether he gave the thing to Lewis? A simple yes or no?

"I . . . not exactly. I sort of still have it. Like I said, I can't talk right now. I'll give you a call tomorrow, okay? Better make that Tuesday. I have an editorial board meeting tomorrow after school. I guess I forgot to mention it, but I'm the news editor of the Gavin Dell paper this term."

Whoopee-shit for him. Didn't he care that curiosity was eating her alive?

His mother was sitting in the living room, not ten feet away, her eyes glued to a book and her ears glued to his conversation. "I'll call you first chance I get, Nicki, I swear. Take care."

Later his mother came to him in his room and pressed her palm against his forehead. "Are you feeling all right, kiddo? You don't seem to be running a fever. Are your allergies acting up?"

"I'm fine, Mom. Do I look sick?"

"Not really." She stepped back to survey him in the way that mothers do. "But you don't seem like your normal bull-by-the-tail self, that's all. What are you studying tonight?"

"Calculus. Honors course. You gave me written permission to take it, remember?"

She nodded. Then she moved behind him and started massaging his shoulders with strong, motherly fingers. Josh loved it when she did this. "I hate to broach the subject," she said, "but we really do need to get cracking on your college applications, kiddo. It's not something we can put off much longer. I know you're committed to finishing your piece on Demon Beef, but some things can't wait.''

"I know. I'll finish the Northwestern application next weekend, I promise. By the way, I had to buy a new battery for my car today. The old one conked out in a parking lot last night. I need about seventy-five bucks to get me through the week, okay?''

Cheryl Nickerson stopped massaging her son's neck and went to find her checkbook. Josh went back to his differential equations, but concentrating wasn't easy.

ii

At 12:15 A.M. he awoke in his bed and stared at the webwork of shadows thrown against his walls by a yellowing New England elm outside his window. The weatherman on the eleven-o'clock news had promised a coastal low-pressure system late tonight, with the likelihood of winds, lower temperatures, and rain. The system had arrived about half an hour ago, rousing the limbs of the old elm and making their shadows dance.

The wind, however, hadn't stirred him from sleep. What had awakened him was the sound of breathing that wasn't his own, the breathing of someone very near.

iii

Lewis Kindred parked his Action Power 9000 next to his bed and plugged in his twenty-four-volt battery charger, ensuring that the wheelchair would be fueled and ready to go in the morning. Then he tucked his damaged left arm against his rib cage and expertly rolled forward onto the bed, ending up in a sitting position with the stumps of his legs protruding only inches over the edge of the mattress. If he needed to use the bathroom during the night, which was probable, he would go crablike on hands and stumps, pulling himself along the hand-rail affixed to the wall in the hallway. He would then hoist himself onto the toilet by grabbing the stainless-steel bar bolted to the wall above it.

A man without legs becomes something of an acrobat.

Before turning out the light, he opened a drawer next to his bed and took out the Colt .45 military service pistol he kept there. He ensured that it was loaded, that it had a round in the chamber, and that the spare magazine was both full and handy. After engaging the safety, he laid the weapon in his lap and switched off the bedroom light, using the remote-control device that his aunt, the landlady, had installed for his convenience.

His eyes adjusted slowly to the dark, seeking out the shifting shadows thrown by the elms and oaks in the yard. Leaning against the wall that his bed abutted, he listened for the sounds he'd heard earlier in the evening, the ticks and scrapes of someone moving around in the darkness of his porch, the squeak of old floorboards outside his front door, the soft rustle of clothing against skin. Someone was stalking him, spying on him, waiting for an opportunity to finish what had begun more than two decades ago on the edge of a rubber plantation in Vietnam.

Throughout the years he'd come close to seeing the man a dozen times—a smear of movement half-glimpsed from the corner of his eye, never straight-on and never in the full light of day. He'd seen enough, however, and *sensed* enough, to know that it was a small man with rat-shrewd eyes and wiry limbs.

He'd seen enough to know it was No Bick.

Lewis didn't doubt the irrationality of this conclusion, but neither did he try to rid himself of it. After all, he was far from alone in clinging to a belief in the preposterous. As a student of philosophy, he'd often marveled how some benighted scientists believed both in science and the Bible. Such folks accepted the paleontological fact of fossils of creatures that lived hundreds of millions of years ago, but still swallowed the biblical version of creation, in which God created the earth mere thousands of years ago. These same scientists would scoff at a theory about where UFOs come from, because nobody could present evidence to support such a theory. But in the next breath they would endorse the idea of an afterlife, though not a shred of evidence existed to support *that* notion. *Compartmentalization of beliefs*, some intellectuals called it. In matters of science, one adheres to a set of strict standards for establishing truth, but in matters of the soul one accepts much looser ones.

The notion that No Bick had stolen one of his severed legs on the battlefield, he knew, was nothing more than a sick fantasy brought on by the trauma he'd suffered. To think that No Bick had stolen the leg to *eat* it was nothing short of psychotic. In another compartment of his brain, however, Lewis believed not only that No Bick had stolen the leg to eat it, but also that he'd followed him from the laterite meadows of the Iron Triangle to Portland, Oregon, U.S. of A., to *finish his meal*.

Like many combat veterans Lewis kept a loaded gun in his home. He'd often bolted awake in the dead of night, shaken by some horrific memory that had wormed its way into a dream, certain for a shrieking moment that he was back in the 'Nam. Falling asleep again required the comforting touch of gunmetal on his fingertips. It wasn't that he feared the North Vietnamese Army anymore. He was worried about something else. . . .

Numbah-one chop-chop. Numbah one, okay. . . . ?

He first detected No Bick's prowling back in 1976, shortly after his mother had died. He'd sold the old family house in Laurelhurst and, at his aunt Juliet's insistence, had moved into this apartment. The prowling nearly always occurred at night. He'd never called the police or told his aunt about the intrusions, because he knew exactly what he was up against. Vietnam had done things to him, left its disease in his heart. And that was a very private matter.

iv

Fear settled against Josh's chest, heavy like an anvil. His ears magnified every sound that filtered into his room from the surrounding apartments and the outside world—the faraway whoop of an ambulance, the whoosh of wind in the trees, the bong of his mother's heirloom clock on the living-room mantel. And close by, the breathing. Steady and smooth, feminine.

It wasn't his mother, and it wasn't his sister, for he knew their sounds. They were his own flesh and blood. And neither of them would hide in the shadows near his bed, that was certain.

Who, then?

Something made him think of the orb. Before going to bed, he'd placed it in the right top drawer of his cluttered desk, not knowing what else to do with it. He would make that decision tomorrow, he'd told himself.

He thought, too, of the gorgeous Millie and her mismatched eyes. He felt again the dizzying power that flowed from those eyes, the authority they conveyed. He remembered the way she'd moved—as smoothly as a shadow but with the power of a lioness. Who was Josh Nickerson to disobey her?

He realized that he was shivering, for under the single sheet he wore only boxer shorts. The sound of rain came to his ears, the pitting and patting of droplets against his windowpane. And the stirring of papers on his desk. The window was open, and a cold wind was wreaking havoc with the loose clutter of the room.

With adrenaline pounding through his veins, he swung out of bed and padded to the window, meaning to close it. He discovered that the screen was missing. Leaning over the sill, he saw the screen on the grass below, the rain pounding icily against his neck and shoulders.

Without knowing why, he opened the top right drawer of his desk and rummaged around inside it for the orb. He heard Lewis's voice in his head, urging him to throw the thing into the river. Maybe he shouldn't put off getting rid of it until tomorrow, Josh thought. Maybe he should get rid of it *tonight*.

The problem was that he couldn't find it. He knew he'd put it in this drawer, which also held old baseball cards, disused pens and pencils, wadded Snickers wrappers. The orb wasn't here now, which was crazy, because no one had come into his room since he'd snapped off the lights, except . . .

"Looking for this?" whispered someone behind him.

The back of Josh's neck tingled, and his heart thundered crazily. He forced himself to turn around, to open his eyes. Millie stood so close to him that he felt the heat of her breath on his bare chest. She held the orb in her fingers only inches from his face. The thing was like a beacon, casting its crimson strings of light over the walls and fixtures of the room.

"*Christ almighty . . . !*"

Millie smiled wickedly, her mismatched eyes coming alive, the left one brown, the right one blue. *Earth and ice*, thought Josh, his mind fluttering like a trapped moth. She wore a simple shift of black, short and cut low at the neck so that the tops of her breasts were visible. Josh couldn't stop staring at them. Her rusty dreadlocks tumbled around her shoulders, and she smelled of some sweet perfume mixed with musk. She wore open-toed stiletto heels, and the red of her toenails matched that of her long fingernails. The glare of her teeth terrified him, but he was getting a hard-on nonetheless.

"Let's not waste time, Josh." She slipped her hand into his shorts and wrapped her fingers around his cock. "I asked you to do something for me, didn't I? Remember what it was?"

"I—I remember. You asked me to give that—the *orb*—to Lewis." She stroked him, for he was hard as a rock already, and he could hear her breathing, her breasts rising and falling.

"But you didn't do it, did you, Josh? You let him refuse it, didn't you?"

"I—I didn't have a choice. He wouldn't take it. H-he told me I should . . ." His hips started pumping involuntarily, heat creeping from his groin upward into his abdomen, downward into his thighs. It was delicious. ". . . throw it in the river."

"It's very important to me that you do what you agreed to do, Josh. I helped you, didn't I? Didn't I save your life? Now it's time for you to help me.'' She pressed the orb into his hand, then caught his other hand and pulled it to her breast. She quickened the rhythm of the stroking. "Try again, Josh,'' she said huskily, urgently. "Make him take it.''

He felt her nipple harden like an olive pit, and in his other hand the orb grew warm. His hips thrust back and forth violently as he fucked her fist, and through his half-open eyes he saw that her body, too, was pumping. He imagined himself pushing her onto the bed, lifting up the dress. Surely she wore no underwear, as she'd worn none last night. He imagined her legs spreading eagerly for him, long and brown, glossy with sweat. He imagined her ankles locking into the small of his back.

"Try again, Josh,'' she rasped, her body shuddering, and Josh's orgasm exploded. He clutched the orb tightly as Millie slipped away, a hissing shadow. In the space of three heartbeats she was gone, apparently having left the way she'd entered, through the open window. Josh stood dazed and sticky, holding the orb, which still glowed red but not as brightly. A chill settled over him as his sexual heat subsided and the glow faded.

Eight

i

IT's AUGUST 17, 1978, early afternoon. It's hot.

The taxi ride from O'Hare Airport to Chicago's South Side takes most of a sweltering hour. Before paying the driver, Paul Tran squints at the sign painted on the dingy plate-glass window of the Italian restaurant and glances again at the slip of paper on which he's jotted the name. This is it—Ristorante

Cacceone. He pays the driver and steps into the summer heat, lugging a small suitcase, his damp shirt clinging to his back.

Inside, the place is nearly empty of customers, for the lunch hour is past. The air is dusky, cool, and fragrant with garlic. A jukebox blares a tune by Three Dog Night, something about old black water and a Mississippi moon. When Tran's vision adjusts to the dusk, he sees a young black man sitting alone in a booth near the rear of the establishment, his nose buried in a book, smoke ribboning upward from his cigarette. Tran recognizes him instantly, though nearly eight years have passed since he's last seen him. Instead of olive-drab jungle fatigues Jesse Burton wears the brown uniform of a delivery service. His once bulbous Afro is neatly trimmed. He seems less bull-like now, less sturdy than when he was a soldier. The creases around his eyes look too deep on the face of a man still in his twenties.

"Hello, Jesse. It's good to see you again. Thank you for agreeing to meet me."

Jesse looks up from the book, hesitates a moment, then grasps the slender hand of the Vietnamese man he knew as No Bick. "Sorry, but I've forgotten what I'm supposed to call you these days."

"I've taken the name Paul Tran—something of my old name, but less foreign sounding to Americans. Better for business, I think. May I sit down?"

Jesse motions him to the other side of the booth and lays aside his book, which Tran sees is a history of early English colonizing in North America. A waiter appears with a pitcher of ice water, and Tran orders a cup of coffee.

Their talk is awkward at first. Jesse asks how Tran found him, and Tran replies that it was easy, though time-consuming. Remembering that Spec-4 Burton was a Chicago boy, he went to the Multnomah County Library in Portland and found the current Chicago-area telephone directories. Jesse's name appeared in none of them, so he copied the phone numbers and addresses of every Burton listed in the Chicago metropolitan area, more than two hundred listings. He started calling the numbers. On the twenty-seventh try he got lucky, and found Jesse's aunt Clarine in Cicero. She gave him the telephone number of the woman Jesse lived with.

"You'd make a good private detective, No B—" Jesse stops himself. "I mean *Paul*. Sorry, man. Old habits die hard." A hint of smile twitches in the corners of his mouth.

"It's okay. If you want to call me No Bick, I don't mind."

"Well, you *should* mind, seems to me. You have a new life now, same as I do. No Bick's in the past, just like the old Spec-4 Jesse Burton. They're dead and gone, and we should let 'em rest in peace."

"But Lewis Kindred isn't in the past. He's the same man he was when he lost his legs. He's home in Portland, and he's very much part of the present. As I told you on the telephone, he's the reason I've come."

At the mention of Lewis Kindred, Jesse's face tightens, and he lowers his gaze to the tabletop. Tran senses his pain and steers the conversation elsewhere, at least for the moment. He asks about Jesse's job, his plans for the future. Jesse replies that he has enrolled in a community college and is studying to become a teacher. If all goes well, he'll transfer to the University of Illinois in Champaign within a year or two, assuming he can save enough by working part-time as a truck driver for United Parcel Service. The GI Bill covers tuition, but it doesn't buy books or pay the rent or put food on the table. Almost as an afterthought he reveals that he's undergone treatment for alcoholism, and has only recently been released from a veterans' rehab center.

"So how about you?" Jesse asks, apparently having said as much about himself as he means to.

Tran briefly tells about his emigration with his wife and daughter to the United States in 1976, leaving out the details of their harrowing escape from Vietnam, the privation that they endured aboard a rust-bucket freighter, and the months spent in a squalid relocation camp in Taiwan. He found a job with a street-maintenance crew in Portland during the day and works as a janitor at night. Having saved every spare penny, he hopes soon to buy out the owner of the janitorial service and launch a business career of his own. He wants to give his family a decent house, nice clothes, a good car. He wants his daughter to have a first-rate college education.

Jesse's face softens, and he tamps out his cigarette. "You went to Portland because you knew that's where Lewis was, didn't you?"

Tran nods. "In Vietnam I overheard him and you talking about your hometowns, arguing over which was best. I don't recall who won the argument."

"How's he doin', anyway? I've sort of dropped out of touch with him the last couple of years."

Tran explains that he's only watched Lewis from afar. He's learned that Lewis's mother died two years earlier, and that an aunt has provided him an apartment in a building she owns in a nice neighborhood called Gander Ridge. Lewis gets around on his own, thanks to a motorized wheelchair, and he has a circle of friends with whom he plays poker at least once a week. As for whether he has any romantic interests, Tran can't say. "You see, I can't approach Lewis myself. He thinks I . . . this may sound strange. I don't quite know how to put it. He thinks—"

"He thinks you stole one of his legs and ate it. I know all about that. I visited him in the 12th Evac before they shipped him back to the world, and he told me what he'd seen right after the mortar round hit. I tried to tell him it was a halluci- nation, all that business about you policin' up his leg and run- ning off with it. He said he knew this in his brain, but not in his heart."

Tran takes a handkerchief from his pocket and wipes his forehead, then dips it into his glass of ice water and holds it to the back of his neck. "I, too, visited him in the hospital, but he was unconscious, delirious. I'd managed to make my way back to Cu Chi from the Ho Bo Woods, and I didn't learn that he'd survived until I checked in with the Triple Deuce sergeant major. Lewis was raving when I saw him, talking to someone that I think was his father."

"His old man was dead. Died a year or two before Lewis went to the 'Nam, as I remember."

"I know. I heard him tell his father, his *dead* father, that he knew I would one day find him, and that I"—this is difficult. Tran's thin face whitens a shade—"will kill him in order to eat the rest of him."

Jesse grinds his teeth and shakes a fresh cigarette from his pack, lights it, and inhales deeply. "A man goes a little crazy, getting shot up like that, losing his legs. He sees things in the shadows, hears things in the dark. You can't hold it against him."

"No, of course not, which is exactly why I've elected to stay out of his life. I don't want to cause him any unnecessary pain. Who can say what might happen to his mind if I were to confront him? How would he react? The sight of me might unleash old nightmares—"

"Or he might pull out a gun and blow your ass away. Lots of combat vets keep guns around, I hear. I keep one myself, under the mattress. Just knowin' it's there helps me sleep at night."

Paul Tran cringes and sips his coffee. The possibility that Lewis might kill him has crossed his mind more than once. This is the main reason he hasn't approached him directly, but has taken to prying, spying, and prowling around his apartment like a thief in the night.

Jesse blows a cloud of smoke into the air and stares into Tran's face. "What's this all about, anyway?" he demands, getting down to the bone. "You call me up out of the blue, tell me you're flying into Chicago and that you want to talk to me about Lewis. You can't talk about it over the phone, you say—it's got to be face-to-face. Well, here I am, and there you are. I've knocked off some sick leave to be here, man, so maybe you ought to tell me what's on your mind so I can get back to work."

Tran bites his lower lip and studies his cup. "Do you remember Gamaliel Cartee?" he asks.

Jesse blinks at the mention of the name. "Yeah, I remember

him. I've made myself forget a lot about Vietnam, but I haven't succeeded in forgetting *him*. What's he got to do with all this?''

ii

Tran relates what happened to him on that sunny afternoon in 1970 as he stood outside a makeshift hooch on the edge of the Michelin rubber plantation, a firefight raging around him. He talked to a man he knew to be dead. The man had a bullet hole in his face, and his flesh had that flat, washed-out grayness that death brings. The man was Gamaliel.

''He walked into the bushes and found a pearl-handled pistol,'' Tran explains softly. ''I recognized it as Lewis's. Gamaliel tossed it to me and told me that Lewis had shot him with it. He wanted me to take it back to Lewis, and to make certain that he knew who'd given it to me. I remember his next words exactly: 'Tell Lewis that our dealings are far from ended. We have much to do together, he and I—much to do.' And then he ran away, but not like any mortal man can run, Jesse. The way he skimmed the ground, he almost appeared to be flying. Seeing a man move like that frightened me more than I can say.''

Disoriented and afraid, Tran hid out in the Ho Bo Woods for the next few days, scuttling around like a hunted animal, living in holes and burned-out tree trunks, avoiding both the Americans and the NVA. Eventually hunger drove him back to Cu Chi Base Camp, where he reported in at the Triple Deuce battalion headquarters. He told the command sergeant major that he'd become separated from the scout platoon during the battle, and that only with great difficulty had he made his way back. The command sergeant major removed his name from the missing-in-action list, but not before asking whether he'd seen anything of another missing soldier, Sergeant Gamaliel Cartee. ''I lied to him, of course, and said I hadn't seen Sergeant Cartee. I couldn't have told him the truth, because he would've thought I was *dinky dau*. I hardly believed the truth myself then. Sometimes I scarcely believe it even now. . . ."

iii

Nearly five years after that sunny, bloody day in the Ho Bo Woods, the war in Vietnam simply petered out. The last American military personnel went home in 1975, leaving behind an almost overpowering silence. No more *whup-whup* of helicopters or ground-shaking eruptions of artillery or clatter of small arms in the night. The victorious North Vietnamese converted the sprawling Cu Chi Base Camp into a "reeducation center," where people either died or learned to talk like Marxists. The whorehouses in Cu Chi all shut down, and the whores seemed to melt away.

Mere days before the fall of Saigon, Tran Van Hai left his wife and infant daughter in Cu Chi and journeyed north to Tay Ninh on foot, a distance of nearly forty miles. He traveled at night and kept to back roads and rice dikes in order to avoid the endless green-and-tan columns of NVA soldiers streaming south for the final battle. During the daylight hours he hid in the same tunnels and spider holes that he'd used as a Vietcong.

His destination was the Holy See of the faith that once virtually ruled Tay Ninh Province, a bizarre hybrid creed called Cao Dai. Its followers worshiped a collection of deities that included Victor Hugo, Lao-tse, Jesus of Nazareth, Sun Yat-sen, and William Shakespeare. Calling themselves the "Third Alliance between Man and God," the priests of Cao Dai staged séances in which they coaxed divine wisdom from their improbable assembly of gods.

Virulent persecution by the Buddhists and Catholics had reduced the faithful to a fraction of the two million who had followed the creed at its height. In 1975, a stalwart core of white-robed monks still lived in the walled cloister of the Holy See in the center of Tay Ninh, where they practiced their faith in chambers bedecked with orchids and the icons of their gods.

Hai wasn't a follower of the Third Alliance, but during his childhood in Saigon he'd heard whispers about an underground sect of Cao Dai priests who supposedly knew answers to questions that normal, rational men wouldn't ask—"questions about the dark," in the words of his superstitious old uncle. Hai had decided that he must find one of those underground priests, having seen what he'd seen of Gamaliel Cartee. "Questions about the dark" had burned in his soul like a fever for nearly five years.

He arrived at the Holy See with his boots worn nearly useless, his feet masses of blisters, his stomach howling with hunger. The monks took him into their cloister with its vined walls and gardens, gave him food, and let him rest. They warned him, however, that he couldn't stay long, because North Vietnamese soldiers routinely searched the Holy See. Someone who was a former Vietcong like himself, a *Hoi Chanh* who had deserted the ranks of the revolution to help the Americans kill his old comrades, could expect to be castrated and hung in a tree to die if the NVA found him.

"I've seen a man whose right eye is blue, but whose left one is brown," Hai told them. "His shadow hisses like a snake. He delights in causing pain, and he—"

"Say no more," said the elder brother, holding up a hand. "We don't speak of these matters here, for we aren't shamans."

"I've been told there are those among your brothers who can answer questions about such things."

"We will take you to the one whom you must see. But you must speak no more of this to us."

The monks shaved his head and oiled it, then gave him a flowing white robe to wear, so that he looked like one of them. A middle-aged monk drove him north from Tay Ninh on a Lambretta scooter, where NVA soldiers marched south on the shoulders of the highway, most with the faces of young boys but with the weapons of men resting on their shoulders. Many waved cheerfully to the two holy men on the scooter.

Half an hour later the monk turned off the road and headed west on a trail that led through tiny hamlets nestled in groves of bamboo and coconut palms. Hai clung nervously to the man's waist, fearing that the trail might be booby-trapped or mined. They entered a rubber plantation that had gone to jungle, and the April sun disappeared behind the overhead canopy. The plantation fell behind but the trail continued, mounting low hills, twisting around languid ponds and ancient, forgotten pagodas. Finally they burst into a clearing where sunlight shone on an abandoned French villa with rusting iron gates and rotting porches. A sturdy jackfruit stood proud in a yard overrun by elephant grass, its branches bending under the weight of fruit. Red jasmine abounded, and crimson butterflies flitted among the blossoms. The driver cut the engine and told Hai that from this point he must go alone.

Hai pushed through the front door of the villa into a foyer that was decaying and green, into a house destitute of the furnishings that once had made it grand. The air was thick with rot. He moved into a drawing room, where he heard the tinkling of wind chimes. Beyond a shattered wall of windows lay a flagstone terrace, where sat an aged man in a robe that should have been white but had long ago yellowed and grayed. The old man beckoned to him, and Hai went. The old man motioned for him to sit at his feet, and Hai sat. Up close Hai saw that he was even older than was first apparent, perhaps ninety. His eyelids drooped like veils over his rheumy eyes, and the flesh of his cheeks hung like the combs of a rooster. Each gnarly thumb had a nail that was at least six inches long. He sat in a wicker chair next to a low table, upon which a candle stood in a plate of molten wax, its flame guttering. His mouth, dry with age, was stained red from chewing betel nut.

With a voice that crackled like dry bamboo he asked why Hai had come.

"I've come to ask your help, Uncle. I'm told that you have knowledge of certain dark things—knowledge from long ago. I've seen a dark thing, but I lack the means to fight it."

"What have you seen, nephew?"

Hai told him about an American soldier who had one blue eye and one brown, a man named Gamaliel. Whose shadow rustled and hissed when he moved, whose passion was inflicting pain. A man who could run like a deer.

He described the globe of red crystal through which Gamaliel controlled the forces of chance. He told about a young lieutenant in the American army who had tried to kill Gamaliel, apparently unsuccessfully, though the wound would have easily killed any normal human being.

Having heard all this, the old man sat silent a long time, the filaments of his beard stirring in the breeze. "Your accent tells me you're from Saigon, nephew. Have you lived all your life in the city?"

"Near the city, actually. Except for the years I spent studying in Europe."

"You're a man of learning, then."

"Some say so, but I want to learn from you. Universities don't teach the kind of knowledge you possess."

The old man chuckled. "No, I don't suppose they do. But let me ask you this: Do you believe in demons?"

"Five years ago I would have said no, but now I don't know what to believe. I'm not Cao Dai or Buddhist. My mother was Roman Catholic, but I've never been religious."

"Religion has nothing to do with demons, nephew. I've been a priest of the Third Alliance for many years, but the things I speak of are much older than Cao Dai, older even than Buddhism and the Catholics. You understand, don't you, that Cao Dai wisdom comes from our gods, and that we receive it during séances? It's *human* wisdom, nephew, gotten from the dead, and it's older than you can possibly imagine. Can you accept this wisdom if I speak it to you?"

"Yes."

The old man kept another long silence, gazing into the deepening shadows of the jungle beyond the terrace, thinking. "Tell me about yourself first," he said finally. "And tell me why you've decided to pit yourself against this man with one blue eye and one brown."

Hai explained that his parents, who were teachers, had fled Hanoi in 1957 to escape socialism, bringing with them their children, an uncle, and an aunt. They'd settled in Cu Chi, near Saigon. Because his parents were teachers, Hai learned at an early age how to study, and his marks were good—so good, in fact, that he eventually won scholarships to study in Paris and London. Ironically, he learned his radicalism in the great universities of the capitalist West, where he immersed himself in the writings of Marx, Lenin, Mao, and Ho Chi Minh. Upon returning home he joined the National Liberation Front. Like so many others, Hai had wanted only justice for his people, and he'd equated justice with throwing out the Westerners.

Years of soldiering with the Vietcong, however, did not harden his political beliefs. He met escapees from the north and learned that life under socialism was a cruel joke, a mere variation of the tyranny that the people of Indochina had endured for a thousand years. He saw that his own Vietcong comrades were not above committing atrocities that rivaled and surpassed anything dreamed up by the murderous president Duong Van Thieu or his lieutenant, Nguyen Cao Ky. War is war, he learned, and anyone who ascribes virtue to its practice is a liar.

After the disastrous Tet offensive of 1968, which the NLF cadre staged as a "final battle" to bring about the collapse of the Saigon government, Hai decided to switch sides. The Americans had virtually destroyed the Vietcong, and the NVA had become the principal vehicle for the national cause espoused by Ho Chi Minh. The Americans, he figured, represented the best hope of ending the war soon, and that was all he wanted—to *end* it. To stop the butchery. To let the tears dry.

Hai marveled now over his own stupidity. With his Western academic degrees and his knowledge of the world, he should have understood the geopolitical realities that barred the Americans from launching an all-out military effort to defeat the NVA. Having read Western magazines and newspapers, he should have grasped that the war had deeply divided the Americans themselves on moral grounds. But he'd failed to understand. And he turned his back on his comrades to *chieu hoi.*

He became a Kit Carson, which meant that he was assigned to an American unit to serve as a special combat adviser, one who knew firsthand the tactics of the Vietcong and the NVA. His job was to prevent the GIs from blundering into booby traps, mines, and ambushes, but he never did that job very well. Seeing the destruction and hardship that the GIs inflicted on the civilian population—some of it unintentional, some of it not—he couldn't muster any sympathy for these brutes. He became silent as stone, responding to Americans' questions with ''No bick.''

He drifted into a fog of lassitude. He ate, slept, and survived. He lived only for the day when the nightmare would end—not for any cause or even for the hope of justice. The fog lifted, however, on a scorching autumn afternoon in 1970 as he witnessed a spectacle of cruelty inflicted by a creature who wore the uniform of an American sergeant and cast a shadow that seemed like a living thing.

''It took five years for me to understand what happened to me that day,'' he told the old man. ''After living those moments again and again in dreams, I understood that I had acquired a new enemy, as well as a new ally. My enemy was the man with mismatched eyes, and my ally was the young lieutenant who had thwarted him. I don't need politics anymore, Uncle. I've found my cause.''

The old man nodded. ''I will tell you all that I know, nephew, but you must understand that my knowledge is incomplete. You're venturing onto dangerous ground, knowing only part of the truth.''

''I've ventured onto dangerous ground before, Uncle.''

''Your enemy is a thing for which we have no name. It lives not only here in Tay Ninh Province, not only in Vietnam or Indochina, but wherever human beings live. This is as it's been since the beginning of time, throughout the whole world.

''Sometimes it simply walks out of the jungle to take up its life among men, or crawls out of a swamp. I've heard some say that it comes out of rivers or lakes.

"It survives by taking the flesh and blood of humans, and it thrives on the anguish it brings to our kind. You are correct that it can twist the forces of chance, and this is why it often robs men in games of cards and dice. Throughout the ages, the various tribes of man have spun legends and fanciful tales about these beings, calling them vampires or werewolves or incubi, and prescribing various concoctions or prayers to stave them off or kill them. But none of these cures is of any use, nephew, for there is but one way to defeat them. You must enlist the help of the dead. . . ."

iv

Jesse Burton listens to the story with mounting annoyance. It's all craziness, this bullshit about talking to Cartee after Lewis put a bullet through the man's head. Why Tran has concocted a story about talking to a dead man, Jesse can't guess. And the part about spending three days in the jungle with an old Cao Dai shaman is almost laughable. *Enlisting the help of the dead.* Who the fuck does Tran think he's talking to, anyway?

Jesse holds up a hand. "I don't want to insult you, but what makes you think I believe any of this? I mean, you gotta know how it sounds, right?"

Tran looks wounded. "You've seen Gamaliel. You saw what he did to the two women in the village near Trung Lap. You've seen—"

"What he did to those women was no worse than what happened to thousands of other civilians in that dirty fuckin' little war. He was an IPW, right?—an interrogator of prisoners of war. He wasn't supposed to be a righteous, upstanding dude."

"You were there in the motor pool when he and Lewis played poker. You saw the power of the red orb."

"What I saw were the tricks of a stage magician, a cardsharp. What I saw was nothing more than . . .'' Images creep into Jesse's mind like thieves—Gamaliel's *shadow*, not black but deep blue, hissing along the ground like a host of predatory bugs; the ruined body of a little whore in Mama Dao's whorehouse; Lewis lying mangled next to the shallow crater dug by a mortar round, bathed in bright blood, with spikes of bone poking through the stumps where his legs had been.

Jesse has tried hard to forget all this, tried hard to forget the fact that he conspired with Lewis to kill Gamaliel. He's let himself believe that they succeeded, even though no trace of Gamaliel's body was found. *Missing in action*, the army said, and Jesse has let it go at that. Any other possibility is simply too horrible to contemplate.

He inhales deeply from his cigarette. *The tricks of a stage magician?* ''I don't see what all this has to do with me,'' he says flatly, a hopeful lie. ''Why dredge it up now? The war's over, and we can't undo any of it.''

''You saved Lewis's life. You carried him to safety. I know that you admired him, and that you care what happens to him.''

''I care, yeah—but what the hell can I *do* for him, man?''

''Listen to me, Jesse. Gamaliel's kind aren't simply born in the way other creatures are. They're recruited from the ranks of ordinary people. The old Cao Dai priest couldn't tell me exactly how this is done, but it has something to do with the crimson orb. The creature presents it to the intended recruit as a gift, allowing him to sample the powers that may someday be his. If the person accepts the gift, then the next phase of the recruitment begins. A demon comes to him as a woman, and they make love. He becomes infected with her disease, and then he becomes *like* her, one of her kind. From that moment on, he will need human flesh and blood to survive. He will have one blue eye and one brown, and he will have powers that normal humans can't even imagine.''

''Are you saying this will happen to Lewis?''

''I'm saying only this: Gamaliel has already tried to give the orb to him. You and I both saw it happen in the motor pool during the poker game. Second, Gamaliel himself told me to tell Lewis that they would have future dealings, which has led me to believe that Gamaliel and his kind haven't given up on Lewis, and that they still intend to make him one of them."

Jesse leans back from the table and shakes his head. "I'm sorry, man, but I can't swallow all this hocus-pocus about demons. If Gamaliel was a monster, then he was only one of thousands of others in Vietnam, and they all wore jungle fatigues and dog tags. As far as I'm concerned, what happened in Vietnam stays in Vietnam."

Tran balls his fists and his eyes become hard. Color rises in his cheeks. "Please let me finish before you jump to conclusions." He reaches into a pocket and takes out a marble of red crystal, about half an inch in diameter. "Don't let it frighten you—it's only a replica. The old priest gave it to me, along with a lacquered box to keep it in."

"What does it do?"

"I'm not quite certain. The old man wouldn't say exactly, except to suggest that it will warn me when the crisis begins. He also taught me how to meditate, how to ready my mind for the truth that will one day come to me. He instructed me to watch Lewis on a regular basis—spy on him, if need be— in order to determine when and if he falls under the influence of Gamaliel's kind."

"So you've been prowling around his apartment, is that it? Peeking into his windows, pressing your ear against the door? That sounds dangerous to me, man. You're going to fuck around and get yourself shot."

"I don't have a choice. If one of the creatures comes to him, I must learn of it."

"Well, you've got to do what you've got to, I guess. What I can't understand is what you want from me."

"You must help me, Jesse. You must help me conduct my surveillance of Lewis."

"How can I do that? I'm here in Chicago, and he's out there in Oregon."

"Call him regularly. Write to him. Rekindle your friendship

with him so that he will tell you if a woman comes into his life.''

"And if that happens, I'm supposed to call you, right?''

"Yes. But you must help me another way, too. You must help me find Gamaliel Cartee.''

"Find Cartee? Are you serious? The man was shot in the head and listed as an MIA. If he's not dead, how in the hell are we supposed to find him, when the U.S. Army couldn't do it?''

"As I told you, he's not dead. I'm certain that he will find his way back to Lewis, if he hasn't already done so.''

"What makes you so sure of that?''

"He himself told me, and he wanted me to pass the message on to Lewis, remember? I haven't done it, of course, and I don't intend to.''

"Just what do you plan to do if you find Gamaliel—spank his hands?''

"If I find him, I will kill him.''

Jesse chuckles bitterly and lights a fresh cigarette. ''You're going to kill a man who can take a nine-millimeter round through his head and run around like a deer, huh? Forgive my curiosity, but just how in the fuck are you going to do that?''

"I'll have help.''

"The help of the dead, right?''

Tran stares silently at Jesse.

"Okay, you listen to me for a change,'' says Jesse, poking the air with his cigarette. "It's true that I admire Lewis Kindred. He showed me how a man stands up for what he knows to be right. He showed me guts and determination. If you want to know the truth, it's because of him that I've finally gotten my ducks in a row. I don't drink anymore, and I don't hang with the homeboys. I'm working and studying in order to make something of myself. I guess you could say that Lewis inspired me.''

"Then you owe him something—''

"Shut up! If I owe him anything, it's an obligation to succeed in what I've started. I'm going to be a *teacher*, man. I'm going to help make the world a little more livable. I'm going to play straight with people, like Lewis played straight with me.''

"In other words, you intend to turn your back on him."

"Wrong! I'll do what you ask. I'll call him on the phone, and I'll write to him. I'll be the friend I should've been all along. But I'm not going to spy on him for you, and I'm sure as hell not going to help you track down Gamaliel Cartee."

Tran's shoulders slump forward, and he closes his eyes. "Then I suppose I have wasted your time," he says, defeated. "I'd hoped you would remember how it was with Gamaliel and Lewis. I'd hoped—"

"Oh, I remember, all right. That's my problem, man. I remember too much. It's time to forget now." Jesse rises from the table, taking with him the check and his book on early English colonies. "I normally don't presume to give anyone advice," he says, turning to go, "but I'll make an exception this once. Get some help for yourself, man. The war is over. You don't have to let it make you sick." As he strides away, he resolves to take that same advice himself.

Nine

i

REX CASWELL KEPT his three-story floating house moored off the posh shores of the Sellwood Bay Club on the Willamette River. His photography studio, darkroom, and weight room occupied the third floor, while the master suite, a study, and a guest room took up most of the second. The main floor, which was for lounging and entertaining, had panoramic windows, two decks, and a gourmet kitchen. The living room boasted as much expensive sound and video equipment as he could cram into it.

Rex Caswell considered himself a man of taste, a connoisseur of life's finer things. He admired style. He wore clothes from Armani, drove a Mercedes 450 SL, and roamed the Willamette on a custom-built cigarette boat with duel V-8s. He worked out ninety minutes a day in his weight room in order to maintain a body that looked thirty instead of the forty-four it really was. He used a tanning lamp to enhance what he considered his "craggy good looks" and pulled his straight blond hair into a stubby ponytail. He wore a gold bead in the lobe of his right ear, but no other jewelry, except for a simple Piaget watch.

Rex Caswell had more style than anyone he knew.

His mainstream photography business was too small to support his commitment to the finer things, but his pornography business was more than up to the challenge. For nearly two decades Rex had photographed young girls in the nude, some as young as thirteen, and dealt the pictures to a nationwide syndicate that published underground "specialty" magazines. The business had provided an embarrassment of riches, not to mention certain side benefits not measurable in dollars and cents.

On Monday afternoon, September 14, 1992, he strolled into his living room and picked up a telephone handset, which was the conventional kind with a cord. Rex didn't believe in cordless telephones, because they were too easy to tap. "Yeah, Mase," he said when someone answered on the other end, "I want you to draw ten kilobucks for me and drop it by the house before seven. I've got a game tonight, and I feel— *special.*"

Mason Benoit, a close associate and Rex's chief liaison to the organized criminals who distributed his kiddy porn, said simply, "I'm on my way."

Within minutes Benoit would fetch ten thousand dollars from a safe in the basement of an apartment building that Rex owned in Maywood Park, which was far away in northeast Portland near the airport. The safe held one of four such stashes of cash that Rex maintained at widely spaced locations throughout the metro area—"surplus money" that he couldn't launder simply because he had too much of it. That was one of the little headaches that came with being a successful child pornographer: you made so much money that you couldn't spend it all.

ii

He poured himself a bourbon on the rocks, lay back in an armchair, and gazed through a panoramic window at the darkening far shore of the river. Maybe tonight would be the night, he dared to hope. He felt more than lucky tonight; he felt *integrated*—the integration of skill and discipline derived from years of practice and study. For the first time in years he felt like he had what it took to beat Lewis Kindred at the poker table.

He'd first played poker with Lewis in 1967 at the Sigma Chi house at the University of Oregon, where they'd both lived. Lewis was a philosophy student, Rex a fine-arts major. Lewis had won big that first night, and Rex had left the table an angry young man. Nothing pissed him off like losing at cards, for he'd always considered himself a damn fine poker player.

He later gave in to a craving for revenge and joined the regular poker group that Lewis had started. The two became "poker buddies," though their cordiality was only a veneer. Rex's revenge never came. More times than he cared to remember, Lewis methodically cleaned him out. More galling than defeat was Lewis's arrogant attitude, his implied assumption that because he could outsmart Rex Caswell at cards, he was the better man.

Thus it went until Lewis graduated in 1969, after which Rex heard that he'd entered the army and gone to Vietnam. Three

years later, after Rex had dropped out of school and started a
fledgling photography business, he and a girlfriend encountered a man with no legs on a sunny spring morning in downtown Portland. The man was driving down a sidewalk on
Broadway in a motorized wheelchair. Rex's mouth dropped
open when he recognized the shrapnel-scarred face of Lewis
Kindred, his old frat brother—broken and mangled and
doomed to a life on wheels. They traded awkward small talk,
asked about each other's lives, though the course of Lewis's
life was painfully obvious: he'd had a bad day in Vietnam.
Who's the better man now, Lewis? Rex yearned to ask. He
savored the sweetness of standing tall next to Lewis's wheelchair, towering over him on his two good legs with a beautiful
young woman at his side, knowing that for all Lewis's suc-
cesses at cards he would never again have what Rex could
daily take for granted.

They talked about cards, naturally, for they'd had nothing
else in common. Lewis had invited Rex to play at the next
regular poker game at the Hotel Fanshawe, probably because
he relished the prospect of fresh money on the table. And more
than twenty years later, Rex still went to the Fanshawe every
Monday night, questing for a vengeance that had yet to come.

"Maybe tonight," he whispered to himself, draining his
whiskey. "It's bound to happen sometime, so it might as well
be tonight."

Ten

i

ONE REASON LEWIS Kindred loved the Monday-night game at the Hotel Fanshawe was that the sharpest poker minds in the city were regulars, meaning that the competition was hot, just the way he liked it. Too, there was never a shortage of "new blood," which meant fresh money for the taking—a conventioning businessman with a fat wallet or an itinerant pro who'd blown into town to test the local yokels. The company was good and the laughs were nonstop.

The owner of the Fanshawe was Tommy Iadanza, one of Lewis's best friends, a Vietnam veteran like himself. To those who didn't know him, Tommy seemed nervous and a little sour, but that was just his way. Tall, thin, and loose-limbed, he had sad basset-hound eyes astride a prominent Roman nose, and a permanent scowl that suggested acute heartburn.

Tommy didn't play poker himself, but he enjoyed hosting the Monday-night game, and he went to great lengths to make the players feel welcome. With help from Carlotta, his wife, he maintained a flow of refreshments from the Huntsman's Bar and Grill downstairs to the playing table. He managed the kitty and administered the bank according to strict rules that every player pledged in writing to honor. He screened newcomers against infiltration by stoolies, since organized poker was illegal in Portland, though Tommy figured the cops knew about the Fanshawe game and just didn't care. This game was squeaky-clean, after all, and nobody ever got shot or stabbed.

The Hotel Fanshawe stood on Third Avenue Southwest near the intersection with Salmon Street, opposite a park full of elms, oaks, and maples. The neighborhood had seen better days but might yet see better ones still, given the pace of development in downtown Portland. Many old hotels like the Fanshawe had suffered the wrecking ball, particularly in the blocks north of here, where the demand was intense for new offices, shops, and parking garages. In 1980, the Iadanzas had

saved the Fanshawe from oblivion by buying it, believing that
a market existed for clean hotel rooms at reasonable rates, even
in booming Portland, Oregon.

On Monday, September 14, 1992, Lewis arrived at the Fanshawe with Alvin Johnson, an affable, rotund man in his late
sixties. Known to his poker pals as "Wisconsin Johnson" in
honor of his native state, he wore cheap wool suits and dark
green sunglasses year-round. He was one of the best poker
players Lewis had ever known, though he had the distracting
habit of eating salted peanuts without removing them from the
shells.

Wisconsin's arch-rival at the poker table was Sidney Grue-
ner, a retired furniture retailer from Lake Havasu City, Ari-
zona, who was as painfully thin as Wisconsin was fat. Sid had
deep, oily eyes that should have belonged to a doctor or a
rabbi, for they hinted at a reverent soul that his mouth tried
hard to deny. He had a hooked nose and thick white hair that
swept straight back from a narrow forehead. The other players
called him "Lake Havasu City Sid."

A third regular was Connie Wierzbinski, a fiftyish woman
who lived on her poker winnings and a stock portfolio she'd
obtained as a result of her third divorce, some twenty years
earlier. Spare and birdlike, she wore Trail Blazers fan clothes
and chain-smoked menthol cigarettes. She had light freckles
on her cheeks and dull brown hair that she wore short, like a
cap.

The card room was on the second floor, directly above the
Huntsman's Bar and Grill. The smells of greasy cooking
sometimes wafted up through the ventilation ducts. A huge
circular table, at least eight feet in diameter, stood in the center, covered with green baize and illuminated by track lights
in the ceiling. Ten straight-backed chairs surrounded it, well
padded for comfort and upholstered in a deep blue broadcloth
that matched the carpet. When a game was in session, Tommy
Iadanza manned a banker's table near the door, which he kept
locked to prevent any curious hotel guests from blundering in.

If a player needed to use the rest room, Tommy gave him a key to the door.

Lewis liked most of the people he played cards with. With few exceptions they were honest, down-to-earth folks for whom poker was a sport and a hobby. This level of competition was free of compulsive gamblers, simply because addicts lacked the temperament and discipline to compete against first-rate players. To survive in this crowd, a player needed complete control of himself. He needed to think logically and unemotionally, to execute complex strategies and tactics that were beyond the poor powers of gambling addicts.

In addition to the regulars, tonight's game included a pair of "occasionals," an amiable young veterinarian from Beaverton and an engineering student from Reed College in southeast Portland. New blood came in the body of an electrical contractor from Florida.

Lewis motored up to the table in his Action Power 9000 and parked in his usual spot. In an overdone British accent he said, "You're probably wondering why I've asked all of you here tonight—"

A wadded napkin bounced off his forehead. "We *know* why you asked us here," said Connie Wierzbinski, having hurled the napkin. "You're after our money!" Her chuckle degenerated into a wheezing smoker's cough.

"Let's not make it easy for him, just this once," groused Lake Havasu City Sid. "I've got grandkids who need to go to college."

Everyone fidgeted to get comfortable while Tommy Iadanza carried a chip bucket from player to player, selling red, white, and blue chips. Carlotta followed behind him with a notepad, taking orders for food and drinks.

"It's Texas hold 'em tonight, same as always," Tommy announced while dispensing twenty-five hundred dollars' worth of chips to Lewis. "No limit. If the board wins, everybody splits the pot. Any questions?"

No one had any. Texas hold 'em was the near-universal choice of serious poker players in America, and everybody in the Fanshawe knew the rules like they knew their own Social Security numbers. A variant of seven-card stud, the game was deceptively simple. The dealer gave each player two "hole" cards, then dealt five communal cards facedown in the center of the table—the "board." A round of betting occurred immediately after the deal, testing the strength of the players' hole cards. Another round occurred after turning over three of the board cards at once. A fourth and fifth round came after the dealer turned over each of the remaining board cards. Players used any combination of their hole cards and the board to make a poker hand.

No-limit Texas hold 'em was popular among the heavyweights for several reasons, not the least of which was that it accommodated lots of players. Lewis loved the game, especially at a crowded table. He was expert in using his position in the betting order not only as a bluffing tool, but also as a means of figuring odds. With so many cards left in the deck after each deal, playing the odds became extremely important. As Anthony Holden, the great British player, had written, a gambler bets *against* the odds, but a real poker player bets *with* them. Lewis was no gambler.

"We're missing Caswell," said Tommy, breaking the seal on a new pack of cards, "but we may as well get this fiasco going. You can deal him in when he gets here." Scowling in his usual way, he set the deck on the table, and the players cut for the deal.

ii

Through the closed door of his room Josh heard the telephone ring, heard Kendra pick it up. *Don't let it be for me*, he prayed, but no sooner had he breathed the prayer than he heard his sister's footfalls in the hall. Two perfunctory knocks, and the door swung open.

"Your latest Coke bottle is on the phone," Kendra announced. "She sounds desperate to talk to you, and more than a little upset. I told her I wasn't sure you were home, but that I'd check.''

Josh really didn't want to talk to Laurel right now, not with the load of worry weighing on him. Having hardly slept last night, he was tired and irritable, and he had a ton of homework.

"So how 'bout it, bud, are you home or what?" Kendra glanced around at the clutter of his room. "God, how can you stand to live in this landfill? Have you no pride in yourself, no self-esteem? Anyway, if I were you, I wouldn't keep this girl twisting in the wind too long. Someone who looks like her isn't going to have any trouble getting dates." Though only fifteen, Kendra was wise in the ways of the world. She herself was built like a Coke bottle, and the boys at Gavin Dell panted after her like adoring puppies. Josh didn't doubt that his little sister was more seasoned in romantic matters than *he* was.

"Tell her I'm not home. Tell her I didn't see her after school because I had an editorial board meeting. Say that I'll call her tomorrow."

"Hey, I'm not going to get in that deep. I'll offer to take a message, okay?"

Kendra pulled the door closed after her, and Josh listened to her retreating footfalls, heard her voice from down the hall as she talked to Laurel. He let out a sigh of relief when she hung up the phone.

Leaning back from his desk, he rubbed his eyes and studied the light fixture on the ceiling, trying to distract himself from the image that flashed again and again in his mind—of Millie with her wonderful mismatched eyes, standing not two feet away from where Josh now sat, her hand in his boxer shorts. He felt her breast against his palm, the nipple hardening. He heard her words: *It's very important to me that you do what you agreed to do, Josh. . . . Try again . . . Try again. . . .*

The whole thing seemed absurd. What was so damned important about the orb, anyway? And why couldn't Millie simply give it to Lewis herself, rather than go through Josh?

He rose from his chair, went to his window, and stared down through the dripping foliage of an elm tree to the pavement of Gander Circle, two floors below. Lights shone in the stately old houses on both sides of the street, for it was still early, not yet 8:30. A shroud of drizzle hung over downtown Portland, muting the lights of the skyscrapers and bridges.

From his window the drop to the yard below was sheer—two floors, at least thirty feet. When craning out the window last night in search of the missing screen, he'd seen no ladder leaning against the house. He'd even gone down this morning to look for marks in the ground, which a ladder would certainly have made in the rain-softened grass, but he'd found none.

He tried to imagine how someone would break into his room through this window without using a ladder. It was possible, he supposed, that the intruder had shinnied up the column from Lewis Kindred's porch and swung over the rail onto the Nickersons' deck, which would have been an awesome feat, even without the wind and rain. To gain his window from the deck, however, the intruder would have needed mountaineering equipment, for the distance was more than ten feet, without handholds or footholds.

And yet, Millie had come in and gone out through that window, wearing a shift and stiletto heels. It was possible, Josh supposed, that she'd lowered herself on a rope from the roof. She could have climbed onto the roof of the house via the fire escape on the far side of the building and secured the rope to one of the chimneys. Then, dangling from the rope, she could have removed the screen, raised the window, and—

Why hadn't he seen a dangling rope when he leaned out to look for the screen?

Another theory down the tubes.

He went back to the night of Ron Payne's murder, when he'd seen Millie strolling on the deck of the singer's apartment. Mere seconds later he'd seen her on the ground, as if she'd jumped or, as Lewis had suggested yesterday, *rappelled* the three-story vertical drop from the deck.

Josh wondered whether the police had found any climbing equipment in Payne's apartment. The news coverage had mentioned nothing about climbing equipment or ropes, but this didn't mean anything. Investigators often withheld such details from the public, not wanting the perpetrator to know just how much they knew.

A coil of fear tightened inside him. He was no longer the disinterested observer of the bizarre realities surrounding Ron Payne's death. Having become involved with Millie, he'd become more than an observer, more than a reporter. He was now part of the story, but he didn't know *which* part.

Decision time. He thrust his hand into the desk drawer and took out the orb, then zippered it into a leather fanny pack. He fastened the pack around his waist, threw on a jacket, and headed out.

iii

Rex Caswell parked his Mercedes half a block north of the Hotel Fanshawe in the closest space he could find. He glanced at his Piaget and saw that he was more than half an hour late. One of his business associates had called earlier from L.A. to discuss expanding their distribution network into Canada, and the guy wouldn't shut up. Oh well, better late than never.

As he entered the lobby he saw an exquisite creature sitting on a divan near the elevator, a light-complected black woman in a mint-green double-breasted jacket with a matching pleated skirt. She had dramatic, rust-colored dreadlocks and silver earrings that matched the buttons of her jacket. *This woman has style*, he told himself, unable to tear his eyes from her. She rose suddenly from the divan and approached him. She had one blue eye and one brown.

"I'll bet you're Mr. Caswell," she said in a soft Southern contralto. "I was told I might find you here."

Rex felt his breath go out of him. "Well—I . . . yeah, I mean *yes*, I'm often here on Monday evenings. I don't think I've had the pleasure.''

"No, you haven't, and neither have I. My name is Millie Carter.'' She offered a slim hand with nails painted the same mint green as the suit she wore. "I'm wondering if you might do me a favor, Mr. Caswell.''

"Please. Call me Rex. All my friends do.''

"Why, thank you, Rex. As I was saying, I would be in your debt if you'd let me accompany you to your game tonight as your guest.''

"To the game? As my guest? Why?''

"I'm very interested in poker, and I've been traveling around to various cities, watching games, learning, even playing now and then. I've been told that this game is *the* game in Portland. Someone gave me your name as the man to see, if I wanted to observe. I do hope you can see your way clear to let me come with you. Who knows? Maybe I'll be your good-luck charm.'' She reached over and smoothed the lapel of his expensive trench coat, which was spotty with raindrops.

Rex stared at her a moment, wondering whether he dared bring her upstairs. He muttered something about this being short notice, something else about the rules prohibiting visitors who hadn't received clearance by the owner of the hotel. Millie smiled dazzlingly, and assured him that she wasn't a police informer. Rex felt a drop of perspiration run down his leg as he laughed with her. Of *course* she wasn't an informer. Of *course* she would be welcome upstairs. He would see to that.

iv

At the poker table Lewis was in his element. Here he needed no strong legs or arms, no flawless, unscarred face. He needed only his wits and his nerve. Each game was a world within a world, where the deck of cards represented anything and everything that fate could fling at him.

But it wasn't a soft place, this world within a world. Poker was tough, heartless. Poker demanded your best shot, and sometimes your best wasn't good enough. Sometimes you lost. This was part of the game, and Lewis accepted the good with the bad, knowing that in the end, he would win. This was *faith*, he supposed, or something close to it.

For Lewis the evening had gone swimmingly. The electrical contractor from Florida had lost steadily, as had the young veterinarian from Beaverton. Wisconsin Johnson was also having a bad night, thanks mainly to three big hands that Lewis had won. Already Wisconsin had consumed half a pound of peanuts in the shells, indicating how nervous he was about his losing streak.

Then Rex Caswell arrived, strutting his costly clothes, his stubby blond ponytail bouncing comically, a gorgeous racially mixed woman in tow. The instant Lewis laid eyes on her, he knew who she was, for her mismatched eyes gleamed like cut gems. She was Millie, the star of the story that Josh Nickerson had told him yesterday. Lewis had seen eyes like hers before.

Tommy Iadanza was hesitant to admit an observer without prior clearance, but Rex clapped him on the shoulder and said, "Tom, please. You don't really think I'd bring a guest that I hadn't thoroughly vetted! I hope you don't think this glorious creature"—he pulled Millie close to the table so that all the players could get a good look at her—"could be a cop, do you? I mean, get a grip. Can you see a lady like this doing close-order drill at a fucking police academy?"

A gust of laughter went up from all the players except Lewis. He couldn't take his eyes off Millie, and she stared straight back at him, smiling faintly as if he and she shared a secret. Lewis felt a stirring in his gut that he'd not felt in a long, long time.

"How about we take a vote right now?" continued Rex. "All those in favor of letting Millie stay raise your hands. . . ." Everybody voted to let her stay.

V

Josh drove to Nicole Tran's house and begged her to come along with him—to where, he couldn't say. He needed to talk, that's all. Nicole told him that he wasn't the only one who cared about getting his homework done. But when she got a good look at his face, and saw the fear and tension tugging at it, she knew that she couldn't turn him out on his own. She pulled on a hooded rain jacket. "We're going for pizza!" she yelled to her mother, heading out the door.

The rain fell in earnest now. Twists of colored light lay on the wet asphalt of downtown Portland, cast there by neon signs and street lamps. Traffic was light. Josh headed down to Front Street along the Willamette and turned into River Place, where he had no trouble finding a parking spot.

"Let's walk," he said, and they got of the car, mindless of the rain.

They ambled north along the esplanade, Nicole's arm hooked into Josh's elbow, alone except for the occasional scurrying couple under an umbrella. Most of the shops and eateries that fronted the river were dark. The lights of the marina looked gauzy through the veil of rain, and the river itself was a black canyon beyond the shore.

Josh told Nicole everything he'd told Lewis Kindred yesterday—the fact that he'd been outside Ron Payne's apartment on the night the singer died, that he'd seen Millie there. That he'd received newspaper clippings from an anonymous sender about similar murders in other cities. He also related Lewis's experiences, real or imagined, with an orb of red crystal and a man who had mismatched eyes.

Then he started to tell her what had happened in his room last night, but he stammered and stalled when he got to the part when Millie put her hand into his shorts. Nicole waited for him to finish, no doubt miffed because he'd withheld so much from her for so long. Josh forced himself to finish the story, and he felt Nicole's grip tighten on his arm. "What she did then . . . well, I guess she gave me a hand job. I wasn't going to say anything about this, but—''

''Jesus!'' Nicole let go of him and stopped dead in her tracks. ''*This* is what you dragged me out on a rainy night to tell me? That Millie gave you a hand job?''

''How could I avoid telling you? It's all part of what's been happening to me.''

''Who in the hell do you think I am, anyway—one of the guys? One of those testosterone-poisoned grunge heads you hang with? You think it's cool to tell me your fucking locker-room stories?''

Josh put his palms to his forehead, shaken by her eruption. ''I thought you'd want to know, that's all. You're my closest bud. If I can't tell you, who can I tell?''

''So, I'm your closest bud, am I? That's great. That's fucking great!'' She whirled on her heels and stomped away. The breeze blew the hood of her jacket back, and her long black hair streamed away from her face. ''Be sure to let me know when you get your next hand job, okay, Nickster? And I'd be especially interested in hearing about Laurel's blow jobs. I hear she's real good at it. I'll want all the gory details.''

Josh trotted after her. ''Nicki, don't turn your back on me. I need to talk to you. I need your help.'' She quickened her pace. Josh had never known a girl who could walk as fast as Nicole without breaking into a run. ''Think about it, okay? Here I am, a normal everyday kid in Portland, Oregon, seventeen years old. I get inspired to write a story about a hometown band. I end up outside the apartment when the lead singer gets killed. I see a mysterious woman. I start getting press clippings in the mail. Then the woman I saw saves me from getting stomped by skinheads and gives me a crystal orb and orders me to give it to someone else. Next thing I know, she's in my room with her hand in my pants, like she's flown in through the window or something—''

He caught Nicole's arm and pulled her around to face him. The rain had drenched her face and hair, but even in the sickly glow of mercury-vapor streetlights she looked great. She also looked pissed off. ''Nicki, don't spaz out on me, okay? This is serious. I've gotten mixed up in something very major and very weird. It's wearing me down. I need your advice, and I''—he dropped his gaze to the wet cement—''and I need your friendship.''

When he dared to look up again he saw that her face had softened. Raindrops ran down her cheeks in rivulets. She no longer looked angry. Only a little hurt.

''What do you want to do, Josh?''

''I've brought the orb with me. I want to throw it in the river, and I want you to make sure I actually do it, okay? Don't let me wimp out at the last minute.'' He nodded over his shoulder at the Hawthorne Bridge, a graceful lacework of black metal over the river, rimmed with feeble lights that looked vaguely like Christmas decorations. ''Up there. We'll go up there and do the job, okay.''

''Okay, Nickster,'' whispered Nicole. ''We'll go up there and do the job.''

vi

Lewis couldn't concentrate. He'd lost five straight hands to Rex Caswell, hands in which he should have folded after the first round of betting. He felt as if his mental calculator had blown a chip, that his ability to figure odds had flitted out through his ears.

Rex, on the other hand, was enjoying an unholy blast of luck. Lewis reminded himself that these things sometimes happen, that players occasionally beat the odds several times in succession. A man on a lucky streak was unbeatable, as the pros all knew, and the only way to handle him was to stop playing and give the streak time to fade.

But Lewis couldn't stop tonight, not with Millie watching. She sat in an armchair against the wall, her slim legs crossed and her chin propped on her fist, staring at Lewis with those unreal eyes of hers. She seemed to be uninterested in everyone else in the room, even Rex, who often turned around to grin at her, celebrating what he probably thought was his great skill at poker.

The first to leave the game was the electrical contractor from Florida, who complimented everyone at the table and expressed the hope that they would let him play the next time he blew into town. The other players smiled, shook his hand, and wished him well.

On the next three hands Lewis lost more than three thousand dollars, all to Rex. The other players were folding early, but Lewis played each hand to the bitter showdown, trying unsuccessfully to bluff Rex into submission. The problem was that Rex was getting the right cards, and he wouldn't be bluffed.

"Jesus, Mary, and Joseph," muttered Connie Wierzbinski after the latest hand, in which Rex had dealt himself a pair of aces and another pair to the board. "What do you gotta do to get a hand like that?"

"You've got to live right, dear lady," replied Rex, grinning, "and take your Metamucil regularly."

"I guess my sins have caught up with me," Connie declared, rising from the table while gathering in her small hoard of chips. "See you all in a week."

Lewis won the next hand, a modest haul, inasmuch as Rex folded early and busied himself with whispering sweet nothings to Millie. Lewis let himself believe that Rex's lucky streak had finally ended, and he resolved to take the asshole apart, piece by piece. This was no-limit Texas hold 'em, after all. People had won fortunes playing this game, and had lost them, too, all in a single night. Rex Caswell had plundered Lewis's game reserves, riding a steed named Dumb Luck, and Lewis meant to make him pay for the ride.

He picked up the deck and shuffled it in his patented one-handed way, for his left hand was good for pushing the option button on a computer keyboard and not much else. The feat was spellbinding to those who'd never seen it before, and Lewis loved doing it. He was the only one he knew who could bring it off—shuffle the deck, cut the cards, and deal, all with one hand. But then he caught Millie's blue-brown stare, and his concentration broke. The deck exploded and cards flew in every direction. Rex Caswell roared with laughter and thumped the table with both hands, while the other players scrambled to pick up the cards.

"God, Lewis," he shouted, "could you do that again? It looked like a fucking tickertape parade in here! Do it again for the folks—*please*?"

Lewis waited for the cards to be collected, grinding his teeth but holding his poker smile. Wisconsin Johnson handed the deck to him, and he tried again. The others waited patiently, riffling their chips as good players do, keeping their faces down. This time Lewis dealt the cards without a hitch.

vii

They stood at a point midway on the Hawthorne Bridge and leaned against the pedestrians' railing, their shoulders touching. Occasionally a car rumbled by, its tires hissing on the wet pavement of the bridge and its headlight beams scooping conical swarms of rain. Staring into the depths of the Willamette River, Josh wondered how many poor souls had slipped over this rail to put an end to whatever tormented them. In his mind he saw human bodies plunging toward the hungry water, flailing and screaming while the wind whined through the girders and wires. He felt a pang of sadness. He supposed that he should be thankful that his problems weren't that bad, that he could conquer his woes merely by dropping a red crystal orb into the water.

Or could he?

"Okay, let's get this over with," said Nicole.

"Right." Josh tugged on the zipper of the fanny pack, which had become stubborn because it had gotten wet. Finally he got the orb, which gleamed dully red in his palm, its innards swirling like miniature cyclones.

It's very important to me that you do what you agreed to

*do, Josh. . . . Didn't I save your life? Now it's time for you to
help me. . . .*

Josh's eyes went bleary, and he felt as if someone had
dropped a chunk of ice down his collar. The sound of Millie's
voice was as clear in his ears as the whine of the wind. He
shuddered.

"Nickster, are you okay?"

"I'm okay. It's just that . . ." The orb now grew hot, almost
too hot to hold. If it grew much hotter, he would either need
to drop it into the Willamette or put it back in the fanny pack.

Try again, Josh. Make him take it, Josh.

He tried to explain to Nicole, but explaining wasn't easy.
He didn't know himself what was happening to him. His mental video screen fluttered to life again, this time with Millie's
grinning face, her blue eye and her brown eye blazing both
with promises and threats. Josh's scrotum prickled, and the
flesh of his back tried to crawl off his bones.

"It's just what, Nickster?"

"She can get to me, if she wants to. She's done it before—
broke right into my room with me in my bed. What'll she do
to me if I throw this thing in the river, huh?"

"I don't believe this. Not fifteen minutes ago you were
straining at the bit to get rid of it."

"Maybe I should do what she wants. Maybe I should try
one more time to make Lewis take it."

"Nickster, I swear I don't understand you."

"I'm scared, okay? I'll admit it. I'm scared shitless of the
bitch."

"Then give it to me. *I'll* throw it in. You can tell her I stole
it."

"*No!* She has ways finding things out. She's not like other
people, Nicki. Somehow she knew that Lewis hadn't taken the
orb when I tried to give it to him. On top of that—Christ, this
sounds weird, I know—but I think she can fly."

"You're raving, Nickster! You're absolutely drooling, do
you know that? You need professional help. If you won't
throw that goddamn piece of glass away, or if you won't let

me do it, then you'll have to deal with the consequences yourself.''

"Please, Nicki, I want you to understand—''

"I understand this,'' she spat, planting her fists on her hips. "You're behaving like a scared little kid. First, you're bound and determined to do one thing, but fifteen minutes later you do exactly the opposite. Grow up, Josh. Join the world of the big people, and stop looking for monsters in your closet.''

"I'm *not* looking for monsters!''

For the second time that night Nicole turned her back on him and stomped away, but this time she didn't let him stop her. The hike back to the car was long and silent and wet. Josh kept the orb in the pocket of his jeans, where he could feel its warmth against his leg.

viii

Rex Caswell stared at his hole cards, his brow furrowed in concentration. The hand had entered the fifth round of betting, "Fifth Street,'' the players called it. All the others had folded except Lewis.

Lewis had a pair of jacks in the hole, and the board showed a jack, a queen, an ace, a four, and a seven. Thus, his hand was three jacks, which was very strong. He studied Rex's face, looking for telltale signs of worry or distress, some indicator that the man was bluffing. A bead of sweat, maybe. A quick sidelong glance. An unconscious pucker of the lips.

He saw all three.

The betting had been heavy, for neither Rex nor Lewis had passed up a chance to raise. The pot now had more than six thousand dollars in it.

"I guess the bet's to me, isn't it?'' said Rex. He glanced at his hole cards one last time, then started counting out blue chips, each of which was worth fifty dollars. He pushed a stack of ten into the pot, and then another stack of ten, and another and another. "I'll raise you two thousand.''

Lewis had barely enough on the table to see the raise, and he pushed a mound of chips forward. "Banker," he called to Tommy Iadanza, who rushed to his side with a bucket of chips in one hand and a ledger book in the other. "If my credit's good, I'd like an advance of ten thousand dollars."

Gasps came from around the table, followed by a general hush. This was no ordinary poker hand, the others all knew now. Someone was about to teach someone else a lesson. The only sound was the purr of Lake Havasu City Sid's chips as he riffled them in perfect arcs from one hand to the other and back again.

"Your credit's good, Lewis," said Tommy. Lewis took a pen from a pouch in his wheelchair and prepared to sign a note.

"Don't fill in the amount yet," said Rex, grinning across the table. "I'll see your ten thousand and raise you fifty—*thousand*, that is."

Now it was Lewis who gasped. What the hell was going on here? Did this dipshit really think he could bluff Lewis Kindred merely by throwing big money at him?

"Rex," said Lake Havasu City Sid, "do you really want to do this? There's already a lot of money on the table. Maybe you should just call, huh?"

"Butt out, Sid. You folded, remember? How about it, Lewis? Are you going to see my raise? If not, you can forget the note and just write me a check for ten thousand."

Lewis happened to glance at Millie, who had leaned forward expectantly in her chair. She watched his every move with fascination, her blue-brown gaze boring into him. He blinked against the intrusion, but those greedy eyes of hers were relentless, insistent. They had unnerved him earlier. They unnerved him now.

"What's the matter, Lewis?" asked Rex, tapping his hole cards with a finger. "Has the game gotten a little rich for you?"

"Don't rush me, okay?" For a mad moment Lewis actually forgot what cards he had in the hole. A twitchy facial muscle plucked at his poker smile. *Two jacks*, his mind screamed. *Two jacks plus one on the board makes three. That's strong, man, real strong.*

But was it fifty thousand dollars' worth of strong?

"Time's up," declared Rex Caswell. "Let's play cards."

Lewis looked up at him and saw trails of sweat running out of his tight blond hairline. Rex's eyes were nervous, despite the forced grin. *The asshole's bluffing*, Lewis said to himself. "I'll see your fifty thousand and raise you another fifty," he declared. "*Thousand*, that is—assuming my credit's good."

Rex's grin fell away, and he quickly looked again at his hole cards. Millie's lips spread into a smile, as if she approved. Her long, slim fingers toyed with the silver bracelets on her wrist, moving them slowly up and down, up and down. Lewis thought of a young woman he'd once known all too briefly, a young whore named Thuy Thanh, the last woman he'd known sexually. He remembered her long, smooth legs, her perky little breasts. Lewis had been a whole man then.

"Another fifty thousand," said Rex Caswell.

"This is no-limit Texas hold 'em," Lewis reminded him caustically. "You wouldn't be playing this game if you couldn't afford it. Hell, fifty grand is probably walking-around money to you, right?"

Rex glared back at him. "Okay, asshole. I'll see your fifty thousand and raise you a *hundred* thousand. How's that, Lewis? Are we having fun yet?"

"Gentlemen, gentlemen," pleaded Wisconsin Johnson, rising out of his chair. "This is getting out of hand. Why don't we—"

"Shut up, you sack of blubber!" Rex spat. "This is between Lewis and me. Let's see if he has the stones to finish what he started. *My* money's green, and if I lose it, I'll fork it over. How about you, Lewis? What color is your money?"

Lewis gritted his teeth. He couldn't back down now, not with Millie watching. He could never hope to have her, or any other woman. But in this one electric moment he would be a man for her. Maybe she would remember him for it.

"For God's sake, Lewis," rasped Wisconsin, "see him and call!"

"Okay," said Lewis, "for the sake of everyone's mental health, I'll see your hundred thousand, Rex . . ." There. That much was done. Lewis was on the line for $210,000. ". . . and call."

Rex blinked sweat off his eyelids and reached for his hole cards. One card came up a ten, and something sucked the air from Lewis's lungs. *Don't let this be . . . !* And the other came up a king. Rex Caswell had a king-high straight, which beat the hell out of Lewis's three jacks.

An eternity of seconds dragged by as Lewis's guts cramped and his throat tightened. The room swam, and the faces of the other players floated in crazy orbits. He felt hands on his shoulder—Tommy Iadanza's—and heard declarations of loyalty from the others, their voices echoey as if the walls of the room were made of brass. He saw Rex Caswell's damnably handsome face, sheened with sweat, smirking.

"I'm a rich man!" Rex shouted, and he turned around to hug Millie. "This calls for a"—Millie had slipped away—"celebration." Lewis saw that she was gone, and he was glad for it.

"I think the game's over for tonight," declared Tommy.

"Damn right it's over," growled Lake Havasu City Sid. "Lewis, do you have a ride?"

"Let's not get ahead of ourselves," said Rex, standing. "There's the small matter of two hundred and ten thousand dollars."

Lewis stared up at him, feeling weak and small in his wheelchair. He started to speak, but his throat was full of mucus. He tried again. "It'll take me a while to raise that much, Rex."

"I don't understand. You're not telling me you played poker with money you don't have, are you?"

"You said my credit was good."

"I said it as a businessman, Lewis, assuming that you—a businessman yourself—would know how much you're good for."

Lewis forced himself to breathe. "I'm good for the money, Rex. But I can't give it to you now. Like I said, it'll take a while to raise it."

"A *while*? How long is a *while*?"

"I don't know. I need to sell my mutual funds and my bonds. I need to borrow some money, talk to bankers, brokers. Three weeks, a month."

"You've got a week. Seven days. Bring the money with you to next week's game."

"Wait just a damn minute!" raged Tommy Iadanza. "You're not talking to some deadbeat here, you're talking to Lewis Kindred. He said he's good for the money, and he needs a little time to raise it. The least you can do is—"

"Shut up, Tommy," warned Rex smoothly. "This is none of your affair."

"The hell it isn't! Lewis is a friend of mine, and I'm *making* it my affair."

"Back off," said Rex with real menace this time. "I'm in no mood for this."

"Well, maybe you're in the mood to get your ass thrown out the window!" Tommy roared. He started forward, but Wisconsin and Sid managed to hold him back, one on each arm.

"Tommy, I can handle this!" shouted Lewis. "I got myself into it, and I'll get myself out."

"That's the spirit," Rex replied. "The King of the Dweebs is owning up to his responsibilities. I like that." He came around the table and put his face close to Lewis's, smelling smartly of sweat and expensive cologne. "There's no need to be down on yourself, Your Majesty. You just got yourself bluffed by a master, that's all. I've been waiting ten years for this night, reading, studying, practicing—ten long, fucking years. I plan to savor the victory. That's why I gave you a whole week to come up with the money. I *need* a week to let the glory of this night sink in properly." He stood like a giant over Lewis, a blond Paul Bunyan in an Armani sport coat. "Don't forget, Lewis—bring the money to the next game. In cash. I don't even want to think about what will happen if you don't.''

He turned and saluted the others, who had clustered in a corner around Tommy in order to hold him in check. "Have a nice evening, friends and neighbors. See you next week." He draped his expensive raincoat over one arm and walked out of the room, whistling. A moment later Lewis heard his laughter echo down the corridor.

Eleven

i

TUESDAY DAWNED WET and wild. Summer road film became slime with the arrival of rain, making the morning rush a bumper-cars event. Airborne radio traffic reporters tried to route motorists around the snarls and the fender benders, but the situation only worsened the harder it rained.

"Be careful driving to school, Josh," his mother told him as she headed out the door to work. "Sounds like everybody in town has forgotten how to drive in wet weather. I'll never understand why the same thing happens every fall." She wore a gray flannel suit, a pink dress shirt with a button-down collar and a flouncy floral-print scarf—very businesslike, Josh thought. Just right for the busy executive but not particularly alluring. He wished that Kendra would give their mother some fashion tips.

"You be careful, too, Mom," he said.

He and Kendra left for school at 7:30, which gave them half an hour. In order to avoid freeways, Josh drove to the top of

Gander Ridge on Montgomery and turned downhill toward Burnside, which he intended to follow into Sylvan Heights, where Gavin Dell School stood on a scenic hillside. Unfortunately, a legion of other westbound commuters had apparently gotten the same idea. A long line of cars inched toward the intersection with Burnside, bumper-to-bumper, left turn signals all flashing blearily. Josh fell into line, swearing under his breath.

"Oh, this is really special," griped Kendra, gnawing a carefully painted fingernail. "I'm going to be late for my chemistry lab. I *told* you we should've taken the Sunset Highway, you dolt. We'd be off the Sylvan exit by now."

"Blather on, stupid one. The freeway's a hair ball in all this rain, which you'd know if you listened to the radio. Leave the driving to someone with a fully developed frontal lobe, okay?"

They arrived at Gavin Dell with minutes to spare, but Josh didn't turn into the student parking lot. He pulled into the front drive and halted to let Kendra out. "So what's the deal?" his sister wanted to know. "Are you cutting school today, or what?"

"I've gotten an upset stomach. I think I had too much pizza last night."

"Just remember to pick me up at three forty-five."

"Keep a tight butt."

"Spare me your adolescent crudities, for Christ's sake." She slid out the door and slammed it behind her.

ii

He returned home and went immediately to his room, opened his desk drawer, and took out the orb. In the gray light of morning it didn't look particularly special, even when he held it up to the window. It was a ball of crystal, and that was all. A glass bauble that caught light in strange ways and gave the impression of movement inside it. Anyhow, he'd decided not to concern himself with the nature of the thing, what it was or what it wasn't. He'd decided to concern himself with giving it to Lewis, as he should have done in the first place.

He phoned his mother at work and told her that he'd come down with a case of the runs, that he couldn't go to school today. He felt otherwise fine, he assured her, and begged her not to come home during her lunch hour to check on him. Yes, he would call her if he needed anything. Yes, he would spend the day resting and drinking plenty of liquids. Then he left the apartment, the orb tucked into the side pocket of his oversized plaid flannel shirt, bound for Lewis Kindred's place.

He used the circular staircase that descended to the front foyer, where a huge crystal chandelier hung from the high ceiling. Turning right on the landing, he entered a short corridor that led to Lewis Kindred's apartment. Two steps away from the door he halted, hearing voices from within. Creeping closer, he noticed that the door was ajar. He heard a woman's voice, which he recognized instantly as that of Juliet Kindred, Lewis's spinster aunt and the owner of Sloan House.

". . . and if I were to give you money, I would be interfering with the work of the Holy Spirit—can't you see that, Lewis? I fully believe that the Holy Spirit has decided to bring you down a peg or two, just to show you once and for all how much you need the Lord in your life."

Josh cringed. He knew how Lewis detested his aunt's blind religiosity and her strident right-wing views.

"Juliet, please don't make this any tougher than it already is," pleaded Lewis. He sounded as if he'd been drinking. "You know I wouldn't dream of asking you if it wasn't an emergency."

"Oh, I can just imagine what kind of emergency it is. You've gambled away everything you own, haven't you? Don't lie to me, Lewis. I've always known this would happen. I knew it years ago when my brother, your father, taught you those horrible, Satanic card games. I begged the Lord to forgive him for polluting an innocent child's mind with the devil's knowledge. And I prayed for you, too, Lewis, that you would turn your back on that filth and give your life to Christ. But you did just the opposite. You immersed yourself in sin, and gave yourself to the secular humanists and philosophers who deny the Lord with every breath. You took to cards and gambling, and when the Holy Spirit intervened, taking your legs from you, even then you hardened your heart.''

"Juliet—will you *please* stop preaching? Why do you need to turn every little issue into an excuse to preach? *Why?*''

Josh pressed his back against the wall of the hallway, half expecting Juliet Kindred to storm out of Lewis's apartment. He envisioned her standing ramrod straight with militant conviction, her long face powdered and rouged, her gray hair perfectly coiffed, her eyes fiery with zeal. He imagined her wearing lots of expensive jewelry, for she believed that Christ wanted His born-again flock to wear their riches as a testimony to His beneficence.

"I preach to you because I love you, Lewis," she answered, "just as the Savior loves you. He wants you to come back to Him. That's why He let you lose your legs, and that's why He's allowed you to lose your money, to show you how hopeless life is without Him.''

"Do you have any idea how ridiculous that sounds—God loves me so much that He took my legs and wiped me out financially? Crimminy, Juliet, why can't you think logically for once in your life? I need help! It has nothing to do with God or religion or why I lost my legs. If you can't help me, or *won't* help me, just say so, but spare me the bullshit about how God loved me so much that He made a double amputee out of me.''

"I'll thank you not to use that kind of language in my house, Lewis Kindred. And if you refuse to let your heart be softened, I suggest you pray to the humanistic philosophers whose books line your shelves, and see whether *they* come rushing to your aid.''

Josh sensed that this was the moment to dart back into the foyer, where he pretended to be fetching the morning *Oregonian* from the row of tubes next to the tenants' mailboxes. Juliet

Kindred rushed out of Lewis's apartment, her sharp chin thrust out and her twiggy limbs pumping, her necklaces swinging. She paid Josh no attention as she swept into the elevator, which stood open. The doors whooshed closed, and she was gone.

iii

"Lewis, are you alone? It's me."

"Come on in. There's a pot of coffee made, if you're interested."

The apartment smelled both of brewing coffee and stale beer. Josh fetched himself a cup from the kitchen and went to the living room, where Lewis sat in his Action Power 9000, staring through a rain-spattered window at the gray morning.

"Why aren't you in school?" Lewis asked, glancing up.

"I need to talk to you, and I can't put it off. Missing a day of school won't wreck my life." The pouches below Josh's friend's eyes looked like bruises, and the eyes themselves were bloodshot and weary. The wrinkles in his sweatshirt and corduroy jeans suggested that he hadn't bothered to undress last night. "Lewis, are you okay?"

"I met Millie last night. Her full name is Millie Carter, or maybe you knew that. She sat in as a spectator at the Fanshawe game. You were right—she's world-class gorgeous. And I put on quite a show for her. I was in rare form, if I do say so myself." He reached into a pouch of his wheelchair and took out a bottle of Beck's, which he tipped to his lips.

"Lewis, what's wrong?"

"Nothing. Nothing's wrong. Everything's hunky-dory. I lost two hundred and ten kilobucks, that's all. Did it all by myself, too, just me and my trusty ego." He took another long pull from the bottle. "Want to hear about it? It's not very uplifting, I'm afraid."

Josh nodded. He tried hard to forget about the red orb in his side pocket, which every now and then seemed to throb.

iv

The intercom in Rex Caswell's study bleeped, notifying him that his "associates" had reached the security gate in the parking lot of the Sellwood Bay Club. He punched a button that electronically unlocked the gate, then glanced out the wide window of his study toward the misty shore. He watched the two men amble down the inclined ramp to the docks, shoulders hunched against the drizzle, hands pocketed in their breakers. Tweedledum and Tweedledee, he thought, though they were nothing alike. Rex never called them this to their faces, of course. Good help was hard to find in this business.

Rex was naked, having just showered after his workout in the weight room upstairs. He often padded around the house with nothing on, liking the unfettered feeling it gave him, liking more the sly glances he drew from Silhouette, his latest squeeze. Her real name was Jennifer Gordon, and he'd found her on the street a year ago, when she was barely seventeen—a blond wisp of a girl with vacuous, oversized eyes. Rex liked his girls young.

He'd told her he was a fashion photographer and that she was pretty enough to have a career as a model (which was almost true). He'd shot several hundred pictures of her doing nasty things with a vibrator, and had made a small fortune on the set. One thing had led to another, and now she lived with him in the floating house. At least for the time being.

The doorbell chimed downstairs, and he pulled on a plush terry-cloth robe. His hair fanned down over his ears, for he hadn't yet banded it into the little ponytail. He went down in his bare feet.

Silhouette had opened the door for Mason Benoit and Lester Pittman and had seated them in the living room. Benoit was an athletic black man of twenty-five, who looked as if he could bench-press a Miata. He dressed conservatively, and spoke in low, polite tones. His choirboy's face suggested that he couldn't harm a flea, but in reality Benoit could harm any living thing that someone paid to have harmed. He would pull the fingernails off a nun, if the money was right. Smart, reli-able, and discreet in his drug life, he was one of Rex's most valued associates.

Les Pittman—"Spit" to those who knew him—was even bigger than Benoit. He looked as if he could press a Miata full of wet cement. Unlike Benoit, he was white, balding, slovenly, and stupid. He had tiny colorless eyes that looked like ball bearings embedded in an oversized cantaloupe. Spit wouldn't harm someone for money or drugs. He would do it because he enjoyed it.

"Don't get up, guys," said Rex, lowering himself into a huge leather recliner. "I won't keep you long. The reason I have this shit-eating grin on my face is that last night I won two hundred and ten large at the poker table."

"The rich get richer," said Mason Benoit, giving a fist salute.

"That's unreal," breathed Spit. "I've never heard of any-one winning that much in a poker game."

"Oh, it's real, all right," said Silhouette, entering with a tray of screwdrivers in frosted glasses. "He's been walking on air ever since he came home last night."

"Thank you, sweetheart," said Rex, accepting his drink. He always enjoyed a screwdriver after working out. "She's right, I'm happier than a worm in a cream puff, but there's one small concern. The geek I won it from hasn't raised the money yet. Says he needs time to sell stocks and bonds, get loans, all the usual excuses. I gave him seven days. I feel it would be ap-propriate to remind him gently of his obligation."

"You want us to twist his crank a little?" asked Spit, look-ing eager. "Maybe put a notch in his ear or somethin'?"

"I said *gently*," Rex reiterated, chuckling. "Don't give him any pain at this early stage. Just scare the living dog-fuck out of him, okay? The pain will come later, if need be."

"Good," said Spit, his tiny eyes dancing.

Rex then picked up a notepad, jotted Lewis Kindred's name on it, and handed it to Benoit. "He's in the phone book. You may want to scope out his habits for a day or two before making contact, in order to decide on the right time and place. When you do it, make it good. Make sure he understands that we take a very, very, *very* dim view of not paying your poker debts on time. Even for guys with no legs.''

"The man's got no legs?" asked Benoit.

"Nothing but stumps. Any problem with that?"

"Me? I have no problem with that. You know me, Rex—I do what needs to be done. The same goes for Spit."

"Good. Now finish your screwdrivers and get out of here. And have a great day, okay?"

"We will, Mr. Caswell," said Spit. "You have a great day, too."

V

"So that's what happened, Josh. I lost control. I let my emotions take over, and my concentration went south. I knew better than to try to bluff that hair ball, but I did it anyway. He had the right cards, and I didn't."

"And now you owe him two hundred and ten thousand dollars?" Josh was incredulous. He tried to imagine what a person could buy with that much money. The sum boggled his mind.

Lewis nodded as if he himself didn't quite believe it. He drained his Beck's and pulled a fresh one from the pouch on the side of his wheelchair. As he poured beer down his throat, a gust of wind huffed at the window, pressing veined spirea leaves against the pane. "Just before you got here I made the mistake of asking my aunt to help me out."

"I know. Your door was open, and I overheard you talking, but I had no idea how much money you were talking about."

"Funny thing is, Aunt Juliet has a ton of money socked away, probably enough to pay off Rex Caswell and not notice it. But will she lend me any? Not on your life. *Unless*, that is, I accept Christ as my personal savior and promise to stop playing poker. Don't you love that? My aunt tried to bribe me into becoming a born-again Christian!'' He laughed bitterly.

"How much are you short?"

Lewis leveled a bloodshot stare at him. "If I sell everything I own and cash in all my equity stocks and bonds—plunder my retirement fund, in other words—I'll still be about fifty thousand short. With my veteran's pension and my small outside income, I don't have the faintest hope of ever paying Rex off."

Josh suddenly hated this Rex Caswell more intensely than he'd hated anyone or anything in his life. Based on what Lewis had told him, Caswell wasn't even a very good player, but only lucky. And luck didn't care about justice, who's deserving and who's not.

Years ago Lewis had taught Josh how to play poker, and he enjoyed the game, but he knew that he wasn't in Lewis's league and never would be. He was good at figuring odds and he could remember the cards as well as anyone, but he lacked the intensity, the go-for-the-jugular aggressiveness, needed to become a first-rate player. "*Why*, Lewis?" he demanded, fighting to keep his eyes dry. "How could you have let it get so out of hand that you lost everything you have? Will you tell me that, Lewis? *Please?*"

"Don't you think I haven't asked myself the same thing a thousand times since last night?" He touched the joystick of the wheelchair, and the contraption hissed to life, moving in the direction of his bedroom. "You'll have to excuse me. I've got an appointment with my broker in an hour. I need to take a shower and put on some clean clothes." He halted the chair abruptly and executed a smooth one-eighty. His face twisted. "Okay, I'll tell you why it happened. When I play poker, I'm as good a human being as anyone at the table. I don't need arms or legs, and I don't need to be pretty. When I play poker, I've got everything I need up here." He tapped his temple with a fingertip. "But last night was different. Last night I tried to be something more than I needed to be. . . ."

"For Millie?"

"How did you know that?" Lewis nudged the chair right

up to Josh's knees, and glared at him. "How in the hell did you know that?"

"I know what she's like, Lewis." The wind gusted again, and the sound of rain at the window intensified. "She's responsible for what happened to you last night. *She* did it to you. Somehow she fixed it so you would lose."

"Don't turn this thing into something it isn't. What happened was my fault, no one else's. I chose to take stupid risks, that's all."

"Man, you don't know what she's capable of—" Josh cut himself off in order to let his brain catch up with his mouth. Could he really say what Millie Carter was capable of and make anyone believe him? This wasn't the time to try.

vi

He watched from his rain-streaked window as Lewis, aided by Tommy Iadanza, left Sloan House to visit his broker. Tommy held an umbrella overhead and steadied the wheelchair while Lewis maneuvered himself into the passenger seat of the Iadanzas' Taurus, no small feat for a man with stumps for legs and only one strong arm.

Josh watched them go, feeling useless. He dug the orb from his pocket and studied it like a gypsy fortune-teller. In its depths he saw himself driving down to Front Street, parking under the Hawthorne Bridge, and walking to the spot on the bridge where he and Nicole had stood last night. He saw himself hurl the orb into the Willamette River, and he didn't stop following it with his eyes until it struck the water and disappeared in a tiny explosion of red.

He damned himself for not doing it earlier. His life had been hell from the moment he'd first laid eyes on the thing. He now understood that it had touched Lewis, too, and deeply. Josh hoped that by throwing it into the river, he could rid himself and Lewis of its influence, and of Millie, too.

Josh having made the decision, the world seemed a little friendlier. Hunger rumbled in his stomach, and he remembered that he'd skipped dinner last night and breakfast this morning. He went to the kitchen, made toast with margarine and marmalade, and poured himself a glass of cold milk. Violating his mother's standing orders, he carried the food into the living room and sat on the sofa, intending to take nourishment before embarking on his mission to the Hawthorne Bridge. Eating made him drowsy, though, and he lay down on the sofa, wanting only a few minutes' rest.

He bolted awake suddenly blinked, and looked at his watch. He'd slept more than two hours. It was almost noon.

A squawking drew his attention to the window. A pair of young crows played in the branches of a Pacific dogwood, their feathers shining blue-black in the sunlight. *Sunlight?* Josh went to the living-room window and saw ragged patches of blue sky between gray boulders of clouds. The rain had passed, at least temporarily. The sun peeked out and poured its yellow warmth onto his face, while steam rose in billows from the lawn.

He heard something, or almost heard it. A breath, drawn and held. Or the shush of a shoe over carpet. He turned and surveyed the living room, which brightened, darkened, then brightened again as clouds toyed with the sun. His mother's heirloom clock sat on the mantel, faithfully ticktocking away the seconds, its short pendulum swinging. The rounded Scandinavian furniture squatted in tasteful groupings, guarded by the expensive lamps and carved teakwood tables that his mother so prized. Over the fireplace hung a moody George Maynard painting of a young girl seated alone at tea, reading a book in the chilly light of a tall window, beyond which a stone steeple was visible, encrusted with snow.

All seemed as it should be: quiet, ordered, clean. Except for a drinking glass that was a third full of milk and a plate with a few crumbs on it, nothing appeared out of place. The young crows chattered boisterously in the dogwood. A car whispered past on the street below, and an airplane droned overhead— sounds barely heard, but *needed*.

His hand went to the side pocket of his oversized flannel shirt and touched the orb. He'd made a decision, and the time had come to carry it out. He would go to the Hawthorne Bridge, and do what he needed to do. He started toward the foyer, but he saw something out of the corner of his eye—a smear of movement, like the tip of someone's elbow darting around a doorsill.

He froze.

Had it gone into the kitchen? The dining room? Had it entered the hallway that led to the bedrooms? His eyes were playing tricks on him, he decided. He inched toward the dining room, needing to verify that nothing was hiding there, that nothing had watched him while he napped.

In the dining room he found only the teakwood table, the china hutch, the clusters of family photos on the wall. Grandparents, uncles and aunts, cousins, all innocent and still. He went to the French doors and stepped onto the sunlit deck. Filled his lungs with the clean smell of rain. Walked to the rail, which overlooked a circular drive that accessed the service entrance to Sloan House.

Beneath an elm sat a black Jaguar convertible, its white fabric top beaded with rainwater and spotted with yellowing elm leaves.

A thread of terror wrapped itself around his spine. He retreated from the rail, wondering why a black Jag should be parked at the rear of Sloan House when none of the tenants owned one, when nobody but the yard-maintenance people ever used the service drive. He wanted to conclude that the car belonged to anyone but Millie Carter, but he couldn't quite manage it.

Was she inside the apartment? If so, how had she gotten into the building without a key? *Stupid questions*, he muttered to himself. He'd seen what she could do. Locked windows and doors meant nothing to her. Of *course* she was in the apartment, and she'd come for Josh Nickerson.

He went back through the French doors into the dining room. Stepping across the threshold, he became conscious of

the structure of the apartment and the house itself, the confin-
ing walls and hallways, the inhibiting doors. Here she could
easily corner him, but there was no other way he could go.
The silence crowded him, felt massive and oppressive.

The door between the kitchen and dining room stood open,
admitting a wedge of sunlight from a kitchen window onto the
beige carpet. The shadows of tree branches wiggled across the
wedge and danced as the breeze blew. A large section of
the wedge went suddenly black, as if someone passed in front
of the kitchen window. Not black, exactly, but deep *blue*. The
shadow was so electrically vivid that the texture of the carpet
disappeared, subsumed in a swarm of beads too small to see.
A profile took shape in the mass: a strong cheek and jaw, a
slender neck, a mass of dreadlocks tumbling onto the
shoulders.

Terror clawed at Josh's throat. He forced his legs into action, forced one foot to follow the other, and charged into the
hallway. His footfalls sounded like cannon on the carpet, and
for a hellish moment he heard the rustle of the shadow behind
him, chasing him. He found the front door, plunged through
it. He pounded onto the second-floor landing, then down the
curving staircase into the main foyer.

He aimed for the front door of Sloan House, beyond which
sunlight ruled, but something steered him into the gloomy hallway that led to Lewis Kindred's apartment. The door was unlocked, as always, and he dived through it, pulled it closed
behind him. He threw home the dead bolt. Knowing the apartment like the back of his hand, he went straight to Lewis's
bedroom, straight to the bed table where Lewis kept his .45.
Lewis had showed him the weapon countless times, demonstrated how to load and unload it, how to engage and disen-
gage the safety switch. *Never touch this thing, Joshua, unless
you plan to kill someone with it—in other words, to save your
life or the life of someone you love.*

Josh whipped the weapon out of the drawer and switched
off the safety. After certifying that it had a full magazine, he
pulled back the slide, which put a round in the chamber. He

eased the hammer into the half-cocked position, went into the studio, and sank into an armchair. Scarcely breathing, he listened to the sounds of Sloan House—the faraway whisper of the ventilation system, the electrical buzz of Lewis's refrigerator, the ticks and snaps of old timbers settling. Above him he heard the squeak of floorboards, which meant that someone was moving around in the Nickersons' apartment.

His flesh crawled. If Millie Carter came for him, he meant to put nine .45-caliber slugs into her.

vii

Lewis Kindred's stockbroker had his offices on the twenty-fourth floor of the PacWest Center, a tall tower with rounded corners, smoked windows, and a dull metallic finish. Tommy Iadanza waited in the reception area and thumbed through a *Forbes* magazine while Lewis met with his broker in an inner office.

The session lasted longer than necessary, since the broker was chagrined upon receiving orders to sell all the mutual-fund shares and bonds owned by one of his favorite clients, investments that represented a lifetime of savings and the hope of a dignified retirement. He asked for an explanation, for some assurance that Lewis knew what the hell he was doing. Lewis candidly told him the reason, which caused the man merely to shake his salt-and-pepper mane and stare out his window. They talked about alternatives, but reached the unhappy conclusion that Lewis didn't really have any—not if Lewis needed to pay the debt immediately. The proceeds from the sale of the shares and bonds wouldn't come close to doing the job, unfortunately. Knowing what he knew about banks and commercial lenders, the broker could offer no encouragement about the prospect of a loan to cover the balance of the debt. The session ended with grim smiles and a long handshake.

Afterward, Lewis and Tommy Iadanza went to the Huntsman's Bar and Grill in the Fanshawe, which had filled to near capacity with a noisy lunch crowd. They sat in a booth near the rear, where the wheelchair wouldn't block traffic.

Lewis loved this place, even though his internist had put it off-limits to him because of the greasy cooking. He loved the enormous back bar with its glossy wood, its long column of booze bottles and the arched mirror. He loved the ceiling fans and the mounted sailfish above the front door, the stuffed animal heads that gazed down from the high walls, and the brass foot rail that spanned the length of the bar. The Huntsman's was comfortable—worn but not worn out, free of artifice and pretense. Lewis remembered the era before the Iadanzas bought the hotel, long before the Huntsman's became a lunchtime hangout for yuppies. In those days there was a public card room in the rear, where a serious poker player could always find a friendly game of dealer's choice. His own father had played cards here, as had Lewis himself as a teenager.

He stared at the menu and wished he was hungry. Because today was Tuesday, the lunch special was Cajun meat loaf. Nothing on the card sounded good, except beer. When Carlotta Iadanza came to take their orders, Lewis asked for a pint of Full Sail Golden.

"That's not much of a lunch," Carlotta chided. "You really should have something substantial, Lewis."

"She's right," said Tommy. "You can't live on beer. Whatever you want, it's on the house."

"Thanks, guys. But I'm not very hungry." Lewis happened to glance toward the front of the café, where a trio of video poker machines stood against a plate-glass window. A middle-aged man in an expensive suit sat at one of the machines, a cigar in his mouth and a long-neck Budweiser in his fist, punching quarters into the machine as fast as it would take them. On the other side of the window stood another man, slight of build and short, dark-haired, his face obscured by shadow and fronds of potted palms. He stared into the Huntsman's Bar and Grill as if searching for someone.

Lewis felt his heart quicken as a familiar old fear took hold.

Before he could draw his next breath, the man darted away, as though his eyes had found Lewis's face and this was all he'd needed.

Numbah-one chop-chop . . .

"Lewis, are you okay?" Tommy asked.

"Me? Yeah, I'm great. Why?"

Tommy and Carlotta traded concerned glances. "You look anemic," offered Carlotta. "Maybe I should bring you the liver and onions, get some iron into you."

Numbah-one chop-chop, okay . . . ?

"Look, there's nothing wrong with me that two hundred and ten thousand tax-free dollars wouldn't cure. And with all due respect, Carlotta-my-love, I'd rather have a spinal tap than a plate of liver and onions."

"Then have a cheeseburger. At least have a cheeseburger."

With his heart still pounding and his neck cold with sweat, Lewis agreed to have a cheeseburger.

During lunch Tommy talked about last night's *Monday Night Football* game between the Dolphins and the Browns, which he'd taped on his VCR and watched in the wee hours of the morning, as was his custom. "You should've seen Dan Marino," he enthused over a fellow Italian. "It's the final ten seconds of the game, right? He hits a wide receiver for a touchdown, and the Dolphins win twenty-seven to twenty-four! I'm saying to myself, 'Oh Mama—there's justice after all. Good triumphs over evil!' I'm telling you, man, there was pandemonium in the stadium. They were throwing their babies off the balconies . . . !"

Lewis listened quietly, taking an obligatory bite of cheeseburger now and then. But he couldn't suppress his awareness of the minutes and hours ticking by, of the fact that already he had less than a week before Rex Caswell would demand what was owed him. By tomorrow morning he would have only five days left.

Three old friends approached the booth and slid in on either side of Lewis—Wisconsin Johnson, Connie Wierzbinski, and Lake Havasu City Sid. They all smiled at him, asked how he was doing, and tried to act as if this wasn't a prearranged meeting. For expert poker players, they were lousy at keeping the telltale signs of conspiracy off their faces.

"I suppose you're wondering what's going on, Lewis," said Lake Havasu City Sid finally. "In a nutshell, we think you got shafted last night. We don't know exactly how it happened, but regardless of how it happened, we think it stinks. Maybe Rex was just lucky."

"If he wasn't lucky, he was cheating," Lewis said flatly. "And to tell you the truth, I don't think he's smart enough to cheat that well."

"We agree. But regardless of how he did it, we think you don't deserve this, Lewis. You're too good a player, and you're too good a person. We've gotten together and decided we want to help you out."

"Help me out? I don't understand."

Sid took out an immaculate white handkerchief and dabbed his oily eyes, then blew his nose. He adjusted his yellow tie, needing to get it perfect before going on. "The four of us— Wisconsin, Connie, Tommy, and I—figure we can help you cover your loss to Caswell. If you can kick in twenty percent, say—that's in the neighborhood of—"

"Exactly forty-two thousand dollars," Lewis said, his voice betraying his annoyance.

"Well, yes. Forty-two-thousand. That leaves a balance of something like—"

"A hundred sixty-eight thousand."

"Yeah, right around that." Sid ran a hand through his thick white hair and glanced around at the others, all of whom kept their stares glued to the vinyl tablecloth, happy to let him handle this. "Lewis, we've all known you a long time. Each of us considers you a friend. What happened to you last night was an accident, an aberration, like getting hit by a bus. We all saw it, and we all felt it—"

"Rex Caswell was lucky, and being lucky is no sin in poker. He beat me fair and square."

"*His* kind of luck isn't right, Lewis," wheezed Connie

Wierzbinski, looking as if she desperately needed a cigarette. "It isn't—*natural*."

"Bullshit. A man wins at poker, he's entitled to get paid by the loser."

"Lewis, if this had happened to any one of us, you'd feel the same as we do," said Wisconsin Johnson, his triple chin gleaming, wagging, his eyes hidden behind dark glasses. "You'd want to help. None of us is what you'd call rich, but we can all dig up some cash, and we're willing—"

"Forget it! Poker isn't a team sport, folks. It's every man for himself, in case you've forgotten, and it's patently unethical to gang up against one player, even if he happens to be a reprobate like Rex Caswell."

"For God's sake, will you stop with the ethics?" pleaded Sid. "We're not trying to gang up on anyone. Our purpose is to keep you from being ruined, Lewis. We care about you, that's all."

"No, that isn't *all*. You also feel sorry for me, right? Poor old Lewis Kindred, trapped for life in a fucking wheelchair. Pretty pathetic, isn't it? Save the women and children and cripples—isn't that what you all mean? Well, here's a flash for you: I lost to Rex Caswell because I played stupid cards and I deserved to lose. I plan to face the consequences like a man, to stand up on my own two feet, if you'll pardon the expression. I don't need your pity, and I don't need your money." He pulled the joystick and backed his wheelchair away from the table, then made for the front door as fast as the electric motor would take him.

viii

Tommy Iadanza parked his Taurus in the front drive of Sloan House, fetched the components of the Action Power 9000 from the trunk, and hurriedly assembled the contraption. Watching through the passenger window, Lewis felt like shit for having lost his temper in the Huntsman's. Tommy had run after him and caught him outside on the sidewalk, had insisted on driving him home. Which was fortunate, because minutes later the rain had begun anew.

"I'm sorry I was such a prick at lunch," Lewis said as Tommy helped him into the chair. "I said some things I shouldn't have."

"Don't sweat it. Anyone who loses two hundred thousand bucks is entitled to be a little owly." Tommy walked alongside the chair as Lewis motored to the entryway of Sloan House. Both were getting soaked, since neither wore a hat or jacket.

"I appreciate what you and the others wanted to do," said Lewis, pushing his key into the lock, "but I hope you can understand why I can't let you do it. My old man taught me that a poker player doesn't do certain things, one of which is pool money against another player. I don't think I could live with myself if I—"

"Lewis, don't kid yourself, and don't kid me, okay? This isn't about your old man's ethics—you know that and so do I. It's about your pride. You don't want to feel dependent, which is understandable. You don't want to be a taker. I can relate to that, and so can the others. Just don't hold it against us for trying to be here for you." He offered a handshake, and Lewis accepted it eagerly.

"Better go in before we both drown," said Tommy. "Do you plan to put in a shift at the Center tomorrow?" He referred to the VIP Center, which stood for Veterans In Progress, a private relief organization that provided counseling and direct aid to homeless veterans. For the past decade both Lewis and Tommy had worked as volunteers one morning a week at the Center's storefront headquarters in Portland's Old Town.

"Sure, why not? I'm not the only guy in the world with problems, right?"

"Great. Pick you up at nine."

Tommy loped back to his car and Lewis let himself into the dryness and warmth of Sloan House. He spun the chair around to lock the door behind him, then paused to gaze through the glass pane as the Taurus swung out of the drive. He sat awhile in the foyer, thinking.

Tommy Iadanza was as good a friend as anyone could hope to find. Lewis worried that he didn't deserve friends of this magnitude. He wondered how his life would have turned out if he hadn't lost his legs. A two-legged Lewis Kindred would probably have gone on to graduate school and a career in academe. He might have shifted gears completely and gone into business or law. Hell, he might have become rich. A two-legged Lewis Kindred would have considered himself superior to someone like Tommy Iadanza, who lacked a college education. He would have traveled in a different crowd and acquired sophisticated friends who never talked with their mouths full, who attended charity events and gave receptions for visiting lecturers. Legs or no legs, Lewis would have been a poorer man for lack of Tommy Iadanza as a friend.

He piloted his chair into the dusky passage that led to his apartment and snapped back to reality when he found the door to his apartment locked, which was strange, because he never locked it, not even when going out. A man with no legs, he believed, was likely to need a neighbor's help one day, maybe with a crisis as small as a dead battery in his wheelchair or one as large as a fire in the building.

Digging for his other key, he felt a tickle of apprehension. He was totally unprepared to find Josh Nickerson in his studio, sprawled in an armchair with the stereo headphones on his head, a can of Diet-Rite in one hand and Lewis's old .45 in the other. The kid's eyes were closed, but he wasn't asleep, for his head nodded to the rhythm of the music that only he could hear. Lewis motored up to the armchair and tapped his knee, and Josh jolted upright. For a harrowing moment Lewis feared that Josh would shoot him, so full of fright were his eyes.

"Wow, I didn't hear you come in, man," breathed Josh, pulling off the headphones and setting aside the pistol. "This looks pretty weird, I'll bet."

"You've got that right. What's with the bullet launcher?"

"This . . . uh . . . is a little hard to explain." He stared guilt-ily at the weapon on the table next to him, then studied his own hands. "I was upstairs in our place, and I fell asleep on the sofa in the living room. When I woke up, someone was in our apartment. I got scared and ran downstairs, and when I saw your door was open, I came here, thinking it was probably the safest place I could be. I locked myself in and got the gun out, in case she—"

"*She?* It was a woman?"

"It was Millie Carter. I don't know how she got in—the place was locked. But this babe doesn't need keys."

"Did she say what she wanted?"

"I only saw her shadow, and I got out of the apartment before she could get me. I've never been that scared in my life, Lewis. I figured I would have a better chance against her down here, using your gun. I swear to God I would've shot her if she came after me."

If he only saw a shadow, Lewis wanted to know, how did Josh know whose it was? Shadows don't wear name tags, last time he looked. The boy's answer dredged up old fears: the shadow was like the one that Lewis himself had described when telling the story of Gamaliel, a shadow that swarmed with bits of living matter. Its color wasn't black but a deep blue. Josh had recognized the profile, the tumble of dreadlocks and the graceful sweep of a broad nose, a profile that could only belong to Millie Carter. Too, he'd seen her Jaguar parked outside in the service drive.

"She's been in the apartment before," Josh went on. "She was there Sunday night, in my bedroom." He described what had happened that night, even the part about the hand job. Lewis's face whitened when he heard how urgently Millie had charged Josh to give the red orb to him. "I wasn't going to tell you all this, Lew. I figured you had enough to deal with right now, and didn't need the aggravation. I was going to do what you said I should do in the first place and throw the orb in the river, but I fell asleep in the living room, and—well, you know the rest."

Lewis dug his fingers into his still-damp hair and suffered an eerie sense of connectedness to another place and another time, a realm where roamed a mysterious black-white man who carried an orb of red crystal and sported an affinity for poker. That creature, too, had tried hard to give the orb to Lewis, and had eventually succeeded—in a way. "Did you do it?" he asked Josh. "Did you throw it in the river?"

"Not yet. I've stayed right here, hiding. I heard Millie's car leave a while ago, but I stayed anyway, because I wanted to talk to you. I hope it was okay if I listened to some of your CDs." He finally noticed Lewis's damp clothes. "So, why are you all wet? Did you drive that thing through a car wash, or what?"

"Do what you planned to do, Josh. Take the orb to the river right now, throw it away, and forget you ever heard of Millie Carter."

"Lewis, I've been doing some thinking. Hear me out, and don't say no until you've considered what I have to say, okay?" He reached into the pocket of his bulky flannel shirt and took out the orb. "In Vietnam you and Gamaliel did an experiment. He laid an orb on your side of the table while you were playing poker, and it made you win, right?"

"He didn't give it to me—not then. I wouldn't let him."

"But it was *with* you when you did the experiment. It was near enough to you that it gave you the power to win."

"That's what he wanted me to believe. What really happened is that he played some kind of trick on me."

"Get real, Lewis. He didn't play any kind of trick on you. The orb has power. You can see that just by looking at it. You yourself used it at the vets' hospital here in Portland, when you beat the guy from New York at cards. You couldn't lose unless you consciously tried to."

"I don't know if that's the way it really was. Just because I remember it that way doesn't mean it actually happened that way."

"Then what about Gamaliel's shadow, and Millie's shadow? And what about the monster he became when he killed the girl in the whorehouse back in Vietnam? You've seen all these things with your own two eyes.''

"It's only what my mind *tells* me I saw. There's a part of my mind that's very sick. It's what Vietnam did to some people.''

"That's bullshit! You're not sick, and neither am I! You've told me dozens of times not to believe in anything I can't see and touch, Lewis. Well, I've *seen* Millie's shadow. And I can *touch* this orb. I can *feel* how warm it is, and so can you.'' He pushed it toward Lewis, causing him to shrink back in his chair as if the orb were some huge, venomous bug. "Listen, man. You can use it to win your money back from Rex Caswell, to get your life back on track.''

Lewis grimaced as if someone had suggested that he cuddle with a dead cat or eat a sandwich made of severed human ears. "There's no way in hell I'll ever touch that thing again! I told you to get it out of here, and I meant it.''

"And what happens when Rex Caswell comes knocking at your door, wanting his two hundred and ten thousand bucks? How are you going to pay him, Lewis—with a smile? Or are you going to sit still and let him take everything you have?'' Josh suddenly seemed much older than his seventeen years. "You don't deserve to spend the rest of your life scraping along with nothing. You've worked too hard to let him turn your whole life to shit. All you need to do is challenge him to a rematch. Tell him you've got the money you owe him, and that you want to go double or nothing. Then you can—''

"Shut up! I've told you I can't touch that thing!''

"Not even to save your own future?''

"I may not be much, but I'm no cheat—not anymore, anyway. It's true, I used the orb once to win at cards, and it made me dirty. I won't do it again. My old man taught me that your life isn't worth a gob of spit if you're not honest, and I've tried to teach you the same thing.''

"You *have* taught me, Lewis. And I believe it, honest to God.''

"So, what would I be if I used that—*thing* to beat Rex

Caswell out of his money? Do I need to spell it out for you? My old man would roll over in his grave.''

"But these are special circumstances. You lost to Caswell because of Millie Carter. You were a *victim*, and you're entitled to even things up.''

"I wasn't a victim, Josh. I was stupid. I lost the game because I lost control of myself." He leaned forward in his wheelchair and took hold of Josh's arm. "I want you to learn from this. Watch what happens to me, and make sure it never happens to you.''

Lewis wheeled around and headed for his bedroom. Before closing the door behind him, he turned the chair to face the boy a final time, his eyes brimming. "Take the orb to the river, Josh. Go while the sun's still shining and there're lots of people around. Go to the river and throw it in.''

Twelve

i

THE NEXT MORNING, Lewis rose well before dawn, unable to sleep. Through his window he could see tongues of mist swirling in the aura of the streetlights on Gander Circle, portending a gray dawn. He took a shower, using a specially designed sling that allowed him to hoist himself out of his chair and suspend himself in the shower stall. Later he toasted an English muffin and switched on his computer to catch up on work that he'd neglected yesterday.

He was tired, for he'd tossed and turned all the night. Shortly after midnight he'd imagined that he heard No Bick rattling a window to test whether it was locked. Lewis had flicked off the safety of his service .45 and sat upright, only to spend an hour listening to his own heartbeat. Time and again he'd forced his eyes shut, only to see the grinning face of Gamaliel Cartee staring hungrily at him across an expanse of green baize. Finally he'd fallen asleep and dreamed that the crystalline orb had somehow gotten into his mouth and he couldn't open his jaws wide enough to expel it. He'd bolted upright in bed, gagging and heaving.

Now he stared at his computer screen for minutes at a time, absently chewing a piece of the English muffin. In his head he heard Josh Nickerson's pleading voice: *You were a victim, and you're entitled to use the orb to even things up. . . .*

What must the kid think of him, Lewis agonized, having seen him at his absolute worst? Beaten, humiliated, and scraping for money? He'd always played the role of mentor to Josh, the wise uncle who wore the scars of worldly experience like merit badges. Lewis had watched him grow from a chubby toddler into a handsome young man, and throughout those years had taken an active part in shaping his outlook and his intellect. Cheryl Nickerson had seemed grateful for this, and had gone out of her way to include Lewis in family activities. She'd occasionally conferred privately with him concerning her son's upbringing, such as whether to enroll him in a program for the gifted, whether to buy him a car, whether to let him get an after-school job. Lewis had come to feel like part of the Nickerson family. He loved Josh like a son.

He clenched his good hand into a fist and pounded it on the desk. Starting this moment, he resolved, he would behave in a way that would make Josh proud of him. No more groveling or sniveling. No more cowering from old memories and harmless baubles of red crystal. Somehow he would dispose of the crisis with Rex Caswell, and he would do it like a man. If lean times lay ahead, so be it. He would survive. From this moment on, he vowed, he would conduct himself as if he were a whole man.

ii

Tommy Iadanza arrived on the stroke of nine to drive Lewis to the VIP Center. The rush-hour traffic had begun to subside by the time they reached Old Town, and they parked in a lot on First Avenue, less than two blocks from the Veterans In Progress Center.

They cut through the heart of the Skidmore Historical District, where quaint nineteenth-century buildings stood on every corner and the streets wore ancient paving stones. Half of one block was a pedestrian square bounded by tall, Neoclassical colonnades that shone whitely in the gray morning. A chilly mist hung in the air.

On one side of the stone-paved square stood the New Market Theater, built in 1875, now the home of New Market Village, a collection of specialty shops and ethnic eateries from which wafted the tantalizing smells of cooking. Across the square stood the Salvation Army's Harbor Light, a large white-brick building where the homeless could get meals, places to sleep, and sermons (not necessarily in that order). Outside the front entrance, scores of whiskered, weather-beaten men awaited the start of the Salvation Army's next breakfast shift, leaning against the white bricks or sitting on the curb, talking quietly or smoking.

The VIP Center on SW Second Avenue was sandwiched between a Greek restaurant called Berbati and a Persian one called the Green Onion. Inside, a dozen or so men waited in the reception area, drinking coffee and eating doughnuts, leafing through magazines or staring at an old black-and-white television set bolted to the ceiling. Most wore drab, dingy clothes, though several were neatly groomed and dressed, having spruced themselves up for their appointments with the VIP counselors. One old man sat in a bent wheelchair while a younger man with one leg dozed in a corner, leaning on his crutches.

Some of these men, Lewis knew, had received referrals from the Salvation Army across the street or from the Rescue Mission on Burnside. Others had heard about the Center from friends or had simply noticed the sign on the door. Two or three appeared to be inebriated, and they would be sent to local detox centers. The VIP staff had standing orders not to deal with anyone who wasn't stone-cold sober. Lewis felt an aching compassion toward all these down-and-out veterans, but his heart went out in a special way to the disabled ones, for he understood their torments as only one of their kind could.

He and Tommy went through the waiting room into an open area sectioned into cubicles, where secretaries labored over word processors and counselors met individually with "clients." At the rear was a closed office with a door plaque that said EXECUTIVE OFFICES.

Suddenly a door burst open, and out dashed a fast-talking, fast-walking woman who weighed probably three hundred pounds. She wore a huge sweatshirt embroidered with a red rose and the phrase ROSE CITY MAMA. She had short gray hair and one of the sweetest smiles Lewis had ever known. She was Audra Fallon, the assistant director of the VIP Center.

Today she was not smiling, however. She barely glanced at Lewis and Tommy as she thundered past them. Behind her trooped a pair of middle-aged men in crisply laundered army field jackets and expensive haircuts. Neither of them was smiling, either. As Lewis and Tommy moved aside to get out of their way, Lewis noticed that each man wore a pin that said VETERANS FOR BUSH/QUAYLE '92.

"One thing we don't need around here is politics," said Audra as she moved past Lewis. "We're here to help veterans, not to campaign for George Bush or anyone else." She halted, pulled open the door to the reception area, and held it wide. "At the risk of being rude, I'm afraid I'll have to ask you gentlemen to leave. We've all got a lot of work to do."

The lead Bush man, the taller of the two, said, "Miss Fallon, I'm afraid I haven't done a very good job of communicating with you. We're not trying to politicize your organization. Far from it. All we want to do is talk with some of your clients and enlist three or four of them to participate in a public-relations project on behalf of the president. Naturally we wouldn't think of doing it without your blessing.''

"It'd really help us out, Miss Fallon," added the shorter one. "This is going to be a close race, as you're well aware. We're putting together some brochures and newspaper ads targeted at veterans—Vietnam veterans in particular—stressing the president's war record and the fact that his opponent doesn't even have one. We need some bona fide vets in the photos—guys who're clearly disabled.''

"Guys in wheelchairs, on crutches, that sort of thing.''

"Right. They'd lend authenticity and generate sympathy among other vets.''

Audra scowled ferociously. "This isn't an advertising agency. This is a charitable institution. Most of our clients are desperate by the time they get here. Many are homeless, jobless, and addicted. They need help, not—''

"*Not* Bill Clinton," interrupted the taller of the Bush men. "They don't need a lying, womanizing draft dodger as their president, Miss Fallon.''

"It's *Missus* Fallon," Audra corrected him. "I'd appreciate it if you'd get it right.''

"I'm sorry—*Missus* Fallon. I'm just making the point that it would be an affront to the men you serve if Bill Clinton got elected president. Here's a guy who maneuvered, schemed, and—''

A man's voice rolled like thunder from the rear of the room, a dark voice that could have belonged to a poet or a drill sergeant or a steel-yard foreman. *"The lady asked you gentlemen to leave, and I think it would be wise of you to do just that."*

He was a burly man with silvering eyebrows and a round face that was black as dreamless sleep. His huge hands looked well accustomed to gripping the wheels of his unmotorized wheelchair. His legs dangled at troubling angles. A monstrous yellow cat curled in his lap, its eyes slitted. *"I trust I don't need to say it again. I'm sure you gentlemen have the decency not to stay where you're not wanted."*

The taller of the Bush men took a step toward the man in the wheelchair. "Excuse me—are you talking to us?"

The eyes beneath the silver eyebrows hardened, and the leathered hands coiled into fists. "You *know* who I'm talking to. Do yourself a favor and get your sorry asses out of here while you still can."

The taller of the Bush men blanched through his store-bought tan. He turned back to Audra. "Is this guy supposed to be your bouncer, or what?"

"He's a man who served his country. He suffered a bullet in the spine and total paralysis of his legs. He has no job, no home, and no health insurance."

"And I drink a fifth of bourbon every day, mixed with milk to keep my stomach from corroding," added the man in the wheelchair. "It helps the pain." By now the room was silent. Lewis could plainly hear the purring of the giant yellow cat in the black man's lap.

The shorter of the Bush men sidled past his partner and made for the front door, muttering something about wanting no trouble. The taller man stuck his nose into Audra's face and glared at her. "If I were you, *Missus* Fallon, I'd hit the fund-raising circuit, and I'd hit it hard. Federal help might be hard for you to come by, from now on." Then he, too, pushed through the door.

Suddenly the black man in the wheelchair laughed uproariously, and everyone in the room laughed along with him, including Audra Fallon. She planted a kiss on his forehead. "Dewey, you're a treasure! I thought I was going to have to wrestle that guy to get rid of him."

"Hey, woman, I've still got what it takes! Once a drill sergeant, always a drill sergeant. It's all in the voice, hear what I'm sayin'? You've got to put *authority* into it!"

Lewis maneuvered his wheelchair next to Dewey's, caught his hand, and shook it. "You made us proud, brother!"

"Want to know somethin'?" asked Dewey. "I was actually hopin' that son-of-a-bitch would try to muscle me, 'cause if he did, I was planning to let him have some of this." He pulled an eighteen-inch-long length of pipe from inside his verminous army-surplus trench coat. "And if that didn't work, I was planning to feed him to Big Sister here." At the mention of her name, the yellow cat opened her eyes, but quickly closed them again.

"Those guys were professional vets," said Tommy Iadanza, drawing a cup of a coffee from the urn. "They're the type who join organizations and march in parades. They tell a lot of war stories and generally act superior to anyone who had the good sense to avoid going to Vietnam."

"And most of their war stories are bullshit," said Dewey. "I'll bet that those two were REMFs, if they were even in Vietnam at all." This brought a smile to Audra's face, for she'd spent enough time with Vietnam veterans to understand about Rear Echelon MotherFuckers.

"Folks, I hate to put an end to this happy scene," said Audra, "but we all have jobs to do. Let's get this train back on the tracks, okay?" She lowered her voice. "Lewis and Tommy, thanks for showing up. I've got three guys for each of you to talk to, all homeless, all detoxed. One of them is missing a leg, so I thought it would be best to steer him your way, Lewis."

She led them back to her office, where she presented three manila file folders to each. The folders contained the Center's files on the men to be counseled this morning. "Do what you can to motivate these guys, okay? I think they're all good prospects."

iii

No one at the VIP Center knew Dewey's full name. No one knew whether he was really a veteran. He was "undocumented," in the parlance of the relief-and-welfare community, and therefore "unvettable." He could produce no military discharge papers, birth certificate, passport, Social Security number, or any other document to prove who he was.

Consequently, nobody could establish whether he was eligible for any public or private assistance programs.

He lived by foraging in Dumpsters and washing windows for restaurants and neighborhood grocery stores. He refused to panhandle, because he didn't believe in begging, though he wasn't averse to accepting the daily charity of the Salvation Army, the Rescue Mission, and other relief agencies. He slept in alleys and doorways, or wherever his wheelchair would fit, meaning that he sometimes slept in the open. On winter nights he slipped Big Sister into his shirt, where she slept next to his skin.

On every Wednesday for the past decade, Lewis had taken Dewey to lunch, usually to one of the take-out places in the outdoor arcade of the New Market Theater. Indoor restaurants had rules about cats and Dewey wouldn't go anywhere without Big Sister. The arcade was partially enclosed in glass like a greenhouse, so they could eat without getting wet on rainy days.

Today they bought lunch at Mai Ly's Oriental Kitchen, then parked their wheelchairs next to an ancient bench made of wrought iron. Dewey shared his chicken and pea pods with Big Sister, who ate greedily, while Lewis picked at an order of Szechuan shrimp.

Dewey noticed the tenseness in Lewis's face and asked what was wrong. Rather than burden him with his real problems, Lewis talked of a man he'd counseled this morning. The guy had lost a leg to a booby trap in the Mekong Delta.

"He'd have a lot going for him if he could only get his head on straight," said Lewis. "He's smart. He's got a couple years of college under his belt. There's no reason he can't make a good living for himself if he stays clean and sober."

"So, what's his problem?"

"First, he's minus a leg. Second, he's a Vietnam vet. He thinks Vietnam vets are an underclass, a pack of losers."

"I hope you told him that's a load of bullshit."

"I told him. And I told him about my old bud in the 'Nam, Jesse Burton, who wrestled with booze and won. Went on to school and got himself a doctorate in education. Now he's holding down a big job with the National Education Association.''

"I remember you talking about him before. Black man, right?''

"Right. I told this guy that the vast majority of Vietnam vets didn't end up on the streets, that they came back to the world and put together respectable lives. Many went to school and became first-class scholars, or doctors, or lawyers—''

"Or bureaucrats. Don't forget that some of them became fuckin' bureaucrats.'' In Dewey's view, bureaucrats merited special places in hell.

Lewis laughed. "Like I was saying, I tried to make him understand that being a Vietnam vet isn't a blot on your life. Only a small percentage of us suffered any severe post-traumatic stress, other than some recurring nightmares.''

"Hey, some of those nightmares can get pretty deadly, brother.''

Lewis nodded, and his laughter faded.

"What time is it?'' asked Dewey, stroking Big Sister's fur.

"Quarter to one.''

"Time for confession. Want to come along?''

They set out across the square, their wheelchairs jouncing over the paving stones. They crossed SW Second and went half a block up Ankeny Avenue, which was more an alley than a street, until they reached the "24-Hour Church of El-vis,'' a narrow storefront with a musty display window. The "church'' was a sidewalk console with a coin slot and push buttons, not unlike an automated teller machine, except it didn't dispense money. Rather, it dispensed a funky religion that glorified shabby plastic images. Not so different, really, from most other religions, in Lewis's view. Behind the glass lay the "altar,'' a dizzying array of photos, figurines, costume jewelry, clippings from newspapers and magazines, mass-produced souvenirs and doodads, most of which concerned Elvis Presley or some aspect of his life and career. A video screen mounted inside the window urged the worshiper to deposit twenty-five cents into the coin slot, then press a button to specify a wedding, a confession, or a sermon.

Yes, people could actually have a "church wedding" right here on the sidewalk, providing someone in the wedding party could come up with a quarter. It had happened more than once.

"Hit me with a quarter," said Dewey, and Lewis did so. Dewey pushed the coin into the slot, selected CONFESSION, leaned close to the microphone, and muttered something that Lewis couldn't hear. A few moments later the computer screen flashed a message of absolution. Dewey backed away from the window, looking cleansed of his sins.

"I feel like a new man," he said. "Nothin' like a little forgiveness to brighten up your day. Now, if I could just talk this thing into giving me a new pair of legs . . . !"

Lewis laughed. "Get a pair for me while you're at it!"

"Well, I guess it's time to go our separate ways, brother," said Dewey, pain glittering in his eyes. "I need to buy a quart of milk." This meant it was time to hit the bottle in earnest, for the pain had flared, and it would grow until he doused it with bourbon.

"I'll walk you to the store," Lewis said.

"That's not necessary. You've got troubles of your own— anybody can see that. Go back to the Center, Lewis. Tommy will be waiting to take you home."

"I don't want to go home just yet. I need some company, and—" Before he could finish, a shadow fell across his face. Standing over him was a balding man in his midtwenties, with massive shoulders and a surprisingly small head. He had tiny, washed-out eyes. A draft animal, thought Lewis, feeling a jolt of fear.

Suddenly the world went topsy-turvy as someone tilted Lewis's wheelchair backward, forcing him to look straight into the blinding sun. He heard Dewey scream his name. Someone caught a fistful of his hair, igniting a rash of pain across his scalp. The draft animal grinned wildly. "How's it goin', Stumpy?"

Lewis caught sight of another man off to his left, a slick-looking man in an expensive anorak and tailored slacks. He was as black and clean as the draft animal was white and slovenly, though not as massive. His smooth face could have belonged to a choirboy.

"Let's not be disrespectful, Spit," said Mason Benoit, moving toward Lewis with something in his hand. "This gentleman is a Vietnam veteran, after all, and the second-best poker player in Portland." He flicked a switch on the thing in his hand, and it started to buzz. It was a battery-powered hair clipper. "He's a man of dignity, can't you see that?"

"How come he's got so fuckin' much hair, and I don't?" asked the balding man, and Lewis knew immediately who had sent them and what they meant to do.

"Luck of the draw," answered Benoit. "How about we take some of his hair and give it to you? Would that make you happy, Spit?"

"It sure would."

Lewis's mind raced as the clipper drew near. The thought of getting his head shaved didn't gall him as much as playing the victim to Rex Caswell's maniacs. Caswell had sent them to deliver a "reminder" about the poker debt he owed, as if he needed one.

Acting on impulse, Lewis jerked back the joystick of his wheelchair, throwing it into reverse and catching Spit by surprise. The chair twisted from Spit's grip and abruptly righted itself. Lewis shoved the joystick forward again and plowed hard into the black man, the motor whining. Benoit lurched against the glass of the 24-Hour Church of Elvis and landed on his ass, dropping the battery-powered clipper.

Suddenly Dewey joined the fray, wheeling into the path of Spit, who'd lunged forward to grab at Lewis. Spit tumbled over Dewey and sprawled onto the sidewalk, bruising his elbows. Big Sister squealed and leaped out of Dewey's lap, but Spit caught her by the scruff of her neck as he scrambled to his feet. The cat bit and scratched, leaving a bleeding wound on Spit's hand. "Son-of-a-bitch!" Spit screamed.

A knot of yuppie types strolled down the opposite side of the street, shirtsleeves rolled up and ties loosened. They'd heard the commotion, but they merely stood and watched, incredibly.

"Forget the fuckin' cat!" shouted Benoit, having scrambled to his feet. He retrieved the clipper from the sidewalk and moved toward Lewis again. "Let's do our fuckin' job and get out of here."

Spit grabbed Big Sister's tail with his free hand and swung the screeching animal against the display window of the 24-Hour Church of Elvis—twice, three times. Smears of blood appeared on the glass. He tossed the twitching corpse into the gutter and rounded on Lewis again.

Dewey had a length of pipe in his hand and fury in his eyes. He jammed the pipe hard between Spit's legs, causing him to howl and double up on the sidewalk. Dewey whipped the pipe hard against the bridge of Spit's nose, and his nostrils spewed blood.

Benoit groped inside his anorak for a gun, but Lewis drove his wheelchair into him at full throttle. Benoit fell across the armrests, arms and legs flailing. Lewis caught Benoit's wrist in his good hand and twisted, causing the black man to shriek and drop the gun. As Benoit flailed to regain his feet, Lewis snatched up the gun from the sidewalk and thrust its muzzle hard against his cheek.

"Make one more move, fuck-stick, and you're dead," he said through clenched teeth. Benoit slid slowly to his knees and knelt on the sidewalk.

By this time Dewey had rained at least a dozen blows with the pipe on Spit's head and shoulders, and the draft animal had collapsed in a bloody mess on the dirty cement. Lewis screamed at him to stop, but he wouldn't have stopped if two mounted policemen hadn't galloped to the curb and grabbed the length of pipe away. Dewey would have beaten the draft animal to death, Lewis was certain.

iv

Later, they sat together in shade of the Neoclassical colonnades in the Market Block, neither doing much talking. Having given statements to the cops, they'd gone to the neighborhood grocery on the corner of Burnside and Third, where Lewis had bought a fresh quart of milk for Dewey.

For the first time ever, Lewis was able to detect signs of inebriation in his friend, who had methodically polished off a third of a fifth of bourbon within an hour, sipping first from the bottle in the brown paper sack and then from the milk carton. Occasionally he paused to stare at the bundle wrapped in plastic beside his wheelchair, the remains of his longtime companion, Big Sister. Lewis saw no tears in his eyes, heard no quiver in his voice. Decades of suffering had drained him of tears, Lewis figured.

"Dewey, I want you to come home with me tonight. The living-room sofa folds out into a bed. I'll make chili and we can listen to some good music, maybe watch a little tube."

"Forget it. I appreciate the offer, but I don't need any sofa that folds out into a bed, and I don't need any chili. I only need to be alone, okay?" His speech was slurred, his eyelids heavy. Lewis worried that he might fall out of his wheelchair.

"Dewey, we're both hurting. Neither of us should be alone tonight."

"Not true. *I* should be alone." He stole another look at the bundle on the ground. "What'll happen to those motherfuckers, Lewis? Will they get what they deserve?"

"I hope so." Lewis didn't believe that this would happen, of course. He'd heard the story that the one named Benoit told the cops after the ambulance had sped away with his pal, the draft animal. They'd been walking quietly along the street, minding their own business, when the crazy old black man in the wheelchair suddenly attacked with a length of pipe for no reason. Benoit had drawn his gun only to break up the ruckus. But the white cripple had slammed his wheelchair into him and taken his gun away, threatened to kill him. Benoit was glad the cops had arrived when they had.

"Know what I think, Lewis? I think they'll both be out on the street before it gets dark. The cops won't believe their story, but you and I aren't hurt, so the only real charge is carrying a gun, which I'm sure that dude didn't have a permit for. Unless one of them is on probation or has a warrant out for him, they'll both be free and walking around before sundown."

"You may be right," Lewis conceded. "On the other hand, you might've hit the big one hard enough with that damned pipe to keep him in the hospital for a while."

Dewey shook his head and said he hadn't managed to crack the bastard's skull, though he'd tried. God knows he'd tried. He looked at Lewis with hopeless eyes. "What am I gonna do without Big Sister, man?"

"I don't know. I wish I could . . ." He saw Tommy Iadanza jaywalking across Second Avenue from the VIP Center, coming to fetch Lewis and drive him home. "Please come home with me. You're in no shape to take care of yourself tonight."

"I've survived out here this long. Nothing's gonna happen to me. If you want to help, lay ten bucks on me so I can get a bottle of decent whiskey."

"I'll give you twenty if you promise to get a roof over your head. I mean it, brother—buy yourself another bottle, but get inside somewhere."

"Whatever you say, man."

Lewis dug out his wallet and gave him the last twenty-dollar bill he had.

Thirteen

i

WHEN HE ARRIVED home from school on Wednesday afternoon, Josh found Nicole Tran in the gazebo behind Sloan House, eating an apple, her nose buried in Camus' *The Plague*. He parked his Escort in one of the two slots allotted to the Nickersons, ambled across the lawn, and eased himself into the vacant side of the wicker love seat in which she sat.

Without looking up from the book, Nicole said, "So, you're alive. Some of us were beginning to wonder."

"It's been what?—two days since we talked?"

"I haven't been counting, actually."

"Lose the attitude, okay? You're starting to sound like Laurel."

She wrinkled her nose and crossed her eyes in a way that had always made him laugh. "God help me if I'm anything like *her*! Check me into the nearest personality-transplant center."

"Hey, it's all right for me to insult my girlfriend, but not for *you*," Josh retorted. "She's not so bad when you get to know her. You're the only one I know who doesn't like her."

"I don't know what you see in her, that's all."

"Aside from the fact that she looks like she just stepped out of a beer commercial, you mean?"

"Aside from that, yes. Not to mention the fact that she lets you do anything you want to her."

Josh gave her a playful punch on the shoulder. "Hey, it doesn't get any better than this."

Nicole rose from the wicker love seat and leaned against the railing that ran around the edge of the gazebo. The sun had begun to slip behind the rim of Gander Ridge, and afternoon shadows stretched across the lawn. Crows and jays cackled in the old cedars that guarded the corners of the property. The air smelled cleanly of the rain showers that had come and gone throughout the day.

"Can I assume that you've forgiven me for the way I acted on the bridge Monday night?" Josh asked.

"There's nothing to forgive."

"You seemed pretty mad when I told you about Millie Carter coming into my room and what she—"

"Let's not dredge that up again, okay? When it comes down to it, I'm the one who should apologize."

"Why is that?"

"Because I don't have any reason to be mad at you for telling me"—she paused, seeking precisely the right words—"for *divulging* certain intimate details of your sex life. You and I certainly aren't romantically involved with each other. Never have been and never will be. In other words, I don't have any basis for being offended. Let's drop it, okay? You forgive me, I forgive you."

"Consider it dropped."

She turned toward him again, her delicate Asian face dark with worry. "There's still the matter of the orb, though. Did you get rid of it?"

Josh felt a pit in his stomach. He'd carried the orb with him today in his rucksack along with his books and notebooks, having promised himself that he would get rid of it as soon as possible, as Nicole and Lewis had both begged him to do. But he knew that he couldn't throw it away yet, because it represented *hope*. It was Lewis Kindred's only means of disposing of his debt to Rex Caswell.

"You didn't do it, did you?" said Nicole, reading his face. "You still have it."

"Nicki, something has happened, something bad. Lewis was playing cards at the Fanshawe, like he does every Monday night, and there was this guy named Rex Caswell, a real slug. . . ."

He blurted the story about Lewis's loss of $210,000 to Rex Caswell. He told about Millie's second visit to the Nickersons' apartment yesterday. And he revealed his belief that Millie was behind Lewis's blast of bad luck at the poker table. Not once did Nicole interrupt him.

"I'm hoping Lewis will come to his senses and use the orb to get out of this mess," he concluded. "I've tried to convince him he should challenge Rex Caswell to a rematch, then use the orb to win back the money."

"What did he say to that?"

"He threw a fit, told me he would never touch the damn thing again. Said that he'd once used it to win at poker, and afterward he felt dirty. He thinks that using it against Caswell would be the same as cheating."

Nicole said nothing for a long time, but only gazed across the lawn of Sloan House. When she spoke again, it was hardly above a whisper. "Nickster, this is scary stuff, and I don't like it. I've never believed in the supernatural before—"

"Neither have I. But you've seen the orb and touched it. You don't have to be a rocket scientist to figure out that it has some kind of power."

"It scares the bejabbers out of me. I wish I could close my eyes, then open them and find out this has all been a nasty dream."

Just then Josh felt something move inside the rucksack, but he told himself that it had only been his books shifting. "It scares me, too," he said, watching a crow wheel across the sky.

ii

He walked with Nicole as far as the front drive of Sloan House. "Nicki, I'm sorry about the grief I've caused you during the last few days. And I'm sorry I didn't get rid of the orb when you wanted me to. I have this sinking feeling that if I'd listened to you, I could've prevented all this."

"I'm not so sure that getting rid of it would've solved anything. You still would've had Millie to deal with. I wonder who she is and what she wants."

"I worry more about *what* she is. She can do stuff that mere humans shouldn't be able to do." He shuddered, remembering

Millie's shadow on the carpet of the dining room. "Hey, why don't you come and split a pizza with me? We can study together later. Kendra's at Spanish club and Mom won't be home until after eight—some meeting or other. I'm not wild about the idea of being alone right now."

"Nickster, I'd like to, but I shouldn't. Things aren't so good at home." Her eyes filled with worry. "It's my dad. He's been acting kind of strange again, and I can tell that my mom is worried. I really should get home."

"Has he started going out at night again?"

Nicole nodded. Over the years her family had suffered stints when Mr. Tran came and went at all hours, missed meals, broke appointments, and generally lived a secret life apart from his wife and daughter. Mrs. Tran naturally had assumed that he was seeing another woman, but Nicole had never believed this. She'd seen torment in her father's face that didn't fit a man who was cheating on his wife. More than once she'd expressed to Josh the fear that her father was mentally ill, that he may even have suffered hallucinations.

"I'm sorry," said Josh. "Go be with your mom. I'll call you later."

"Thanks for understanding."

She headed down the hill toward the Tran family's house. Josh watched her for a moment, and a new worry seized him. He and Nicole were seniors in high school, and next year they would each head to college in different directions. If things went as hoped, Josh would study journalism at Northwestern in Chicago. Nicole would attend Stanford near San Francisco, seeking a degree in literature. If they were lucky, they would get together on holidays for a few hours at a shot.

Would they drift apart, he wondered, as he'd been told that most childhood friends do?

Josh slung his rucksack over his shoulder and let himself in through the etched-glass doors of Sloan House. The elevator in the foyer stood open, and though he usually bounded up the stairs four at a time, he felt bone-tired today. He'd taken three steps toward the elevator when Lewis Kindred's voice stopped him.

iii

"It's about time you got home." Lewis sat in the deep shadow of the corridor, clutching a bottle of Full Sail Golden in his fist. "Got a minute?"

"I do if you've got a Diet-Rite in your fridge."

Lewis motioned him inside his apartment.

They traded small talk for a time, during which Lewis asked how school was going, how he was getting along with his girlfriend, how things were with his mother and sister. Josh answered each question thoroughly and tried not to show his worry over how Lewis looked—wrung out, bleary-eyed, and half-drunk. The wastebasket next to the computer desk held at least six empty beer bottles.

"Enough of the happy horseshit," said Lewis. "You're probably wondering why I'm drunk at four in the afternoon, right?"

"Yeah, I am."

"You'll know soon enough. Did you get rid of the orb?"

Josh took a deep breath. "Lewis, I couldn't do it. I wanted to, believe me, but I kept it because I thought you might change your—"

"Good. I need it."

"You what?"

"I've thought about your suggestion that I use it to win back my money from Caswell. I've decided you were right."

"You have? Lew, that's great! I've got it right here." He hoisted his rucksack onto his lap and pawed through it until his fingers found the orb, smooth and warm. He pulled the thing out. Lewis wedged his beer bottle between the stumps of his legs and reached for it unsteadily, his hand trembling.

The instant his fingers made contact with the orb, his face paled.

"I want you to know something, Joshua. Today, something ugly happened to someone I care about—a man who lives in a wheelchair like I do. Rex Caswell sent two of his no-necks to *remind* me of the money I owe him, and while they were doing it, they killed an old flea-bitten cat. That cat was the only real family my friend had left. He lost her because of me. After it happened, I suddenly understood that I had to do something."

He coughed and went on, his eyes moist. "Let's face it—I don't have a prayer of raising all the money I owe Caswell. I can raise two thirds or maybe even three fourths of it, but no matter what I do, I'm going to be at least fifty thousand short. He'll keep on leaning me, threatening me, hurting me any way he can in order to force me to come up with the rest. It'll occur to him that the best way to do this would be to hurt the people I love, so that's what he'll do. And do you know what *that* would mean?"

Josh swallowed. "What?"

"I'd have to kill him."

Josh's neck went prickly. "You don't mean that, man."

"I *do* mean it. If Caswell hurt you or one of your family, or Tommy Iadanza or Carlotta or one of their kids, I'd load up my old Colt forty-five and I'd find the son-of-a-bitch, and I'd pump a full clip into him."

Josh wanted to be sick. "You can't do that, Lewis. You can't even think it."

"You're right," said Lewis, holding the orb next to his cheek. He stared blindly as he talked. "That's why I've decided to take your advice. I need to challenge him to a rematch. We'll play five-card draw, one-on-one, and if I have this thing with me, I won't lose. I'll get my life back, and I'll be able to face the future without the prospect of living under a bridge. But I'm not doing it just for me. I'm doing it for everyone I care about. Understand?"

"I understand."

Fourteen

i

Twenty-four hours after Josh Nickerson handed the orb to Lewis Kindred, a stiletto-shaped powerboat eased into a slip outside a posh floating house at the Sellwood Bay Club, her big engine burbling. Mason Benoit hopped from the deck onto the dock and tied her next to the monstrous cigarette boat already in residence. Benoit's partner, Spit Pittman, clambered after him, his head a mass of bandages, his face a hodgepodge of purple-and-green bruises. He had two huge black eyes.

They made their way to the lower deck of the house. Inside they found Rex Caswell nervously pacing the living room. He wore an expensive-looking silk shirt and well-tailored slacks, which was normal attire for him on a weekday afternoon. But he also wore a shoulder holster with a Glock 9mm pistol in it.

"Sit down," he ordered, and Benoit and Pittman did so. He stared at each of them, Spit with his masses of bandages and bruises, then Benoit with his wrist brace. "Look at you guys—supposedly the best muscle available on the West Coast. Steel men, I was told, pumpers of iron. Reliable. I believed every word of it, and I put out major bucks to get you and keep you in the manner to which you've become accustomed. But what happens when I send you to do a simple little job like laying some tough talk on a guy with no legs? One of you fucking near gets his head pounded in and ends up being hauled off in an ambulance! The other gets his *wrist* sprained."

"Kindred has a strong right hand, Rex," protested Benoit.

"Shut up! I'm the guy who pays the bills, so I'll do the talking, okay?" The muscle in Rex's neck bulged like towing cables. "Right now I'm trying to figure out what the future holds for two dipshits who attack a pair of disabled veterans in wheelchairs, in downtown Portland over the fucking noon hour, yet. Not only do they get themselves beaten up, but they get arrested! What am I supposed to think of guys like that?"

"Rex, what happened yesterday was a fluke," pleaded Benoit. "We're not even going to be prosecuted, wait and see. They confiscated my gun—so what? Nobody got hurt except Spit, and the DA doesn't have the time or resources to—"

"I said shut up!" Rex's right hand darted to the shoulder holster, and his fingers played over the handle of the Glock, but he didn't pull it out. "Neither of you should've been carrying a piece in the first place, because the job didn't call for it. Even Spit knew that much, for Christ's sake. I would've expected a little more from you, Mase. Don't I pay you enough? How in the hell do you afford that boat tied up out there, huh? Or that town house of yours in Northwest? Or that BMW you drive? Where does the money come from, Mase— from your nine-to-five job designing computers in Beaverton? Or from your brain-surgery practice? I'll tell you where it comes from . . . !"

"It comes from you and your dirty pictures of kids, Rex. I know that, and I appreciate it."

"You're damn right it comes from me! And don't I pay you enough to—"

The telephone bleeped. Rex shouted for Silhouette to pick it up, but it continued to bleep. He swore when he caught sight of her through the glass doors beyond the kitchen, contentedly smoking and drinking on the sunlit deck, oblivious to the phone. "Fucking airhead," he muttered, and he went to answer it himself.

ii

Lewis clutched the phone in his sweaty fist and listened to the buzzes on the other end. All day he'd rehearsed for this moment, having actually written out his lines and read them aloud over and over again. He'd even tested various inflections in order to get his delivery perfect.

"Hello!"

He sounds mad, Lewis thought. "Rex, this is Lewis Kindred. Remember me?"

Dumbfounded silence. Then: "Uh, yeah. Lewis. Of course I remember you. Think I'd forget an old frat brother, especially when he owes me a couple hundred large? How'd you get this number, anyway?"

"Tommy Iadanza at the Fanshawe. He's got all the telephone numbers of the Monday-night crowd. I talked him into giving me yours."

"I see. Well, to what do I owe the pleasure of a call from the Stumpmeister himself?"

"Just thought I'd call to tell you that I've raised the money I owe you."

Another silence. "You *have*?" Lewis smiled, because Rex sounded terribly deflated. "You raised two hundred and ten K in three days? No way."

"Yes way. I'm sitting here looking at it, actually." In truth, he was staring at the orb, telling himself that he'd not seen it move.

"I gotta say it, Lewis—I didn't expect you to pull it off. What did you do—blackmail somebody or grease a rich uncle?"

"None of your business, Rex. You should take the money and thank the gods of poker that they gave you one night of pure, unmitigated luck."

Rex laughed loudly. "Is that what you're telling people, big guy? That I had a lucky streak?"

"I don't have to tell anybody anything. People were there. They saw what happened, and they talk."

"Are you saying that people think I just had a wild spin of luck?"

"Well, what do you expect? We've been playing poker together for something like twenty years, and every night until last Monday you've left money on the table, *big* money often as not. Then suddenly you're unstoppable—not to mention that I get an attack of the stupids and play the worst cards I've played since I was thirteen. So what? Every hack gets at least one lucky streak in his life, and you've had yours. Nice for you, too bad for me. But hey, it's not the end of the world.''

Lewis listened to heavy breathing over the line, Rex laboring to keep his temper. "You're really something, Lewis. For a guy who's lost more than two hundred thousand dollars, you talk awfully big.''

"Oh, but I do more than talk, Rex.''

"Yeah? Meaning what?''

"I'll give you a chance to show what you're made of, my friend. I'll take a rematch, if you're up for it. We'll play draw poker, just you and I, with an ante of, say, fifty thousand dollars. We'll each put up another hundred large as a side bet. The game will stop when one of us gets scared or tired. What do you say?''

"You've got to be out of your goddamn mind. Why would I do that when I'm more than two hundred thousand up? Sounds to me like you're chasing bad money, Lewis.''

What the hell is this? Lewis worried. *Is Rex Caswell getting smart?* "You would do it, Rex, because you need to prove that you're good. I say you were lucky Monday night. I say you couldn't do it again in a million years.''

"Why should I give a fuck what you say? Who listens to you anymore? You've been beaten, remember?''

"You're right, nobody listens to me. Forget I mentioned it. Give me your address, and I'll bring the money to you tomorrow. Or if it's more convenient, I can meet you at a bank or something.''

Silence, long and deathly. *His wheels are going around,* thought Lewis. *What he decides will determine whether I have a life left.*

"Wait a minute," said Rex. "I'm not afraid to go another round with you, not even for high stakes. If that's what you want, Lewis, I'm game. Bring enough money to play poker this time, you son-of-a-bitch, because I'm not taking any more IOUs.''

"How about next Monday night at the usual time and place? But don't drag along those no-necks who jumped my friend and me yesterday in Old Town. If I see one of them, I'll rip his leg off and beat him to death with it.''

"I'll be there, and I'll be alone. Remember what I said, though. Bring the money. I'll want to see it before we start.''

"Don't worry," Lewis assured him, "I'll bring plenty of money." His stare wandered to the orb, which sat in its place, its innards swirling. *And I'll bring something else, too.*

iii

Shortly after midnight Nicole Tran laid a blanket over her mother, who'd finally fallen asleep on the living-room sofa, exhausted after three consecutive sleepless nights. Nicole had kept the vigil with her, sitting in an Ethan Allen swivel chair for hours on end, listening to classical music and reading her school assignments. Again her father hadn't come home, but had left his downtown office promptly at five and gone out without leaving a message for his wife or daughter.

During past periods of such strange behavior, he'd sometimes returned in the small hours of the morning, slipping in through the rear door, climbing the back stairs to his den and locking himself in. Nicole had learned the uselessness of knocking on his door.

Only recently had her mother confided in Nicole, disclosing her suspicions about the possibility of another woman. In many ways Nicole's mother was the traditional Vietnamese *ba*, the dutiful and long-suffering wife who never questioned anything her husband did, but she'd lived in America long to acquire some Western feelings about a wife's rights and entitlements. Her Vietnamese nature tugged her in the direction of quiet forbearance, while her American side insisted on confrontation and resolution. Nicole hated seeing her mother torn like this, but she couldn't hate her father for causing the pain. She simply couldn't believe that his behavior had anything to do with another woman. It had to be something *else*.

Nicole stood over her mother a long moment, listening to

her regular breathing, glad that she'd finally fallen asleep. As the final strains of Mozart's Symphony No. 26 came over the stereo, Nicole heard the closing of a door at the rear of the house, and knew that her father had come home.

She climbed the front staircase to her room, which was on the second floor at the front of the house. She collapsed onto her four-poster bed and lay silent a moment, eager for sleep but afraid that it would not come. The *sound* came again, a rapid-fire thumping—almost like the drumming of human fingers on a wooden surface, except it couldn't have a human source, because the rhythm was too machinelike. She'd often heard this sound in the night, and several times she'd followed it to the locked door of her father's den. Pressing her ear against the door, she'd heard something else beneath the beating: her father's voice, moaning in Vietnamese. He sounded fearful, almost panicky, as though he was suffering some horrible dream or hallucination.

As she'd done before, she left her room and entered the dark hallway that led to the rear of their beautiful old Queen Anne house. She came to the door of his den, tested the handle, and found it locked. Once again she heard the soft sounds of a man sobbing and moaning from within. Nicole longed to go to him and offer a daughter's comfort, to assure him that she would be here for him whenever he needed her. But the locked door kept her out as it always had before.

iv

Despite the fact that Lewis Kindred had the orb in his possession, the earth continued to revolve on its axis. Birds sang and human beings went about their daily business, all of which reassured him. He convinced himself that he hadn't entered into any kind of Faustian bargain, that using the orb would not damn him to eternal torment or cause the downfall of Western civilization. He would do with it what needed to be done, then dispose of it forever. Life would be good again.

On Friday morning he motored into his studio, where a desk calendar told him that it was September 18, 1992. Only three more days until the rematch with Rex Caswell.

Three days to-day, between Hell and Heaven . . . !

He smiled. The line was from Dante Gabriel Rossetti's dark and unnerving poem "Sister Helen," an artifact of his courtship of Twyla Boley, way back in ancient times. Twyla been an ardent worshiper of the Pre-Raphaelite poets of the mid-nineteenth century. Lewis had spent hours pretending to listen raptly to her reading of George Meredith, Algernon Charles Swinburne, and the Rossettis.

Throughout the weekend he tackled his contract work, managing to finish several projects and start another. On TV, newscasts came and went, as well football games, sitcoms, movies, and ads. The world spun on. In Portland, preparations were under way for Oktoberfest in countless pubs and restaurants. Local churches buzzed about next week's Billy Graham Crusade in Civic Stadium, mere blocks from Sloan House. In France, voters were deciding whether they liked the Maastricht Treaty. George Bush and Bill Clinton went at each other tooth and nail.

While waiting for Monday night and the Big Event, Lewis kept to himself. Several poker associates called with invitations to games, one of which would likely have proved lucrative, but Lewis declined. He wanted no poker until he next cut the cards with Rex Caswell.

Josh knocked on his door late Sunday night, shortly after Lewis had stuck an Eric Clapton CD into the CD player. "What's with the locked door?" Josh wanted to know as Lewis let him in.

"I've been a little jumpy after what happened in Old Town. I'll give you my spare key." Lewis locked the door again and led the way into the studio, where Josh plunked his lanky frame into his usual spot, the cushy armchair next to the computer table. Lewis opened a drawer, took out his spare key, and handed it to him.

"All set for the big showdown tomorrow night?" the kid asked.

"I'm not looking forward to it, but I'm ready." Several days earlier Lewis had related in great detail how he'd issued the challenge to Caswell, how Caswell had snapped it up like a hungry dog after a T-bone.

"I need to ask you something, Lewis, and please don't say no. Can I come along with you tomorrow night?"

"No way."

"Lewis, I want to come along."

"I've just told you, Joshua, you can't."

"Why?"

"Because it won't be clean, wholesome fun, that's why."

"I'm not into clean, wholesome fun. I need to be there."

"Forget it."

"But you'll want some moral support, Lewis. You'll need a friend, right?"

"Wrong. Tommy will be there, and most of the others, too, I think. My cheering section will be more than adequate."

"Lewis, I *need* to come along," pleaded Josh, suddenly straightening up in the chair. "I'm going to write about all this someday. I've got to see it happen with my own eyes. It's not good enough to get it secondhand."

"You're only seventeen. This is going to be an adults-only affair." Lewis avoided looking at him and studied the joystick on his wheelchair. "It won't be suitable for kids."

"Why? Because there'll be strong language? Because there'll be adult themes? I was old enough to save the orb for you, wasn't I—old enough not to throw it away, like you kept telling me I should?"

Lewis stared into Josh's clear, green eyes. *He's no little kid anymore*, said a voice deep inside him. He asked himself what could happen in the card room of the Fanshawe that would be too lurid for the tender eyes of a seventeen-year-old, especially if that seventeen-year-old was Josh Nickerson. He could think of nothing.

"Okay, damn it, you can come along. But don't tell your mother about this, okay?"

"Mom wouldn't be a problem if she knew about it. But if you don't want me to tell her, I won't." He got up from the chair and stuck out his hand. "Thanks, Lewis. You won't be sorry."

Lewis shook his hand and thought that Josh's grip was noticeably firmer than he remembered it.

V

Rex Caswell conscripted Mason Benoit to chauffeur him downtown to the Fanshawe, telling him to pack a piece, inasmuch as Rex would be carrying three hundred thousand in cash. "No need for you to come inside," he said, stepping out of the Mercedes in front of the old hotel. "Park somewhere close and stay with the car. I'll call you when I'm ready."

"No problem, Rex."

Rex strode into the lobby of the Fanshawe, his custom-made eel-skin attaché case thumping his thigh with every stride. He patted the breast pocket of his Armani blazer to certify that he'd brought his cellular phone. His own pistol bulged comfortably in his armpit. He was ready for anything, and he felt good. He felt *integrated*.

When he saw Millie Carter rise from the sofa near the elevators, he nearly swallowed his tongue. She wore a burgundy silk jumpsuit that left her brown shoulders bare. Her lipstick looked like liquid pearls. She was even more gorgeous than when he'd last seen her. She smiled as he approached, her teeth a storm of white. His knees went weak.

"Rex! It's good to see you again. How *are* you?" She offered her hand, and he took it. She leaned close to him, and he caught a whiff of citrus-flavored perfume. "I assume there'll be another game tonight. Interested in having a tagalong again?"

Rex cleared his throat and collected himself. No woman over the age of seventeen had ever affected him like this before. "Well, Millie—it *is* Millie, isn't it?" He knew damned well what her name was. Her mismatched eyes had haunted his dreams every night for the past week. "I don't quite know what to say. I'd thought you'd abandoned me last week. One minute you're with me at the poker table, and the next minute—*poof!*—you're gone. I didn't know what to think."

"I'm sorry about that, Rex, but something came up, something of a—uh—shall we say, *feminine* nature. By the time I got back from the little girls' room, you were long gone."

Rex lowered his face and stared at her through his blond eyelashes. "Sweetheart, give me some credit."

She ran her tongue over her lips. "You've got to admit that I brought you luck last week. Why not think of me as your walking, talking good-luck charm?"

"How do I know it wasn't the lucky pair of socks I put on before leaving the house?"

"Come on, Rex. Have you ever won like that before? You don't really think a little old pair of socks could bring you two hundred and ten thousand dollars from one of the best poker players in the country."

Rex couldn't make himself angry at her. Suppose it *had* been pure luck that produced his win over Kindred. If Millie had been the source of it, then he would be crazy not to have her by his side tonight.

"You've talked me into it, Millie. But I warn you: if I win again tonight, I'm afraid I'll have to keep you."

vi

Before the game started, Josh made mental notes about the room and the people in it, for he'd been serious when telling Lewis that he meant to write about this night. He meant to remember the details. If Tommy Iadanza had let him, he would have taken real notes in the spiral notebook he'd brought along, but Tommy had worried that some in attendance would feel uneasy if someone sat in a corner and wrote things down.

The Fanshawe crowd were as Lewis had often described them. The rotund Wisconsin Johnson, wearing a cheap wool suit, popping peanuts into his mouth with the shells still on them. The immaculate Lake Havasu City Sid with his thin face, white mane, and solemn eyes. The freckled Connie Wierzbinski in her Trail Blazers sweatshirt and baseball cap, whose smoker's hack rattled her spare frame and left her gasping every few minutes.

Lewis wore a crisply laundered button-down shirt and corduroy jeans with the cuffs tucked under his stumps, his hand clamped around the handle of a battered briefcase that sat on the floor next to his Action Power 9000. The briefcase contained a thousand hundred-dollar bills, which represented a good portion of Lewis's liquidated retirement fund, neatly bundled into stacks of fifty. Earlier in the day Tommy had arranged for him to cash his broker's check at the U.S. Bank branch down the street.

Watching Lewis, Josh thought, *He's on autopilot. He's functioning but he's a million miles away.* Lewis's gray eyes had a glazed-over look that meant his brain was busy with something he'd found in one of his philosophy books. Josh had seen the look many times.

vii

The door opened, and Rex Caswell made his entrance with his briefcase in his hand. Behind him—tall and elegant in her simplicity—came Millie Carter, moving languidly like a swan. She smiled at Lewis through the haze of Connie Wierzbinski's cigarette smoke, then smiled in turn at everyone in the room, including Josh Nickerson, who, when he saw her, instantly looked anemic. Rex noticed the effect she had on the boy, and laughed. Millie took a seat along the wall, not directly behind

Rex but off to his right, which gave her a clear view of Lewis.

Her hour at last, between Hell and Heaven! thought Lewis.

Tommy Iadanza explained what would happen tonight. Lewis and Rex would play a private one-on-one game of no-limit five-card draw with an ante of fifty thousand dollars. The players would make a side bet of a hundred thousand. They would cut for the deal, and the winner of each hand would deal the next one. A game with stakes like these wasn't likely to last long, so everyone present was welcome to play Texas hold 'em after it had concluded. As always, drinks and eats were available from the Huntsman's Bar and Grill.

Wisconsin Johnson, Lake Havasu City Sid, and Connie Wierzbinski sat next to each other on Lewis's right, all nodding their encouragement to him. For some absurd reason they reminded him of the chorus in a Greek tragedy, positioned at the edge of the stage. Lewis wondered who the hero would be, recalling that heroes don't fare well in Greek tragedy. Nestled in the front pocket of his jeans, unnaturally warm and vibrating, was the orb—the deus ex machina, the divine solution. It wouldn't swoop down onto the stage, as in Greek drama, but would stay hidden in Lewis's pocket, resolving the conflict in his favor, if things went according to plan.

Tommy Iadanza produced a new deck of cards still in the wrapper and passed it to each player for his examination. Then he broke the seal and placed the deck on the table.

"Before we cut the cards, I want to see the money," Rex declared. "I want to make sure you brought enough to pay me what you owe me."

Lewis hoisted his battered old attaché case onto the table, pressed the lock buttons, and lifted the lid. The money shone greenly under the track lights, and the chorus murmured. "There's more than enough here, Rex," he lied. "By the way, I assume that *you* brought cash." Rex stared at the open case and chewed on his tongue, apparently weighing whether to insist that the money be counted. "I won't demand that you show me your money," added Lewis. "If you say you have it, I'll take your word for it."

"All right, let's ante up and get this show on the road."

Lewis and Rex cut the cards, and Rex won the deal. Lewis took out ten packets of hundred-dollar bills and flipped them into the center of the table, one by one, staring Rex in the face. In the corner of his eye he could see Millie, perched on the edge of her chair with her legs crossed, riveting him with her two-colored gaze. Rex finished shuffling and slapped the deck down in the center of the table so that Lewis could cut the cards a final time, which he did. Rex then started to deal.

As the cards slid softly from the deck over the baize, Lewis involuntarily glanced at Millie, his attention drawn to her despite his best efforts to shut her out. He absorbed a full blast of her heat and cold, her total and incomprehensible duality. He felt both revulsed and attracted. He plunged into a vivid dream scenario that featured him in bed with her, his hands running over her breasts and pulling away her clothing, her full lips on his, her tongue against his, her legs entwined with *his* legs—

"Are you going to pick up your cards, or what?" Rex Caswell asked.

Lewis's eyes stung, because he hadn't blinked them in God-only-knew how long. A bead of saliva ran from the corner of his mouth as his orgasm pounded, and he was barely able to hold himself motionless lest everyone in the room detect what was happening to him. The orb, warm in the front pocket of his corduroy jeans, pressed against his stiff cock. Millie smiled faintly as she rocked back and forth in her chair with only a hint of motion, unnoticed by everyone but Lewis.

I've been fucking her! the nonrational compartment of his mind screamed. *I don't know how this is happening, but I've been fucking her . . . !*

"What's the matter with you, Stumpmeister—are you having some kind of seizure?" Rex glared at him. "Pick up your cards and play poker, okay?"

Lewis picked up his cards, but when he saw them, he felt immediately sick. Rex had dealt him a potential double-ended straight—the deuce of clubs, three of hearts, four of diamonds,

five of hearts, and jack of spades. The odds were five to one
against his drawing either an ace or six to complete a strong
hand. What sickened him was the fact that he'd seen this hand
in another life, in a dark and dirty Quonset building in a vile
place called Cu Chi Base Camp. His opponent had been a man
named Gamaliel.

Pinheads of sweat popped out on his forehead as the orb
again pressed into his groin, a thing alive. He dared another
glance at Millie, who sat with her eyes closed, her full lips
contorting slightly as if they controlled the movements of the
crystal. The dream seized him again. He saw himself push his
face into the tender mound between her legs, inhaling the spic-
iness of her vagina. He felt her mouth close over his cock, her
tongue thrashing its head and stirring him to a frenzy.

"The bet's to you, Stumpmeister. I'd like to finish this hand
before I reach retirement age, if you don't mind."

One of the chorus said, "Don't let him rush you, Lewis.
You're entitled to think things over."

Lewis heard himself say, "Five hundred dollars." He saw
the fingers of his right hand cull out the jack and set it aside,
meaning to discard it.

"Five hundred dollars," repeated Rex, scowling at his
cards. "Where're your balls, Lewis? Don't you have any more
faith in your cards than that?"

Lewis's balls were busy right now, as was his tongue. The
dream was as real to him as this poker game. He had another
orgasm, this one even more wrenching than the first. He felt
it down to his *toes*.

"I *said*, I raise you ten thousand dollars," barked Rex, repeating what he'd said thirty seconds earlier. "Are you sure
you're capable of playing tonight, Stumpmeister? You're acting like you've dosed up on something."

"I'm okay," said Lewis, staring at Millie. She opened her
eyes and rolled them at him dreamily, as if to say, *That was
good, Lewis. But I'm not finished with you, lover. Not by a
long shot.* "I'll see you and call."

Rex dealt him another card, then dealt himself one.

Lewis lay on his back now, and Millie was astride him, her willowy body slick with sweat. She worked his cock into her, mewling sweetly as she did so, then pumped him furiously, her sweet breasts jouncing. He saw that she, too, was on the verge of orgasm. She screamed loudly enough to shatter windows throughout the city. Lewis howled as he came, causing earthquakes and tidal waves. His hands and arms tingled; his legs and feet tingled. *He was whole again. . . .*

He glanced at his new card, though he needn't have, for he knew what it was—a six, which gave him a six-high straight.

"What do you say we wrap this up right now?" Rex suggested. "It's clear you're not having a good time, Lewis. Tell you what let's do. Let's skip the last round of betting and call. We'll keep the bets we have on the table, but let's up our side bet from a hundred thousand to double or nothing what you already owe me. That would bring the total pot to . . . let's see. . . ."

"Five hundred and forty-one thousand dollars," said Lewis. His poker smile came back. He felt virile and strong. He almost believed that he could rise out of the wheelchair, walk across the table on his own two feet, and kick Rex Caswell in the teeth. "Sounds good to me, Rex. Let's do it."

Rex hesitated and glanced again at his cards. He breathed heavily and loudly through his mouth, as if he were lifting weights. "Half a million bucks and change," he said aloud to himself. "Did you bring enough to cover a bet as big as this?"

"It doesn't matter, Rex. I'm not going to lose. I don't have the money here, but I'm good for it."

"You cocksucker! Didn't I tell you to show up with enough cash to play the game? How do I know you can cover the bet and still pay me what you owe me?"

Movement from Rex's right caught Lewis's eye, Millie's hand settling on Rex's arm, causing him to start as if jolted with a cattle prod. Millie leaned close. "I'll cover him if he's short, Rex. If you win, I'll have the money for you within the hour." Rex gaped at her, and Lewis noticed dark circles in the armpits of his Armani sport coat.

"That's good enough for me." Rex turned back to the table and showed his cards one by one, revealing what Lewis knew them to be—a full house, jacks over nines, the same hand that Gamaliel Cartee had turned over in Cu Chi, a fact that defied mathematical probability. Anguished groans came from the chorus.

"Sorry about this, asshole," said Rex, grinning. "Seems like the poker fairy hit you with the loser stick. Want to know something? Within a week's time, you've taken care of my retirement!" He started to laugh. "That's almost three quarters of a million dollars you owe me! When are you going to learn, Lewis? You're history, man! Your day is over! *Le roi est mort, vive le roi!*" He wiped his tearing eyes with a linen handkerchief.

"I hate to be a wet blanket," Lewis said, "but you're being a little premature." He reached down to turn over his own hand, which only moments ago had been a six-high straight, a loser to Rex's full house. First card: a six. Second card: a six. Third card and fourth cards: both sixes. The orb had worked its magic and, having done so, lay inert and cold in Lewis's pocket.

Millie's laughter cut through the air as Rex Caswell stared stupidly at Lewis's four sixes—laughter that was husky and full, not totally feminine. Lewis cringed. *Why laughs she thus, between Hell and Heaven*?

"You cheating cocksucker!" hissed Rex. "You set me up! You knew this would happen . . . !"

"Wrong. You set yourself up. You dealt the cards. You suggested the double-or-nothing side bet."

"We've only played one hand! We can't quit after only one hand. This doesn't prove anything. It doesn't prove you're a better player than me."

"You're probably right about that, Rex. It only proves I'm richer, at least for the time being. Well, I'm tired, folks. I think I'll get out of here while I'm ahead, go home, and make myself some hot chocolate."

The others came out of their collective shock and jumped

up from the table. They slapped Lewis on the back, cheered, and whistled. They called for drinks from the Huntsman's, and Tommy Iadanza declared that drinks were on the house.

"I assume you brought enough money," said Lewis to Rex, "to cover your loss. In addition to what's on the table, you owe me four hundred and twenty thousand dollars. If you don't mind, I'll take it now."

Rex trembled with rage, his nostrils flaring. He clenched his hands into fits. Lewis wouldn't have been surprised if he pulled a gun out of his coat and started shooting. "I only brought three hundred thousand. I can give you the rest tomorrow."

"I don't understand. You're not telling me you played poker with money you don't have, are you? Is that what you're telling me, Rex?"

"I *said*, I can give you the rest tomorrow. What the hell do you want from me?"

"You've got an hour," said Lewis, savoring this turnabout. "Bring the money here and give it to Tommy. I'm making him my representative."

"I can't get it in an hour! I have to drive clear across town, then back again. It's humanly impossible—"

"An hour," Lewis insisted. "Have the money here in an hour, or I'll come for you." He backed his Action Power 9000 away from the table and drove it around to where Rex sat. He and Rex confronted each other chin to chin. "Don't disappoint me, Rex. I suggest you call one of your muscleheads and get the ball rolling. You now have"—he glanced at his watch— "fifty-eight minutes and forty-three seconds." He then pulled the orb from his pocket and spun his chair around to confront Millie Carter. He tossed the orb into the air twice, three times, then held it tightly in his fist. "I'm glad you came tonight," he said to her. "I hope you found all this entertaining."

"Very entertaining," she answered, eyeing the orb. "I'd say your good-luck charm performed admirably."

Lewis tossed it to her, and she caught it smoothly, not taking her gaze from his. "This isn't mine," he said. "Give it back to its rightful owner, whoever that is."

"But *you're* its rightful owner now."

"No! Not now, not ever." Lewis looked around for Josh, who leaned against the far wall of the room, looking pleased. "Let's go. It's been a long night, and you've got school tomorrow."

Tommy Iadanza stepped forward, dug into his pocket for his keys, and handed them to Josh. "Take my car. When you get him home, stay with him. I'll call when this fuck-stick delivers the money." He nodded to indicate Rex, upon which Rex got to his feet and strode from the room, slamming the door rudely behind him.

Lake Havasu City Sid had gathered up the cash and had stuffed it into Lewis's attaché case, which he now handed over to Tommy. "Better put this in your safe for tonight. I'll arrange for an armored car to pick it up and take it to the bank in the morning. Is that okay with you, Lewis?"

It was. Lewis thanked Sid, then thanked them all for showing up tonight, for giving him their help and comfort when he needed it. He pledged that from now on he would try to be as good a friend to them as they'd been to him.

Millie rose from her chair, still holding the orb in her hand, and walked over to Lewis. She smiled with her ivory teeth, and a hush fell over the room. "I'd be happy to buy you a drink, Lewis. My way of saying congratulations. You name the place."

"I don't deserve congratulations. I'm not proud of what I did tonight."

"Oh, but you should be. You've taken a major step toward a new life, toward freedom and power. You should revel in it." She put the orb to her lips and kissed it.

"I'm afraid I can't go anywhere with you," he said. He pushed hard on the joystick of his wheelchair, and the chair carried him quickly from the room.

Fifteen

i

UPON ARRIVING HOME with Josh, Lewis locked himself in the bathroom, stripped off his clothes, and climbed into the shower hoist. He lingered under the jets of water for nearly forty-five minutes, making it as hot as he could stand it. He lathered and washed vigorously, rinsed and lathered again, then did so yet again. But he couldn't wash away the crawling sensation of having wallowed in a nest of maggots.

He pulled on a clean pair of underwear (the ones he'd worn earlier were semen-soaked), a freshly laundered sweatshirt, and a pair of gym trunks. He got into his wheelchair and motored into the kitchen to fetch himself a beer.

When the telephone rang, Josh picked it up and plugged a finger into his open ear, since Lewis had plugged a Dire Straits CD into the stereo and had turned the volume up loud enough to compensate for the hearing he'd lost in Vietnam. Lewis saw the relieved expression on the boy's face and knew that the caller was Tommy Iadanza, that the news was good. Rex Caswell had delivered the money.

After the album had played, Lewis and Josh sat across from each other in the studio, neither saying much, though each sensed that the other had a lot to say. Lewis knew that the boy's head swarmed with questions about what had happened tonight, and although Lewis felt obliged to explain certain things to him, he doubted whether he could reveal all he knew, or all he feared.

Finally Josh spoke up. "It was scary, wasn't it, Lew?"

"Yeah. It was."

"But there's nothing to be scared of now, is there? Everything came out okay."

"I don't know, Josh." Lewis couldn't bring himself to lie, not here beneath the portrait of Lyle Kindred, an honest man who'd tried hard to raise an honest son.

"You don't think Rex will try to get back at you somehow,

do you? The guy's got to be smarter than to hurt you now, not after what happened in front of half a dozen witnesses. If he came after you now, the cops would know exactly who to nail, right?''

"It's not Rex I'm worried about.''

Josh kneaded the fabric of his bleached denims. "It's Millie, isn't it? You're afraid we haven't seen the last of her.''

"I don't know what to be afraid of anymore.''

"Some things just aren't supposed to happen, are they? Good-luck charms aren't supposed to work, and shadows aren't supposed to be alive.''

A nut of pain took root behind Lewis's eyes. He took a deep swig of beer. "What I did tonight wasn't right. I got dirty. I would've gotten less dirty if I'd called up my aunt Juliet and told her that I'd accepted Jesus as my personal savior, just so I could get my hooks on her money.''

"You don't really think she would've given it to you, do you? Not two hundred thousand dollars . . .''

"You're right—she would've thought up some reason why God wants me to suffer for my own good. But that's not the point. By using the orb, I let somebody touch me, Josh . . .''— if the kid only knew—''somebody filthy. Now I've got the filth on *me*.''

"But you gave the orb back to her. And she accepted it, didn't she? Shouldn't that count for something?''

Lewis wondered how he might explain the way he and Millie had connected tonight, how their souls had locked together in sexual fury while their bodies sat quietly at a poker table. How could he describe the hellish exhilaration he'd felt when at the moment of orgasm he discovered that he had two strong legs? He'd been whole again. Somehow Millie and the orb had done that to him, *for* him.

No, he couldn't tell Josh these things.

Josh stood up and stretched, though it wasn't really late. In his baggy jeans and flannel shirt, he looked gawky and thin. He moved to Lewis's side and laid a hand on his shoulder. "For whatever it's worth, Lew, I think you did the right thing.

But if it wasn't the right thing, then I'm as much to blame as you are, because I talked you into it.''

Lewis smiled at the thought of laying a portion of his guilt on the shoulders of a seventeen-year-old boy. ''You didn't talk me into anything. I made my own choices. I pay my own way, same as everyone else.''

''Whatever happens, I'm going to be here for you. You won't be alone. Count on that. Okay?''

At this moment Lewis couldn't have loved this kid any more intensely if he'd been his own son.

ii

The night deepened. When Lewis Kindred's ceiling ceased to creak, he knew that all three members of the Nickerson family had gone to bed. When David Letterman's chatter faded from the ventilation ducts, he knew that the young stockbroker on the second floor had likewise turned in for the night. The D'Arcys across the way had gone to bed early, and no sound had come from their direction for hours.

Lewis sat upright on his bed, propped with pillows, his eyes wide against the dark. At his side lay his old service .45, locked and loaded with the safety switch engaged.

No Bick was on the veranda outside his window, a skulking man-shape that several times had slipped past the bedroom to try windows elsewhere in the house, to test the outer doors front and back. Lewis had sensed desperation in his movements, an urgency to find a way in and finish what he'd begun more than twenty years earlier.

The man-shape rose before the window once again, and Lewis's wide eyes caught the dull gleam of streetlight reflected from something metallic, the blade of a knife or the barrel of a gun. His hand found the .45, and he thumbed the safety switch off. As he raised the pistol, his heart ached with the certainty that Vietnam had found him at last and had come to claim him. In a way, he'd never left Vietnam at all. Part of

him was still there—a part that he'd given to the Black Virgin.
Vietnam had followed him home, haunted him in dreams, terrorized his nights, and sought his complicity in evils that he
couldn't begin to understand. No Bick was part of it. And
Millie, too.

Lewis Kindred and Vietnam were one.

He leveled the pistol at the shape beyond the window, his
heartbeat thumping in his ears. Whatever might happen tonight, he meant to go down fighting.

The man-shape took something from a bag, a tire iron or a
crowbar or a baseball bat—Lewis couldn't quite make it out—
and reared back to shatter the window. Lewis decided to hold
his fire and let him come so close that he couldn't possibly
miss. The man's arm raised with the tire iron or crowbar in
one fist, the knife or pistol in the other, and Lewis struggled
to breathe.

What happened next nearly convinced him that he was
dreaming. Red light exploded from a source somewhere behind the man-shape, like a Fourth of July pyrotechnic. No Bick
whirled around, startled. The orb orbited his head slowly,
flinging out strands of light. It halted near the windowpane, as
if to bar the way. No Bick's mouth was agape in terror, his
eyes stupidly wide. The orb hung inches from his face, bob-
bing on an invisible wave.

"Don't worry, Lewis," whispered someone close. She
crouched next to his bed, having slipped in like a shadow.
"He can't hurt you now. He'll never try to hurt you again, I
promise."

The orb moved toward No Bick's head. Upon touching his
skin, it flashed white like a miniature nova, showering sparks
onto the veranda. No Bick's hands flew to his forehead and
his mouth yawned. He flailed like a man possessed, twitched
as though electrocuted, until he collapsed to his knees. Lewis
scrambled toward the foot of his bed, sick with the horror of
finding Millie Carter next to him in his room, but needing to
see what was happening to No Bick. Seconds later the orb

wheeled and sailed upward, leaving No Bick to flee like a wounded animal.

Lewis turned back to Millie, who stood upright now, tall and beautiful in the quarter light of the street lamps on Gander Circle. He opened his mouth to challenge her, but his voice was gone. He raised his pistol and pointed it at her, but she only giggled and tossed her rusty dreadlocks in a playful way. "You're not going to shoot me, are you, Lewis? After what we've been to each other?"

Her hand found the snaps that the held her jumpsuit in place. The garment fell away, and she stepped out of it, wearing only a bra of black lace and matching panties. Lewis forced a swallow as his eye wandered over her full breasts, her belly, the curve of her hips. Sweat dripped into his mouth from his upper lip, and his hand could no longer hold the pistol steady. Millie unsnapped the bra, freeing her proud breasts. Her hands slipped beneath the lace band of her panties, pushing them down. And then she was naked.

"What we had tonight at the card table was wonderful, Lewis," she whispered, her eyes gleaming blue and brown. "But it wasn't enough. It wasn't enough for you, and it certainly wasn't enough for me."

Lewis let the pistol drop to the mattress.

Part Three:

Pleasures of the Flesh

Sixteen

i

IT'S JUNE 3, 1983, in Portland, Oregon, a Friday. It's early evening.

Paul Tran sits at the desk in his study, his hand resting on the lacquered box that an old Cao Dai shaman gave him eight years earlier. Inside it lies an inanimate marble of red glass. He lifts an edge of the box and hears the marble strike the interior wall with a sharp thump.

How will this warn me? he wonders for the thousandth time. After all these years, he worries that his memory of the shaman's orders might be faulty. A piece of glass is just a piece of glass—isn't it? *Best not to worry about these things*, he reminds himself. *Best to meditate as the old man taught me, and let my questions answer themselves.*

The telephone rings, shattering his meditation. It's Jesse Burton, of all people, calling from Champaign, Illinois, where he attends graduate school. Five years have passed since the two of them met in a dingy Italian restaurant in Chicago to discuss certain dark things from their mutual past. They haven't talked since that day.

They trade pleasantries, ask about each other's families. College and maturity have softened Jesse's rough edges. He's married now, with a son. His wife teaches school, and he plans to continue his graduate studies toward a doctorate in education.

Tran relates that he has become a naturalized American citizen. He has bought the janitorial service that hired him when he first arrived in Portland, and the business has grown substantially under his guidance. He has acquired a house on the same street where Lewis Kindred lives. He tells about his own little daughter, who is eight and very bright, the light of his life.

Jesse finally asks the question that has lurked just beneath the surface of the pleasantries: has Tran found Gamaliel Cartee?

Tran answers that he has not, but the search continues. He explains that he has queried the Veterans Administration and the U.S. Army in order to obtain Gamaliel's home address prior to entering the service, which would have been a logical starting point—the location of the man's home and family, his childhood friends, his schoolmates. After all, Gamaliel might have contacted someone from his past life, and that someone might know his whereabouts today. But the government won't give out personal data on soldiers missing in action, so this avenue of the search is closed.

Tran hired a private investigator, who launched the usual missing-person inquiries with credit agencies, driver-licensing bureaus, and direct-marketing organizations. The investigator found that nowhere in the country has anyone named Gamaliel Cartee established a credit rating, obtained a driver's license, or ordered an item from a catalog. Nobody with that name has committed any crimes or served time in a correctional institution. Nobody with that name has bought any insurance. The private investigator concluded that Gamaliel Cartee is either living under another name or that he is indeed missing in action, as the government claims.

Tran now haunts public libraries in his spare time and pores over telephone directories of America's major cities. He has found some twenty Cartees in the phone books of big cities like New York, Detroit, and Los Angeles, and he's placed calls to the households of that name. But no one among the Cartees he's found thus far admits to having heard of Gamaliel.

In the meantime he has continued spying on Lewis, but he's seen no evidence that a female of Gamaliel's kind has entered Lewis's life, which is a small comfort.

"And you still plan to kill Gamaliel if you find him?"

No response from Tran, except telling silence.

"I've got to hand it to you," says Jesse, "you're dedicated. I just hope you don't end up serving a life sentence for murder. This is like a religion with you, isn't it?"

"It is my cause."

"Don't you ever wonder whether it's all a bunch of mumbo jumbo? I mean, suppose it's all a bad dream."

"Whenever that suspicion rises, I remember the last time I spoke with Gamaliel. He'd been shot in the face, and he was dead. But yet he *wasn't* dead. I remember how I felt then, listening to his voice and looking into his eyes. I knew that I must fight him, if for no other reason than to protect Lewis from him. Lewis was a good man, and he still is. Nothing has changed, Jesse."

"You've seen a miracle, in other words. An evil one, but it's still a miracle, right?—and that's the basis of your faith."

"I have only a sense of right and wrong, as nearly everyone does. I know that I cannot let Gamaliel and his kind go unchallenged."

"When we met in Chicago, you suggested that I reestablish contact with Lewis, and I've done that. You wanted me to let you know if he ever told me about a woman in his life, remember? Well, we talk on the phone probably once a month, and I always make a point of asking him if he's seeing anyone special. He only laughs when I ask, and it's a bitter laugh, if you know what I mean. I think he's given up hope of ever having a woman again."

"A woman of Gamaliel's kind won't care that he has no legs, or that he's covered with scars."

"No, I guess not. But I learned something from Lewis the other day that you might want to know. For some reason we talked about Gamaliel—I don't know why, but his name just came up, like some people talk about the devil. It was weird. Anyway, he mentioned that Gamaliel was from Louisiana, probably New Orleans."

Excitement worms inside Tran. "How does he know this?"

"He prides himself on recognizing accents. He says Gamaliel had a touch of Creole in his speech. To me the man just sounded like a southerner, but Lewis had a roommate in Officer Candidate School who grew up in the Mississippi River Delta, and Gamaliel sounded just like him, he says. Have you checked out the New Orleans phone book yet?''

"No, but I'll do it immediately."

"What if you don't find a listing for any Cartee?"

"Then I'll go to Louisiana."

"And do what—start knocking on doors and asking if there's a monster in the house?"

"I'll go to the state capital and ask to see the state voting lists. That's the right of every American. Such lists include the addresses of the voters, I'm told. . . ."

ii

It's June 8, 1983, the following Wednesday, midmorning.

A Greyhound bus speeds south from Baton Rouge toward New Orleans with a full load of passengers. In the seat next to Tran sits a young mother with a squalling infant in her lap, but Tran doesn't mind. Noisy children have never annoyed him.

He could easily have afforded a ticket on a commuter airline, but Tran is Vietnamese, even though he carries the label of a naturalized American citizen. In Vietnam, people ride buses. They ride three to a seat, if need be. They carry along live fowl in wicker baskets, and none of the other passengers complains about the crowding or the noise or the smell. Unlike Americans, Vietnamese have no concept of personal space.

Upon arriving in New Orleans, he takes a taxi to a cheap hotel near the French Quarter, a place the driver has recommended. He rides with his window open, and the humid Mississippi River Delta air washes over his face. Something about this city reminds him of Saigon, though New Orleans is much tidier in its Western way, less ramshackle or hectic. Saigon and New Orleans were both capitals of French colonies, once upon a time. Their shared heritage glimmers in the architecture of old buildings and the names of streets.

He calls his wife from his room and gives her the name and number of the hotel, in the event that she must reach him. He has called her at least once a day since leaving Portland abruptly on Saturday. This is a business trip, he's told her, a chance to meet investors who may be interested in franchising his janitorial business in the South. He knows that she hasn't believed him, and he doesn't blame her, for the story sounds contrived even to himself. After hanging up the phone, he tells himself that one day he will compensate her for the anguish he's inflicted on her these past seven years. He has no idea how he will do this, but he vows to find a way.

He's exhausted. He has slept only in fits since flying to Baton Rouge from Portland on Saturday. Now his body demands real sleep. He draws the curtains against the bright afternoon sun and lies fully clothed on the bed, intending to sleep only for an hour. He wakes to the ringing of his telephone, finding that afternoon has faded to evening. Red neon light penetrates the closed curtains, blinking the name of the hotel.

"Paul, it's me—Jesse Burton. I'm downstairs in the bar."

"Here—in New Orleans? How . . . ?"

"Why don't you join me? I could use some company right now, and so could you, I'll bet."

Five minutes later Tran enters the bar, which a quivering neon sign identifies as the Continental Room. Jesse sits in a tight booth with a potted candle on the table, nursing an iced tea. The place is dark and quiet. The only other customer is a black man in a business suit at the bar, sipping a shot of bourbon. When Jesse sees Tran, he rises and motions him over, offering a handshake. He has gained weight since Tran last saw him, but he looks healthier, less worn. He wears a green golf shirt.

"Better get yourself a drink, man," says Jesse, lighting a cigarette. "Do your nerves good. I'm sober these days, so I don't drink anything stronger than this. But that doesn't mean my friends have to suffer."

Tran forces a smile and slides into the opposite side of the booth. "You consider me your friend?"

"Sure, why not? I'll even pay for your drink."

Tran orders a cognac, sips it, and grimaces as the liquor

burns his throat. The next sip feels better, though. And the next better still.

"Aren't you going to ask me how I found you and what I'm doing here?" Jesse asks.

"I suspect you telephoned my home, and my wife told you where to find me. As to why you've come, I'm at a loss."

"When we talked on the phone last week, you mentioned how you felt when you last saw Gamaliel—he had a bullet hole in his head, but he was still alive. I guess I know how you must've felt, because I've had the same feelings. I saw what he did to a whore in Cu Chi, and I saw him do magic during a poker game. I've seen his shadow, same as you. What you might not know is that I was in on the plan to kill him. It was Lewis and I. We set it all up."

"I didn't know, but it doesn't surprise me."

"I'd almost managed to forget it all, man, and so has Lewis, I think. But after you and I talked, I remembered something Lewis said to me back in the 'Nam, after Gamaliel killed the girl at Mama Dao's. It was something like, 'As long as Gamaliel exists, there'll never be a good place, not for you and me.' I know now that he was right."

"But why are you here? You have your family, your studies."

"Do you remember our old CO in Triple Deuce—Colonel Gilbert Golightly?"

"Yes, I remember."

"After we got our asses kicked by the NVA, he put me in for a Congressional Medal of Honor, because I carried Lewis to a clearing where a Medevac chopper could land. I didn't get the medal, but I've never cared about that, because I've always felt that if anyone should've gotten a medal for what happened that day, it was Lewis. He tried to rid the world of Gamaliel, and he's paid for it big time, losing his legs and all. He's still paying for it. I guess I owe it to him to help finish the job."

"You no longer think I'm insane?"

"I've never thought that, no matter what I've *said*." Jesse blows smoke across the potted candle and stares a moment into the cloud with vacant eyes.

He tried to call Tran in Portland, he explains, but Tran had already flown to Baton Rouge. A business trip, Mrs. Tran said. So Jesse hopped the next plane out of Champaign, but by the time he landed in Baton Rouge, Tran had already been there and gone. So Jesse called Mrs. Tran again, and learned that her husband had gone to New Orleans. She supplied the name of this hotel, and Jesse caught the next commuter flight out of Baton Rouge.

"Doesn't it bother you to miss your classes and to be away from your family?" Tran asks.

"Spring quarter just ended, man, and I've got the summer off. As for my wife, I told her an old army buddy needs my help, and she bought it. Didn't even ask who the old buddy is. I didn't mention, of course, that he's a former Vietcong." Jesse grins across the table. "I don't know if I'll be much help to you," he adds, "but I figure you can use the moral support. And who knows, if you find Gamaliel, it might be handy to have an old street fighter from the South Side of Chicago with you."

Tran inhales the fumes of his cognac and nods. It does indeed feel good to have an ally.

"You found something in Baton Rouge, didn't you?" Jesse says.

Again Tran nods.

A name on a voting list in the secretary of state's office. A voter named Claudette Cartee, one of forty-four Louisiana voters with that surname. But how did he know that she was the one?

A *feeling,* he explains. A cold certainty that gripped him the moment his eyes landed on her name.

"The old Cao Dai shaman taught me how to meditate," he tells Jesse. "All these years I've followed the meditation regimen he prescribed, not really knowing whether it would produce any results. When I saw Claudette Cartee's name on that list, however, I knew instantly what the meditation has done for me. It has sharpened my intuition, deepened my innate knowledge of this world. It has allowed my unconscious to touch a realm in which time, space, and matter coalesce. I don't quite know how to explain this, Jesse, but I didn't need my physical senses to learn that Claudette Cartee is the mother of Gamaliel. I just *knew*. And I copied her address in New Orleans. . . .''

iii

They rent a car and buy a map of the city. Jesse has visited New Orleans several times and has become familiar with the downtown area between Carrollton and Broad avenues, so he drives. He also knows the neighborhood around Tulane University, where he has attended several conferences for graduate students, an area the locals call "Uptown." Like any competent tourist he can easily find his way in and out of the fabled French Quarter. The search for Gamaliel Cartee's mother, however, takes him and Tran far afield of the landmarks.

Night has transformed the inner city of New Orleans into a warren of dark side streets and alleys where knots of black men loiter on the corners, their boom boxes thundering, their eyes following the shiny rented Chevy with a look that Tran cannot decide is menace or curiosity. Claudette Cartee lives in a tenement on a shadowy street where every upper-story window has a clothesline strung to a fire escape. She's a stooped black woman with a Creole lilt in her speech, whose eyes brim with a lifetime of hardship. Much to Tran's surprise, she readily invites him and Jesse into her apartment, where the only source of light is a bare bulb dangling from the ceiling. Plaster peels from the walls, and the floorboards are buckling.

She hasn't seen Gamaliel since he joined the army in 1969, she says. He wrote no letters to her, never phoned home. Actually, she can't remember whether or not she owned a phone in those days. Times were better then, but not much. Gamaliel simply vanished from her life upon entering the army, leaving her to wonder whether he survived the war. Something in her tone suggests that she isn't really curious about what happened to him.

Jesse asks whether the U.S. government ever notified her that Gamaliel had been wounded, killed, or missing in action. Her answer is an emphatic no.

Then she reveals that Gamaliel isn't her natural son. The boy came to her at the age of fifteen, sent by her distant cousin Melusinne, who lives on the bayou outside Jean Lafitte, near Lake Salvador, some twenty miles south of New Orleans. Melusinne is a witch, she adds almost as an afterthought—what old-timers on the bayou call a *sorcière*. If Jesse and Tran want to know about Gamaliel, she suggests that they visit Melusinne.

They request directions to Melusinne's place, and Claudette obliges. Tran writes the directions down and reads them back to her, for they involve roads and paths far off the beaten track. Neither he nor Jesse wants to get lost in some remote, alligator-infested bayou.

The old woman rises from her chair and retreats into her bedroom, then returns with a cigar box in her hands. ROI TAN PANATELAS, says the ornate script. Tran wonders if she's about to offer cigars. She hands the box to Jesse, who opens it and finds it empty but for a ball bearing about the size of a marble. Tran's eyes widen with silent knowledge.

"Take this to Melusinne," the old woman advises, "and she'll know you come to her with faith in your heart."

iv

The next morning Jesse raps on the door of Tran's room at exactly eight o'clock. They eat a light breakfast in the hotel's coffee shop and set off in the rented Chevy, carefully following Claudette Cartee's directions.

The area immediately south of New Orleans isn't as rural or as backwoodsy as Tran expected it to be. Scattered among the bayous and lakes are communities of contemporary homes, mini-malls, and commercial strips. Near the community of Jean Lafitte, though, the countryside is more as he had envisioned southern Louisiana—lush forest interspersed with shadowy swamps, long stretches of empty road, and quietude thick enough to put in a bottle.

Jesse turns onto a potholed road that leads to a cluster of low, gray buildings with sagging porches, one of which is a U.S. post office, another a bait-and-tackle store with a neon Miller Lite sign in the window. The rest are houses, bare of decoration and surrounded by junk cars and appliances. A pair of dusty black kids lie on the hood of a derelict Mercury and watch the passing Chevy with suspicion.

Jesse parks in a lot outside the post office. Upon stepping from the air-conditioned car into the humid air, they hear the distant crowing of a rooster. Beyond the lot, the town gives way to bayou, where majestic swamp oaks and cypresses preside in ragged cloaks of Spanish moss. As Tran watches, an egret skims the water and wheels into the noontide sunlight.

With their shirts sticking to their backs, the two men set out on the path that leads southward from the parking lot along the edge of the swamp, as Claudette has instructed. Jesse carries the empty cigar box in his hand and the ball bearing in his pocket. Swatting mosquitoes becomes as automatic as putting one foot in front of the other. Occasionally the path forks, and Tran consults the slip of paper on which he jotted Claudette's instructions. The farther they go, the thicker the gloom becomes. Jesse says he wishes they'd brought a flashlight and a bottle of bug repellent.

"Coming back on this path could be a real adventure after the sun goes down," Jesse says. "Sort of brings back the old days, doesn't it?"

"You mean the war?" asks Tran.

"I mean Vietnam. Where else do you get mosquitoes like these?"

They march on for another five minutes, neither talking. But then Jesse says, "I need to know something, man. Lewis is sure that you deliberately let the platoon get ambushed on the day he lost his legs. I've told him a hundred times that you didn't—that you were as surprised as any of us. But he thinks . . ."

Tran halts suddenly and stares deep into the swamp, his jaw clenched. From somewhere deep inside himself he dredges up the courage to say the truth. His voice shakes. "This isn't easy for me to admit, but I did suspect that we'd come to a very dangerous place on that day. I saw many signs that the NVA were near—indentations in the brush, fresh-turned earth, human scat. . . ."

"But you let us circle our tracks there anyway?"

"I wanted something bad to happen, not so much to you, but to me. I'd lost all hope for myself, for Vietnam. I'd fought on both sides of the war, and found each as bad as the other. I'd seen Gamaliel and saw the evil he could do. For a little while I simply didn't care about anything anymore."

"So you decided to let the NVA chew us up." Jesse's eyes are full of disbelief and accusation.

"I didn't know for certain that they were there until we'd stopped and circled the tracks. You and Lewis had gone ahead on foot. That was when I smelled cooking—boiling rice and fish, the kind of food NVA soldiers ate, and I knew that the smell came from a tunnel in the ground. I came to my senses then, and tried to get word to Lewis that we'd come to a very bad place."

"Yeah, I remember. You told T. J. Skane and he called us on the radio. But by then it was too late." The accusation in Jesse's eyes turns to pity.

"Too late, yes. Lewis lost his legs because I didn't warn him soon enough."

Jesse touches Tran's shoulder. "So you're out here in this fucking swamp for the same reason I am. You owe it to Lewis. You need to kill Gamaliel because you need to make things right."

"No!" Tran pushes away the hand. "Not just for Lewis. For *everyone*. For you and your boy, for my little girl, for everyone who walks on this planet. We can't let Gamaliel take anyone else.''

"Okay. Whatever you say.''

They walk on in silence.

The path becomes squelchy, then downright muddy. They come upon the cabin sooner than Tran anticipates. It stands on the edge of the bayou, enshrouded by a moss-draped swamp oak. A rowboat lies moored to a decrepit dock that has lost a third of its planks. The building itself is in reasonably good repair. Overhead utility lines indicate electricity and a telephone. A late-model Jeep Wrangler stands near a small attached shed, wearing a bumper sticker that reads: A WOMAN'S PLACE IS IN THE HOUSE—OF REPRESENTATIVES.

"Can you believe someone drove that truck in here?'' Jesse asks. "I wonder what they used for a road.''

The whine of insects seems to intensify as Tran stares at the cabin, and he feels a darkness creep over him, a sense of misadventure more acute than anything he's felt since putting his family on a small boat to rendezvous with a freighter in the South China Sea. Suddenly the door of the cabin swings open, and a woman steps out with a shotgun cradled in her arms.

"I trust you haven't come with mischief on your mind,'' she calls out from the dusk of the porch.

Jesse raises a hand to wave. "Are you Melusinne Cartee?''

"I am.''

"We're here at the suggestion of your cousin in New Orleans, Claudette Cartee. We want to talk to you. It won't take long, I hope.''

Melusinne steps into the light of the afternoon, wearing a New Orleans Saints T-shirt, sensible shorts, and Etonic running shoes. Tran had expected her to be as stooped and wrinkled as her cousin Claudette, but the *sorcière* doesn't look older than forty. She carries herself proudly, though she's somewhat overweight. Her facial features are strong and finely drawn, her skin very dark, her eyes bright and lively. She wears her hair in a teased bunch at the crown. The Ithaca shotgun in the crook of her arm looks as if it belongs in a display case.

"If Claudette sent you, it's about Gamaliel, isn't it?"

A knot hardens in Tran's stomach. "Yes, it is," Jesse confirms.

Melusinne motions them forward, indicating the open door. "Come in. I've got some lemonade made and a pot of gumbo on the stove. Y'all might not be hungry, but you sure as hell must be thirsty. Hot and humid today. Probably stay like this till mid-November. Whereabouts are you boys from?"

"Illinois. Name's Jesse Burton, and this is my friend Paul Tran. He's from Portland, Oregon."

"He doesn't look like he's from Portland, Oregon. Looks like he's from China or Thailand."

"I'm Vietnamese," says Tran. "I'm a naturalized citizen."

"Well, I don't care where you're from, Mr. Tran, or what you are. You're welcome here."

They enter the house, which seems very dark at first, but Tran's eyes quickly adjust. On the walls hang the kind of things one might expect in the house of a *sorcière* in the Louisiana bayou—the bodies and heads of dead animals, all expertly stuffed. Cats of several varieties, a fox, an owl. A small alligator, a wild boar, and—Tran gulps—the mounted head of a man. The owner of the head looks to have been seventy or older when he died, though his wrinkles could be attributable to post-taxidermic drying. His nappy hair is pure white, his skin a healthy black that looks eerily alive. The facial expression suggests contentment after a life of toil, but the glistening glass eyes convey a restiveness that makes Tran's flesh crawl.

"That's my old great-granddaddy." Melusinne chuckles, closing the door behind her. "He was born a slave and lived to the ripe age of a hundred and two. It was his wish to have his head mounted after he died, so his surviving kin could look at him and remember the things he taught them."

"What kind of things?" asks Tran.

"The kind you're here to ask me about." She winks and shows them to chairs at a heavy oaken table in the part of the room that serves as a kitchen. While she fetches glasses for iced tea, Tran notices a state-of-the-art stereo system along one wall, a Sony television set with a VCR, a respectable cloth sofa with a matching armchair. A door leads to a bedroom, presumably. Nearby are new-looking appliances, including a refrigerator with an ice dispenser.

"How long have you lived here?" Jesse asks, accepting a tall glass that clinks with ice cubes.

"Longer than I care to admit, and longer than you'd believe. This property's been in my family since the Reconstruction, but I'm the only Cartee who cares about it. That's why there's nobody here but me. I guess you could say that I'm the only one with an interest in carrying on my great-granddaddy's work. By the way, you can smoke, if you want to." She sets an ashtray before him and takes the chair opposite.

Tran wonders how she knew that Jesse is a smoker.

"I suppose my cousin told you that I'm a *sorcière*."

"She did," Jesse answers. "She also advised us to bring some things to you, said they'd let you know that we come with faith in our hearts." He sets the empty cigar box on the table and fishes in his pocket for the ball bearing, which he places next to the box. "For you."

Melusinne smiles. "Oh, these aren't for me, Mr. Burton. They're for *you*."

"I don't understand. What use would I have for these things?"

"You'll find out soon enough. The fact that you brought them tells me what I need to know about you. Now drink your lemonade before it gets all watered down."

Tran sips slowly from his glass and relishes the cold on his throat. He can't remember when lemonade tasted so good. Jesse lights a cigarette and contentedly blows out smoke, looking relaxed despite the fact that Melusinne's dear old great granddaddy gazes down at them from the wall.

"Tell me," says Melusinne, "have you met Gamaliel personally?"

"We both have," Tran replies. "It was over twenty years ago in Vietnam."

"Vietnam. Aha." The fact that Gamaliel went to Vietnam seems to make perfect sense to Melusinne, but she doesn't say why. "You didn't play cards with him, I hope."

"I'm afraid I did," Jesse admits. "Lost my ass, too, if you'll forgive the vulgarity."

She laughs. "I hope it wasn't a hardship for you."

"It wasn't. A friend of mine won the money back for me."

Melusinne grows serious. "He won the money back from Gamaliel—is that what you said?"

"Yes."

"Were you present at this game?"

"Yes, we both were. I think I can even remember the winning hand. Four sixes to beat Gamaliel's full house."

"Did Gamaliel, by any chance, make a gift to your friend before they showed their hands? It would've been a ball-shaped piece of red glass, small enough for a man to carry in his hand."

"Yes, he did," says Jesse, trading glances with Tran. He describes the experiment that Gamaliel proposed to Lewis Kindred, which entailed only that Lewis keep the crimson orb near him while they showed their cards. Lewis won the hand, of course, and won big. Afterward Lewis forced Gamaliel to take the object back, as if he sensed something unclean about it.

Jesse relates all that happened after the game. He tells Melusinne about the atrocity at Mama Dao's whorehouse. How he and Lewis conspired to kill Gamaliel. About the catastrophe in the Ho Bo Woods, where many good men died and Lewis lost his legs. The sorcière listens intently and sympathetically, conveying her concern with appropriate nods and frowns.

She rises from the table to stir the pot of gumbo on the range, then turns back to them. "This friend of yours, this Lewis. He's in danger."

"Yes," answers Tran. "He is the reason we've come to you. I have reason to believe that Gamaliel may try to . . . to harm him."

"Gamaliel will try to nurture what he has planted," says Melusinne. "It may already be too late for your friend."

"What do you mean, too late?" asks Jesse. "Too late for what?"

Melusinne sits at the table again, reaches across it, and links hands with both men. "What I'm about to tell you may be difficult to believe, even though you've both met Gamaliel and seen his shadow. You've seen what he can do with the orb, *non?* And you've heard your friend's description of what he can become. Remember these things if your belief starts to slide away."

She begins by telling them that her family has suffered through an association with Gamaliel's kind for generations, maybe because so many Cartees possessed mental gifts that had led them to dabble in the occult. Whether such dabbling actually attracted Gamaliel and his ilk, she can't say. All she knows is that Gamaliel walked out of the swamp one day, and knocked at her door—a gangling teenager who wore nothing but the filth of the bayou on his skin. Having heard stories of such beings from her old auntie and her granddaddy, she recognized him immediately for what he was. His mismatched eyes were a dead giveaway.

"You see, all his kind have mismatched eyes. I don't know why, and I doubt anyone does. Gamaliel's kind can be white or black, or even like you, Mr. Tran—yellow. They can be male or female, big or small. But they *all* have one eye blue and the other one brown. Gamaliel himself seems mixed, a mulatto, I'd say."

"What did he want from you?" Tran asks.

"Not much more than a place to stay for a while, a loan of some money for clothes, some food. He'd been in the swamp a long time. He was ready to come back into the world."

Why had a teenage boy had been living in the swamp? Jesse wants to know. And where was his family?

His parents were long dead, probably for many generations, Melusinne explains. Even though he looked young, he wasn't. "You see, Gamaliel's kind live a long, long time. But

sometimes they get tired, and they need to go off and be alone,
to sleep, maybe to hide—I can't say. It's like hibernation, you
understand? Sometimes they go off and let folks forget that
they even exist. They hole up in caves or bury themselves in
swamps, and stay for years at a time. And when they come
out again, it's as if the aging process has reversed. They're
like young kids starting out in a new life.''

They need the trappings of humanity in order to live among
humans, Melusinne adds. Each needs a family, a background,
a last name—what a spy would call a ''legend''—in order to
function in society. The Cartee family and its antecedents in
the Caribbean and Europe have met these needs for Gamaliel
since long before anyone could remember. Why? Melusinne
doesn't know. Perhaps because of some covenant struck long
ago.

''It's not like we're a part of his life,'' she hastens to point
out. ''Gamaliel has always taken what he's needed from us
and then gone his way, often to the far corners of the world.
He doesn't really need much more from us than our name,
just a jumping-off point, a place to start from. Like others of
his kind, he makes money, a *lot* of money. And you can just
imagine how he does it.''

''The orb,'' ventures Jesse. ''He uses the orb to win at cards,
am I right?''

''Card games, or the stock market, or real estate. Or business ventures of other sorts—anything that involves chance.
What he does may depend on his frame of mind at any given
time. The orb gives him the power to succeed at whatever he
undertakes. Ultimately, though, he ends up back in the bayou,
where he hibernates. My old granddaddy used to say that he
does this because he gets into so much hot water out there in
the world, and he needs to lie low for a while, just to let the
trouble blow over.''

The last time he came out of the swamp, Melusinne put him
up in her cabin for a month or two, until he decided he wanted
to go to New Orleans. She sent him to her cousin, Claudette,
who kept him for more than three years. They lived as if they

were mother and son until Gamaliel went off and joined the army.

Jesse's cigarette has burned down to the filter, and he stubs it into the ashtray. He lights another and glances up at the stuffed man's head. Tran's eyes follow, and for a horrible moment he believes that the old gentleman has begun to smile faintly.

Jesse mentions that during his tour in Vietnam, a string of serial murders occurred in the vicinity of Saigon. Is it possible? he wonders—

"Young women?" interrupts Melusinne. "Horribly mutilated?"

"Yeah. Like I told you a minute ago, Lewis and I . . ." Jesse clears his throat, and takes a sip of lemonade. The eyes of the old former slave have unnerved him. "We became convinced that Gamaliel was the killer, based on what Lewis saw at the brothel in Cu Chi City. He was certain that the . . . *thing* he saw in the act of killing that young whore was Gamaliel."

Melusinne lowers her face. "And that's why you conspired to kill him, yes. It *was* he who killed the girl—there's no doubt of that. You see, that's how his kind lives. They kill. They eat human meat and drink human blood."

Tran's throat tightens with the horror of this truth. He has heard it before from an old Cao Dai shaman in a forest outside Tay Ninh. But having heard it before doesn't lessen the sting.

Melusinne continues: "Their lives go through cycles that few understand. During some periods they need to kill only seldom, maybe every second or third year. In other periods, or cycles, they need to kill at least once a week. I think it depends on . . . on . . ." This seems painful for her. Tran waits, his scalp pricking. "I think it depends on whether the thing is trying to reproduce."

She tightens her grip on their hands. "Not like mortal humans, you can be sure of that. Actually it's not reproduction at all. You see, they don't bear young. The only way they can make another of their kind is to convert a human being."

Melusinne has never personally witnessed the process, but

has only heard about it, mainly from her auntie and her granddaddy. She doubts that either of them had actually witnessed
it, either. Her knowledge is less than perfect, but what she
knows, she tells.

Not just any human being can live the life of Gamaliel's
kind. A suitable candidate must be intelligent, resourceful, and
angry. Gamaliel gravitates to one whose anger is pure and
deep, whose rage can be tapped to fuel the transmogrification
when the time is right. An attractive candidate is one whose
anger is righteous and unselfish, not self-centered or petty.
Other than these, there is only one prerequisite: the candidate
must have tried to kill the monster, not only proving that he
possesses the fortitude to kill, but also to achieve the needed
level of intimacy with the beast. To Gamaliel's kind, killing
is the most intimate act of all.

Lewis tried to kill Gamaliel Cartee by putting a bullet
through his face, Tran reflects. And Lewis was a man who
burned with righteous anger—anger over the senselessness and
brutality of the war. Over the fact that he himself had been
forced to fight it.

It all makes sense: Lewis met the criteria of an ideal
candidate.

Melusinne explains that the monster initiates the process by
presenting the chosen one a gift, the crimson orb, regardless
of whether the chosen has yet tried to kill him. If the chosen
accepts it, the orb imparts its evil energy to him, infecting him
with it, giving him a taste of the powers in the offing. *Acceptance* is the key, because the change can't happen unless the
chosen embraces it.

Melusinne believes that many a victim embraces the orb
because it enables a man to achieve virtually anything he
wants—wealth, professional success, acclaim. The orb gives
him power over his life, which is more seductive than any
drug.

Tran rises to stretch his legs. He feels old and tired at this
moment. He's no longer the strong young man he'd been in
Vietnam. He glances at Jesse, and he, too, looks old.

"How do we fight him?" Jesse asks.

Melusinne motions Tran back to his seat as she herself gets up. "Wait here." She goes to the door and opens it, letting in a crescendo of insect music. "I'll be back soon. For your own good, stay where you are and don't touch anything."

In the time required for Jesse to smoke another cigarette Melusinne returns, her arms full of a curious cargo. She sets a round baking stone on the table. Onto it she heaps dried sticks and wood chips. From a burlap bag she takes a basketball-size clump of dark soil, which she's apparently just spaded from the ground. As Jesse and Tran watch, she pulls apart the clump until liberating a pouch made of oilcloth. Inside the pouch is an object that causes Tran's breath to catch in his throat like a fish bone—a miniature coffin of glossy oak, not more than five inches long. It has tiny brass handles and hinges long ago tarnished over. Carved into its convex lid is an intricate cross with the Sacred Heart of the Holy Virgin at its juncture.

"My daddy buried this a long time ago," Melusinne announces. "It was the work of my great-granddaddy, the one up there on the wall. My daddy made me promise never to disturb it unless I could be sure that the time was right. And I think it is."

She places the ball bearing that Jesse brought into the empty cigar box, closes the lid, and hands the box back to him. "Keep this closed tightly. I suggest that you hold it against your chest." She scoops up the dirt in which the coffin had been buried, and pushes it into a circle on the surface of the stone, humming a guttural tune that has no discernible musical pattern. After stacking the twigs and wood chips within the circle of dirt, she lays the miniature coffin atop the stack. She strikes a wooden farmer's match, and Tran becomes conscious of how far the sun has fallen. The room has darkened to a velvety texture that he suspects is peculiar to places like the bayous of Louisiana and the tropical fields of Vietnam. He glances up and sees the jittering reflection of the flame in the glass eyes of Melusinne's great-granddaddy. He could swear that the old man's eyelids are widening.

"There's but one way to kill Gamaliel's kind," whispers Melusinne, lighting a stubby candle that she has placed on the edge of the table. "A mere mortal can't do it himself. You need the help of the dead. Come close now."

Tran and Jesse lean forward, bringing their faces toward the mound of sticks with the tiny coffin on it, Jesse pressing the cigar box to his chest with both hands. Suddenly they hear a faint scratching. Something is inside the coffin, something alive. Tran hopes that it's a small animal, a rodent or a large insect.

Humming her low, toneless song, Melusinne brings the candle to the mound and sets the wood afire, as Tran has feared she might. The scratching intensifies, as if whoever or whatever lay in the coffin knows what's about to happen. Flames lick the slope of the mound and spread around it, yellow and white, shades of violet and blue. Puffs of smoke spill upward, spicing the air.

"Closer," whispers Melusinne, beckoning. "You must breathe the smoke and fumes. Don't be afraid."

But Tran *is* afraid, and he can see that Jesse is, too. The scratching becomes frantic. Tran worries that at any moment he will hear a tiny voice scream for mercy.

The flames began to scorch the outer surface of the coffin, producing tart smoke that rouses an itch in his sinus cavities. Melusinne's humming becomes a moan, a deep grumbling that sounds unnervingly masculine. Through watering eyes Tran stares at the coffin as the scratching became more frantic, and he knows that he's witnessing something unspeakable.

Suddenly Melusinne's eyes pop open and she ceases her moaning. Perspiration beads her face and runs down her cheeks in glistening jewels. "Look beyond the *known*, Jesse," she whispers urgently to the black man. "Feel beyond yourself . . ."

Just then the edge of the coffin glows orange, and a piercing squeal issues from it as the fire penetrates the wood. The varnish blisters and peels. Molten satin drips through gaps in the wood before curling and flaming into nothingness. The squeal rises to a shriek that slices through the smoke to the core of Tran's heart, shattering any hope that the occupant of the coffin is a small animal like a mouse or a rat, or even a baby alligator—*anything* but a human being. For the shriek is indeed human, or close to it.

"... turn your heart inward and outward. Inhale the message that seeks you!"

The reek of burning flesh floods into Tran's lungs. He's tasted it before, in the Ho Bo Woods, where he watched men burn and die as tracer rounds laced the air around him, as mortar rounds dropped with bone-crunching detonations. These are the fumes of unreason, burning his throat and turning his gut. This is the stench of a life snuffing out. The colors it generates in his mind are those of hopelessness and pain.

The squeal dies suddenly, and Tran's eyes go to the wall where the old man's head hangs on its mount. A milky fog soaks up the dancing light of the fire, but he can just make out the face, the eyes, the nappy white hair. The facial expression hasn't changed, but tears flow from the dead man's eyes.

Suddenly the cigar box that Jesse holds next to his chest begins to pop and thud, as if the ball bearing inside it has come to life. The popping becomes more rapid and rhythmic, more powerful, until the box literally shudders in his hands as the ball bearing hurls itself against the cardboard walls. The sound is almost enginelike. Later, Jesse will tell Tran that he felt ghostly energy resonate through his body, warming him, opening his heart and mind to possibilities that he'd never before contemplated.

"Look beyond the known, Jesse," Melusinne says again, her face streaked with sweat and tears. "Feel beyond yourself. Inhale the message that seeks you. . . ."

Suddenly the popping dies and the ball bearing rolls to a corner inside the cigar box, where it lies silent.

Seventeen

i

THE WEATHER ON Wednesday morning, September 23, 1992, was in keeping with Rex Caswell's mood—foul. Curtains of rain swept across the Willamette, driven by a wind that roused a chop on the river and set the floating house to shaking. A solitary gull stood on the railing of the deck, bedraggled in the downpour, taking refuge in the lee of the house.

Having lain awake since well before dawn, Rex got up and put in a halfhearted workout in his weight room, then soaked in the hot tub while rain thrummed against the skylight above him. He went downstairs shortly after 8:30, drawn by the aromas of coffee and simmering Cream of Wheat. Silhouette, bless her teenage soul, had made breakfast.

"Sorry I've been such an asshole the last few days," he said between bites of cereal. "Losing all that money to Kindred has done evil things to my mind."

"So why don't you get back at him?" the girl suggested. "You have ways of getting back at people, don't you?" She brought her hand across her throat, as if it was a knife.

"Have him killed, you mean?"

"Sure, why not? You know people who can do that kind of stuff, I bet. What about Mase and Spit? Those two reprobates would do anything you asked them to." She reached across the table and squeezed his hand. "Seems to me that a little revenge might improve your spirits."

"I'll think about it," he pledged. "I'll definitely think about it."

ii

He punched the buttons on his cellular phone as he drove away from the Sellwood Bay Club, the Mercedes's single wiper sweeping rapidly across the windshield. As a telephone rang in Mason Benoit's town house in northwest Portland, Rex thought about what Silhouette had suggested over breakfast. It was true that he hated Lewis Kindred enough to kill him. But killing was too good for Lewis. Rex had something else in mind.

A woman answered the phone on the other end, her voice dreamy with drugs or booze or both. One of Mase's little sluts, probably. "Put Mason on," Rex ordered, and the woman did as she was told. Benoit came on the line, sounding full of piss and vinegar, a real top-of-the-morning guy.

"I'm on the c-phone, so watch your mouth," said Rex as he turned north on Macadam Boulevard, heading toward the center of town. "I want you and Spit to meet me at the Metro on Broadway as soon as you can get there. I've got a little chore for you guys. Whether or not you fuck it up will determine whether you and I keep our relationship. And don't bring any heavy metal, okay?"

Benoit acknowledged the order. Heavy metal was code for guns.

iii

Metro on Broadway lay a few steps below street level, directly across the street from the Portland Hilton in the heart of downtown. It consisted of a large common area crammed with tables, ringed by eight or ten walk-up kitchens that served "gourmet" fast food. The crowd at midmorning was light, since the coffee rush had long ago subsided. Rex had no trouble finding a table in an isolated corner.

Mason Benoit and Spit Pittman arrived together. Benoit still sported a bandaged wrist, but Spit had dispensed with his head bandages, leaving sutures and bruises open to the air. They spotted Rex immediately and joined him at his table.

Rex got right down to business. He wanted Benoit and Pittman to do two simple things: first, find an elegant woman named Millie Carter, whom he described in great detail. Second, he wanted them to relieve her of a certain object, a globe of red crystal about the size of a billiard ball.

"This Millie bitch is the one who wanted to be your walking, talking good-luck charm, am I right?" asked Benoit.

"That's right," Rex confirmed. "She's says she's new in town, which may be true, because I can't find her name in any of the local phone books."

"And may I ask what's the significance of this ball of red crystal?"

Rex started to answer the question, but held back. How would it sound, he wondered, confessing to these guys that he believed in magic? Two nights ago at the Fanshawe, after humiliating him with his demand for payment within an hour, Lewis Kindred had pulled the mysterious red ball out of his pocket, tossed it several times in the air, and flipped it to Millie. *"I'd say your good-luck charm performed admirably,"* she'd replied, gazing at Lewis with her witchy eyes. Lewis had then said something, but Rex couldn't remember what it was, didn't care. What was clear to him was that Lewis had used a charm to win the game. It was also clear that Millie had somehow been involved.

Rex could explain all this to Benoit and Spit, but he doubted that he could make them understand. *You had to be there*, he told himself. Rex had decided that he wanted the red ball for himself, and, Millie too, if he could get her. It only seemed fair, after what he'd suffered.

"Just get the crystal for me," he replied. "If Millie won't give it to you, I'll approach her myself, assuming you can locate her for me. One way or another I want to get my hands on the thing, the sooner the better."

"You've got it bad for this bitch, don't you, Rex?" Benoit chuckled, grinning. "Which do want worse, the bitch or the crystal ball?"

Rex didn't dignify the question with a response.

Eighteen

i

IN THE DAYS following the poker rematch at the Hotel Fanshawe, Josh Nickerson buried himself in schoolwork and extracurricular activities. He spent at least four hours every weeknight poring over books or doing homework assignments on his computer. He put in extra hours at the editor's desk of his high-school newspaper. He even filled out his college application forms and gave his room a thorough cleaning, much to his mother's happy surprise. On Saturday evening he took his girlfriend, Laurel, to see *Sneakers* (starring Robert Redford) and afterward treated her to a pizza. On Sunday he acquiesced to an afternoon with his father and sister at the Oregon Museum of Science and Industry on the east shore of the Willamette, the first such "custody visit" he'd allowed in several years.

On Thursday morning, October 1, a full ten days after the rematch, he woke up feeling guilty for not having contacted either Lewis Kindred or Nicole Tran in all that time. He scolded himself for not keeping the promise he'd made to Lewis: "*Whatever happens, I'm going to be here for you. . . .*"

Josh remembered, too, that Nicole's father had begun behaving strangely again, coming and going during all hours of the night, causing pain and worry for Nicole and her mother. Josh felt as if he'd neglected Nicole as well as Lewis in his effort to crowd out the memories of Millie Carter and her orb of red crystal. Equally troubling was the fact that neither Lewis nor Nicole had contacted *him*.

He vowed to set things right, starting today. Starting right now.

He clomped down the rear stairs of Sloan House and entered the dusky passage to Lewis Kindred's apartment. Though rain had fallen throughout most of the night, the morning had dawned with patches of blue. A beam of cold sunlight slanted through the cut-glass door in the foyer.

Accustomed as he was to barging right in, Josh tried the doorknob and found it locked, then remembered that Lewis had gotten jumpy and had started locking the door after Rex Caswell's no-necks attacked him and Dewey in Old Town. Lewis had given him a key, but Josh had left it in his room this morning, having forgotten that he would need it. When he raised a fist to knock, someone jerked the door open so quickly that air rushed past him into the opening.

Millie Carter stepped around the edge of the door and presented herself, having known somehow that he was about to knock. The blood drained from Josh's face as his eyes took her in. She wore a long robe of hunter-green velvet, with one bare thigh poking through the folds. Her blue eye caught the color of the robe and shone almost green, while her brown eye gleamed with a reddish cast. Her teeth were as white as ever.

"Josh, it's so nice to see you. Lewis and I were just talking about you."

"I—uh—is Lewis here?"

"Yes, of course, but I'm afraid he's indisposed at the moment. Why don't you come back this afternoon after school? You'll be going to school today, won't you?"

Josh's stomach tried to crawl up through his throat. *Indisposed?* What the hell was that supposed to mean? All the fears he'd tried so hard to suppress for the last ten days broke out of their cages and fluttered through his mind like panicky bats. "Uh—yeah. Right." He gulped. "I'll come back later." He spun from the door and plunged toward the sunlight in the foyer of Sloan House, needing that sunlight as much as he'd ever needed anything in his life.

ii

"I talked to Greg on the phone last night," Kendra said as Josh swung the old Escort out of the parking lot of Gavin Dell School. Kendra called their father by his first name as she called their mother by hers, which Josh knew made her feel *very* grown up. "He thought it was really cool that you spent the day with us last Sunday. I told him I thought you had an excellent time at the museum."

Josh joined the queue of cars waiting to turn onto Barnes Road, which would take them on a circuitous route through wooded hills back to downtown Portland. The sun had managed to poke through a layer of pewter-colored clouds. "I'm glad he thought it was cool. I just hope he doesn't expect these little outings to become a habit."

"Isn't it about time you stopped hating him so much? I mean, we're not little kids anymore, and he *is* our dad. And he's paying our way through the most expensive private school in the state. It seems to me that it wouldn't kill you to show a little gratitude."

Josh didn't want to talk about his insurance-executive father. He was intensely worried about Lewis at the moment. All day his brain had hatched theories to explain why Millie had been in Lewis's apartment this morning, undressed and looking oh-so-domestic. None of the theories were comforting.

Upon arriving at Sloan House, Josh pulled into the front drive and let his sister out at the main entrance. Then he drove down the block to Nicole Tran's house, parked at the curb, and walked up to the front door of the dignified old Queen Anne.

He rang the doorbell. Nicole answered after what seemed a long time, and Josh's heart sped up when he saw her. She was lithe in white denims and a bulky red sweater, her hair resting in graceful swoops on her shoulders. Though she smiled when she saw him, he read hurt and tension in her face.

"Nickster, I'm glad you're here," she said, pulling the door wide. "You're probably pissed I haven't called you, huh? It's my dad. He came home in the wee hours a couple of weeks ago, so sick he could hardly stand up. My mom and I managed to get him upstairs to bed, but he's been flat on his back ever since."

"He's been in bed for two weeks?"

"Maybe not that long—I don't know. I've lost all track of

time. Until a few days ago he'd hardly been able to keep anything down. Even now he can't handle anything stronger than apple juice and a little fruit.''

She led him through a paneled hallway into the kitchen.

''What does the doctor say?'' Josh asked.

''He won't let us call a doctor, not even the Chinese acupuncturist he normally goes to over in Vancouver. My mother won't leave his side, so I've been cooking their meals and taking them upstairs on a tray. My schoolwork's in the toilet, as you can probably imagine.''

''Where's your mother now?''

''Up there with him. Where else?''

''Who's running the janitorial company?''

''The foremen, I guess. They've been calling at least six times a day, needing decisions on one thing or another, but Dad won't take their calls. I don't know how much longer things can go on like this.''

''Nicki, you've *got* to call a doctor. Anyone who's so sick he can't get out of bed for two weeks needs professional help. Apple juice and fruit aren't going to do the job, okay?''

''I can't disobey him, Nickster. He's my father.''

''But the guy can't be in his right mind. He needs someone to do his thinking for him. Otherwise he could die, Nicki.''

''Yes, I *know* that.'' She twisted away from him and sat down on a tall stool next to an island counter in the kitchen. ''Nickster, I need to say something.''

Josh took the stool next to her. ''Say it. I'll shut up and listen.''

''I can't do what my father has forbidden, not even when I know I should. That's not my way. I'm not like a lot of Asian kids who think it's cool to trash everything their parents stand for. If my dad tells me not to call a doctor, I can't call one.''

''Any idea what made him sick?''

''There *is* something,'' she answered. ''He has a weird burn right in the middle of his forehead. It eventually scabbed over, and it looks almost healed now. He had it when he stumbled in that night.''

"What kind of burn?"

"I don't know. How many kinds of burns can there be? I asked him how he'd gotten it, but he won't tell me anything." She caught Josh's hand. "Nickster, he seems scared of something. I don't know what it is, because he won't talk about it. Now I'm scared, too."

"Hey, it's okay. I'm going to be here for you."

Nicole let go of his hand and slid off the stool. "Come on. There's something I want you to see."

She led him out of the kitchen and up the rear stairs of the house. When they came to the second-floor landing, she pressed her finger to his lips, telling him to be quiet, then signaled him to follow. They proceeded to a heavy door of dark-stained oak, which Nicole opened with a key that she took from a pocket. They slipped inside, and she eased the door closed and locked it behind them.

The grayness of the afternoon diffused through a pair of shuttered windows at the far end of the room, providing barely enough light to make out the furnishings. An ornate wooden desk presided at the center of the room. Behind it sat a rattan chair with a flared back. Bookshelves lined the walls, crammed with volumes that appeared both old and new, hardbound and paperback, thick and thin. At one end was an alcove with a low altar, upon which sat a jade-colored Buddha, rotund and smiling. Flanking the Buddha were framed photographs of people who Josh supposed were ancestors of the Trans. Here and there lay groupings of small tables and cabinets that held clutters of carved Asian gods, ceremonial fans and candle-holders, brightly colored lamps and lanterns. Among them were statues of Jesus and the Virgin, both of which seemed out of place.

"What is this place—an Asian cultural exhibit?" Josh whispered.

"It's my dad's study." Nicole tugged him toward a table, where sat a stoutly woven wicker basket. She opened the basket and carefully took out a small lacquered box with a hinged lid. "I'm not sure what this is. Maybe a jewelry box or something. My mother has one similar to it, but she keeps old snapshots of her family in it, not jewelry. I think they're fairly common in Asia.''

Some meticulous Vietnamese artist had painted miniature portraits of notable personages on the lid, some of whom Josh recognized. Among them were Jesus, Shakespeare, and Sun Yat-sen. Josh was certain that another face belonged to Victor Hugo, of all people, right next to an Oriental gentleman that he was willing to bet was either Lao-tse or Confucius. On the sides of the box were mystical scenes in which monkeys featured prominently.

"Strange mix of people," Josh observed, studying the portraits. "I didn't know that the Vietnamese were into Shakespeare and Hugo.''

"The paintings probably have some religious significance. Cao Dai, I think. All these people—Christ, Shakespeare, Sun Yat-sen, and all the rest—are Cao Dai gods. The priests contact them in séances and ask for their wisdom about how to live their lives. My mother once explained it all to me. She had an uncle who became a Cao Dai priest. Big scandal in a Buddhist family.''

Nicole opened the lid, and Josh flinched. Inside was a small marble of bright red glass, about the size of those that American kids used to play with. Unlike Millie Carter's much-larger orb, the marble appeared lifeless. "Remember when I told you about the sound I've sometimes heard at night after Dad comes home and locks himself in here—the thumping sound?''

Josh nodded. He recalled her saying that the thumping was rapid and prolonged, almost machinelike.

Nicole closed the lid of the box and shook it back and forth several times so that the marble thrummed against the lacquered sides of the box. "That's the sound," she said, "except when I've heard it before, it's been much louder and faster.''

Josh took the box from her and shook it himself several times, taking care not to do it too loudly. "You're sure about this?''

"I've never been more sure of anything in my life. The

lacquer gives it a tone that's very distinctive, and I'd know it anywhere. I just can't figure out how he makes it happen."

"Didn't you say that he moans or chants when the sound starts?"

"Right, but it's always been in Vietnamese, so I can't understand what he's saying. Sometimes he sounds downright terrified. Hearing him makes the hair stand up on my neck."

When Josh peeked into the wicker basket from which Nicole had taken the lacquered box, the hair stood up on *his* neck. Resting on the bottom in wads of insulating tissue was a semi-automatic pistol, its grips made of pearl-colored plastic. He brought it out, an ugly thing that looked bluntly lethal. He examined it carefully, squinting.

"Chinese characters etched on the barrel," he said, turning it over. The thing was heavy. "Christ, it's loaded, Nicki."

Lewis Kindred had taught him how to handle the old service .45 that he kept in the drawer next to his bed, and this pistol was of similar design. Josh discharged the ammo clip from the handle, then pulled the slide back, ejecting a bright brass cartridge from the chamber. The cartridge skittered across the Oriental carpet, and the slide stayed back, locked in the open position. The gun was harmless now. Josh spotted Western printing near the trigger guard, and he barely made out a serial number followed by "K-54."

"I have no idea why he keeps that thing in here," whispered Nicole. "My dad's brother sent it to him after we'd moved to the States, I think. I was just a little kid. I'm glad I've never touched it—I didn't realize it was loaded. Nickster, it gives me the creeps. Put it away, okay?"

Josh was deep in thought. Hadn't Lewis shot Gamaliel with a Chinese-made K-54 pistol, one that had pearl grips? This couldn't be the same weapon. Why *should* it be, for the love of God? "Nicki, does your dad know you've been in here?"

"Are you kidding? I sneaked his keys out of his pants pockets after Mom and I put him to bed. I didn't work up the guts to let myself in here until a few days ago, and then I made

sure that both he and Mom were asleep before I did it. I hope
they're asleep now.''

"So you just started rummaging through all this stuff, is
that it?''

"More or less. I was hoping to find something that might
shed some light on what has happened to Dad, some clue about
where he's been going at night, or who he's been seeing. I
don't know exactly what I was after. This room has been a
part of my dad's life that's been a mystery to me. Once I got
in, I went through his desk, then moved on to the file cabinets.
Then I started on the trunks, and I finally got to this old
basket.''

"Find anything else of interest?''

"Not really. A lot of Vietnamese stuff, things from temples
and pagodas, even rubbings from grave markers. The desk is
full of what you'd expect—pens and pencils and stationery.
It's strange, though, that Dad would collect so much religious
junk, because he's never seemed like a religious man.''

Josh picked up the cartridge from the floor, pressed it into
the clip, and pushed the clip back into the handle of the pistol.
Then he released the slide, and it sprang forward, loading a
round into the chamber. "It's loaded now, just like it was
when I took it out of the basket. Remember that if you ever
take it out again. I'm going to put it back where it was, okay?
Then you put the box and the marble back the way they were.
Let's do it and get the hell out of here.''

iii

They sat for a long while in a chair swing on the rear porch,
saying little. A breeze whispered through the elms and maples
that shaded the Trans' backyard. Josh remembered that when
he and Nicole were in the third grade, they'd built a tree house
in the maple at the rear of the Trans' property, using lumber
that they'd pilfered from a construction site. For several years
the tree house had functioned as their refuge from hassles and

aggravations, a place where they could talk and read and bitch privately about things in general.

Josh rose from the chair swing and ambled down the steps of the porch, following a stone path that led toward the tree, which reared huge and yellow against a bleak sky. Staring into the mass of leaves, he wished that he and Nicole had a such a place today, now—a retreat where they could hide away and feel safe. But this was impossible, he knew, because the older you got, the less safe you became. And the more likely you were to die in an accident or become excruciatingly sick. Or lose someone you loved. Life followed the rules of mathematical probability, and the rules weren't pretty. If you were lucky, you got old and decrepit. There was no such thing as safety.

Josh searched in vain for some trace of the tree house, but saw not so much as a protruding rusty nail. The tree house was gone, having vanished as completely as a forgotten dream.

"My dad took it down about three years ago," said Nicole, drawing alongside him. "The planks were starting to rot, and he was afraid some little neighbor kid would climb up into it and fall through."

Josh glanced at her and smiled. She was doing it again—reading his mind, or seeming to. No one in the world knew him as well as she did. "Guess what: I came over here today to say I'm sorry for not getting in touch with you for so long. I even had my excuse ready. Want to hear it?"

"You bet I do."

"I've been trying to stay so busy that I don't have time to worry about anything, especially anything associated with Millie Carter. I've been spending every spare minute on school stuff, and I didn't come up for air until today. It occurred to me that I hadn't talked to you in a long time, or Lewis, either."

"Has it worked? Staying busy, I mean?"

"Sort of. Before leaving for school this morning, I thought I'd drop in on Lewis to say hi. Like I said, I hadn't talked to him since before I last talked to you."

"And how is he? Winning half a million dollars hasn't

turned him into a jerk, I hope.'' She managed a grin.

"Nicki, I didn't see him. I knocked on his door, but . . .''
This was hard. Josh suddenly felt like a little kid who'd lost
his best friend. ''. . . someone was there. Sh-she told me that
Lewis was indisposed.''

"No way it was Millie Carter,'' Nicole whispered. ''It
wasn't Millie Carter, was it?''

"It was.''

They stared at each other for a long time as the wind rattled
the leaves in the maple where they'd once built a tree house.

Nineteen

i

WHEN LEWIS FELT his Action Power 9000 tilt backward,
he instinctively leaned forward toward the computer screen,
but relaxed again almost immediately, knowing that he was in
capable hands. The wheelchair pulled away from the computer
desk, turned, and headed toward his bedroom.

"Hey, I've got work to do here,'' he protested, laughing.
"I'm already a week behind on that personnel manual, and
it's for one of my best clients!''

"What I have in store for you will be much more fulfilling
than any old personnel manual,'' cooed Millie Carter, maneuvering the heavy chair through the bedroom door. For some
reason she enjoyed pushing Lewis in it, though he could easily
drive himself around without help from anyone. ''Surely
you're winning enough at poker these days to justify putting
your computer into mothballs. Besides, you should be devoting

your energies to selecting your next target, because at the rate you're going, you'll soon outgrow little old Portland, Oregon, charming city though it may be.''

This was true. Lewis had played poker nearly every night since his big win against Rex Caswell, and the results had been the same, though not as spectacular. He'd played in posh downtown hotels, in the back rooms of ancient saloons in northeast Portland, and in smoky card rooms on the Washington side of the Columbia. He'd played with local high-rollers, professionals, amateurs, and well-heeled out-of-towners. He'd played anywhere he could find a game except the Hotel Fanshawe, where he could never again play cards, he knew.

With Millie at his side and the orb in his pocket, warm and throbbing, he'd been unstoppable. Millie was right: he couldn't go on winning like this much longer and expect to be allowed back in the local action. He would soon need to sally forth in search of fresh victims. Maybe north to Seattle, then up to Vancouver, BC. Or south to the San Francisco Bay, where you could always get into a rich game if you knew the right folks. Eventually, he supposed that he would hit the Mecca—Las Vegas, where he could win enough in six months to live like a smiling pig for the rest of his life.

Life had more to offer, though, than hot card games and money, even for a man with a bad arm and no legs. He'd rediscovered this with Millie. In the eleven days since she'd first shown up in his bedroom, having somehow crept in as silently as a shadow, he'd ceased to ask himself, *Why?* He'd stopped asking himself what she could possibly see in him, a ragged old Vietnam vet with a radically truncated body. He'd simply accepted her explanation about wanting a man who used his mind for something more than deciding how many six-packs to buy for the weekend or whether to bet against the Dallas Cowboys next Sunday. And she'd said something poetic about ''the tempest in his eyes,'' where his feelings spun like tornadoes—anger and love and compassion, but especially *anger*. Millie loved men who could muster righteous anger, she'd whispered one night. And Lewis's anger was the most righteous she'd ever found.

He lay on his bed now, propped on pillows, naked and unashamed of his stumps and scars. He watched her undress in the glow of the lamp on the table next to his bed. She'd gone out today as she had every day since that first night, apparently to her own place, wherever that was, and had returned wearing a long burgundy shift with a belt of finely tooled leather. The shift undulated when she moved and gave tantalizing hints of what lay beneath it. Around her neck she wore a necklace of brightly lacquered charms molded in clay—jungle animals, miniature roses, sunbursts, stars, and crescents.

The leather belt fell away. She laid aside the necklace. She pulled the dress over her head, revealing high-cut panties and a bra of matching red satin. In this light, had he not known her, Lewis wouldn't have been able to discern whether she was a lightly complected black woman or a well-tanned white woman. Not that such distinctions had ever mattered to him. What mattered was that she was a woman, and that she'd given him what he'd given up wishing for.

After tossing the dress aside, she playfully shook her dreadlocks, which jounced like ropes over her shoulders. She stared at him with her mismatched eyes, her lips parted, her broad nostrils flaring with every breath. Lewis wondered if she saw him as he actually was, or if she saw what he might have become if a mortar round hadn't taken so much of him away. Her eyes gave no clue.

She unfastened the bloodred bra, twisting slightly, giving him a quarter profile of her breasts and the curvature of her back. Suddenly the bra was gone, and Lewis thrilled again to the sight of her brown areolae, perched like dollar-sized hillocks on her breasts. Her nipples reminded him of olive pits, and he longed to take them in his mouth and suck them, lick them, and coax them to hardness. Last night she'd taken his cock in the cleavage of those breasts and squeezed it between them, heaving up and down until his orgasm thundered like a summer storm.

Her hands slid down her sides and dipped into the indentations above her hips, converging on the flat pan of her abdomen. One long finger toyed with her navel, a nodule that stood out from the surface of her skin, then slipped into the panties to the mound of black hair that grew there. Lewis's breath became short and rapid as her finger went where he desperately wanted to go, inside her. A sigh escaped her mouth as she prepared herself thus. Finally she pushed the panties below her knees and stepped out of them.

Lewis shivered with delight as she stood upright, long-limbed and dusky. Showing him every inch of herself. She planted a foot on the mattress, revealing a trace of her pink orchid. He beckoned to her, and she lowered herself onto him slowly, allowing her nipples to play in the hair of his chest. Her hips settled against him, and his good hand found her buttocks as her hands found his cock, hard as a railroad spike. Spreading her thighs wide, she took him into her a little at a time, her pelvis gyrating in lazy circles, all the while probing his tongue with her own.

ii

The orgasm was a doorway into an alternative gestalt where reality mixed with memories and dreams. As his genitals pumped life stuff into Millie, warmth spread from the center of his body to the tips of his extremities, right down to the phalanges of his hands and feet. Every fiber of nerve tingled. Every square inch of skin prickled as his consciousness expanded. Suddenly he and Millie were walking arm in arm down Montgomery Street from Gander Ridge, the evening air cooling their faces, their shoes whooshing through fallen leaves.

Thirteenth Street, a left turn, down to Jefferson.

Left again.

A short hike across the bridge that spanned I-405. Beneath them a ribbon of red taillights streamed in one direction, and a river of white headlights rushed in the other.

Down into Goose Hollow they went, laughing now and drinking in the night air. Behind them loomed the towers of downtown Portland like jeweled spikes against a purpling sky, while ahead rose the wooded hills of Washington Park, spangled with the lights of expensive homes. Lewis wondered if he'd died and gone to heaven.

They walked into a torrent of congestion. People were everywhere, young and old, bustling and jostling, getting off chartered buses, stepping out of cars and vans, bright-eyed and rosy-cheeked from the autumn chill. There wasn't a parking space to be had, but this wasn't a problem for Millie and Lewis, because they'd *walked*. They were *pedestrians*. Lewis gloried in the undeniable reality that he had legs and feet, that he was wearing tan Rockport walking shoes and white athletic socks. That he was *walking* around Goose Hollow with a gorgeous woman on his arm. His left hand was as supple and strong as his right one, and the ringing in his ears was gone. He was a whole man.

The human current flowed toward Civic Stadium, where banks of floodlights cast an aura high into the evening sky. The Reverend Billy Graham was in town, and Christians were rallying from every corner of metropolitan Portland by the scores of thousands to hear his message of hope and salvation—this despite a survey that showed Portland to be the second least-churchgoing city in America. Every few hundred feet stood someone with a pink-and-blue badge that identified him or her as a representative of the Billy Graham Crusade. This person's job was to hand out pamphlets to passersby. The pamphlets contained information on how to ensure the salvation of one's immortal soul, among other things.

Lewis accepted one of the pamphlets, which bore the headline WE'RE PRAYING FOR GREATER PORTLAND, and tossed it into the next trash bin he met. Millie laughed and asked why he hadn't at least read it.

"Because these people don't know what the soul is, much less how to save it," he answered. "I doubt that anyone does."

They walked on, giggling like a pair of high-school kids, despite Lewis's growing feeling that someone was following them. He glanced over his shoulder twice or three times but saw no one who looked mysterious or threatening.

They ate a light dinner at the Cajun Café in quaint northwest Portland. Their table was next to a window on the street, which let them watch passersby and wonder aloud whether they were poets, painters, sculptors, songwriters, pimps, or hookers. Lewis washed down his blackened redfish with two pints of Bridgeport Oktoberfest. Gazing at Millie over snifters of brandy, he remarked that her skin was the color of café au lait. She smiled and toyed with a dreadlock.

They walked back toward Gander Ridge, past Civic Stadium, where Billy Graham's sermon had just ended. The neighborhood reverberated with the strains of "Just As I Am," the reverend's trademark theme hymn, played during the "altar call" that followed every sermon. A huge choir sang the hymn over and over as Billy exhorted listeners to come down from the grandstands to the altar, where they could formalize their acceptance of Jesus by filling out forms and making appointments for follow-up counseling. Those who'd already been saved streamed out of the stadium into the streets, creating a traffic jam of biblical proportions. Lewis and Millie veered away from the stadium, and again Lewis suffered the skin-crawling sensation of being followed.

"There's nothing to be afraid of, Lewis," Millie said softly. "Relax and enjoy yourself. You were made for this."

They skirted the athletic field of Lincoln High School, and the sensation of being followed diminished as they left the bright lights behind. Lewis followed Millie's advice and gloried in the miracle of owning two legs again, of simply strolling down a sidewalk on a fall evening.

Suddenly his sphincter tightened and his throat went dry. At the intersection ahead, a cluster of senior citizens waited for the traffic light to change, all sporting pink-and-blue badges that said WE'RE PRAYING FOR GREATER PORTLAND! Prominent among them, taller by inches than all the other women and several of the men, was Lewis's aunt Juliet, her face narrow and white, her silvery hair cropped close.

When she saw him, her eyes widened stupidly and her mouth fell open. A shade of pure horror passed over her rouged cheeks as her brain processed the sight picture on the sidewalk—her nephew, the double amputee who'd rejected Christ in favor of godless humanism, standing on two legs with a woman of color holding his arm.

Amazingly, Juliet maintained her composure and walked with her friends across the street to a chartered bus that waited at the far curb with its engine idling. The bus had a huge poster of Billy Graham's face on its side. A long line of elderly Christians waited to get aboard. Juliet glanced back at Lewis several times while crossing the street, several more times once she'd gotten into line. When her eyes met his, Lewis's heart fluttered, and he heard his aunt's voice in his head, pronouncing with divine authority that every miracle has its price.

iii

Lewis awoke just after dawn and levered himself upright in bed, leaned forward on his stumps, and looked out his window. A light rain was falling through a shroud of fog that obscured the buildings and bridges of downtown Portland. Lewis edged off the mattress into his wheelchair and unplugged its batteries from the charger. He piloted the chair from the bedroom into the bathroom, where he used the handrails on the walls to position himself on the toilet in order to take his morning whiz. This done, he got back into his chair, washed his hands and face, and threw his robe over his lap to hide his stumps.

Next stop, the kitchen. He smelled coffee brewing and good things frying. Millie had risen at least an hour earlier than he, and had made breakfast, as she'd done on every other morning since coming to stay with him.

"I have a tray for you in here," she called from the studio. Lewis smiled to himself: believer in equality for women though he was, he had to admit that these southern women certainly knew how to take care of their men. He could become accustomed to this kind of treatment, if he wasn't careful.

Millie had prepared an exquisite-looking omelette for him, with bacon, toast, and a wedge of melon. She sat in the armchair next to the window, her velvet robe swept around her. Her mismatched eyes seemed almost luminous in the grayness of the morning.

"You're spoiling me," Lewis told her. "I'm starting to wonder how I ever got along without you, or if I ever could."

"You deserve some tender loving care," she answered, raising her coffee cup in salute. "I feel privileged to be the one to give it."

Lewis tackled his breakfast with gusto and savored every bite. "I'm glad my internist can't see me now," he said. "There's more cholesterol in this meal than I'm allowed for the whole month."

"Cholesterol isn't something you need to worry about anymore, Lewis. Our kind have more important things on our minds."

"Is that so?"

"Trust me, and enjoy your breakfast." She smiled angelically, set aside her tray, and got up from the armchair. She wandered toward the low bookshelves that stood against the inner wall of the studio and stooped to eye one book or another. "Tell me, did you dream again last night?" Lewis had described the dreams that attended their lovemaking.

"As a matter of fact I did dream last night. And it was great, as usual. Except—" The part about meeting his aunt Juliet came back to him, and it gave him a chill.

"Except what?"

He set down his fork, having lost his appetite. "Nothing. We'll talk about it some other time, okay?"

"Okay." She turned back to the bookshelves, and he watched her lips move as she mouthed the names of the authors. Nietzsche, Dewey, Foucault, many others, the names of the greatest thinkers in history among them. "Lewis, why does all this matter to you—this philosophy? What does it do for you?"

"It helps me decide what to believe about certain things that I think are important."

"What sort of things?"

"Oh, like what qualifies as truth and what doesn't."

"And what qualifies as good, I suppose. And evil, too."

"Those, too."

"Why are they important to you?"

"They're important to all of us, or at least they should be," he replied, carefully thinking out each word. "Knowing about these things can help us decide how to live together, what kind of institutions to build and which to get rid of. Philosophers help us decide what we want to be, it seems to me."

She smiled, her eyes glittering. "The answers you're after are really very simple, Lewis. There isn't any truth—only what people *say* is truth. And that can change on a daily basis. The same is true of good and evil."

"Well, if it isn't Thoroughly Postmodern Millie?" Lewis said sarcastically, saluting her with his coffee cup. "As long as you're handing out answers to cosmic questions, can you tell me if the soul actually exists, and if it does, what it's made of? That one has bothered me for a long time, and I'd like to get it cleared up."

"There's no need to be snide. I'm only trying to help you. You see, I, too, have spent a great deal of time and effort looking for the very answers you're looking for. Of all the philosophers I've read, the only one who came close to providing a useful answer was Schopenhauer, and I suspect he stumbled upon it without knowing why."

"*Schopenhauer?* Care to enlighten me?"

"The *will*, Lewis. Schopenhauer emphasized the *will* as the center of existence, the force behind all movement. He was right."

"Whose will?"

"Yours, mine. Ours. The only ones that count." She moved

to the opposite wall and studied the framed photographs that hung there, paying particular attention to the ones of his family. "Are these people your parents? I see a strong family resemblance."

"Yeah, I'm a chip off the old block. The one below is my brother, Ken."

"And who are these men?" Her finger touched the frame of a group picture that showed Lewis in the midst of his closest Vietnam buddies.

"The tall ugly one making the peace sign is me, believe it or not. The little blond fireplug is Danny Legler, the skinny black one is T. J. Skane, and the big black one is Jesse Burton. The guy in the cowboy hat is Scott Sanders. They were all in my platoon in Vietnam."

She backed away from the wall a step, viewing the photos from a longer perspective. "They're dead, aren't they—the men in this picture? And your parents? Your brother is dead, too, isn't he?"

Lewis bit his lower lip, surprised at the grief that stirred to life somewhere near his heart. "Yeah, they're all dead, except for Jesse and me. He's very much alive and living in Chicago. We talk on the phone a couple times a month. How did you know about the others?"

Millie turned to face him, her eyes hard. "You should get rid of these pictures, Lewis. The dead aren't of any use to anyone, and it's not healthy for our kind to dwell on them." She snatched the three photographs off the wall, leaving behind three ghostly rectangles where the paint had faded around the frames. "Life is for the living, and you would do well to remember that." She strode into the kitchen, apparently meaning to dispose of the photographs.

"Wait just a damn minute!" shouted Lewis, chasing her in his wheelchair. "I care about those pictures! I care about those *people*! You don't have any right to—"

"I'm only doing what's best for you. I'm trying to give you the benefit of my own experience. The dead should be left alone, avoided. You'll understand this someday." She tossed the pictures into the basket, and Lewis heard a shattering of glass.

"You bitch! Those pictures mean something to me! You can't just throw away the memories of people you love. Who the hell do you think you are?"

"Lewis, listen. It's time for me to leave you now. I've done all for you that I can, and you've got to do the rest on your own. Don't worry, because it will come naturally. I doubt that you could stop it if you tried. All you need to do is relax and let it happen."

"Leave me? I don't understand. Are you saying it's over between us?"

"I'll see you from time to time, of course, and we'll share our experiences and memories like two old friends . . ." Her face darkened with what Lewis took to be regret. She lowered her eyes. ". . . but I can't say any more right now. It would only confuse you. You're confused enough as it is, I can see." She bent down to him and kissed him, then strode from the kitchen down the hall to the bedroom.

Lewis motored after her, pleading with her to tell him why she must go. And what had she meant, he demanded, about having done all for him that she could, and that now he must do the rest? The rest of *what*?

She halted at the front door of the apartment, having dressed in her burgundy shift and a white raincoat, an overnight bag in her hand. "Lewis, you asked me whether the soul is a real thing. I can tell you that it is. It's real, and it's made of energy—nothing less, nothing more. I suspect that the real question on your mind is whether the soul survives the death of the body, so I'll answer that for you, as well. Yes, Lewis, the soul survives. It's made of energy, and it survives. Good-bye."

With that she pulled the door open and went away.

Twenty

"GOD, AM I glad it's Friday, or what?" exclaimed Kendra Nickerson as she climbed into the passenger seat of her brother's Escort. "After the week I've had, I *need* this weekend in a major way. I've had no social life at all since school started, and all my teachers are total homework freaks."

Josh wheeled out of the tenants' lot and turned onto Gander Circle as a KINK newscaster wrapped up a story about a nighttime curfew for juveniles that the Portland police had announced to curb gang violence. Josh was about to gripe that the Crips and Bloods were ruining the lives of everybody under twenty-one when he caught sight of Millie Carter walking along the sidewalk about half a block ahead, her white raincoat visible against the gray morning. He slammed on the brakes.

"For God's sake, Joshua, what're you *doing*?" demanded Kendra. "Are you trying to kill us both? Why are we stopping, anyway? We're going to be late for—"

"Shut up, Kendra." His tone was steel cold, and Kendra shut up. Josh watched Millie Carter walk briskly down Gander Ridge, her dreadlocks swinging with every stride, until she arrived at her black Jaguar, which was parked on the street near the base of the hill. From this distance Josh could barely see her, for the fog now roiled like smoke among the houses of Gander Ridge.

"Joshua, who's that woman? Do you know her? Why are you behaving—"

"I said shut *up*!"

The Jag's taillights switched on, and the sleek car glided away from the curb. Josh turned off his headlights. With the fog as thick as it was, he figured that he could follow Millie without her knowing it.

ii

The house was a Mediterranean-style villa that stood behind
a phalanx of hemlocks and cedars on a hillside in northwest
Portland. The stucco had crumbled away here and there, exposing dirty bricks. The eight-foot stucco wall that surrounded
the property appeared similarly neglected.

"Well, whoever she is, she must be rich," Kendra declared
sourly as Josh halted the Escort near the entrance gate. A moment earlier the barred gate had parted to admit the Jaguar and
had closed behind it, apparently remote-controlled. "Can we
go to school now? We can still get there before second period
if we cruise. I don't mind telling you, Joshua, that I'm not
exactly ecstatic about being taken on a wild-goose chase."

Josh ignored her and got out of the car. He leaned around
the wall and peeked through the bars. The Jag sat in the drive,
looking starkly out of place in the seedy, overgrown surround-
ings. The house had been grand in its day, but Josh could see
that it had fallen on hard times. Mounds of needles and leaves
covered the grounds, broken here and there by colonies of
weeds. Ivy grew in a ragged riot over the front entrance, completely covering the doors of the four-car garage, meaning that
its doors hadn't been raised in years. The windows of the
house were dark. The place looked deserted.

Josh got back in the car and drove past the gate, following
the wooded lane as it curved around the hillside. Occasionally
the foliage broke to afford a vista of the valley below. He
stopped the car at a point where the lane switched back around
the hill in its descent, got out, and gazed upward through a
soft rain. Above him, besieged by ivy and holly near the crest
of the hill, was the stucco wall that surrounded Millie Carter's
crumbling villa.

If someone wanted to enter the property unseen, he said to
himself, he could do it here.

iii

The silence in the aftermath of Millie's departure was deaf-
ening. It lay on Lewis Kindred's heart like a stone, almost as

heavily as the loneliness. The ringing in his ears had grown so loud that at first he didn't hear the doorbell, and when he finally did hear it, he decided not to answer. But the caller persisted, and he gave in.

He was unprepared to see his aunt Juliet on the other side of the door, angular and tall, her face anemic except for patches of rouge on her cheeks. They stared at each other wordlessly until Lewis nudged his wheelchair into reverse and waved her in. Juliet sidled past him into the living room and sat on the edge of the sofa, stiff-backed.

"Can I get you anything?" Lewis asked, endeavoring to be civil. He felt inclined to patch things up with her. She was, after all, his only living relative.

"I attended the Billy Graham Crusade last night," she said in a voice that crinkled like tissue. "It's something I've been looking forward to for months. Our church chartered a bus, and we went as a group."

"It must've been nice for you. You're lucky it didn't rain."

"It didn't rain because many of us prayed that it wouldn't."

"Ah. The power of prayer."

"I *saw* you. You were with some *Negro* woman, and she was fawning all over you. Right there on the sidewalk outside the stadium."

Lewis gripped the arm of his chair to keep from shaking. "You're mistaken, Juliet. I didn't go out last night."

"Don't lie to me! I saw you, and you saw me!" Without warning, she pulled his bathrobe open and gasped when she saw the gnarls of truncated flesh and bone.

"J-Juliet, please," Lewis protested, pushing the robe back into place, his face warming. "I don't know what you think you saw last night, but . . ." But what? He *had* met his aunt last night, except the meeting had occurred in a dream—a vivid, fully textured dream, to be sure, but a dream nonetheless.

"How did you do it?" she demanded, thrusting out her chin. "Have you gotten artificial limbs without telling me? Is that what you've done, Lewis—gone up to the veterans' hospital and gotten yourself fitted with wooden legs?''

"You know that I can't use prosthetics. The muscles in my back were too cut up by shrapnel. I would never be able to maintain my balance.''

"Then how? How could you have been *walking*?''

Lewis stared stupidly at her, his brain reeling. If she'd actually seen him last night in Goose Hollow with Millie, then he hadn't been dreaming at all. And this meant . . .

"Lewis, you know I believe in miracles. I've prayed for miracles all my life, and I've seen them happen more times than I can count. I've seen people healed of addictions and afflictions of all kinds. I've seen others turn their lives around with the Lord's help and become living, breathing witnesses for Him. And when you think about it, Lewis, the birth of every child is one of the Lord's greatest miracles, that is, if some Satanist abortionist doesn't get his hands on the mother before she can deliver. So when I saw you last night, I didn't think for even one moment that I was hallucinating, because I've never doubted that the Lord could give you back your legs in the twinkling of an eye, if He wanted to. After all, He healed a paralyzed man in Capernaum—told him to take up his bed and walk, and the man did just that. And if He was able to create the entire universe in six days, then He'd certainly have no trouble making you a whole man again. What I saw last night, though . . .'' Her breath went out of her. She paused to take another, slow and deep. "What I saw last night wasn't *God's* work.''

Lewis stared at his ficus tree. Rain tapped diffidently against the window, casting squiggly shadows on the leaves. "What you're saying is crazy, Juliet. You're getting yourself all worked up over a mistake. I tell you, I didn't go out last night.''

"Lewis, listen to me. Not every miracle comes from heaven. Some come from hell. God doesn't work a miracle and then take it back. Last night you had legs, and your left arm looked perfectly normal. Today you have no legs, and your arm appears as full of scars and as stiff as it's ever been. Do you know what this means, Lewis? It means that the devil has touched you. The devil has given you a miracle and taken it back again for a reason that I don't even care to know. And he won't be satisfied until he's taken your soul!''

''Stop it.'' He glared at her, but his anger quickly faded. For a crazy moment he actually envied Juliet's ability to attribute every problem to the ''devil,'' and to trust wholly in the opposite absolute, the ''Lord,'' to provide the solution. He knew that she really did love him, and tried to imagine how it must terrify her to see evidence of Satan's touch on the body of her nephew, the only family she had left. ''I'm sorry. I didn't mean to scream at you.''

''Lewis, give yourself to Jesus before it's too late. Pray with me now, and we'll ask the Holy Spirit to minister unto you.''

''Juliet, please. You know I can't do that.''

''But you *can* do it. In Matthew eleven, twenty-eight, the Lord says, 'Come unto me, all ye that labour and are heavy laden, and I will give you rest.' All you have to do is say, 'Lord, here I am. Take my sin away and make me Yours.' If you pray that simple prayer, you're guaranteed a life that won't end, not even when you die.''

''Juliet, this isn't a problem that can be solved by prayer.''

''But prayer can solve *any* problem. If you're worried about that Negro woman, don't be. Because even if she's Satan's vessel, she can't stand up against the power of prayer. She might be a demon sent from hell, but she's no match for the Lord. Scripture says, 'Thou believest that there is one God . . . the devils also believe, and tremble.' That's the secret, Lewis—*believe!* If you believe, the devils will tremble.''

''She's not Satan's vessel, damn it, and she's not a demon sent from hell! How can you judge her when you haven't met her?''

''I'm sorry. I shouldn't've jumped to conclusions. I'm just trying to—''

''I know what you're trying to do, and I appreciate your concern. It's been a long time since I've told you how grateful I am for all you've done for me, letting me live here, installing all the special equipment in this apartment. Since Mom died, you've looked out for me, and I've often taken it for granted. I haven't been the best nephew, Juliet.'' He moved the chair close to her and reached for her hand, but she drew back as if he carried diabolical contagion. ''I hope that someday you and I can get closer, but right now—'' He massaged his brow, rubbed his eyes. ''Right now I'm going through a bad time. I'm pretty sure I can handle it myself, but I need to be alone. I hope you'll understand if I ask you to leave.''

Juliet's gray face became even grayer, except for the patches of rouge. Something in her eyes told Lewis that she verged on giving up all hope for him. ''I understand.'' She stood up, squared her shoulders. ''I hope you'll call me when you've finally become desperate enough, Lewis. And remember that little prayer. The Lord is as close as that little prayer, if you need Him.''

iv

Mason Benoit and Spit Pittman arrived at Rex Caswell's floating house shortly before noon. After Silhouette had given them each a screwdriver, Rex asked Benoit what they'd found out about Millie Carter.

''She's moved in with your old homey, Lewis Kindred,'' answered Benoit.

''*What?* You've got to be shitting me!''

''Sorry, my man. I'm just telling you what we found out, that's all.''

Rex strode to a panoramic window that fronted the river and stared a full minute at the far shore. ''What does she see in him? The son-of-a-bitch doesn't even have any legs! He doesn't even have two good hands! Are you absolutely positively fucking sure about this? She's actually *living* with him?''

''It certainly looks that way. We staked out Kindred's place three nights in a row—cold nights, I might add—sitting in the car across the street from his apartment, waiting for her to come out. But she never came out until late the next morning. A couple of times she went grocery shopping. Couple of other times she went out to get some clothes.''

"So how do you know what they were doing in there?"

"Rex, get real. Those two are an item. Kindred never goes anywhere without her. They've shown up together at card games all over town, and Kindred has been winning big time. They arrive together, they leave together, they go back to Kindred's apartment. The babe doesn't come out till the next morning. I'm sorry, but I can't believe that they're spending all that time playing Mr. Potato Head.''

Rex swallowed most of his screwdriver in one gulp and scowled. "You say he's been winning big time?"

"That's what we hear. Plays almost every night—east side, west side, Vancouver. He's been so hot that people don't want to get into games with him anymore. Hey, I'm surprised you haven't heard about this. You're supposed to be tuned into the poker crowd, aren't you?"

"I've been out of circulation for the last couple of weeks."

"Understandable. If Kindred had done to me what he did to you, I'd be a little embarrassed to show my face."

Rex ground his teeth. "What about the crystal? Did you get it?"

"No," answered Benoit, trading glances with Spit.

"Why the hell not?"

"Rex, think about it. Why would the bitch give it to us, anyway? We're a couple of perfect strangers to her. Besides, you said you'd approach her yourself, if we located her. Well, we located her. You can find her any evening at Lewis Kindred's apartment. I'd advise calling first."

"You're right, I did say I'd approach her myself. Maybe that's exactly what I should do. I should've known better than to give the job to you jerks."

"Rex, you gotta chill, man," Benoit whined. "We did what you asked us to do, right? We found the bitch. If there's something else we can do for you—something within the realm of feasibility, that is—all you've got to do is say it. We work for you and with you, okay?''

Rex closed his eyes. Countless times Lewis Kindred had condescended to him, humiliated him with snide little comments, treated him like shit. In his mind he saw the irksome smirk that Kindred wore when he played poker, the one that widened whenever he scooped Rex's money from the table. Rex knew its meaning: *I've got no legs, and I'm still more man than you are*. Now Lewis had taken Millie Carter from him.

"I want to hurt this guy," Rex declared. "I want it badly, you understand?"

Spit and Benoit nodded.

"The problem is, I can't do it directly or the cops will be all over me."

"You've got that right," agreed Benoit. "It's only been— what?—eleven days since Kindred wiped you out at the Fanshawe. That's not long enough."

"I've got to be indirect about it. The thing to do is to put the hurt on somebody he's close to, somebody who . . ." Rex's face brightened as his mind worked. He sat down in his favorite chair and tilted it back so he could gaze at the ceiling. "I think I've got it. How's your wrist, Mase? All healed?"

"It feels fine, Rex."

"And how about your head, Spit? Are you fully recovered from getting worked over by that old dirtball in Old Town?"

"I've still got some bruises," answered Spit, "but my brain's back to normal, I'm happy to say."

"Good. I'll tell you gentlemen what I want you to do. I want you to put the major hurt on that old derelict friend of Kindred's, but this time use your heads. Do some planning, and make fucking sure that nobody but nobody can get back to me with it."

"Are you serious about this?" asked Benoit.

"Damn right, I'm serious. Send him up in flames. I want you to hurt him so badly that Lewis Kindred will never sleep again."

"We hear you, Rex," said Spit. "When we're done with him, he'll look like he belongs under the sneeze guard at Tony Roma's."

"You've never told us to do anything like this before," said Benoit. "We'll need to bring in some types from out of town, since Spit and I have a history with the guy. The cops are likely to check us out if something ugly happens to him. I know people in L.A. who'll be glad to help, but it'll cost you some greenies. Are you sure this is what you want?"

"It's what I want," Rex replied. He knew that his hatred had blinded him, but he didn't care. Sometimes a man needs to act on his feelings, or he might tie himself in knots and strangle himself. "If you don't have the stones for it, I'll get someone who does."

"We've got the stones for it. I just want to make sure you know what you're asking."

"Just fucking *do* it!"

Benoit stood up and buttoned his jacket around him. "Consider it done, Rex. You're the man. And what the man wants, he gets."

V

Lewis called Tommy Iadanza shortly after one in the afternoon and asked for a ride downtown. Tommy asked how the hell Lewis was. The Fanshawe crowd had missed him at last Monday night's game, and they'd started to worry. Lewis promised to fill him in later about everything that had happened since the big rematch with Rex Caswell, and apologized for staying out of touch for so long. He owed his friends better than this, he confessed. Tommy said he would pick him up in an hour.

Lewis bathed, shaved, and made himself as presentable as he could. He put on a newly laundered button-down sport shirt, a crewneck sweater, and a fresh pair of khaki slacks, the cuffs of which he tucked neatly under his stumps. Then he went to the computer desk in his study and took out the orb, the only thing that Millie had left behind.

The sight of it, the feel of it against his palm, roused a strange sense of unreality. He'd read enough psychology over the years to know the symptoms of schizophrenia. A schizophrenic loses touch with the world and manufactures his own reality, one that seems totally authentic to him. The manufactured reality may be so terrifying that it radically disrupts his life. Lewis knew that he could not possibly have grown legs and walked around Goose Hollow, but a huge part of his mind insisted otherwise. And this morning his sick mind told him that Aunt Juliet had seen him in the body of a whole man, something he knew wasn't possible. The only explanation that made any sense to him was schizophrenia.

He wondered how much time he had left before the disease progressed to the drooling, blithering stage, how long before it reduced him to cowering in closets to escape the relentless biting of the butterfly lizards. Or loitering on street corners, picking invisible french fries out of the air. It was only a matter of time, he concluded, before his worst nightmares became as real to him as the air he breathed, which meant that he needed to make good use of the time he had left.

vi

The waiting room of the Veterans In Progress Center was standing-room-only, but Lewis and Tommy didn't need to wait long. Audra Fallon soon poked her head through the inner door and ushered them into her office. She gave Lewis a huge hug and asked where the hell he'd been for the past two weeks. Good counselors were scarce as hen's teeth, especially those with Lewis's background. And why hadn't he returned her calls? Didn't he listen to his answering machine anymore?

"Audra, I'm sorry," he said, opening the old Samsonite briefcase he'd brought along. "I should've called. These last few weeks have been tough ones—I won't bore you with the gory details.''

"Oh, but I *love* gory details.''

"Maybe some other time.'' He took a letter-size manila envelope from the briefcase and handed it to her, causing her broad brow to wrinkle. "I want the Center to have this,'' he said. "I know that cash contributions are a little awkward, but don't worry—it's not ill-gotten.''

"Don't believe him,'' quipped Tommy Iadanza. "It's the proceeds from a string of whorehouses he owns throughout the Pacific Rim.''

Audra opened the bulging envelope and gasped. She withdrew several packets of hundred-dollar bills and turned them slowly. "Lewis, there's got to be ten, fifteen thousand dollars here.''

"Twenty thousand on the nose. I've had a lucky streak in poker lately. I figured you can make better use of the money than I can.''

"I—I don't know what to say. The money couldn't come at a better time. But I've got to wonder whether—''

"Audra, don't even think of trying to talk me out of this. It's what I want to do. It's what I *need* to do.''

"Whatever you say, Lewis. I just want you to know that what you've given in the past—your time, your skills, your caring—these are all priceless. The money's nice, yeah, but it's no substitute for *you*.''

Lewis dropped his stare to his stumps. "That's something else I need to talk to you about, Audra. I won't be doing any more counseling, I'm afraid. I'm not the kind of person who should be telling someone else how to get his life together. . . .''

vii

They found Dewey just where Audra Fallon had said he would be, at the south end of Tom McCall Park, his wheelchair

braced against the rail so that he could stare at the river, which
lapped at the cement wall twenty feet below. Lewis's heart fell
when he saw him. Dewey looked achingly alone. Passersby
gave him hardly a glance as they strode past on their good
legs or glided by on their costly mountain bikes. Only the
pigeons and gulls paid him any heed, for he'd shared with
them whatever he'd had for lunch—a sandwich from one of
the greasy spoons in Old Town, judging from the wadded paper sack in his lap. Or maybe a day-old croissant handed out
by a kindly baker. The pigeons waddled around Dewey's chair,
patrolling for missed crumbs.

Dewey straightened up when he heard the whisper of Lewis's Action Power 9000. "I'd know the sound of that contraption anywhere," he said, offering his hand. Tommy shook it,
and then Lewis. Dewey's handshake was uncharacteristically
weak.

"How's it going?" Lewis asked, trying to sound cheerful.
"You've been behaving yourself, I trust."

"Soldiering on, same as you." The whites of his eyes had
yellowed, and he slumped in his chair like an old man.

Lewis apologized for having missed his usual Wednesday
rendezvous, but Dewey only looked away. "I've got
something for you," Lewis said, opening his briefcase. "You
won't want to take it, I know, but I'm going to give it to you
anyway." He tossed a bulging manila envelope into Dewey's
lap.

"What've you got that I could possibly want?" Dewey tore
at the end of the envelope with stiff fingers. He gaped at the
contents of the envelope, his whiskered jaw falling open.

"Looks like your scrounging days are over, sarge." Tommy
laughed. "There's twenty thousand bucks there. Enough to
take care of you for a long, long time, if you handle it right."

Dewey scowled at the money and folded the envelope
closed. "Where'd it come from?"

"I've been on a lucky streak in poker. Bunch of high rollers
from out of town thought they could bluff me off a double-
ended straight."

"Then it's your money, not mine." Dewey tried to hand it back.

"Negative. I want you to have it. Before you get all pissed off and insulted, let me tell you what I propose. I'll give the money to Tommy here, and he'll take care of it for you. No sense carrying this kind of scratch on the street, right? You'd last about ten minutes in Old Town before some *chiva* dealer put a blade in your ribs. Anytime you need some of it, go to Tommy at the Hotel Fanshawe down on Third and Salmon, and he'll give you as much as you want. He'll act as your bank."

"Except I don't pay interest," Tommy put in, winking. "I'll put it in a real bank, if you want."

"And that's all there is to it? No catches?"

"No catches," Lewis confirmed. "But I'm going to suggest something to you, Dewey. Let Tommy invest the money for you. Let him help you find a place to live—"

"I've already got a damn place to live."

"I'm talking about a roof. I'm talking about three squares a day and some help for your pain. You need to get in out of the cold, and you need to quit pounding down a fifth of bourbon a day."

"Anything else I need to do? Maybe I need to quit cussin' and start washin' behind my ears? Maybe I need to trim my fuckin' toenails every week?"

"Don't get mad. I've already told you there're no catches. The money's yours. If you want to spend the rest of your life sleeping under the Burnside Bridge and eating out of garbage cans, then have at it. I'm only trying to give you a shot at something better, that's all."

Dewey stared at the river, saying nothing. A hundred feet away, a brightly painted stern-wheeler insinuated itself next to the pier, looking like an artifact of the last century. A crowd of dark-suited executives chatted and munched lobster salad inside its glass-paneled salon.

At length Dewey opened the envelope and fished out a hundred-dollar bill, which he handed to Lewis. "I'll take the

money under one condition. You bring me another cat, one
who looks like Big Sister. That C-note ought to cover it. Don't
worry about tryin' to find one as smart as Big Sister was, or
as nice looking, either. All she needs is to be warm. The nights
are starting to get cold around here.'' Then he folded shut the
manila envelope and handed it to Tommy.

viii

After watching Dewey roll south along the river and disappear among the traffic going into and out of Old Town,
Lewis and Tommy retired to the Huntsman's Bar and Grill for
a beer. They sat quiet awhile, sipping and staring at the ancient
photos on the walls.

"Are you going to get him a cat?" asked Tommy at length.
"Our old tiger stripe is about to drop a load of kittens, and
you're welcome to one of them. Hell, you're welcome to *all*
of them."

Lewis thanked him, but declined. He planned to pick up a
cat from the Multnomah County Humane Society tomorrow
and take it to Dewey right away, one that looked as much like
Big Sister as he could find. It seemed important not to wait.

"Something's bothering me," said Tommy, scratching his
jaw. "The way you were talking to Audra and Dewey was
like you're planning to join the French Foreign Legion. That
business about not counseling vets anymore—not being the
right kind of person. What the hell was it all about? I mean,
here you are, giving away money by the truckload and acting
like you're tying up loose ends, getting ready to die—it's
enough to make your friends worry."

Lewis chuckled dryly. How do you tell a friend that you're
going off your rocker, that you've been hallucinating wildly,
and that you can't distinguish fantasy from what's real?

He hoisted his Samsonite briefcase onto the table, opened
it, and took out a final manila envelope. He tossed it across to

Tommy and grinned when he saw his friend's basset-hound eyes become round as dollars.

"What the fuck is this?"

"Twenty thousand dollars, coin of the realm."

Tommy blew out a sigh of exasperation. "Lewis, I think you're about a hundred ants short of a picnic."

"Just take the money and do something good with it. Use it toward the kids' college, if you want. Or put it into restoring the Fanshawe. Or better yet, take Carlotta to Venice like you've always wanted to do, and give her the romantic vacation she's always dreamed of. I don't care what you do with the money as long you take it."

"Lewis, this goes beyond—"

"The *hell* it does, Tommy. It doesn't go beyond all the years you've put up with me, hauled me around with my wheelchair, carried me up and down stairs, included me with your family and friends. It doesn't go beyond all the good conversation we've had, the jokes we've shared—even the shitty ones—"

"Lewis, I can't take this."

"You don't have a choice, man. The money's yours, no strings. You'd do the same for me, if I asked for it. Subject closed."

ix

Before heading back to Sloan House, they made a final side trip, this one to the Hawthorne Bridge, which was only a few blocks from the Fanshawe. Tommy walked alongside Lewis's chair in a light drizzle, asking no questions. When they arrived at the midway point, Tommy said, "If you'd wanted to go across the river, we could've taken a nice dry car."

Lewis halted and dug into his anorak for the orb, which he brought out and held a moment in his hand. Tommy exclaimed under his breath when he saw the thing. "Remember this?" Lewis asked.

Tommy nodded as an eighteen-wheeler thundered across the

bridge, flailing them with spray. Over the thunder of the truck he shouted, ''You gave it to Millie Carter on the night you clobbered Rex in the rematch. She called it a good-luck charm, as I recall.''

''If it's good luck I've been having, I hate to think of what bad luck must be like.''

''What the hell is it made of? Why does it shine like that?''

Lewis's lips tightened as he searched the far horizon. Above the vista of urban clutter hung webs of rain clouds that hid Mount Hood, which stood in the east like a sentinel. He wished he could see the volcano now, for the sight of it might have given him confidence that what he was about to do might save him. He'd once trusted Nui Ba Den, the Black Virgin of Vietnam, and she'd betrayed him. So the gods and goddesses of volcanoes owed him something, he told himself—if he could only make himself believe in them.

He reared back and flung the orb as hard as he could away from the bridge and followed it with his eyes until it disappeared many stories below.

Twenty-one

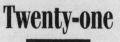

i

JOSH BEGAN ANOTHER near-sleepless night in a state of alertness for noises from the apartment below, where he feared that Millie Carter was working some kind of evil magic on his friend. Though he lay stone still and barely breathed, he heard nothing beyond the ordinary small sounds that issued from the nooks, crannies, and heating ducts of Sloan House. Finally he

got out of bed, switched on his computer, and booted the Demon Beef story he'd worked on for so many months.

Reading through the draft, he quickly concluded that this
story was no longer about Demon Beef or Ron Payne, but
about Millie Carter and her crystal orb, as well as Lewis Kindred and Josh Nickerson himself. The story read more like a
cheap horror yarn than a piece of investigative journalism.

Josh knew that this wasn't the kind of meaty, real-world
stuff that a fledgling investigative journalist should write. Because of his own direct involvement, the story lacked an ob-
jective viewpoint, which—as his teachers had reiterated
endlessly—was a critical element of good reportage. Yet he
continued to peck at the keyboard, laying down the facts as
he knew them, finding that with every keystroke his commitment to finishing the story hardened. Someone needed to tell
it through to the end, he felt. Someone needed to unravel its
mysteries and lay them bare. He resolved to be that someone,
to discover the whole truth about Millie Carter. Not only to
warn the world about her, but also to find some way of fighting
her, maybe even beating her.

He ate breakfast alone, since his sister was sleeping in after
a late date and his mother had gone to the Multnomah Athletic
Club for an early workout. Halfway through his microwaved
French toast, he decided that he needed to talk to Lewis, even
at the risk of another encounter with Millie.

He hurried out of the apartment and thumped down the rear
stairs. Reaching the first landing where the stairs curved
sharply to the right, he glanced out through the diamond-paned
window that faced the center of the city. A block away, just
visible at the end of a corridor of pines and oaks, a Tri-Met
bus had halted at the intersection of Gander Circle and Montgomery, its side panel adorned with a huge color photo of the
Trail Blazers' Clyde Drexler in midflight to a slam dunk.
Lewis Kindred had driven his Action Power 9000 onto the
power lift of the bus, and the lift was rising slowly. Josh
watched as Lewis maneuvered the wheelchair through the
door, as the door closed after him. The bus pulled away.

Resting his forehead against the windowpane, Josh blew out a sigh. Lewis was apparently functioning with some degree of normalcy, which was reason to be glad. Still, Josh was antsy as hell to talk with him. As he slowly climbed the stairs again, he mulled over an idea that had come to him again and again since he'd followed Millie to the old villa in northwest Portland. To act on it meant unconscionable risk, he knew, but *not* to act had become unthinkable.

He thumped back down the stairs and hurried out through the foyer, headed for Nicole Tran's house.

ii

He parked the Escort on the shoulder of the narrow road at the base of the hill and leaned out the window, his face turned up toward the stucco wall that curved along the crest. "That's where we'll go over it," he said to Nicole, who was crouched over to lace a hiking boot. "We'll leave the car here, where it won't make anyone suspicious."

He reached beneath the seat for his trusty Coleman flashlight, which he slid into a side pocket of his bulky flannel shirt. He checked the other pocket to ensure that he'd brought his notepad and a ballpoint. Nicole wore old jeans with holes in the knees, a dark cable-knit sweater, and a navy breaker. With her long black hair tucked under a knitted watch cap, she looked like an elfin cat burglar.

"Sure you're up for this?" he asked.

"I'm up for it only because I can't let you do it alone. But I want to go on record that I still think it's a stupid idea. And a dangerous one."

Josh grinned crookedly and put on his Twins baseball cap—backward, naturally. Persuading Nicole hadn't been easy. Josh had explained that he needed to find out who Millie Carter was. He needed to discover her background, where she'd come from, how she lived. *Know your enemy*, someone famous had once said (or had it been Lewis?). A person's household possessions said much about her, as every investigator knew. Josh needed to check out the pictures on Millie's walls, the quality of her furniture, the back issues of magazines she read, the medicines in her cabinet, and—

"And the brace of rottweilers she keeps to guard against people like you," Nicole had thrown in. "You realize that breaking and entering is a crime, and that we're close enough to eighteen to be tried as adults. We could go to prison, Nickster."

They wouldn't get caught, he'd declared simply. Yesterday's reconnaissance had told him that Millie parked her Jag in the front drive of the villa, and that the garage hadn't seen any use for years, judging from the ivy that overgrew its doors. He would check to see whether the Jag was present before deciding whether to go on in. Nicole had scoffed, but in the end she'd agreed to come along, and Josh had detected a glitter of excitement in her eyes. Like him, she'd sensed a *wrongness* about Millie Carter from that first moment when they'd encountered her in the alley in downtown Portland. And having heard all that had happened since that night, Nicole, too, felt the need to take action.

iii

Climbing the hillside to the stucco wall took longer than Josh anticipated, for yesterday's rain had slickened the ground. When they reached the top, their hiking boots were cakey with mud, their jeans soaked from slogging through wet sword ferns. They stopped to catch their breath and gaze over the valley below, where industrial northwest Portland sprawled beneath a thin haze.

The immediate neighborhood was bucolic. Shrouded in trees, upscale houses stood back from the winding lanes, their tiled and cedar-shake roofs just visible through gaps in the greenery. Early autumn had touched the deciduous foliage with bits of yellow, and though some leaves had fallen, the trees were far from bare. Mount St. Helens hunkered in the north, her blunt summit silvered with new snow. The morning sky had brightened as the cloud layer thinned.

They went over the wall with the help of a young oak tree that had grown just outside it. Josh hoisted himself into the vee from which a branch grew away from the trunk, then eased himself onto the top of the wall where a mason had mortared pieces of broken bottles and jars into the surface. He cautioned Nicole not to cut herself.

They entered what was once an Italianate garden but which decades of neglect had reduced to a hodgepodge of weeds. The ground was spongy with decaying leaves and needles. Moss grew on the aged terra-cotta statuary, and a riot of blackberries had taken over the fountain. A flagstone walkway wound from the garden toward the house, which cowered in the dusky shade of hemlocks and cedars.

A covered veranda swept across the rear of the structure, where some earlier owner or tenant had dumped old furniture and appliances. A trellis had long ago rotted away and collapsed onto a rusty refrigerator, which stood with its door open like a mute beggar.

After circumnavigating the house to ensure that the front drive was empty of Millie's Jaguar, Josh and Nicole crept into the veranda and halted next to a splintered armoire, listening hard but hearing nothing except the rustle of a breeze in the foliage and the squeak of branches against stucco. They moved to the rear door, which Josh tried and found securely locked.

"Now what?" whispered Nicole.

"We try the windows." These, too, were locked and heavily curtained.

They climbed an exterior stairway at one end of the veranda to an open second-floor deck, which was empty but for mounds of yellowed needles and moldering leaves. Glassed-in French doors fronted what appeared to be a large sitting room, though the glass was so dusty that they could hardly see through it. The French doors were locked, as were the windows that flanked them.

"I suppose we could break the glass," Josh said, glancing around in search of a suitable heavy implement.

"*No!* What if there's an alarm system? The cops would be here in a New York minute."

"I suppose you have a better idea."

"I have an idea. I'm not sure it's a better one."

She went to the far end of the deck, scissored over the railing, and edged close to the wall. Leaning away from the railing, she swung a foot onto a second-floor window casement. Stretching, she grasped the upper edge of the casement and pulled herself aboard, kneeling precariously against the windowpane on one knee. Josh held his breath, fearing that she might fall into the thicket of junipers below. But she didn't fall. She reached downward until her fingers found the edges of the windowpanes and pulled upward. The window slid open, because the owners of the house had apparently overlooked the need to lock it, considering its location. Nicole rolled through it.

Josh let out his breath. Before he could turn around, one of the French doors creaked open behind him, revealing Nicole's grinning face. "What're you waiting for? Let's get this over with. I'd just as soon not be here when Millie comes back."

The room was bare of furnishings except for a tattered sofa with knots of upholstery herniating through rips in the cushions. The floral wallpaper had faded to near colorlessness, though occasional rectangles of brightness betrayed spots where pictures had once hung. Josh and Nicole passed through into a balcony that overlooked a long interior hall, where daylight filtered in through dingy windows. A chandelier festooned with webs hung from the ceiling, its brass lanterns green with tarnish. A long Persian runner stretched beneath the balcony into the front entrance, covered with dust and grime except for a comparatively clean strip down the very middle.

"Are you sure she actually *lives* here?" whispered Nicole. "This place is the pits."

"No, I'm not sure, now that you mentioned it. All I'm sure

of is that she came here yesterday. I suppose the house could belong to someone else.''

"Oh, that's just great! You're telling me that we may have broken into a house that doesn't even *belong* to Millie Carter.'' Nicole shook her head incredulously. ''We might as well see what's downstairs, now that we're here.''

They tiptoed down a curving staircase to the main hall, cringing whenever a step squeaked. They found the dining room, which adjoined the main hall, and beyond it another room that had many built-in shelves, most sagging precariously—a library, once upon a time. At the rear was a large kitchen, where cupboard doors hung askew on their hinges and rodents had left their scat among baseball-sized dust bunnies.

"Look at this," whispered Nicole, having wandered back into the hall. She pointed to the Persian runner with its strip of comparative cleanness. ''Somebody walks down the middle of this rug on a regular basis.''

"No shit, Inspector.''

"And she turns here, before getting to the kitchen . . .'' She pointed into a short adjoining corridor, where the parquet wood flooring had a path that was similarly free of dust and grime. ''. . . and goes into that room.'' A pair of walnut doors stood shut, their brass handles gleaming in the sparse light.

"How much do you want to bet that the room is locked?'' Josh asked.

"A large pizza at Pizza Oasis says it's not. Care to do the honors?''

Josh shrugged and tried not to look scared. He walked slowly to the doors, put his hand on the cold brass, and pushed. A metallic clink stung the silence of the empty house, and the door swung inward.

"You owe me a large pizza at Pizza Oasis,'' whispered Nicole with a sly wink. ''I'll want at least six toppings, including anchovies.''

Josh stepped into a high-ceilinged room made gloomy by heavy brocaded drapes over the windows. He saw that this room was very different from the others they'd explored thus far: it appeared thoroughly lived in. To his left was a massive stone fireplace, its mantel paneled in walnut, its firebox heaped with fragments of a still-warm log. Half a dozen ornate armoires stood against the outer walls, one with its doors open, revealing a collection of women's clothing. Here and there were exquisite old chests of drawers, and in a far corner sat a lady's vanity well laden with cosmetics, lotions, and perfumes. Pieces of luggage lay open on the floor, costly-looking stuff made of good leather, lined with heavy satin. Articles of clothing lay about on padded sofas and chairs, as if their wearer had slipped out of them and simply cast them aside. A large round table stood before the fireplace, attended by an authentic-looking Tiffany floor lamp and six high-backed chairs.

"So this is where she lives," breathed Nicole. "It's a little messy, but at least it's not filthy like the rest of the house. No stereo, no TV, though. I'd go crazy."

"It doesn't make any sense. Why have a mansion if you're only going to use one room?"

"It has a temporary feeling, don't you think? Like a hotel room. It doesn't look like she's even finished unpacking."

Josh tried the light switch next to the door, and the Tiffany lamp lit up. "She apparently does some reading, and maybe some writing," he remarked, eyeing the stacks of file folders and envelopes on the table. He poked though a jumble of papers, among which were bank statements and bills for credit-card purchases. "This is Millie's place, all right. These bills came to her by name, and to this address. *Jesus*—Nicki, look at this . . . !" Millie Carter's checking-account balance at First Interstate Bank in Portland was fifty-six thousand dollars and change.

"She's definitely not hurting for money," said Nicole.

"And look at *this*—statements from mutual-fund accounts, stockbrokers. . . ."

"From all over the country. Houston, Las Vegas, New Orleans . . ."

"God, she's rich! Nicki, she's a millionaire!"

"I don't see why that comes as a surprise to you. You don't

live at this address unless you've got plenty of money.''

"But why doesn't she fix the place up? I mean, why let a mansion like this fall down around your ears if you've got the money to make it nice?''

Nicole checked out the clothes in several of the wardrobes and pronounced them on the cutting edge of fashion, then did likewise for the jewelry in the vanity. Josh pawed through one of several valises stacked on the floor.

"Here's a letter from the realtor who sold her the place,'' he announced, holding aloft a sheaf of paper. "They closed the deal early last winter. Listen to what this guy says: 'Though the villa is in some need of restoration, I can guarantee that it will satisfy your requirement for privacy.' *Some need of restoration*—can you believe it? She paid cash, almost five hundred thousand dollars. And look—the letter was sent to an address in Las Vegas, which must be where she lived before moving here.''

They went on with their separate searches for the next ten minutes, neither of them knowing exactly what to look for. Josh occasionally jotted notes in his little spiral book.

Suddenly he started to choke noisily, causing Nicole to forsake her exploration and go to him. "Nickster, are you okay? Did you get something in your throat? Can you breathe?''

He waved her off, saying that he'd merely swallowed wrong, but his face had turned horribly red. He'd opened one of the valises and had pulled out several sections of newspapers, each of which had a hole clipped in a page. "I don't believe this,'' he rasped. He coughed again, took more deep breaths. "Look at these, Nicki.''

She took the section of newspaper that he held out, but didn't see anything particularly frightening about it. "It's a newspaper that someone has clipped,'' she observed, sticking a finger through the hole in the page and wiggling it. "What's the big deal?'' Josh handed her another, and a third, and a forth, all with similar holes scissored into them. "I'm sorry,'' Nicole confessed, "I still don't see what the problem is.''

"Remember the mysterious newspaper clippings I got in the

mail over the summer? They all concerned murders that were just like Ron Payne's. The first one came in June, right after we got out of school, a piece from the *Atlanta Constitution* about a night watchmen who was so badly mutilated that the cops thought a big dog might've done it.''

He pulled a section of newspaper from the bundle that Nicole held and pointed to the heading in the top corner of the page. Sure enough, it was the *Constitution,* and the date corresponded to the clipping that Josh had received in the mail— June 19, 1992.

''I'll buy you *two* large pizzas from Pizza Oasis if the clipping I got doesn't fit this hole,'' he added. ''The next one came a month later from the *Des Moines Register,* and it was about a dentist who picked up some babe in a bar and took her to a hotel. He ended up in pieces, just like Ron Payne and the night watchman in Atlanta.'' This section, according to the heading, had come from a July issue of the *Register.* ''Then, in August, I got one from the *Burlington Free Press*, in Burlington, Vermont''—he showed her a clipped section of newspaper, pointing to the heading— ''about a sales manager of a car dealership, ripped to pieces in his hot tub. And a month later I got one from the *Sacramento Bee*''—this one corresponded to the final section that Nicole held in her hands— ''about a windsurfing instructor from Lake Tahoe, found dead in his car outside Sacramento, California, more or less in the same condition as the others.''

''What're you saying? That Millie Carter sent you the clippings? Why would she do that?''

''I don't have a clue.''

''Where were the envelopes mailed from?''

''The postmarks were from the actual cities where the murders happened, which makes me think—wait a minute! Let's do another take of her credit-card bills.''

Josh rummaged through the stacks of papers on the writing desk and pulled out billing records from MasterCard, Discover, and American Express. He ran his finger down each list, occasionally circling an entry with his pen.

"Just as I suspected. In June she bought a round-trip ticket on United Airlines to Atlanta. In July, she went to Des Moines, Iowa. I can't find an entry for Burlington, Vermont, but *here*—" He shuffled a sheet to the top and made another circle with his pen. "Here's a trip to Sacramento on Alaska Airlines. And the dates all match!" He laid the papers on the desk and stared at Nicole, his face paling. "That's three out of four, Nicki. She went to three out of the four cities where murders took place."

"Murders like Ron Payne's."

"She was physically there at three out of four, and I'd bet all my college tuition money that she went to Burlington, too, even though I can't find the record."

"She might've lost that particular bill. People lose stuff like that."

"Now the question is whether she actually *killed* those guys. You'll recall that I saw her in Ron Payne's apartment the night he got killed. It almost takes a leap of faith to think that she wasn't involved in those murders somehow, even though we can't assume she did the actual killing. But she was *there*, in each of the cities! And she was *here* in Portland when Payne got snuffed!"

"We still don't know why she sent the clippings to you."

Josh's mouth went dry. He understood now that he *meant* something to Millie Carter. He *meant* enough to her that she'd sent him the clippings.

"Nicki, listen. The night Millie saved us from the skinheads—remember how it happened?"

"How could I forget? I still dream about it"

"She knew who we were. She called us the Dynamic Duo of Gander Ridge."

"That's right! You asked her how she happened to come by when she did, and she said that it was no coincidence. She'd been *looking* for us!"

"And that means she knew us before we were even aware that she existed. I got the feeling that night that she'd set the whole thing up, didn't you? It was like she was manipulating us.''

"Let's get out of here, Nickster.''

"No, we've got to finish this. We've got to look for anything that might actually connect her to the murders, something besides newspapers with holes in them.''

"Okay, but let's hurry.''

Nicole went back to searching the armoires and the luggage while Josh busied himself with the contents of the valises. He found nothing else of interest, only more credit-card bills and correspondence with realtors concerning the sale of a condo in Las Vegas and another in St. Thomas, Virgin Islands.

Nicole made the next startling find and called to him.

"Wow, it's like a war museum,'' Josh whispered, staring into the wardrobe she'd opened. Scores of photographs lined the inside surfaces of the doors and shelves, snapshots taken of soldiers doing what soldiers do. Lounging and loitering in foxholes and bunkers. Marching or smoking and joking, playing cards. Clowning, and drinking beer. Or, in a more serious vein, firing their weapons in scenes of combat. They were shirtless and ponchoed, helmeted and bareheaded, young and old, but mostly young. Scattered among the snapshots were portraits in frames of various soldiers in various wars, swarthy men with strong faces and unsettling eyes, veterans of the Second World War, the First World War, the Spanish-American War, even the American Civil War.

On shelves and in various nooks and crannies of the wardrobe lay more substantial artifacts of war. Ammunition clips and empty shell casings. Bayonets, several looking very old. Sabers that looked older than the Revolutionary War. Even a Renaissance-era cutlass.

On a horizontal rack hung a dozen or so military uniforms, one of which was a set of U.S. Army "Class A's,'' consisting of a forest-green jacket with matching trousers, gleaming brass insignia, and gold-threaded sergeant's stripes on the sleeves. Above the left breast pocket of the jacket were rows of ribbons and medals. Josh recognized several, because he'd seen some like them on Lewis Kindred's old army uniform. Lewis had explained their significance to him.

"Whoever owned this one," said Josh, pulling the uniform off the rack, "was a Vietnam vet." He touched a metallic badge that had a silver musket embossed on a blue field, encircled with an oval-shaped wreath. "That's a Combat Infantryman's Badge. And this little yellow ribbon is a Vietnam campaign ribbon. This guy must've been some kind of hero—he's got a couple of Bronze Stars with Oak Leaves and a Purple Heart." He placed the uniform back on the rack and pawed through the others, one of which looked like that of a World War I–era doughboy. When he looked up at Nicole, he saw that her lower lip was trembling. "You okay?" he asked.

"Nickster, did you see the nameplate on the first one?"

Josh retrieved the first uniform from the rack and held it up. Above the right pocket hung a rectangle of glossy black plastic with CARTEE emblazoned in white letters. He quickly hung the garment on the rack again.

"That's the name of the man Lewis tried to kill in Vietnam, isn't it?" said Nicole.

Josh nodded, and unconsciously wiped his palms on his jeans. "Cartee," he said, barely aloud. "Carter. Cartee, Carter. Cartee . . ."

"I know what you're thinking. They've got to be related, right? Millie *Carter* and Gamaliel *Cartee*. Otherwise, why would she have his uniform?"

"The names are too close for coincidence, that's for sure. I can't believe I didn't think of it before. Maybe they were brother and sister. Or cousins."

"How about father and daughter?"

"I'll believe anything."

His eyes found one of the photographs that hung on the interior surface of the wardrobe door. It was a faded color portrait of a striking man of indeterminate age, as young as twenty or as old as thirty-five, hard looking in a lean way. He grinned into the camera with dazzling white teeth. He had the features of an African and the complexion of a Greek or an

Arab, and despite the fact that the picture had faded, Josh could plainly see that his left eye was brown and the right one blue. Just visible above the right pocket of his Class As was his nameplate: CARTEE.

"He looks enough like Millie to be her twin brother," Josh said.

"Nickster, you're right about wanting to write about this. Promise me you'll do it, and that you won't let anything stand in your way." Nicole riveted him with her dark eyes, reaching to him in a way she'd never done before. It touched him.

He suddenly knew something that had only been a half-formed notion before, one that had always slithered from his grasp like a wriggling eel: he loved her. Not as a friend loves a friend, but as a man loves a woman. He loved her with a pounding, insistent urgency. Whatever he'd felt for his nominal girlfriend, Laurel, paled next to what he felt for Nicole.

"Promise me," Nicole pressed. "Write about it and make sense of it. It'll take someone like you to do it. Not just anyone could."

"I promise." He needed to kiss her, and was about to try, when they heard a sound in the distance. An old water pipe, perhaps. Or the thump of a tree branch against the roof. Or the slamming of a car door outside in the drive.

"We've got to get out of here!" Josh whispered. He moved toward the door, pulling Nicole with him.

"But she'll know we've been here!"

"Too bad! We don't have time to straighten up!"

As they entered the main hallway, they heard a clank of metal against metal, the throw of a dead bolt in the foyer that echoed like a pistol shot throughout the empty rooms. "Not that way," breathed Josh. "She'll be in before we can make it up the stairs."

"*Where,* then?"

"This way!" He led her toward the kitchen, remembering a doorway that he'd figured must open to a room that fronted the veranda. They passed through a musty-smelling pantry and burst through a wall of cobwebs into a long parlor that was

empty but for a pile of warped boards and a rotting snooker
table. A glass-paned door gave onto the veranda, where derelict furniture and appliances were barely visible through misty
glass.

Josh tried the door and found it locked, as before. "It's a
dead-bolt lock that takes a key. We can't open it." He stared
at Nicole helplessly as the scuff of footsteps echoed from beyond the pantry. Nicole stared back at him, biting her lower
lip.

Josh pulled her into the pantry, where they'd passed a de-
scending stairway into what must be the cellar. The one remaining option was to hide down there in the dark. If they
were lucky, Josh reasoned, they would find a coal chute with
an opening to the outside, or an exterior entrance through a
ground-level door, like many old houses had. But Nicole hung
back when they reached the maw of the stairway, her hand
suddenly going as cold as ice in his. "I can't go down there,
Nickster."

"We don't have a choice! There's nowhere to hide up
here!"

"I can't! It's too dark! It smells horrible!" A foul odor
wafted up from the darkness below, a latrine kind of smell that
brought to mind human waste, unwashed skin, unbrushed
teeth.

"Nicki, she's coming. . . ."

More footsteps came from behind them. Curious footsteps
that stopped to listen with a cocked head. To glance around
with hungry eyes for clues of intrusion. To sniff the stale air
with flaring nostrils. Footsteps that knew someone had been
here, *still* was here.

Josh dragged Nicole down into the darkness. With his free
hand he took out his flashlight, but he didn't dare to snap it
on yet, because Millie might detect its glow from the top of
the stairs. Nicole trembled like a terrified kitten.

With every step downward the stench became thicker,
warmer. For a hideous moment Josh imagined that they would
step off the foot of the stairs into a holding tank full of semi-

liquid filth, stuff more vile than vomit, more poisonous than sewage, in which something sharklike swam in patient circles, a meat eater. Yet, he forced himself downward, pulling Nicole after him until they reached the bottom, which was as firm as hard-packed earth, thankfully. He let himself breathe again despite the stink.

He snapped the flashlight on, and its beam knifed into the darkness, revealing more or less what he'd expected. An antique-looking boiler hunkered in its corner on the right, from which pipes led along the ceiling in every direction to radiators in the rooms above. Stacks of crates stood against sweating concrete walls, probably full of household wares that long-dead people had once thought valuable. And on all sides were piles of toys and play gear from childhoods long forgotten, judging from the cobwebs and rust and mildew. Tricycles and bikes, a badminton set, croquet mallets, a deflated football, a chipped and faded rocking horse that would have looked at home on a carousel, and much more. Josh headed toward an inner doorway at the far end of the room and snapped off the flashlight, causing Nicole to gasp and squeeze his hand hard enough to hurt.

"It's okay," he whispered. "I'll lead you. Don't let go of me, okay?"

"That's the one thing you don't have to worry about."

He started forward into the pitch-blackness. The stink became stronger, and Josh needed to breathe through his mouth to keep from gagging. The flashlight contacted something solid, and Josh tested it with his fingers, finding the splintery wood of the doorjamb. As he and Nicole edged around it, his face encountered a stiff web, and the terrified spider scurried across his cheek into his hair.

Above them the planks of old flooring squeaked and snapped, footsteps in the kitchen. Another creak, closer. In the pantry now. Another, in the parlor that fronted the veranda. Then, nothing. Had Millie stopped to listen and sniff?

Josh heard a wheeze in the darkness behind him and tightened his hold on Nicole's hand. Another wheeze, the begin-

ning of a cough. Josh squeezed again, and Nicole pressed
herself against him, trembling.

"Nickster," she whimpered into his ear, "that wasn't me."

Josh's heartbeat hammered in his temples. "Nicki,
please. . . . !"

"I'm not kidding, it wasn't me. There's someone behind
us!"

A scuffing came next, then a muffled grunt, the sounds of
struggling. Josh heard breathing that wasn't his or Nicole's,
for she was so close that he could feel the air from her nostrils.

"Nickster, turn on the light!"

"I can't!"

"You've got to! I'm going to lose my mind and start
screaming, if you don't. I can't stand this!" She shivered, and
Josh could feel the terror that had started to tear her mind
apart. He had no choice. He raised the flashlight and positioned
it over her shoulder. He snapped it on.

The beam knifed across a face that he didn't accept at first,
because it seemed so wrong for here and now, a face that
gazed into nothingness with empty, senseless eyes. It belonged
to one of the skinheads who'd attacked them in the alley behind Southwest Thirteenth Street, the one Josh had thought of
as Fireplug. Slouching, head hung forward, Fireplug literally
looked dead on his feet, except for the fact that he slobbered
piteously. Behind him stood his four pals in similarly witless
conditions. Pimples, his face a dermatologist's nightmare, the
arm that Millie had broken hanging at an absurd angle. Next
to him, the blond Hitler, scraggly and drooling. Behind him
the two others.

All five were bunched together in the dark like mannequins
stored in the stockroom of a department store, mute and motionless as if they'd been cast in wax.

Nicole clapped a palm over her mouth and screamed into
it, her breath whistling through her fingers. Josh felt his bladder start to let go, but he somehow held it.

The stubble on Fireplug's face had grown into an uneven
beard, as had most of the others'. His brown leather jacket had

collected a thick layer of dust. A spider had spun a web between the tip of Pimples' nose and the chrome swastika pinned
to the flap of his army-surplus field jacket. All five thugs had
dark stains on the fronts of their jeans, indicating that they'd
voided themselves, which accounted for the stink. And all bore
the marks of the drubbing they'd gotten two weeks ago at
Millie's hand in the alley—contusions and abrasions from
slamming into brick walls or asphalt paving.

Nicole got herself under control, though she still clung so
close to Josh that she seemed to be trying to climb into his
clothes with him. "What's wrong with them? Why are they
just standing there like that?"

"I don't know. I think they must be under hypnosis or
something."

"But it looks like they've been standing there for *weeks*.
There's dust all over them, and—*God*, it looks like fungus!"
Josh beamed the light against Fireplug's cheek, where a
splotch of discoloration suggested a colony of something fun-
goid. Josh decided that things might indeed start to grow on
your skin if you stood for weeks at a time in a dark, damp
cellar.

"Millie did this," he declared. "She put them under some
kind of spell, or poisoned them, slowed down their meta-
bolisms—I don't know. She has powers, Nicki. I've told you
that. She can come through locked doors, for Christ's sake. If
she's on your side, you can win at poker, and if she's not . . ."
He rubbed his eyes, fighting a headache. "I'm not surprised
she can do something like this. Like I said before, she set us
up in the alley that night, sicced these guys on us like a pack
of dogs, then came riding to the rescue. When she was finished
with them, she put them into storage."

"But *why*?"

"If we knew that, we wouldn't be here."

Fireplug coughed again and took a rattling breath. As they
watched, his eyes turned toward them, and his head raised. His
lips stretched into a yellow-toothed grin, and his eyes became

homicidal slits. His body jerked, as if he was trying to break out of an invisible plaster cast.

"This isn't good," whispered Josh. "We've got to get out of here."

"The stairs are the only way."

"Then we'll take the stairs."

"But what about Millie?"

"Do you want to stay here with these guys?"

Josh hauled Nicole toward the mouth of the stairway, clicking off the flashlight when they reached it. He hesitated a moment at the first step to let his eyes readjust to near-total darkness. How ludicrous it seemed, to think that they would have any chance of escaping Millie. She would probably do to them what she'd done to the skinheads or to Ron Payne or to those other poor guys about whom Josh had read about in the newspaper clippings.

"Josh!" Nicole's shriek jarred him, and he whirled with the flashlight, snapping it on. Fireplug stood scarcely a yard behind Nicole, having broken out of his spell and moved after them. He'd pulled a long bayonet from his pocket and poked it forward in a herky-jerky parody of a thrust, the blade making contact with Nicole's arm.

Josh's rage exploded. He swung the heavy Coleman flashlight at Fireplug's head with all his might, felt it crunch against bone. The lens dissolved in an explosion of shards, and the light died. Fireplug bellowed like a bull as he went down. Josh launched himself up the stairs, pulling the shrieking Nicole after him, and he looked back only when they'd reached the top. Fireplug had crawled to the first step, his face awash in blood from the gash on his forehead, his hands clawing upward.

"Are you hurt?" Josh asked Nicole. "Did he get you with the knife?"

"It didn't even break the cloth of my jacket. I'm okay."

They turned left through the pantry and stole into the kitchen, trying not to let their hiking boots thud against the tiles. They peered into the hallway before entering it, looking for any sign of Millie Carter, but saw nothing except motes of dust floating in the gloom. They moved slowly toward the front of the house, hand in hand, each step an ordeal of creaky flooring. They halted at the intersection with the short hallway that led to the room where they'd found Millie's possessions. If something was about to happen, this seemed a likely place.

Josh pressed his back against the wall and peeked around the corner. What he saw nearly turned his blood to slush. Millie Carter stood outside the door of her room as if waiting for them, her head cocked quizzically so that her reddish dreadlocks splayed about her shoulders. Her eyes shone as if they were themselves sources of light. She wore pleated tan trousers, a superbly tailored black blazer, and earrings made of large chromium chain links. She could have been a lawyer, dressed as she was, or a bank executive or a model, if not for her eyes, if not for the grin that parted her lips to reveal teeth that didn't look quite human.

Josh tasted fear as he'd never known it. He sprinted toward the front hall of the house, holding tightly to Nicole's hand but having no time to tell her what he'd seen. They bounded up the curving staircase to the room with the French doors, through which they'd entered the house. Nicole was a fleet runner, fortunately, and she didn't stumble or slow him, but actually overtook him on the staircase.

Josh braved a glance backward when they reached the second-floor balcony. He saw Millie in full pursuit, hauling herself hand over hand along the banister with her body stretched nearly horizontal. She moved with a liquid grace that was almost eellike.

They crashed into the room at the top of the stairs and headed for the French doors. From behind them came a rustling, like a billion flesh-eating insects scuttling over cardboard. Josh knew it was the sweep of Millie Carter's shadow. He'd just opened one of the doors when she caught them. Nicole screamed as something razor sharp sang in the air, the swipe of a claw. Josh caught a glimpse of Millie in another form, a thing so misshapen that her tasteful black blazer was in shreds. A thing with a head that was mostly mouth. He muscled Nicole out the door and plunged down the exterior stairs onto the veranda. Dodging a fallen trellis, he made for the garden with Nicole in tow, her whimpers piercing him, the sunlight nearly blinding him.

They found the stucco wall and somehow got over it, then plunged down the hill to the roadway below. They reached the Escort, scrambled inside it, and locked the doors. Josh fired the engine, slammed the transmission into first gear, and popped the clutch, causing the front wheels to spray gravel.

"We made it!" he hollered jubilantly, thumping a palm on the steering wheel. "We made it, Nicki! We're alive and in one piece! Do you believe it?" He swung the little car around a curve, driving much too fast. He was drunk on adrenaline and close to hyperventilation. "I thought we were dead meat back there. When she caught up to us at the French doors . . ."

"She let us get away," Nicole put in. "You know that, don't you, Nickster? She could've had us, but she let us get away."

Josh slowed the car to a sane speed and glanced over at Nicole. His heart missed a beat, for she was as white as an autumn mist, and she hadn't stopped shivering. She'd lost her watch cap. Her beautiful mane of raven hair no longer flowed down her back, but ended at neck length in a diagonal slash.

Josh saw that Millie's claw had made contact. He saw too that Nicole's breaker had a long gash across the shoulder, and that the seat in which she sat was drenched in blood.

Twenty-two

i

THIS GUY WILL *be more than a match for Dewey*, Lewis said to himself while filling out the Humane Society's paperwork. The twelve-week-old kitten had yellow fur like Big Sister's and similar greenish eyes, but there the similarity ended. "Little Brother" wasn't female, and he showed no inclination to spending two thirds of his life asleep. The nice lady at the Humane Society provided a cardboard carrier free of charge.

With the carrier perched on his stumps, Lewis rode a Tri-Met bus south from the Humane Society shelter in northeast Portland to a Max light-rail station and caught the commuter train across the river. He got off the Max on the First Avenue side of the Skidmore Historical District, which teemed with a cheerful crowd of Saturday Market shoppers and sightseers. Food stalls were everywhere in the stone-paved square, tucked in among watercolor artists and hawkers of Indian jewelry and builders of hang gliders.

Keeping his eyes peeled for Dewey, Lewis drove his Action Power 9000 through the maze of stalls. The clouds had dissolved, leaving a sparkling blue sky and shirtsleeve weather. He checked Dewey's customary spot in the shade of a white colonnade, but found it occupied by someone else. He crossed Second to the VIP Center, where none of the staff had seen Dewey since yesterday. Feeling a twinge of unease, Lewis borrowed the VIP Center's phone and called Tommy Iadanza to ask whether Dewey had shown up to draw from the stash of money that Tommy was keeping for him. But Tommy reported that nobody at the Fanshawe had seen him, either.

Lewis spent the rest of the afternoon driving his wheelchair up and down the length of Tom McCall Waterfront Park, hoping to see Dewey with his chair parked against the railing. But the old veteran had apparently forsaken his usual Saturday haunts. Lewis's unease grew.

He bought a can of Nine Lives at a 7-Eleven on the Espla-

nade and fed a third of it to Little Brother, then headed back
to Old Town. By the time he returned to the Skidmore District,
the Saturday Market crowd had thinned and the vendors had
headed home. With the afternoon waning and a chill gathering,
he cruised by the Salvation Army's Harbor Light, which had
attracted more than a hundred scruffy, tired-looking men who
waited on the sidewalk for this evening's dispensation of charity. Dewey wasn't among them.

"L.T., is that you, man?" The voice came from behind him
among the men standing in line outside Harbor Light. Lewis's
heart leaped, for it was an achingly familiar voice, but it wasn't
Dewey's. *"L.T., wait up, will you?"*

Lewis spun his wheelchair around and saw a lanky black
man quit his place in line to shamble toward him. The man
wore street-dingy painter's pants, layers of moth-eaten sweat-
ers, and a pair of cloggy workman's boots. His jaw was rough
with stubble that looked like tungsten filings, his face the color
of hickory. He stopped before Lewis's chair and pulled off his
sunglasses and his Los Angeles Raiders cap. "Don't you recognize me, L.T.? Take away twenty years' worth of wrinkles
and gray hairs, and it'll come to you."

Lewis stared at the grinning face in disbelief. He'd last seen
T. J. Skane twenty-two years ago in the Ho Bo Woods of
South Vietnam, immediately after a rocket-propelled grenade
had blown the young GI off his track. T. J. was burning then,
a dervish of fire. Lewis saw him go down, saw him cease
writhing. He learned later from Lieutenant Colonel Gilbert Golightly that T. J. had died. On October 17, 1970, Specialist-4
T. J. Skane of East Los Angeles, California, had become a
KIA—"killed in action."

Yet here he stood, unscarred beyond the effects of life on
the street, his 'fro having thinned and grayed but his body fit
looking for a man in his forties. In his black eyes shone a
simple joy for having stumbled onto an old pal after all these
years, Lieutenant Lewis Kindred, his platoon leader. The man
who'd gotten him killed.

Lewis's mouth worked, but nothing came out. *It's drooling*

time, he heard a voice in his head say. *Time to find a reputable shrink and get some psychotropic medication.*

"Who's your little buddy here?" asked T. J., sticking a finger through an airhole of the carrier. The kitten bit him, but he didn't seem to mind. "How you been, L.T.? You look pretty much the same, except your hair's a lot longer and a lot grayer. I heard about you gettin' your legs blown off, but somebody said you'd been doin' okay since gettin' back from the 'Nam. I hope that's true."

Lewis managed to nod. "And how have you been, T. J.?"

The black man laughed and stuck his cap back on his head. "I guess you could say I've been doin' okay, considerin'. . . ." He indicated the Harbor Light building with the motion of his head, as if to say, *This is my life.* "I was hittin' the drugs and the booze pretty good when I got out of the army, and I ended up in the California joint for stealin' a mail truck and tryin' to sell it. Can you believe that, L.T.? A *mail* truck. That's how fucked up I was. I was gonna sell it and buy skag with the money!" He chuckled the infectious way Lewis remembered.

"Anyway, I was never able to keep a job after I got out of the joint, and next thing you know, I was on the street in East L.A. with my hand out. Well, I'm tellin' you, man, East L.A. is no place to be out on the street. I mean, it's worse than the fuckin' Ho Bo Woods or the Iron Triangle. So I started travelin' around a lot, stayin' awhile here and there, tryin' to keep both halves of my ass together. I drink a little Night Train now and then, mostly when the weather gets cold. But I'm no drunk anymore, and I'm sure as hell no junkie." He folded his sunglasses and tucked them away, for the sun had plunged below the West Hills. "I never hurt anybody, L.T., so you don't have to be scared of me. I don't even hit up old friends for handouts."

Lewis wondered whether this was what T. J. would have become if he'd lived. An addict and a felon, a panhandler. Or was this grinning, good-natured man a fragment of a reality that Lewis had misconstrued all these years, a vision of the world twisted by the gnarled fingers of mental illness? Swallowing a sob, Lewis found T. J.'s hand, discovered it to be made of flesh and bones. "I—I thought you were dead," he said, his voice pinching. "You and Danny Legler, and Scottie Sanders—"

"Well, I'm happy to say I ain't dead, L.T., and I'm happy you ain't either. Know somethin'? For a white dude you were all right. I'm talkin' about the day you stopped that IPW motherfucker from thumpin' up on a little girl and her old granny. What was that motherfucker's name? I can't remember it— somethin' strange."

"Gamaliel," Lewis said. "Gamaliel Cartee."

"Yeah, that's it. Interrogator of Prisoners of War, a fuckin' Eye Pee Dub-yew. That was one nasty dude, I don't mind sayin'. Anyway, I remember how you got in his face and told him to jack down, and how that old lifer—what was his name?"

"Markowski."

"Right—Frank Markowski, the platoon sergeant. He tried to chill you out, but you weren't havin' any of it, and you drew your forty-five and pointed it at Cartee's head and told him to let the girl go, or you'd blow his fuckin' brains out. I gotta say it, man, that was one of the best things I ever saw in my life. The motherfucker let the girl go, and the good guys won a round for a change." Laughing, he moved close and laid a hand on Lewis's shoulder. "You didn't deserve what happened to you, man. I mean, if anybody deserves to have both his legs, it's you, L.T."

Lewis struggled to keep the tears back. "Thanks, T. J. I've told myself the same thing a thousand times, but it helps to hear it from you. I can almost believe it now."

ii

Lewis offered to buy dinner at one of the walk-up kitchens in the New Market Theater. He'd been responsible, after all, for T. J's losing his place in line at the Harbor Light. T. J. at first declined the offer, but Lewis could see in his eyes that he was hungry. Lewis bought him two slices of pizza and one for himself. They ate where Lewis and Dewey normally had their Wednesday lunch.

Lewis was about to ask where his old friend planned to stay tonight, when T. J. suddenly said, "It's strange meetin' you out on the street like this, L.T. Of all the people in the world, I would've never expected to see you on the sidewalk outside the Harbor Light. You've got a home to go to, right? A house, an apartment, somethin' like that?"

Lewis nodded.

"Then why ain't you there? It can get dangerous around here at night. You ought to be home, sittin' in front of the tube, sippin' on a beer."

Lewis explained that he was searching for a friend, an old Vietnam veteran named Dewey. A black man in a wheelchair. Dewey had lost his cat, and Lewis wanted to give him another—Little Brother.

T. J. stopped chewing and stared at Lewis. "I know that old dude. In fact, I was talkin' with him just this afternoon, not ten feet from where we're sittin' right now."

"You saw him here—today?"

"That's affirm. He had himself a brown paper bag with a fifth of bourbon in it and a quart of milk, sittin' right over there beside that big pillar, just as content as could be."

"I spent the afternoon scouring the whole damn neighborhood for him. I don't see how I could've missed him."

"Hey, you better feed that little monster something," said T. J., pointing to Little Brother. "He's makin' an awful racket!"

Lewis set the carrier on the ground, dug out the remainder of the Nine Lives he'd bought this afternoon, and fed it to the kitten. "How did he seem? Dewey, I mean. Was he in good spirits? He wasn't sick, was he?"

"He seemed fine, except he had an appointment he needed to keep."

"An appointment? With who?"

"Said he needed to see a man about a cat, and that he had a long way to travel. Said he had to go to a warehouse up past the Broadway Bridge."

T. J. estimated this had happened about an hour and a half ago, maybe two. Lewis apologized for needing to hurry off, but he was worried about Dewey, who hadn't been himself lately. Lewis needed to find him.

"Man, I can't let you go up there by yourself. No tellin' what kind of trouble a man in a wheelchair might get himself into up in that neighborhood. I'm comin' with you."

"I can't ask you to do that, T. J."

"You didn't ask. I offered."

iii

They crossed Burnside into Chinatown. Darkness stole ashore from the river as they made their way ever deeper into the bowels of the city, where lurked dealers of crank, crack, and *chiva* (the street term for Mexican tar heroin). Loitering in the black pockets of alleys and doorways were the homeless, the addicts, the street punks, and the child whores who sold "dates" for the price of a Big Mac and a hit of crack. Whenever possible, Lewis avoided their glistening stares.

By the time they reached Union Station, downtown Portland's only Amtrak stop, the Action Power 9000 had begun to run out of both action and power. Lewis's afternoon-long search for Dewey had depleted the battery.

"It's okay, man," said T. J. "I'll push you."

"Man, this thing is heavier than hell. I can make it into the railroad depot and call a friend to come and get me."

"Why should you do that? You've already got a friend."

They continued north toward the Broadway Bridge with T. J. pushing the heavy wheelchair as easily as most people push shopping carts. The neighborhood gave way to an industrial quarter that was colorless for lack of neon and lonely for

lack of traffic, where long expanses of chain-link fence
guarded factories, warehouses, and parking lots for various
industrial fleets. T. J. pushed Lewis along as if he knew exactly
where to go, edging ever closer to the river, until they crossed
Front Avenue near Terminal Number 1. They skirted a vast
expanse of asphalt—a warehouse parking lot, where half a
dozen eighteen-wheelers lay side by side, their engines idling
as their drivers napped in their bunks—to the rear of a dock
facility, where loading cranes towered against the night sky
like colossal steel insects.

Lewis rode silently in his chair, his hands holding tight to
the carrier with Little Brother inside it. He decided to give in
to the gestalt, knowing that the psychological configuration
was greater than the sum of its parts, and therefore greater
than his ability to resist it. The vision defied logic and contra-
dicted all rationale. Had the pattern begun with the first appearance of Gamaliel Cartee, he wondered—back in 1970,
after a civilian bus struck an explosive device on the road to
Trung Lap? Had the spectacle of mass death and gore so weakened his mind that his unconscious created its own reality,
using phantasmagoric elements like red crystalline orbs and
flesh-eating monsters to supplant the outrages of the real
world?

How much of his life had been real? he wondered.

Darkness closed around him, and the wheelchair began to
jounce as T. J. pushed him ever faster along the graveled
shoulder of the road they'd taken. Strings of light lay on the
far shore of the river. Lewis craned backward to get his bearings and saw the twin crystal spires of the Oregon Convention
Center. To his left loomed the facades of warehouses like low
concrete cliffs, punctuated here and there by unfriendly yard
lights.

"Look up ahead, L.T. You see what I see?"

Several hundred yards in front of them, the road took a hard
left turn at the riverbank, where a barrier of chain-link fence
prevented anyone from venturing closer to the water. Someone
had parked a car on the shoulder, gotten out, and hung

something dark and heavy on the chain links.

T. J. sped up, his logger's boots crunching on the gravel. Lewis was able to make out the figure of a man spread-eagle against the fence, his wrists and ankles lashed to it. Two other men were dousing him with liquid from five-gallon cans.

It can't be gasoline, said Lewis to himself. *Nobody would do such a thing*, not even in the utterly graceless world of the nineties, where kids carried Uzis and routinely gunned each other down in school yards.

But it *was* gasoline. One of the two flicked a butane lighter and held it close to the struggling man on the fence, and suddenly the world was bright with flame. T. J. halted so quickly that Lewis nearly flew out of his chair. The pet carrier skittered off his lap onto the gravel. The two men threw their five-gallon cans over the fence and scrambled into the car. Screams filled the night as fire bit flesh. A starter wound and an engine gunned. The car lurched onto the pavement and sped away, its taillights leaving bloody streaks across Lewis's vision. T. J. grabbed up the carrier with Little Brother in it, and the screams reached a hellish pitch.

Lewis knew that voice. It called his name, pleaded for help. Lewis *wanted* to help. He grabbled for the joystick, his tears blinding him. The voice belonged to Dewey.

Lewis found the joystick, and the battery had just enough power to push the chair to within twenty feet of the inferno, close enough to get a lungful of the sweet stench. He'd tasted that ghastly smell before. He'd watched T. J. Skane burn to a meaningless pile of charred sticks one afternoon in the Ho Bo Woods. Now he was watching Dewey burn away, a human X with arms splayed like a crucifix, spindly legs stretched below. A horror beyond reason.

"*Do* something, T. J.!" Lewis shrieked, flapping at the night with his good hand. "Throw dirt on him! Smother the fire! We can't let him—"

More lights stabbed the night, white and red and blue, rotating beacons and headlight beams that cast harsh shadows across the walls of warehouses. Cop cars and fire trucks. Ambulances. Sirens shredding the darkness. Milling figures in uniforms, shouting orders to one another. Two-way radios crackling.

Lewis saw a man with an extinguisher spray foam on the motionless, silent form of Dewey. Watched competent-looking people study the lifeless body and shake their heads. Watched a pair of white-clad paramedics carefully take the body off the fence. Watched TV news teams from four local stations shoot footage and conduct interviews of cops and firemen.

Too soon, it was over. Night reasserted its claim as beacons and lights switched off, as emergency vehicles left the scene. T. J. Skane, inexplicably, had vanished.

A young cop approached Lewis, his blond hair disheveled and his eyes too weary looking for someone his age. He asked whether Lewis had seen what had happened. Yes, Lewis answered, his entire body having gone numb, though deep within him flickered an ember of rage. He'd seen it all.

iv

They sat in an interrogation room with soundproofing tiles on the walls and a one-way mirror at one end. The room had a convenient electrical outlet, which enabled Lewis to recharge the battery of his wheelchair during the interview. He was not a suspect in the murder of Dewey, the cops told him again and again. He was, however, a potentially valuable witness.

The young blond cop hung up the telephone he'd just used and pushed it out of his way. He lit a cigarette and blew smoke toward the ceiling. His nameplate identified him as L. McGillivray.

"The Salvation Army doesn't have a record of having served anybody named T. J. Skane," he said. "They're pretty good about keeping records of these things. You're sure it was the Harbor Light where you met him, and not one of the other shelters?"

Lewis sipped from the Styrofoam cup of coffee that Mc-

Gillivray had given him. Yes, he'd met Skane outside the Harbor Light. They'd eaten pizza together, because Skane had missed the dinner shift. Maybe T. J. hadn't gone to the Harbor Light before tonight, and maybe this was why the Salvation Army had no record of him.

"What I'm really wondering is where he disappeared to," said McGillivray. "The fire call went in almost immediately, thanks to the attendant on the Broadway Bridge. From his perch up in the bridge house, he saw the fire break out right away, and he was sitting at a phone. That's why there was a truck on the scene within five minutes—"

"Which was more than enough time for Dewey to die."

"Yes, Mr. Kindred, and it's a tragedy. But my point is, where did Skane go, if he'd been pushing you along the road in the wheelchair? Did he run back the way you'd come? If he'd done that, then certainly one of our guys would've seen him, because that's exactly the kind of thing they look for— people running from the scene. If he'd run the other direction, *I* would've seen him, because that's the route I took. And as you know, I didn't see anybody running away."

"Then maybe he's still out there somewhere. Maybe he's hiding in or around one of the warehouses. There must be a million places to hide in that neighborhood."

McGillivray massaged his eyeballs through clenched lids and took another pull from his cigarette. "You're right. And any minute one of the security cops who works out there is bound to see him and call us. In fact, it should've happened by now."

"Why don't you just come right out and say it? You think I made up the part about T. J. Skane, right? That I know more about this thing than I'm letting on? Well, I don't! I've told you everything I know, everything I saw. I don't know why T. J. took off, and I don't know where he went. I wish I *did* know, because his eyes are probably better than mine, and maybe he saw more than I did. I'm not holding anything back from you, Officer McGillivray. I can't tell you any more than what I've told you, I swear it."

"You didn't see what kind of car the suspects had, and you can't describe either of them, except that they were both males. Is that right?"

"For the nineteenth time, that's right."

"And you don't have any idea where your friend T. J. Skane might've gone?"

"If I knew, I'd tell you. I hope you find him, honest to God I do, because he's got Dewey's cat. Do me a favor when you find him, will you? Call me. I'd like to get the cat back."

McGillivray stared at him a long time with his tired eyes. "I will, Mr. Kindred. I'll call you, and you can get the cat back."

Twenty-three

i

JESSE BURTON, PH.D., had seen many substandard schools over the years, but he'd seen few that compared with Hancock Central Elementary in Sneedville, Tennessee. Throughout the building were spots on the cinderblock walls where the mortar had crumbled to let in the daylight. The teachers doubled as janitors, which accounted for the grime that coated the floors, desks, and fixtures. The school district had no money for books and crayons. To buy paper towels and toilet paper, the school held regular fund-raisers.

Welcome to Appalachia, thought Jesse.

The story was no rosier across town at the Hancock County High School. Here, the tiny library could neither afford to buy new books nor to participate in an interlibrary loan program.

Having only recently received her first computer for the library, a donated IBM, the principal hoped sometime soon to get software to run it, as well as some training. Until then, the computer sat untouched in a corner.

The poor get poorer.

As he drove his rented car the seventy miles back to Knoxville, where he planned to catch a plane home to Chicago tomorrow, he dictated his thoughts onto tape: "The cause to upgrade education with computers is in big trouble, especially in poor schools. My survey shows that inner-city schools and many rural schools just don't have the money or the training to acquire and maintain the machines. . . ."

As a research fellow with the National Education Association, Dr. Jesse Burton had ramrodded a three-year study on how to put personal computers to use in American schools. He'd traveled throughout the country from his home base in Chicago, observing the ways administrators and teachers applied computer technology in running schools and teaching courses. His findings had troubled him deeply: despite remarkable claims of progress by the federal government, which had spent more than a billion dollars during the past eight years to help public schools compete in computer skills with the rest of the industrialized world, an alarming percentage of American schools used antiquated and obsolete computers.

As a black man who'd struggled most of his life to overcome the weight of poverty and disadvantage, he cared intensely for the kids who attended schools like Hancock Elementary, whether they lived in desperate little towns like Sneedville or raging inner cities like south Chicago, where he himself had grown up. Education, Jesse believed, was the only effective weapon against poverty and the evils it spawned.

He drove into Knoxville on Highway 11 and followed the arrows to Interstate 40, which took him downtown, then followed more arrows toward Dickenson Island Airport on the Tennessee River. He exited to the Holiday Inn where he would stay and work on his report until tomorrow's early-morning flight to Chicago. He turned in the keys to his rental car and checked the reception desk for messages, and was surprised to find one from Shandelle, his wife.

"Yeah, it's me, babe," he said when she answered his call-back. "What's up?"

A man had called several times for him, she reported, from out in Portland, Oregon. He had a slight foreign accent, and he sounded very upset. He'd insisted that Jesse return his call at the earliest opportunity and had left a number.

"It wasn't Lewis Kindred, was it? The only other guy I know in Portland is . . ."

No, it wasn't Lewis Kindred. Shandelle knew Lewis's voice. This man left his name, and she'd written it down with the phone number. Jesse waited while she located the notepad. *Paul Tran*, the man's name was. As Jesse wrote down the number, he felt something cold in his heart.

ii

Josh's eyes wandered around the hospital room, soaking up details. He studied the MediLogic patient monitor on the rack above Nicole's bed, with its spiky lines of green light bouncing across its screen, which signified her failing heartbeat, labored respiration, weakening blood pressure. He studied the flowers in their pots on the windowsill, on the bed stand, on the dresser. He studied Nicole's once beautiful face, yellowed by jaundice and tight with the agonal throes of some nameless, unspeakably virulent disease. He studied her hands, knotted into claws.

Josh needed to remember every horrific little detail down to the color of the carpet and the pattern on the bedspread, because he intended to call up this scene in his mind many times as his own worthless life wore on. He intended to relive this night's full blast of desolation. Nicole's dying was incomprehensibly unjust, because he, the less worthy, would continue to live.

He meant to suffer for that injustice. He would pay the price for having been so stupid as to discount the danger of breaking into Millie Carter's house, for having dragged Nicole along on the adventure despite her well-reasoned misgivings. He would atone for having been blind to his own love for this girl, for having pushed it down and ignored it for so long, and having deprived them both of the joy it would have brought them.

Suddenly she reached out and gripped his hand. She tried to speak. Josh's tears flowed into the corners of his mouth as he leaned close.

"You owe me a large pizza," she whispered. "We had a bet, remember? About the door. You said it would be locked, and I said—" Pain pinched off her words. She'd refused to let the doctors increase the dosage of morphine, because she wanted to remain lucid up to the end. She'd told Josh that she wanted to look at his face while taking her final breath.

"Just get better," Josh croaked, "and I'll buy you a gourmet pizza every day for the rest of your life. In fact, we can have a wedding *pizza* instead of a wedding cake—how's that sound? We'll get a big one, like ten feet across, right? We'll get anchovies on it, and extra cheese. . . ." Grief overwhelmed him. He lowered his head and cried.

Nicole lay still a long time, silent except for her raspy breathing. What was left of her raven hair spilled over a white pillowcase. Josh pressed her hand against his cheek, clenched his eyes, and tried to fathom how the last two days could have happened in a world that purported to be governed by the rational laws of science.

Nicole had suffered a deep slash across her left shoulder, as if someone had swiped at her with a sickle. Josh couldn't be certain of this, but he believed—based on what he'd seen out of the corner of his eye in a frantic fraction of a second—that Millie Carter had struck Nicki with a claw. It had happened when he and Nicki dashed through the French doors onto the upper deck of the villa. The blow had sliced through Nicki's long black hair, shortening it at a crazy diagonal, cutting through her clothing as if she'd been wearing paper. She'd bled profusely, and Josh had rushed her to the emergency room of Good Samaritan in northwest Portland.

After suturing the wound, the emergency-room resident, an intense young man named Dr. Chaklai, had kept Nicole for observation. He clearly didn't believe her and Josh's insistence that she'd cut herself on a rusty nail while squeezing between the slats of an old fence. No rusty nail he'd ever seen was capable of shearing a girl's hair off while inflicting an eight-inch gash in her shoulder, he'd said.

By four o'clock on Saturday afternoon, Nicole had worsened. Infection had spread from the wound throughout her body. Her skin turned yellow and the whites of her eyes became orange with jaundice as the disease attacked her liver. Dr. Chaklai administered the maximum allowable dosages of every antibiotic at his disposal, then called in specialists who ran test upon test, looking for bacteria, viruses, malignancies, even death-cap-mushroom toxins. They found nothing. The antibiotics had no discernible effect.

By Sunday morning the disease had attacked her pancreas and kidneys. She developed pneumonia. Her pulse weakened. The doctors hovered over her with ashen faces while her mother prayed at her bedside. Her father, apparently, was himself too weak to visit his daughter's sickbed, which required that Mrs. Tran divide her time between her husband and her dying daughter.

On Sunday evening, Josh's mother and sister arrived at Good Samaritan in time to hear Dr. Chaklai pronounce the situation hopeless, for the disease had so riddled Nicole's vital organs that total renal shutdown was inevitable within twenty-four hours. Still, Nicki welcomed her visitors with what passed for a smile.

All through Monday she'd hung on, and Josh had stayed with her when her mother needed to go home in order to care for her father. But now, late on Monday evening, he could see that she'd used up her reservoir of strength, that she had only minutes left.

They were alone. Her mother was en route to the hospital, having received a call from the doctor. Nicole opened her eyes and smiled through the agony, a ground-glass grin that cut Josh to the quick. "You promised that you would finish—" She cringed as new pain lanced through her, and Josh cursed the disease silently. "—f-finish writing the story," she whispered. "You'll do it, won't you, Nickster?"

"Nothing's going to stop me."

"And you'll write more stories, won't you? You'll become a writer. You're so good at it, Nickster—you've *got* to do it."

"I'll do it. I'll do it for you, Nicki."

"For us."

"For *us*."

Her yellowed eyes filled with tears that ran in rivulets down her cheeks. "We had some great times, Nickster. I wouldn't trade a single minute of what we've had for an eternity with somebody else. I mean that—I really do. I guess you know that I've loved you all these years, huh?"

"I know. And I've loved you, too. I just wish—"

She touched his lips with a fingertip. "Don't say it. I wish it, too. But it's enough that we have each other right now, isn't it?"

Josh couldn't speak. He could only nod.

"You won't forget me, will you?"

"God, no. I couldn't forget you, Nicki. You'll always be my girl, right? And we'll always be the Dynamic Duo of Gander Ridge."

Nicole's grip relaxed suddenly, and the frightening tautness in her face gave way. She exhaled and didn't draw another breath. Her gaze never left his, not even as death stole her smile.

Twenty-four

i

As NICOLE TRAN lay dying in Good Samaritan Hospital, Lewis lay awake in his bed, having tried and failed to take refuge in sleep from the madness of his waking life. The shock, the grief, and the anger over Dewey's horrible death weighed on him like an anvil strapped to his back.

He'd simply lacked the strength to visit Nicki in the hospital. Cheryl Nickerson had phoned on Sunday afternoon to notify him of the girl's mysterious illness and the dire prognosis, but every time he tried to muster the energy to go out, his head swam with nausea and he became faint. Frustrated, he could only hope that Josh was bearing up, and that Nicki wouldn't linger too long in excruciating pain. His heart went out to both of them and their families.

Rain pattered against his windows, a sound that ordinarily would have nudged him over the threshold of sleep. But it didn't do the trick tonight. Eventually his thoughts gravitated to Millie, and when finally he fell asleep, he dreamed of her. They walked together in the rose gardens of Washington Park during a rainstorm, devouring the bursts of color with their eyes. Bloody reds, honey yellows. A hundred shades of peach and a thousand of orange. Against the grayness of the day, the color of the roses was delicious.

He asked her how much of himself a man could lose and still be himself. A man didn't become someone else, did he, simply by losing, say, his legs? Or suppose that a man lost his arms *and* his legs. Or suppose that he lost his entire body except for that section of his brain that housed sentience and intellect, assuming that doctors could keep that morsel alive. At which stage of loss did a man lose *himself*?

Millie smiled at him with her wonderful blue-brown eyes. *Lewis, you never lose* just *your legs,* she said. *You always lose more than you think you do. But no matter how much you lose,*

*you're still you. Only one thing can truly change you into
someone else.*

The dream gradually knitted with reality, and Lewis became
aware of his aching bladder. He'd drunk far too much beer
before turning in. He got out of bed and padded to the bathroom, stood before the toilet and pissed, leaning with one hand
against the wall. Not until he flushed the toilet did he understand that he wasn't still dreaming, that he actually stood in
his bathroom on two good legs. He whirled to the mirror and
stared dumbfounded at the reflected image—a man in his
youngish forties, tall and slim, hairy of chest and slightly silvered around the ears. The gray eyes were steady, the jaw only
slightly scarred.

"Who are you?" he asked aloud. He discovered that his
ears no longer rang, that his left arm was as good as his right.
"Who *are* you?" he demanded again, leaning close to the
mirror. He ran his fingers over his cheeks, down his neck,
across his shoulders. He pushed his hand down into his shorts,
and his cock suddenly stirred with a tickling hunger.

He dashed out of the bathroom into the bedroom, his heart
thudding, expecting to find Millie there. But the bedroom was
deserted except for the patter of rain. "Millie!" He ran to the
kitchen, to the living room and the studio, only to find that he
was alone in the apartment. How could this be happening, his
brain screamed, without Millie?

The answer came to him almost too easily. When a man
makes love to a woman, he keeps a part of her with him, as
she keeps a part of himself. Their two bodies exchange not
only sweat, but also the juices and oils of sex. Their minds
touch, and each gives the other a fragment of his or her es-
sence, some kernel of "self." Yes, he'd kept a part of Millie,
and that part—whatever it was—made possible the change
he'd just undergone.

Joy washed over him like a flash flood.

He was ravenous, for he hadn't eaten today, or yesterday,
either. He went to the closet and pulled out his best pair of
Levi's Dockers and slipped his strong, unscarred legs into

them, one at a time. He put on his best sport shirt and shrugged into his favorite lambs' wool sweater.

Then he remembered that he had no shoes, no socks, no footwear of any kind. He hadn't needed such things for more than twenty years. But now he had *feet*, damn it, and he couldn't go out without shoes. He recalled again the night he and Millie walked down to Goose Hollow, and the exultation he'd felt upon looking down and seeing a pair of tan Rockport walking shoes. He'd worn white athletic socks—not exactly chic, but comfortable. If the dream had produced footwear then, it could certainly produce footwear now.

He went back to the closet, pulled open the sliding door, and searched the area where Millie had hung her things while staying here. Sure enough, a pair of tan Rockports lay in the corner at the far end of the closet, and with them several pairs of new athletic socks.

ii

Legato Ristorante was off the lobby of the plush Metro Plaza Hotel on Broadway. Though nominally Italian rustic, the decor was in fact "California Modern," which featured polished oak and marble, dark upholstery, and lots of potted plants. Several steps down from the reception desk lay the bar, where long windows offered patrons a lower-than-street-level view of passing pedestrians.

Lewis walked in on his own two feet, grinned at the maître d', and requested a table for one. For a moment he felt certain that someone had followed him, but when he turned to stare through the glass doors of the entryway, he saw nothing suspicious. Had he also heard something—a half-familiar *rustling*, a sound from a forgotten dream or a previous life? No. He'd heard nothing like that.

A pair of well-dressed women lounged at a far table, nursing fruity-looking drinks in skinny glasses. When one of them, a blonde in her early thirties, glanced up and locked stares with

Lewis, he knew that he was indeed hungry.

But not for food.

"On second thought," he said to the maître d', "I think I'll just have a drink in the bar."

iii

The blond woman was Megan Venton, a buyer for Nordstrom's who traveled extensively in her work, enjoyed aerobics, and never missed an episode of *L.A. Law*. She wore a tan jacket with peaked lapels over a matching shirt and a white T-shirt with a simple gold necklace. Very *now*, Lewis thought, aching for her. *She's not my type. She can hardly put together a complete sentence, but here I am, turning on charm I didn't know I had. . . .*

Megan's brunette friend, a fellow buyer named Stacey Something-or-Other, recognized the chemistry afoot and departed, pleading an early day tomorrow. Forty-five minutes later Lewis and Megan checked into the Metro Plaza, using her American Express Gold Card.

"Drink?" offered Lewis, holding up a bottle of Scotch from the honor bar. "We've got everything here from bourbon to aquavit."

"No thanks, Zeb," she replied, slipping her arms around his neck. He'd told her he was Zebulon Councilman, and that he was the business agent for the American Association of Philosophy Writers, AFL-CIO, out of Van Nuys. The bullshit had come off the top of his head like water out of a tap, and Megan had lapped it up. "I'm not up for a drink right now, but I might be up for something else."

They kissed deeply, and Lewis savored the sweetness of her mouth. Without breaking the kiss, they moved to the bed, which seemed big enough for four couples. They glided down onto it. His hands moved to her breast and found that under the T-shirt she wore no bra. He massaged her breasts gently, while his hunger built to a level of urgency that frightened him. This was more than normal sexual hunger, more intense even than the craving he'd felt for Millie. What scared him was the growing certainty that he was powerless against it.

They broke the kiss to peel off each other's clothing. "You're married, aren't you, Zeb?" she whispered. "That's why you wanted to use my credit card when we checked in. You don't want your wife to see the bill."

"You're too smart for me, Megan. Sorry."

"Oh, I'm not mad. I think that adults should give themselves the freedom to do what comes naturally. I mean, why should we feel guilty about using our bodies in the way the good Lord intended?" She ground her pelvis against him and parted her legs.

"I couldn't agree with you more."

"You'll wear protection, won't you? It only makes sense in this day and age."

Lewis suffered a bolt of panic. He hadn't bought condoms in over twenty years. His face must have said as much.

"It's okay, Zeb. I've got some."

She rose from the bed to fetch her purse, totally naked now. Lewis watched her go. She was tall and well muscled, smooth in her movements like a cat, thanks to aerobics, no doubt. He full breasts bounced tantalizingly with every movement. The hair in her pubic mound showed her to be a true blonde. After rummaging a moment in her purse, she returned to the bed with a foil square in her hand. She tore it open and removed the condom.

"Let me do this for you," she said, smiling.

Lewis rolled onto his back and closed his eyes, worrying that he might suffer an accidental orgasm. *Think about poker,* he said to himself. It had worked when he was young. Megan gasped, causing him to raise himself on his elbows.

"What the *fuck* . . . ?" she breathed, covering her mouth. Lewis saw that his erect penis was almost five times its normal size, so long and thick that no normal woman could possibly take him. He stared at it openmouthed, not knowing whether to laugh or cry.

"I don't believe this!" Megan exclaimed. "What *are* you, some kind of freak?"

She tried to jump from the bed, but Lewis caught and held her. He felt something spread through him, an excitement, an overpowering hunger that set his heart to thundering and his muscles to twitching. Megan's face contorted in panic as she beheld the change.

Lewis could smell her terror. It was like an old dream that waited to be touched and fondled to life. He prodded it with his mind, prodded it again, and it burst forth—bestial and brutal, the incarnation of a dream that belonged in hell.

Before Megan could scream, Lewis reached out with a mental tentacle and seized her will. She could do nothing now except cooperate. She couldn't struggle, couldn't scream, could only breathe.

He hoisted her up on all fours and mounted her from behind, driving his monstrous cock into her up to the hilt. The shuddering of her wounded body only fanned his excitement. Blood was suddenly everywhere, the smell of it tickling his nostrils. Sweat poured off his forehead into his eyes, but through the blur he could see that his fingers had lengthened and that each had a long, curving claw. Megan's skin showed cruel marks wherever he'd touched her.

The hunger twisted inside him, demanding nourishment, even as his cock and balls sent signals of impending orgasm. Not knowing exactly what he was doing, he bent low and bit into the woman's left shoulder, ripping away meat with his teeth. Blood filled his mouth, so rich and sweet that it nearly blinded him with pleasure. He chewed, swallowed, bent for another bite, and felt his jaws crush her clavicle. As each mouthful of flesh slid into his stomach, it produced a rush that made him want to roar his exultation to the stars and planets, for this was more than nourishment. This was *power*.

His orgasm rocked him to near senselessness, and when he pulled out of Megan, he saw that he'd reduced her to a clutter of wet meat.

Twenty-five

i

THE MANILA ENVELOPE was identical to the four that Josh Nickerson had received from an anonymous sender throughout the preceding summer. The only clue to its origin was the postmark: Seattle, October 3, 1992. It had arrived on Monday, two days earlier, but Josh hadn't noticed it until now, for he'd spent Monday at Nicole's deathbed, watching her slip away.

ii

He'd spent the day after her death in his room, shunning all company and ignoring his mother's plea for him to eat something, anything. She'd begged him to talk to her and cry with her, to take advantage of the fact that he had a family who yearned to help him shoulder his grief.

But he'd not wanted any help from his family, especially his father. The hotshot insurance executive had arrived at the apartment on Tuesday evening, summoned by his ex-wife to make a stab at doing whatever fathers are supposed to do at times like this, Josh figured. Greg Nickerson had pounded on the bedroom door for nearly thirty minutes, gently at first but ever more loudly as his frustration grew. He'd called upon Josh to "snap out of it," and to "stop sniveling like a little girl." Josh had ignored him.

He'd played no CDs, never turned on the television or the radio. He'd perused no magazines and read no books. He'd wanted no distraction from the pain, no intrusions into his impossible vision of a life with Nicole. If he concentrated hard enough, his heart lied, he might bring the vision to life.

How could she possibly be *gone*? The bitter truth of her death seemed out of sync with creation as Josh Nickerson knew it. He wanted no part of a world in which Nicole could actually die.

He envisioned being in bed with her. He visualized what they would have done together, her lithe little body pressed close against him, her strong legs wrapped around him, her tongue mingling with his. He tasted her, experienced her. Half-asleep with this luxurious dream, he masturbated and awoke to an orgasm that fouled the sheets and blankets. Then he lay for a full hour and sobbed like a little boy.

iii

The envelope contained a newspaper clipping from the *Seattle Times*, dated October 3, Saturday. It described the gory murder of a forty-six-year-old lawyer aboard his sailboat at Seattle's Shilshole Marina on the shore of Puget Sound. A spokesman for the police said that the assailant had literally ripped the man to pieces. An initial examination of the scene by a forensics team suggested that the murder had occurred sometime Friday night. The spokesman said that this was the most brutal, gut-turning homicide that anyone in the department could remember.

Friday night. Josh's mind started to click. *Millie Carter did this.* Why she'd gone to the trouble of mailing another clipping to him, he couldn't imagine.

He pieced together the likely sequence of events. Millie flew up to Seattle sometime on Friday, after Josh had followed her to the villa in Northwest. She located a victim, maybe picked him up in a bar as she'd done with several of the others, or struck up a conversation with him on the street; who could know? Then went with him to his boat and tore him to pieces with her claws and teeth. Josh wondered if she fucked the guy first. She stayed the night in Seattle. After the morning paper hit the streets, she bought a copy, clipped the story about the murder, and mailed the clipping to Josh. She hopped a plane back to Portland, arriving scarcely forty minutes later. She drove home from the airport and caught a pair of intruders in her house. For some reason she let them escape, but not until she'd sliced open Nicki's shoulder, using the same claws she'd used to disembowel that poor guy in Seattle.

Josh seethed. A world without Nicki was damn near unbearable, but a world with Millie Carter in it was even worse. A thing as evil as Millie Carter, a thing so toxic that a scratch from its claw would kill you, couldn't be allowed to live.

The LED readout on his clock radio said 10:15 A.M. Today was a schoolday, but he'd stayed out for the third day in a row. No telling when he would go back, if ever. School didn't matter anymore.

After listening for any sign that either his mother or his sister was at home, he carefully opened his door and peered out. Taped to the doorjamb was a Hallmark card in a peach-colored envelope, featuring a dreamy landscape executed in chalks. He read his mother's penned note, which welcomed him back to the world of the living and informed him of a baking dish in the refrigerator that contained scrambled eggs with onions, fried potatoes, and bacon bits—one of his favorites. All he needed to do was to pop the dish into the 'wave and blast it for sixty seconds. Oh, and by the way, she loved him. And so did Kendra. *See ya soon.*

Josh couldn't remember the last time he'd eaten—Sunday, maybe? Almost four days ago? The thought of food made him nauseous. He doubted that he would be able to eat until after he'd killed Millie Carter.

iv

He let himself into Lewis's apartment with the key Lewis had given him several weeks earlier, and found the place so quiet that at first he thought no one was home. As he crept toward the bedroom, however, he heard a snore that could only be Lewis's. He stood fossil still for a moment, listening for the breathing of another person. Hearing none, he moved forward again, half expecting Millie to fly out of the bedroom with her claws spread like giant spiders, her mouth stretched

into a slavering grin. Before coming here, he'd walked around
the grounds of Sloan House and looked for her Jag, but he'd
seen no sign of it. Millie wasn't here, he was certain, but he
couldn't shake the fear that she might be lying in ambush.

Lewis's blinds were shut, so his bedroom was dusky. Josh
went quickly to the table next to the bed, carefully pulled open
the drawer, and took out the old Colt .45. He paused to gaze
down at his friend, who slept with his face turned to the wall,
a light blanket covering him. Something wasn't right.

He tiptoed toward the door and stepped on something that
almost caused him to lose his balance—a shoe, one of the
casual "walking" kind that middle-aged men seemed to like.
Its mate lay two feet away.

Shoes. What did Lewis Kindred need with *shoes*?

He turned back to the slumbering form on the bed, where
Lewis lay in a tangle of blanket and sheets, the outline of his
body obscured among the folds and valleys of cloth. From this
angle, Josh could almost make himself believe that under the
blanket Lewis had two good legs.

V

He left Sloan House through the rear entrance, which stood
wide open. In the service drive was a huge United Van Lines
truck, into which three beefy men were loading furniture, appliances, and cardboard boxes. Off to one side stood the landlady, Juliet Kindred, and the young stockbroker who lived on
the second floor next to the Nickersons. They chatted amiably
in the cool late-morning sunlight. Josh surmised instantly that
the guy was leaving Sloan House, maybe because he'd decided
to marry and his wife-to-be wanted a house, not an apartment.
Or maybe his company had transferred him to another city.
Josh didn't care, and he didn't stop to chat.

As he drove into Northwest, he felt weirdly detached from
the sights and sounds of the world around him. He felt de-

tached from *himself*, as if he'd graduated to a plane of existence on which the familiar old Josh Nickerson didn't exist. He no longer cared about writing the story of Millie Carter and all her evil doings, for the time had come to give up writing and *act*. After all, he was no longer a mere observer, but a player, a victim. He'd lost Nicki, and nothing of his old life mattered anymore. Josh Nickerson had become someone else.

He parked the Escort where he and Nicki had left it on Saturday morning, on the shoulder of the road at the base of the hill, where the stucco wall marked the rear property line of Millie Carter's villa. He sat silent a moment, staring into the thicket that grew almost to the edge of the gravel. His hand went to the passenger seat, which was crusty with Nicole's blood, and remained there a moment as his fingertips searched for some lingering sensation of her touch. Tears pooled in his eyes. Anger constricted his chest.

He checked the pistol to ensure that it had a round in the chamber and that the hammer was in the half-cocked position, which was as good as engaging the safety switch, Lewis had taught him. He got out of the car and sprinted across the road.

He trudged up the hill as Nicki and he had done four days earlier, fending off damp fronds of sword fern. Here and there he noticed indentations in the soil that Nicki's boots could have made, and his heart weltered. He hauled himself into the young oak tree and went over the wall, then made his way through the tattered Italianate garden. He climbed the exterior stairs at the far end of the covered veranda. Using the butt of the pistol and disregarding the possibility of an electronic alarm, he knocked out a pane in the French door, reached through it, and freed the lock. Just that quickly he was inside the house, a criminal bent on committing a capital crime.

Down the curving staircase he went, and into the front hall, where dust and grime on the windowpanes polluted the incoming daylight. Where filaments of spiderwebs fluttered from chandeliers. He walked quickly into the foyer, squinted through the dirty glass of the doors into the front drive, and saw Millie's Jaguar with its chrome gleaming in the sunlight. He followed the Persian runner toward the rear of the house, not caring about the thump of his hiking boots. As he reached the juncture with the short hallway that led to Millie Carter's one livable room, he pulled out the pistol and thumbed the hammer back.

She waited for him just inside the walnut doors, wearing her green velvet housecoat. She stood next to the heavy round table, bathed in the glow of the Tiffany lamp, grinning at him with what might have been triumph or contempt—Josh couldn't read her blue-brown eyes. She was beautiful, and Josh loathed himself for thinking so.

"I knew it would be you," she whispered. "I've waited for this moment a long, long time. I never had any doubt that it would eventually come." She stepped away from the table and moved slowly toward him.

"*Why?*" Josh asked, his voice shaking.

"Why? That's the question of the ages, isn't it? Has it ever occurred to you that human beings are the only creatures on earth who ask it? Of all the sentient organisms on the face of this planet, there isn't one other that presumes a need to know the reasons behind events—not even whales or porpoises or chimpanzees, or any of the super-intelligent species. Only human beings feel a need to know the *why* of anything. It sets them apart."

"Why did you kill Nicki?"

Millie moved to within an arm's length of him, close enough that he could smell her perfume. Her dreadlocks were the color of cinnamon. "She was an encumbrance. She would've held you back, Josh. You didn't need her."

"Who are you to decide what I need?"

"I'm the one who loves you and your delicious anger. I've taken it upon myself to take your future into my hands. I *need* you. I've never needed anyone as much as I need you, not even Lewis."

Josh began to feel dizzy. Images whirled and swirled in his mind like wind-driven snowflakes, put there by Millie, he suspected. Wonderful images, frightening ones, carnal ones. This was another aspect of her power—the ability to put things into the heads of others. How else could she have manipulated both Lewis Kindred and Rex Caswell during a poker game in which she wasn't even a player? How else could she have manipulated five Nazi skinheads and then turned them into mannequins? Staring at her through blearing eyes, Josh wondered whether she was feeding on his anger.

Something she'd said in the downtown alley came to him: *"Never try to hold your anger in, Josh. Always let it out. Let it grow. Let it become strong and hard."* She'd wanted him to feel rage so she could feast on it.

"Why did you send me those newspaper clippings?" he demanded, pointing the pistol at her forehead. "Tell me, or I swear to God I'll blow your brains out!"

"There's no need to threaten me, Josh."

"*Tell* me!"

"I'm not sure I can. I knew that you'd seen me on the night of Ron Payne's rather messy demise, and I suppose that I wanted to connect with you in some indirect way. The time simply wasn't right for me to approach you straight on. And I did it to confound you, confuse you. To make you *angry*. It was a labor of love, Josh, I swear. You see, I'd been watching you for a long time. I'd pretended to be enamored with Ron Payne and his cohorts in that insane band, but it was really *you* I was interested in. By staying close to the band, I could stay close to you."

"Why me? What have I ever done to you?"

"Nothing. I had an initial interest in Lewis Kindred, which goes back many years. We had unfinished business, he and I, which I'm happy to say we've concluded successfully. When I started watching him, I couldn't help but notice you, since you and he are such close friends. I knew that you were an excellent prospect, just as Lewis turned out to be."

"You used the skinheads, didn't you?" Josh said, gulping. "You used them in order to get to me. Couldn't you have found an easier way, a simpler way? If you just wanted my help in giving the orb to Lewis—''

''That wasn't the only reason. I needed to fan your anger, Josh. I needed to give you a reason to let it erupt.''

''So you could use it, right? You feed on anger like normal people feed on burgers and french fries!''

''That's not entirely true. I *sample* a person's anger before I move in on him, because I need to find out what kind of person he is. Not everyone passes the test. Ron Payne is a good example. He was a very angry young man, but his anger was selfish and visceral and pointless. By tasting it, I discovered that he was shallow and weak, not a good prospect. He turned out to be good for only one thing—a meal. Not like *you*, Josh.''

''That's the second time you've used that word—*prospect*. Prospect for what?''

Millie's grin became wider, toothier. ''You'll find out soon enough. I'm afraid that I might already have told you too much.''

''You killed the men in those news clippings, didn't you? And you're *still* killing. You fly around the country every month or so, and you kill someone. Never in the same city twice, because you don't want to set a pattern. You killed those men, then you clipped the stories from the papers and sent them to me. And you killed Ron Payne.'' Josh wiped sweat out of his eyes with his free hand and breathed deeply to banish the quiver from his voice. ''Is that what you have in mind for me? Am I a good prospect to become an animal like you— a cold-blooded murderer?''

Millie's nostrils flared. ''You understand very little right now. In time you'll understand everything, and then you won't be quite so willing to condemn me.''

''Is that what you think?'' Josh lowered the heavy pistol. ''I've got news for you, bitch. I'll always condemn sick animals like you, and I'll *never* become like you.''

''Then the loss is yours. You have such potential, Josh. You're strong, tough-minded, resourceful. Your anger is the kind that could serve you, unlike the anger of so many others.

You would do so well with the gifts I offer.''

Josh turned to leave. He no longer wanted to become a killer. He remembered the promise he'd made to Nicole in this very room, that he would pursue and realize his dream of becoming a writer. ''I don't want anything from you,'' he said to Millie, spitting the words. ''I don't want any part of you or the things you do.''

''Don't go! I can give you what you never had with Nicki. I can give you what she could only give you in your dreams. You've dreamed of holding her body close to you, haven't you?—of putting your hands . . .''

She let the hunter-green robe fall to the floor and stood naked before him. Josh couldn't help but stare. A trickle of sweat ran between her breasts and over her rib cage. She played with herself, kneading her breasts so that her nipples stood rigid, and sluicing her fingers into the cleft below her pubic mound. Moaning hungrily, she showed himself to him.

''This is what you wanted to do with her, wasn't it, Josh? You wanted to kiss her here. You wanted to run your hands over her—''

Josh felt his groin come urgently alive. His anger thundered deep inside him as he remembered that he would never be able to live his dream with Nicole.

''Do it to me, Josh. Come to me, and come inside me. Do to *me* what you wanted to do with her. It'll be good, I promise. It'll be so much better than anything you would've had with her. She can't compare with me, Josh. You'll be glad she's dead.''

Josh raised the pistol again. He squeezed the trigger, heard the weapon bark, and saw fragments of Millie's brain shower the Tiffany lampshade. She slipped to the floor and lay still in a spreading lake of blood, harmless now, her perfect forehead ruined by a bullet. Acid rose in Josh's throat. Gagging, he whirled and fled to the sunshine.

Twenty-six

i

PAUL TRAN'S WIFE ushered Jesse Burton into the room where her husband lay sick, and Jesse stood at the bedside with his hands clasped respectfully in front of him. Jesse was as Tran remembered, except his closely cropped hair now had a sprinkling of gray. The decades had broadened him, rounded him, left signs of wear, but he hadn't lost the marble hardness of his black eyes.

"Jesse," Tran said, offering his trembling hand, "it's good to see you again. Thank you for coming."

The big man's face broke into a sad smile, and he took Tran's thin Vietnamese hand in his huge black one. "Your missus told me about your daughter, Paul. I can't tell you how sorry I am."

"She was a wonderful child, so beautiful, so good to us," Tran said. "She died at the hand of Gamaliel or someone like him." Jesse clamped his jaw tight when he heard this.

Tran waved him into a chair beside the bed, and his wife brought tea. He asked about Jesse's family and his work, for they hadn't talked since parting in New Orleans after visiting a *sorcière* naméd Melusinne in a Louisiana bayou, and that had been nearly nine years ago. Jesse reported that he'd earned his doctorate in education, that his work involved the use of personal computers in public schools. He had two sons now, and his wife had become a successful writer of children's stories.

Tran pointed to the bed table, where he'd placed his lacquered box with brightly painted Cao Dai iconography on its lid. The lid was open, and inside lay the marble of red glass. "Do you still have your cigar box and the steel bearing?" he asked.

Jesse nodded. "It's in my suitcase. I've kept it all these years, hoping I'd never need it. But I guess I knew deep down inside that this day would come." He picked up Tran's lacquer box and turned it over in his hands, examining it. The marble rolled around noisily inside. "Did it warn you?" he asked.

"Yes. It behaves in exactly the way the ball bearing behaved in your cigar box, when the *sorcière* cremated the small coffin. I suspect it's psychokinesis brought on by awareness of the presence of another mind."

"Gamaliel's mind?"

"His or the mind of someone like him. The theory isn't really scientific, but it's more palatable than spirits and demons, wouldn't you say?"

"Yeah. I'd just as soon not deal with spirits and demons."

On the night of September 21, the marble went mad, Tran told Jesse. Never before had the marble been so full of energy. The intensity of the experience convinced him that Lewis Kindred was under deadly assault by a determined force, that the time had come for a showdown.

He armed himself with a tire iron and the K-54 pistol that Lewis had used to shoot Gamaliel, which Tran's brother had kept for him and sent to the United States after Tran emigrated with his family. He went to Sloan House and began his surveillance.

Lewis came home to his empty apartment shortly after eight o'clock, accompanied by his young friend Josh Nickerson, who also was a close friend of Nicole. Several hours later Josh left the apartment and went home to the apartment directly above Lewis's. Hours passed, and the night grew chill, but Tran held his position behind the clump of azaleas outside the veranda near Lewis's apartment, certain that a confrontation would occur before the night was out. A few minutes after 1:00 A.M., he saw a shadowy figure approach the front entrance of Sloan House, a tall woman with hair that shone like copper in the glare of the streetlights. She took out no key, but merely put her hand to the door and pushed it open, then disappeared inside. Tran's stomach fluttered, for he knew that the doors of Sloan House were the self-locking kind. Without a key, a visitor needed to call a tenant on the intercom to gain entry, but the woman with the coppery hair hadn't done this.

More movement, this time inside Lewis's apartment—the flicker of a shadow in the window of his studio, which was next to his bedroom. Tran waited for what seemed an eternity, then ventured out of his hiding place and entered the veranda. He tried the windows and found them locked. He tried the other windows, tried the rear entrance of Sloan House and the front entrance (the one the woman had used), but found them all locked. He returned to the veranda and took the tire iron out of the bag, having decided to smash the window and get directly to the heart of the matter. If he found Lewis in bed with a creature who owned both a blue eye and a brown one, Tran meant to kill them both and try to escape, for Lewis would be beyond hope. If Lewis *wasn't* in bed with such a creature, then Tran meant to escape if he could, leaving him to live on into his dotage, with luck.

He raised the tire iron to strike at the windowpanes, but became aware of a red glow that ate the darkness like acid eats silk. An orb sailed around from behind him and hung before the window, barring his way like a miniature sun. Tran had seen one like it before, in the motor pool of Triple Deuce Mech in Cu Chi Base Camp, on the night that Lewis Kindred and Gamaliel Cartee played poker. He knew who it represented. He tried to strike at the thing with the tire iron, but it darted forward and pressed itself against his forehead. A shower of sparks erupted, blinding him. The heat seared his skin and lanced through his skull into his brain. Beyond this moment he remembered only pain.

ii

The sun sank below Gander Ridge, leaving a sky the color of ripe cantaloupe. Tran and Jesse talked about whether it was actually possible to call forth the dead to help them fight Gamaliel's kind.

Calling forth the dead, Tran suggested, was probably a metaphor for reaching deep into one's mental storehouse to find the proper psychic weapon. In his study of Eastern religions and cults over the years he'd found numerous references to mental phenomena like psychokinesis, the ability to move objects with thought, and physioplasty, the ability to contort one's body into monstrous shapes. Too, he'd read case studies about types of schizophrenia that cause a person to believe that he's a monster—a vampire or a werewolf or a demon. Psychologists had documented cases in which subjects committed unspeakable acts of murder and mutilation, even cannibalism, because they believed that they were monsters.

"Perhaps Gamaliel's kind are merely schizophrenics who have mastered psychokinesis and physioplasty," he ventured. "I hope that this is so."

"If that's the case, how did Gamaliel come alive again after Lewis put a nine-millimeter bullet through his head?" Jesse asked.

Tran closed his eyes and lay back on his pillow. "I've found no possible explanation of this, Jesse. I'm afraid there is none." He opened his eyes again and reached for Jesse's hand. "We would be honored if you would stay with us. My wife will prepare a room for you."

"You've just lost your daughter, and the funeral is tomorrow. I don't want to impose on you now. I'll find a hotel nearby, so I can be available if—"

"It isn't an imposition, Jesse. You are my brother now, my ally. I had planned to confront the evil alone, but this—" His hand went again to the blister on his forehead. "—this has robbed me of my strength. I know that the battle will require concentration and mental power. But this sickness, whatever it is—I know that I'm not up to the challenge on my own. With you, though, I can do it. Together we have the necessary strength, of this I'm certain. Stay with us. Please."

Jesse agreed to stay with the Trans. But he wanted to see Lewis, and he wanted to do it soon.

Twenty-seven

i

Rex Caswell lay in bed with the wispy Silhouette, his brawny limbs entwined with her thin, pale ones. By the light of the rising sun he leafed through the Wednesday *Oregonian*, skimming stories about the presidential race, the fighting in the Middle East, and South Africa's agonizing struggle to end apartheid. Suddenly he bolted upright, startling the girl, and stared at a police sketch in the Metro section. The headline of the story read:

POLICE HUNT SUSPECT IN GRISLY HOTEL MURDER

The sketch was from a description given by a woman who had seen the suspect in Legato Ristorante, the restaurant in the hotel. Rex scoured the story for some reference to the guy being in a wheelchair, but there wasn't any.

The face belonged to Lewis Kindred.

The suspect, according to the story, had told the woman and her friend—the victim—that his name was Zebulon Councilman, and that he worked for some philosophy writers' association in California.

That sounds so much like him, Rex thought. He remembered that Lewis was a philosophy major at the University of Oregon, and that he loved philosophy almost as much as loved poker.

Then Rex came to his senses. How could Lewis walk into a ritzy restaurant on a pair of legs that he didn't even own and put the moves on a sweet young thing, then walk her next door to the Metro Plaza, strip her naked, and tear her up into little pieces? Lewis Kindred couldn't make it to a men's room without space-age technology. Moreover, police artists were notoriously bad. The resemblance between Lewis and the face in the picture had to be coincidence, Rex told himself.

ii

Throughout the day, Rex tried to put the police artist's sketch out of his mind, but failed. Just how much was possible, he wondered, if a man had the red crystalline globe in his pocket? Did the crystal give its owner powers that went beyond the poker table? Did Millie Carter come with the crystal, or was it the other way around? Speculations fluttered through his head, both scaring and exciting him.

That evening he met Mason Benoit for a drink at the Benson Hotel in downtown Portland, one of his regular haunts. They sipped their brandies in an alcove off the wood-paneled lobby, their conversation covered by live piano music.

"In case you're curious," Benoit said, "our old homeboys from California are safely out of the country. One is in Costa Rica and the other's in Cabo San Lucas. Neither of them will set foot in the States for at least six months. With what you paid them, they should be able to live like kings." He referred to the two men he'd hired to toast a homeless black man in a wheelchair, a man known simply as Dewey.

"That's one crime that'll never be solved," Benoit went on. "No clues, no surviving family to press the issue. Just one less derelict to clutter up Old Town. Can't say the same thing, though, about that slaughter two nights ago at the Metro Plaza. The cops'll get that dude, mark my words. The city's in a fucking frenzy over it, have you noticed? Worse than when Ron Payne got himself done last spring."

"Did you see the police artist's sketch in today's paper?" Rex asked.

"I did."

"Who did it look like to you?"

"Promise not to stop liking me for being a lunatic?"

Rex nodded.

"It's Lewis Kindred."

Rex studied his glass and smiled indulgently. "Lewis must have an evil twin, eh? Speaking of Lewis, I haven't given up on getting that red crystal. When I *do* get it, I'm going to play one more round of poker with him, and I'm going to take him for everything he has. I may even call our homeboys back from their vacations and give them some work to do, depending on the mood I'm in. Or I may let Lewis twist in the wind for the rest of his worthless, poverty-stricken life.''

"What's the point of it? You lost some big bucks to Kindred, sure, but you're not hurting for money. Why do you care about mashing some pathetic middle-aged double amputee?''

Rex toyed with his ear pin. "Nobody makes an ass of Rex Caswell and gets away with it, Mason. You should know that by now—especially not an arrogant prick who doesn't even have a pair legs to stand on. I've taken his shit way too long.''

Benoit blew out a sigh. "There's no way you're going to get the crystal from Millie Carter. I've never said this before, Rex, but she's one spooky bitch. When Spit and I were following her and Kindred around, I sometimes got the feeling that she could stare through solid walls with those damn unmatched eyes of hers. She's a good one to steer clear of.''

Rex's face brightened as an idea hit him. "Maybe we don't need to concern ourselves with her. I don't know why I didn't think of this before.''

"Think of what?''

"I should be concentrating on the *kid*, Lewis's little pal—what's his name? Joshua! Josh, he calls him. For years I've been hearing Lewis talk about him like he's his own son. They live in the same apartment building, and the kid practically grew up on Lewis's doorstep. Lewis talks about how good in school the kid is, what girls he dates, where he plans to go to college. To hear him talk, this Josh is the hope of the twenty-first century. And Josh was at the Fanshawe the night of the rematch.''

"You're thinking he probably knows something about the orb?''

"He was there when Lewis took it out of his pocket and tossed it back to Millie, right after the game. And there was something else, too—something I hadn't remembered until just now. Millie Carter had an *effect* on that kid.''

"Hey, she has an effect on everybody."

"But not like this. You should've seen him. When we walked into the room, he took one look at Millie and got white as a sheet. There's a history between those two, I'm sure of it."

"What's this got to do with the orb?"

"I'm telling you, Mase, the kid and Lewis are close. If either Millie or Lewis has the orb, that kid will have access to it. And something tells me—call it intuition, or call it knowing people—something tells me that Josh will cooperate with me. I'll use him to get the orb, and I'll worry about Millie later."

"Sounds like a good idea," said Benoit, signaling the waiter to bring another round of Courvoisier. "Use the kid and stay away from Millie. I'm serious about this, Rex. That bitch is bad news. I don't know how I know this, but she can hurt a man. She can hurt a man real deeply."

Twenty-eight

i

THE HUNGER WOKE him long after nightfall. He swung his legs over the edge of the mattress and planted his feet solidly on the carpet. For a long time he sat still in the dark, tasting the coarse pile of the carpet through the soles of his feet. *You never know what you've got till you've lost it,* he mused.

> *This little piggy went to market.*
> *This little piggy stayed home. . . .*

He wiggled his toes. He massaged the instep of one foot with the big toe of the other. He played joyfully with his feet, visualizing the miraculous articulation of tarsus, metatarsus, and phalanges, conjuring images and anatomical terms that hadn't entered his mind since his high-school biology class studied human anatomy. The components of the human foot. *Navicular. Os calsis. Cuboid . . .*

And thanks to the fact that the ringing in his ears was gone, he could hear a dripping faucet in the bathroom. And his left hand was still limber and strong, his left arm as good as his right. He was whole.

The hunger growled and squirmed, promising some horrible consequence if an appropriate feeding didn't occur soon.

He'd dreamed of Millie while asleep, a long, sweaty dream in which she'd approached his bedside and slowly peeled away her clothes. She'd knelt before him and let him lick her nipples to hardness. She'd encouraged his mouth downward, into her navel, then farther down still as she arched over him, humping his face. She'd kissed and licked him around his midsection, and had taken one of his testicles into her mouth at the very moment his tongue slithered over the lips of her sex. For a primal moment he was certain that an orgasm would thrust him into transcendental ecstasy, but it never happened. Sounds intruded from far away, the bleep of his telephone and the buzz of his answering machine. The dream withered. He heard his own voice tell the caller that he couldn't come to the phone right now, but to leave a message.

"Lewis, are you there, man? It's me, Jesse Burton, at— uh—nine-fifty in the evening. You've got to talk to me. I've come all the way from Chicago, and I'm here in Portland. I've got to see you, Lewis. It's important. . . ."

Vietnam is chasing me, Lewis told himself. The voice in the machine was Jesse's, yes. And Jesse was Vietnam. As the hunger was Vietnam. As Millie and the orb and Gamaliel Cartee had all been Vietnam.

I've been slipping in and out of a psychogenic fugue. I don't really have legs, even though I can feel them and see them as plain as the nose on my face. But seriously, folks, I may not even have a face . . .

He'd laughed out loud as the machine cut off Jesse's pleas.

. . . or arms or hands. I may not even have a head. For all I know, I may not even be alive. Vietnam may have already eaten me!

How much of himself can a man lose before he becomes someone else? Some*thing* else?

ii

The White Eagle Café and Saloon on North Russell, the cabdriver had said, was famous for straight-ahead live rock and roll on Wednesday nights. The establishment stood in a dismal industrial quarter near the east shore of the Willamette River, an area that once boasted a lively maritime trade. In the old days, the building had housed a brothel.

No punk or grunge at the White Eagle. No spikeheads, skinheads, or Gothics. The crowd was middle-aged professionals, blue-collar types, and bikers (some of whom merely dressed the part, others who lived it), the common denominator being a love of good old-fashioned rock music played live and loud.

The place was also haunted, said local legend. Patrons sometimes complained of harassment in the men's room by a poltergeist, supposedly the spirit of a prostitute brutally murdered in an upstairs bedroom by a drunken john. A recent patron had reported that something had thrown him against a wall, while another claimed to have had his penis bitten. No one had established with certainty that the ghost was responsible for either attack.

In his college days, Lewis had been a frequent customer of the White Eagle, but he'd never encountered the ghost. Maybe he would encounter her tonight, he thought hopefully, flushing the urinal after emptying himself of his third pint of Widmer Oktoberfest.

He made his way from the rest room back to the bar, dodging couples on the dance floor, eager to get back to the business at hand. Halfway across the floor he halted to glance behind him, certain that he'd heard something among the layers of music blaring from the stage—a rustling or a hiss. But he saw nothing out of the ordinary among the sweaty dancers, no one following him or hiding in the shadows.

Kaycee waited for him on a bar stool. She was a raven-haired beauty in fire-engine red lipstick and the tightest Levi's he'd ever seen. He'd met her an hour ago, and she'd taken a shine to him. Everything that came out of his mouth, it seemed, was magic to a woman's ear.

Kaycee Logan, her full name was. A dental hygienist from an eastern suburb of Portland, divorced at thirty-five. Mother of three, but you wouldn't know it from the tautness of her ass. Lewis figured that within the hour he would be fucking her to death. Literally. And then . . . well, he didn't want to think about it. His hunger was like a blast furnace.

"How 'bout I buy you kids a drink?" someone asked as Lewis reclaimed his bar stool. He turned and saw a square-jawed man in his forties, tall and rawboned, easy blue eyes, wavy brown hair. The man would have looked comfortable in a wide-brimmed Stetson and cowboy boots, but he wore a corduroy sport coat over a button-down shirt, the gear of an urban professional out on the town.

Lewis suffered a thrill of panic. The man was Scott Sanders.

"*Doctor* Scott Sanders," the guy said, beaming, as if he'd heard Lewis say the name in his head. "I'm an osteopath these days. Got myself a clinic out in Beaverton. It's good to see you again, L.T. I mean that. I think about you a lot."

Lewis's mouth dried as a scene from the distant past flickered in his mind. He saw tracer rounds slashing the sky above the Ho Bo Woods, felt the crunch of incoming mortar rounds and rocket-propelled grenades. Specialist Scott Sanders, a medic of Lewis's scout platoon, jumped into the bushes where Lewis and Jesse cowered from the blizzard of hot metal. Sanders's uniform was gory with the blood of a wounded GI to whom he'd ministered moments ago, and Lewis's uniform was crusty with the blood of Gamaliel Cartee.

"Thought you were a goner, L.T.! Where you bleedin' from?" At that moment a bullet ripped through Scott's chest and blew his heart out through his back. His face went slack, and his forehead thudded onto Lewis's shoulder.

"You're dead," said Lewis, having regained control of his mouth. "You're not here. I saw you die."

"Never trust what you see, L.T." The late Scott Sanders chuckled. "The eyes will lie to you every chance they get. Now, why don't you introduce me to your date?"

Lewis heard himself say Kaycee's name, then Scott's name. Heard himself describe Scott as a former rodeo rider from Wyoming. All-around cowboy. Got drafted and sent to Vietnam, where he—

"Where I was a medic," Scott interrupted. "That's what got me interested in medicine. When the army turned me loose, I went back to school and stayed there until I made something of myself, as they say. I miss rodeoin', but my wife hates the smell of livestock, so I s'pose it's a good thing I'm into what I'm into. Ever been to a rodeo?"

Kaycee had. In fact, she *loved* rodeos, but she'd never met an actual cowboy before. Had Scott ever ridden a bull? Or a bucking bronc? Scott explained that an all-around cowboy masters a wide range of rodeo skills, including calf-roping, saddle-bronc-riding. . . .

Thus went the conversation until the band took a break. Kaycee excused herself to visit the ladies' room, pronouncing her lipstick in need of attention. Lewis's hunger raged like a fever.

"Fine-lookin' girl," said Scott, saluting her with his whiskey glass as she clicked away across the dance floor in her tight Levi's and spike heels. "You're a lucky man, L.T. I hope you treat her right."

"Tell me," Lewis said, "do you ever see anyone else from our platoon? I mean like Jesse Burton or T. J. Skane? Or how about Danny Legler? Ever run into any of those guys?"

"I doubt that I see as much of them as you do, L.T."

"Why's that?"

"Because I suspect that No Bick has sent them to you. Just like he sent me."

Lewis's flesh went cold. "You've seen No Bick?"

"Haven't you?"

"Now and then, I guess." Lewis stared at Scott Sanders. The guy should be moldering in a coffin, six feet deep in some veterans' cemetery in Wyoming, but here he was, having become what Lewis would have expected him to become if he'd survived Vietnam. "No Bick's here in Portland, you know. The little son of a bitch stole one of my legs the day I got them blown off in the Ho Bo Woods. Took it somewhere and roasted it on a spit, then stripped the meat off and ate it. Probably ground the bones to powder and drank them with rice wine." Lewis took a swig of ale to douse the fire in his throat. "Now he wants the rest of me. He creeps around my apartment at night, rattling the windows, looking for a way in. He carries a pistol and—"

"Lewis, do you really believe that?"

"Why the fuck shouldn't I believe it? I believe in *you*, don't I? I'm sitting here drinking with you, listening to your voice even though I know you're deader than dinosaur shit. Besides, I know what I've seen."

"And I've told you your eyes will deceive you, and so will your other senses, if you're not careful. You can't take things at face value, L.T."

Lewis became angry. "Okay, why don't you tell me the truth, damn it? If I can't believe anything I see or hear, I'll let you be my eyes and ears. I'll believe whatever you tell me, I swear."

"It's not that easy."

"No, I didn't think so."

"The truth is inside you, L.T., where it's always been, where you've always found it before."

"The truth about what?"

"About what's right and wrong, good and bad. The only truth that counts. Remember the time you stopped Gamaliel

Cartee from torturing a young girl and an old woman in—where the hell were we? Somewhere north of Trung Lap, I think. It was the same day that a big mine blew up a civilian bus and killed something like ninety civilians. The Old Man brought in Cartee to—''

''I remember, Scottie. Let's not relive it down to the last fucking detail, okay?''

''I understand. The point is that you did what you did because of what was *inside* you. You knew right from wrong, and you didn't need anybody to define it for you, least of all the damn army. You didn't buy all that military bullshit about how it's okay to do something ugly and outrageous if it saves GIs' lives, or if it means fewer people get killed in the long run, or if it shortens the war. You knew that it was wrong to beat up a little girl and an old woman, period. You knew that no amount of rationalizing would make it right. And you had the guts to do something about it, which isn't true of everybody, I'm sorry to say.''

''I don't see what that has to do with the here and now.''

''I'll make it as plain as I can. You can't avoid taking responsibility for the things you let yourself do, Lewis, even in a dream. If you decide to let yourself become—well, you know what I mean. If you let yourself become—''

''No, I *don't* know what you mean! Become what?''

''I'm talking about whatever killed the girl in the Metro Plaza a couple of nights back. If you let yourself become *that*, then you can't avoid living with the responsibility.''

Lewis felt wobbly. He gripped the edge of the bar to keep himself from keeling over. ''That night at the hotel—it didn't happen. It was all part of a psychogenic fugue, a dream. I can't be held accountable for what happened that night.''

''I wish that was true, L.T. If there's any hope for you, it lies in your freedom to choose goodness over''—he coughed, not liking what he had to say—''over whatever it is you're about to choose.''

Lewis held tightly to the bar. The room was tilting oddly. ''Hey, I don't have the ability to choose anything anymore,'' he protested. "I'm a schizo, Scottie. Understand? I have fugues and fantasies and dreams. I'm a fucking *victim*!"

"Not so," whispered Scott, leaning close to him. "You chose to do what you did to that girl, because you needed it to become a whole man. Eating the meat and drinking the blood was the price of a permanent pair of legs."

"You're lying!"

"You know I'm not. You knew the truth from the beginning. Millie Carter gave you the first taste of wholeness, but to keep it, you need to do what she does, what Gamaliel does."

"She's not like Gamaliel, and I could never become like Gamaliel!"

Scott forced Lewis around so that he faced the dance floor, where Kaycee Logan strode across toward the bar from the ladies' room. Her hips lurched with every step, and her breasts jiggled beneath her knitted top. She smiled when she noticed that both Scott and Lewis were watching her.

"What do you feel when you see her?" hissed Scott in Lewis's ear. "Is it what a normal man feels? What do you plan to do with her after you get her into bed tonight?"

Lewis's stomach cramped, nearly causing him to double over, but Scott held him firmly atop the stool. The sight of Kaycee fanned the hunger to white-hotness, and sweat dripped from his jaw. He couldn't deny what he wanted to do to her. He couldn't deny knowing that a bellyful of her flesh and a snootful of her blood would give him the nourishment he needed. Eating flesh, drinking blood—this was the price of owning a real man's body, and he knew it. He'd *chosen* it.

"No!" He convulsed on the bar stool, but Scott held him steady. "I can't let it happen again, Scottie!"

"I'll help you get through it, Lewis. I'll help you be strong. . . ."

"What's going on here?" asked Kaycee, staring at Lewis and Scott as they clung to one another. "Is this what I think it is?"

"K-Kaycee, I think you'd better go," Lewis managed. "All

of a sudden I don't feel so well.''

"I'm sorry to hear that," she replied. "Well, thanks for the drink. I hope you two are very happy together." She clicked away on her tall heels, pouting with disappointment.

iii

Scott guided Lewis out to the sidewalk, where a dense mist sucked up the light of the street lamps. The night was dark and wet. Lewis leaned against the grainy bricks of the White Eagle and breathed heavily, his clothes sopping with sweat.

"Wait here," said Scott. "I'll call you a cab. Will you be okay for a minute or two?"

"I'll be okay." Before Scott could duck back inside the White Eagle, Lewis caught his sleeve. "What about you? Are you coming with me?"

"Where I'm going, I don't need a cab." He grinned in the way Lewis remembered, then went inside.

A minute turned into two minutes, then five, then ten. Lewis concentrated on keeping himself from collapsing onto the filthy sidewalk. Many times the heavy front door of the saloon swung open, letting people in or out, but if anyone paid any attention to the sick-looking man leaning against the bricks, Lewis didn't know it. His hunger turned into nausea, and he was glad, because now he was incapable of harming anyone. He shuddered to think what he would have done to poor Kaycee if Scott Sanders hadn't come along.

Good old Scottie Sanders.

If there's any hope for you at all, it lies in your freedom to choose goodness. . . .

Lewis realized that he was slipping down the wall. A familiar old squeal filled his ears, and when he tried to steady himself with his left arm, it crumbled under him. He went down hard on his ass, biting his tongue, and sat for a full two minutes amid the cigarette butts and the used hypodermic needles before realizing what had happened.

The hunger was gone now. His head was clear. Gone, too, were his legs. Gone were the little piggies.

. . . and this little piggy cried wee-wee-wee . . .

Through a blur of tears he saw two sets of feet approach from the curb, a pair of huge wing tips and a pair of Nike cross-trainers. He lifted his eyes, feeling lower than he'd ever felt in his life. A legless vet on a filthy sidewalk outside a saloon. Total degradation.

He saw two faces. His vision cleared as the tears fell away, and he recognized Josh. With him was Jesse Burton.

They got down on their haunches, took his hands in theirs. Lewis tried to smile. "I have no idea what this is all about," he said, his voice shaking. "But am I glad you guys showed up!"

"We're going to take you home, Lew," said Josh. "If you want to go, that is."

"Are you kidding? I've never wanted to go home so bad in my life."

"I've got your wheelchair in the car. Wait right here, and I'll bring it."

"How did you . . . ? I mean, why are you here?"

"Jesse called me," said the boy. "I'll let him explain everything." Josh jumped to his feet and jogged away to fetch the wheelchair.

Lewis tightened his grip on Jesse's hand. "How long has it been, man?"

"Too long. Sorry I haven't come before this."

"No sweat, GI. We all have our crosses to bear."

"I tried to call you earlier tonight, but if you were there, you weren't picking up."

"I couldn't answer. I didn't want you to see . . ."

"I know."

"You do?"

"Lewis, listen to me. I'm staying with the Tran family who live down the block from your apartment house—"

"The *Tran* family? You mean Nicole Tran's family? You know them?"

"I do now. After I called, I decided to pay a visit to you in person. I was just leaving the Trans' house when I saw you—" Jesse swallowed. "I saw you *walking* down Gander Circle. Naturally I didn't think it could be you."

Lewis chuckled bitterly, picked up an empty Rockport shoe with a white athletic sock inside. He held it out. "You like these? They're comfortable as hell. You ought to try a pair, Jess. I'd give you mine, but I think your feet are too damn big."

Jesse sniffed and wiped moisture from his eyes. "I followed you," he went on. "I jumped into my rental car and followed you down the block, because I couldn't have kept up with you on foot. You were going fast, L.T., faster than a normal man could've gone, I think. Maybe it was my imagination."

"No, it wasn't your imagination. When I've got legs, I can walk faster than most people can run. Know what else? I think I could probably go up the side of a building, if I wanted to. Amazing, but true."

Jesse had followed him down Gander Ridge and across the freeway to the campus of Portland State University. Lewis had headed north into the heart of the downtown business district. Somewhere near the Center for the Performing Arts, he'd hailed a cab, and the cab had brought him here to the White Eagle.

"I followed you inside and watched you put the moves on that lady with the tight jeans. I thought about approaching you, but I was afraid of how you might react."

"I don't blame you. I can be a very ugly guy when I've got legs. But hey, does that lady have a nice ass, or what? As I recall, you were quite the hound in your day."

"You've had too much beer, L.T."

"You may be right. Or hell, you may be wrong. It's possible that I haven't had nearly enough beer. It's possible that I need something much stronger."

Jesse explained that he had used the pay phone inside the

White Eagle to call Paul Tran, who was Nicole's father. Paul, unfortunately, was too weak to make the trip to the White Eagle, but he'd suggested that Jesse call Josh Nickerson, who was Lewis's best friend.

"Josh seemed like he knew me," said Jesse. "He said you often talked about me and the others in the scout platoon. Said you've got a picture of us hanging on your wall."

"Yeah, Josh knows you, all right. He knows T. J. and Leg and—" Lewis grabbed Jesse's arm and squeezed it hard enough to make the big man cringe. "Tell me something, Jess. Tonight, inside the bar—did you see me talk to anyone besides the lady with the ass? He would've been a guy about your age, about my height when I have legs. He was a white guy—"

"Corduroy sport coat? Brown hair?"

"He's the one. Did you recognize him? Do you know who he was?"

"I didn't get close enough, Lewis. Should I have known him?"

"It was Scott Sanders. He kept me from becoming—" He shut his eyes. No way could he confess this just yet, especially not to Jesse Burton. "He saved my ass, Jess. Someday I'll try to explain it to you, assuming I can ever believe it myself. He said No Bick sent him to me. Can you believe that? Even more strange, he said that No Bick sent *you*. It didn't make any sense, I know, but—"

"He was right. No Bick *did* send me to you."

"I guess I've had too much beer after all. I thought you just said—"

"Lewis, No Bick sent me to you. He's here in Portland. His name is Paul Tran now, and he lives down the street from you. Nicole was his daughter. . . ."

Twenty-nine

i

THE FOLLOWING AFTERNOON, a drizzling Thursday, Josh drove his Escort to the Mount Calvary Cemetery rather than ride with his mother and sister in the family car. He and Nicole had covered so many miles together in this old junker that he felt as if a part of her would always live in the passenger seat. He wanted to be alone with that part of her, if only for the few minutes the drive took.

The graveside service for Nicole Tran was a secular "meditation," led by a family counselor that her father had retained for the occasion. Long after the other mourners had trickled away, Josh stood on the edge of the open hole and stared at the glossy mahogany coffin, feeling a vast emptiness inside him. Only when he heard the engine of an approaching backhoe, the gravedigger coming to fill in the hole, did he wander down the hillside toward the road.

Halfway down the hill, he turned back toward the grave, the moment that the backhoe pushed damp brown earth into the hole. A torrent of emotion almost drove him to his knees, but someone caught him from behind and steadied him with strong hands. He turned and saw the wrecked face of Millie Carter, mere inches from his own.

Josh's scream congealed in his throat. He tried to push her away, but she was far stronger than he. Her face was the color of a bottom-feeding fish, the whites of her eyes a sodden yellow. She had a neat bullet hole in her forehead that Josh himself had put there, surrounded by brown scorch marks from the muzzle flash. She wore a white raincoat, its hood covering her head but for a few stray hanks of dreadlocks that dangled over her face like snakes. On her feet were white sneakers, spotted with stains that might have been blood. Except for her eyes, which glowered brown on the left and blue on the right, she looked dead. She *smelled* dead, too, thanks to bugs and fungus and bacteria. Millie Carter was a walking dead woman.

"I have something for you," she said, her throat rattling. "It's something special. A gift for a very special young man." Grinning with her white teeth, she reached into her pocket and brought out an orb, maybe *the* orb. From it shot sprays of red light that played across her raincoat like living things. She pressed it into his palm, and its warmth sickened him. "It's yours now, Josh. Keep it, and use it. You've *earned* it."

Millie let loose of him and whirled away, her feet scarcely skimming the wet green turf on the hillside.

ii

Without lowering the binoculars from his face, Mason Benoit said, "Give me the phone." Spit Pittman reached across the steering wheel, snatched the cellular phone from its cradle, and pressed the button that dialed his boss's number. By the time he handed the phone to Benoit, Rex Caswell's phone was ringing in his floating house.

"Rex, it's me," said Benoit. "Spit and I are at the Mount Calvary Cemetery near Sylvan Heights. The kid and his family went to a funeral, and we—"

"A funeral? Whose funeral?"

"How the hell should I know whose funeral? We just followed them here. We're maybe two hundred yards from the grave, parked on the road. The kid stayed behind after everybody else left, like maybe he was real close to whoever died and wanted to spend some time at the grave."

"Has anyone seen you?"

"No, it's dead out here, if you'll forgive the expression. It's a Thursday afternoon, and the weather's shitty. But listen to this, man. Josh walks away from the grave, like he's headed for his car, right? And who do you think dashes out of the trees and grabs him? None other than the talented and lovely Millie Carter. It happens while I'm watching with binoculars, and I can see everything that goes on—''

''Millie's out there at the cemetery? Right now?''

''No, she's not here now. I don't know where she is. Let me finish. The kid struggles with her like he wants to get away, and I can see why, because she looks like death warmed over. I mean, she looks like she belongs in quarantine. She doesn't let him go, just holds on to him tight, right there on the side of the hill with the rain coming down in buckets. It's like she's got the strength of a Cape buffalo. And then—are you ready for this?—she pulls a ball of red glass out of her pocket and hands it to him. The kid acts like he doesn't want to take it, and staggers around for a few seconds, like someone has hit him with a baseball bat. Then Millie runs over the hill like an antelope, and that's the last we see of her.''

''She's strong as a Cape buffalo and runs like an antelope? I thought you said she looked sick.''

''Rex, she looked worse than sick. But I've never seen anyone run like that before—almost like *flying*. It gave me the fucking creeps.''

''Where's Josh now?''

''Sitting on a damn gravestone in the rain, staring at the crystal.''

Rex was silent a moment. ''Is there anyone else around?''

''There was a guy here with some kind of tractor to fill in the grave, but he did his thing and split. Like I said, it's a Thursday afternoon, Rex. People don't visit graves on a Thursday afternoon in the rain.''

''Take it from him. Do it now.''

''You mean the crystal? Just walk up and take it from him?''

''Make sure nobody sees you. And be nice about it, if you can. Offer the kid some money.''

''How much?''

''I don't give a fuck how much! Offer him a hundred dollars, a thousand dollars. I'll reimburse you.''

''What if he doesn't want to sell it?''

''Then *take* it from him. Listen, Mason, I don't care how

you do it. Just get the goddamn orb and bring it to me. You understand?''

Mason Benoit understood.

iii

The managers of this particular cemetery allowed no traditional gravestones; only the kind that lay flush with the turf—metal and marble plates in the ground with the decedents' names and dates engraved on them. Josh sat on one, his knees drawn up to his chin and his arms wrapped tight around his shins. The rain had matted his auburn hair and penetrated his heavy wool hunter's jacket, but he felt neither the wetness nor the chill. He sat here because he needed to make sense of a life that was disintegrating before his eyes.

He stared unblinkingly across the hillside into the valley below, where lay suburban Washington County, which from this perch looked like a sea of cloud. Down there were hundreds of thousands of ordinary, everyday people who lived blessedly humdrum lives. For them, reality was fighting traffic, paying credit-card bills, paper-training the puppy, whatever. Few of them had ever killed another human being, he was certain. And not one, he was willing to bet, had killed someone only to see her alive again the next day.

His life had slipped into a pit, where the rules were different from the ones normal people live by. He could no longer count on creation to behave as he'd always expected it to behave. Here, in the bottom of the pit, a double amputee could grow his legs back, as Lewis Kindred had done last night. An orb of red crystal could make you unbeatable in poker. A beautiful black-white woman could transform herself into a beast with toxic claws.

And Nicole Tran could die.

Two men trudged up the hill, one holding an umbrella. They were big men, but one was *incredibly* big and dumb-looking, the white one. The black man looked intelligent but not particularly friendly.

"You must be Josh Nickerson," said the intelligent one, offering his hand. Josh didn't accept the handshake, but sat still on the cold grave marker. Something didn't seem right about these two. "Today's your lucky day, Josh. You're about to make some money."

The orb throbbed in Josh's hand, and grew noticeably warmer. He suffered a vision of freshly shed blood pouring from a vat into a deep, dark pit. The black man bent low and smiled at him. "Are you up for doing a little business?"

"I don't know who you are."

"Let's say I represent a man who's willing to relieve you of something you don't really want, and he's ready to pay you handsomely for it. I'm talking about the thing you're holding in your hand. That ball of glass Millie Carter gave you."

"What does he want with it?"

"Seems to me that's his business. He asks no questions of you, and you ask none of him."

Josh felt sick. *When is it going to end?* He raised his eyes to those of the crouching black man's, and saw a glitter of something that frightened him. Something cruel and without feeling. "Does he know what it can do? It's no ordinary piece of glass, you know. It can be dangerous."

The huge white guy stepped forward and prodded Josh's butt with an athletic shoe that looked as though someone had urinated on it. "Let's not waste any more time, dude. Our man wants to buy that fuckin' thing. You want to sell it or what?"

The black man produced an eel-skin billfold and took out a pair of hundred-dollar bills, which he held in front of Josh's face. "Ever hear of 'caveat emptor,' Josh? It means that the buyer takes all the risk for any merchandise he buys. My employer knows all about caveat emptor. In fact, he practices that principle in his own business life. It means you don't need to worry about what this little ball of glass can do or what it can't do. Once you've sold it, you're free of all responsibility. Now, what do you say? Let's do a deal."

Josh wondered whether the orb would allow transfer of its ownership to someone other than the one to whom the Millie-thing had given it. Interesting question, this. "I won't sell it to you," he said, causing the white guy's muddy little eyes to narrow menacingly. "I'll *give* it to you."

"Seriously?"

"Seriously. God knows I don't want it." Josh pushed the orb toward him, and Benoit reached for it eagerly, but when his fingers closed around it, his eyes widened. "Damn it, what's it doing?" He dropped his umbrella. A stream of red sparks shot out from between his fingers. He screamed and flipped the orb into the air. The white man grabbed for it and caught it like a baseball, but as soon as his hand closed around the orb, he screamed at the top of his lungs. His hand became a nest of sparks. He shuddered and twitched as if undergoing a violent electrical shock, and for a moment his tiny eyes actually rolled back into his head.

"Spit, drop the fucking thing!" screamed Benoit. "Drop it before it kills you!"

"I—I—I c-c-can't! I c-can't let g-g-go!" The orb hauled Spit off the ground to a height of six or seven feet, and he flailed helplessly in the rain like a man suspended by his thumbs. Hot sparks continued to shoot out from between his fingers, streaming to the ground like microscopic suns. "H-h-help me, Mase, for God's sake! I c-can't b-breathe . . . !"

Mason Benoit grabbed Josh by the collar of his sopping jacket and jerked him to a standing position. "You're doing this! Stop it right now, hear me? Make that thing let go of Spit, or I'll twist your fuckin' head off!"

"I can't! I'm not doing anything!"

Benoit let him have the back of his hand, and Josh's head snapped to one side. He heard vertebrae pop in his neck, saw stars explode behind his eyes. He tasted blood on his lip.

"You're doing it!" Benoit roared. "It's some kind of re-mote-control device! You can make it leave Spit alone! Now *do* it!"

"I can't, I tell you! I wish I could!"

Benoit drove a fist into his stomach, causing Josh to fold up like a lawn chair. He buckled forward, choking and heaving, but Benoit hoisted him up again. Through tearing eyes he saw Spit fall to the ground, his hands released. The orb settled gently to the earth and lay still in the wet grass.

Benoit maneuvered Josh into a hammerlock and held him. "Nice going, you little shit. You've just pissed off the West Coast distributor of wholesale trouble. Spit—you okay?"

The hulk got slowly to his feet. "I think so," he answered. Josh saw recent sutures in his scalp, half-hidden by hair that hadn't yet grown out. Someone had apparently worked him over with a blunt object. "What're we going to do with this little puke?"

"That remains to be seen." Benoit reached into his coat for his cellular phone. "Hold him. I need to talk to Rex."

Spit took over the hammerlock while Benoit consulted someone who Josh assumed was Rex Caswell. Josh didn't hear the entire conversation, because Spit levered his left forearm so tightly against his shoulder blade that muscles and tendons screamed with pain. Finally, Benoit tucked the c-phone away, and Spit loosened the hammerlock slightly.

"Okay, listen up," said Benoit. "You're going to pick up that ball of glass and put it in your pocket. You're going to keep it out of sight and safe, hear? Move!" Spit let Josh go, but stayed close to him as he walked the few steps to where the orb lay innocently in the grass.

Josh hesitated before picking it up, fearing that it might do to him what it did to the human gorilla, but then he realized that this wasn't likely. Millie had meant the orb for *him*, just as Gamaliel Cartee had meant another orb for Lewis Kindred. Josh couldn't give it away. He doubted that he could throw it away, either, as Lewis had tried to do. It would always come back, just as Lewis's orb had always come back. Josh plucked the thing from the grass, held it a moment to confirm that it would spew no fireworks. It wasn't even warm. He slipped it into the pocket of his baggy black pants.

"Now we're going for a nice ride in my nice new BMW,"

announced Benoit. He shoved Josh in the direction of the cemetery road. "You'll ride in the trunk, of course. I think you'll find it reasonably comfortable. Most people do." From behind him came Spit's rough laughter and a metallic click that sounded like someone cocking a pistol.

iv

"Lewis, somehow I'm going to get you out of this," vowed Jesse Burton as he pulled the door open to leave. "Paul Tran and I will figure something out, I promise. Try to get some rest now, okay? And don't worry. I'll check back with you tonight."

Lewis waved feebly from the living room, where he sat next to his beloved ficus tree, slumped in his wheelchair and looking like a character out of Kafka. "Thanks, Jess. Thanks for everything."

Get me out of what? he thought, watching the door close. *Insanity? Hell?* He wondered whether Jesse meant to get him a shrink or a shaman. Or both.

He motored into the kitchen and fetched a Beck's from the fridge, opened it, and drained half the bottle with a single chug. He belched and chuckled under his breath. Jesse and No Bick. What a combo. *Oops*, not No Bick these days—but *Paul*. Paul Tran, the former Tran Van Hai, once a Vietcong sapper, today a tycoon in the janitorial business in Portland, Oregon. *And* devourer of severed legs, don't forget.

Not so, Jesse had insisted. Paul hadn't eaten Lewis's leg. And he hadn't followed Lewis from Vietnam to devour him, but to *save* him. To save him from Gamaliel's kind. Paul Tran had summoned Jesse to help in the effort.

The story that Jesse had told him last night would have sounded ludicrous to anyone who hadn't lived in Lewis Kindred's skin for the past twenty-two years—a story that began with Paul Tran's visit to a renegade Cao Dai priest in Vietnam. Jesse and Tran had consulted a *sorcière* in southern Louisiana years later, and they'd learned some particulars concerning the creature whom he and Lewis had known as Gamaliel Cartee, a creature who ate human flesh and drank human blood. But hadn't Lewis known this in his heart all along? Was any of this news to him?

He no longer trusted his ability to differentiate reality from black fantasy. Vietnam had eaten most of his mind and soul, he was certain, leaving precious little for him to hang any hopes on. So what the hell? Let Paul Tran and Jesse Burton carry on with whatever mumbo jumbo they deemed appropriate. Like chicken soup, what could it hurt?

He had serious worries, though, about Josh. The kid had suffered too much. His young face had become a mask of pain and barely controlled panic. Lewis had studied that mask last night, after Jesse and Josh brought him home from the White Eagle. Josh had quietly listened to Jesse's account of his involvement with Paul Tran, grimacing now and again as if he itched to tell a story of his own. Several times he'd stared straight at Lewis, his green eyes brimming with a *knowing* that Lewis expected him to blurt out at any moment. But Josh had kept it in, bottled up like a restless genie. He'd winced whenever Jesse mentioned Millie Carter, and had nodded unconsciously upon hearing that Paul Tran believed that she was of the same kind as Gamaliel.

And today, thought Lewis, feeling an ache in his heart, *Josh is burying Nicki.*

Lewis motored back into his living room and halted before his window, beyond which gray October ruled. As usual in autumn, Mount Hood lay in hiding behind her veils of rain. Lewis longed for a glimpse of her face, thinking that the goddess owed him that much, at least.

"And why do you think she owes you anything?" asked someone behind him. Lewis knew instantly who it was. The Louisiana accent was unmistakable, as was the ability to hear his thoughts. He maneuvered his chair around to face Millie Carter, who sat on the sofa. At her feet lay a small zippered tote, suggesting that she'd come prepared to stay.

She looked impossibly sick, a terror of rancid meat in a white raincoat. She'd wrapped a flowered silk scarf around her head, but something awful had seeped into the silk from her forehead and stained it. "Really, Lewis. I can't look that bad. You should see your eyes. They're big as half-dollars."

"Millie, what's happened to you?"

She shrugged theatrically.

"How did you get in?"

"The same way you would've, through the door. As you should know by now, locks don't bother me much."

"Why did you come back?"

"I was *drawn* back. By you. I sensed that you're struggling with yourself, Lewis, and I came back to help you one more time. I feel a responsibility toward you."

"*Help* me? I don't understand."

"You've resisted the hunger, and you've reverted back to"—she waved a hand at him contemptuously—"*this*. It must be horrible for you, having regained the fullness of life in a whole body, and now being forced to . . . well, you know what I mean. Fortunately you're not beyond help. Another taste of me will put you on the track again."

Lewis suffered a jolt of revulsion. He was certain now that Millie was dead. Someone had killed her, maybe shot her in the head. She meant to share her contagion with him, which could only mean . . .

He gagged. "Millie, please. Not this."

She rose from the sofa and loosened the belt of her raincoat. As she stepped toward him, the coat fell away, leaving her naked. The sight of her like this had once driven Lewis into a frenzy, but not anymore. Now she was a walking carcass.

She probed his mind. Lewis knew that she'd always been able to do this. He'd done it himself to an innocent young woman named Megan Venton to keep her suitably silent and docile while he tore her to pieces. To his horror, Millie seized that part of his will that controlled his sexual nerves and muscles. Instantly he was hard and ready.

"P-please, Millie, I'm begging you. Don't do this to me."

"Someday you'll thank me, Lewis. You're not thinking straight right now, but after you've joined our ranks, you'll look back on this moment and thank your lucky stars that old Millie came back to you."

Lewis reached for the joystick of the wheelchair, but his hand rebelled. It belonged to Millie now, as the rest of him belonged to her. She undid his belt. She worried his jeans and shorts down over his stumps, then grabbed a handful of his shirt and raised him up to her with one hand.

"I'm giving you a great gift," she snarled. "It's more than *power*, Lewis. It's beauty and wellness and near-unending life. We have no cripples among our kind, no ugly ones or weak ones. We have no sufferers of hay fever or high blood pressure or AIDS. No depressives or neurotics, no sick ones of any ilk. We have only strong, beautiful specimens who can become anything they choose to become, for they alone control their lives."

Lewis wished he could faint. Millie's stink was overpowering, her flesh clammy and slick with bacterial goo. She was a nightmare with a brown eye and a blue one.

She lay down on the sofa, spread her legs, and pulled him over her. "Isn't this what you've always wanted, Lewis—control over your life? You can confess it to me, for I've seen everything in your mind, and I know all there is to know about you. It's the reason you play poker, isn't it? The reason you've worked so hard to master the game. Poker gives you the illusion of manipulating chance and making it serve you. Your daddy taught you that skill and self-control can defeat the tyranny of randomness, that it doesn't matter whether you're 'lucky' or 'unlucky.' This may be true at the card table, but it's woefully untrue in life—unless you become one of us. With us, Lewis, you really *can* control chance. You can make fate your servant. But only if you become one of us . . ."

Images streamed into his mind from Millie's, but it wasn't the blissful kind of dream he'd experienced before while they were locked together. Millie's mind was a psychic receiver that picked up signals from distant reality and focused them at whatever point she chose, in this case the video screen of Lewis's mind. The subject of her psychic monitoring was Josh Nickerson. And the picture Lewis saw made him want to scream.

V

The car stopped and the trunk yawned open, admitting a wave of harsh daylight that stung Josh's eyes. Spit hauled him out, causing him to bump his head sharply against the trunk lid. The pain was intense, but he tried not to show it.

"We've got a real tough dude here." Spit chuckled, pushing him toward an old door of corrugated aluminum. "He'll *think* he's tough by the time we're through with him!"

An alley, thought Josh, glancing around. *Old part of town. Strange smell in the air like—hops. We're at a warehouse near a brewery*. These details might come in handy later, if not to tell the police, then to write the story of this adventure. Assuming he lived through it.

Inside the door was a cavernous room that smelled of dust and mildew, high windows painted over to keep the place dusky. Benoit and Spit led him to the far end of the warehouse, steering around broken wooden pallets and mounds of decaying cardboard crates. Spit unlocked a scarred wooden door that flaked eight or ten layers of old paint. Beyond it was a small room lined with gray concrete blocks and a single fluorescent light fixture in the ceiling. In the center of the stained concrete floor were two metal folding chairs, facing each other, one of which held a well-built man who wore a stubby blond ponytail, a gold bead in the lobe of his right ear, and two thousand dollars' worth of Armani clothes. He had hazy blue eyes and an immaculate tan. Rex Caswell.

On the floor beside his chair sat a long leather case that might have held photographic equipment, a musical instrument, or an expensive fly rod. Or it might have held a gun. Josh shuddered.

"Good afternoon, Josh," said Rex. "Welcome to my little warehouse. I don't use it for much more than a tax dodge these days, but who knows? I may fix it up, turn it into lofts for artists and poets. There's money in that these days, as long you as don't rent to artists and poets. Why don't you have a seat?"

Benoit nudged Josh forward, and Josh sat in the vacant metal chair. Spit locked the door and left the key in the lock, a cobra-skin key packet dangling from it. Benoit bent low to Rex and whispered a long explanation of something into his ear. Rex nodded several times, and said, "You're sure no one saw you."

"Trust me. No one saw us."

"Good." Turning to Josh, Rex smiled and said, "A little bewildered by all this, aren't you?"

"No."

"No? Then tell me what you think is happening here."

Josh fetched the orb out of his pocket, and found that it had come alive again. Rex eyed it with wonder as its innards swirled like miniature holograms of the galaxies. Flecks of red light leaped from its surface and flitted across the faces of all in the room.

"It's about this," Josh said. "You want it. And I want to give it to you. But you think I'm playing some sort of game with it, that I can turn it into a weapon through remote control or something. You've brought me here to scare me into stopping the game."

Rex pursed his lips and nodded. "I'd say you've hit the nail on the head, Josh. You're a smart lad. Now that you've defined the problem, how do you suggest we solve it?"

Josh did his best imitation of a smile. "I wish I knew. I wish I could just hand it over and never see it again. But I'm not sure I can do that."

"Well," said Rex, planting both hands on his knees. "I was hoping for something better from you, smart as you are. Since you can't come up with a suggestion, let me make one." He picked up the leather case next to his chair, pressed three latch buttons, and lifted the cover. Inside was a short, ugly shotgun. Its metal parts gleamed an oily gray, its stock a flat black that looked almost like rubber.

"Josh, this is a Mossberg riot gun. The way it's customized, you can set the choke to bring down an elk at thirty yards, or you can spray a pattern wide enough to take out a football team." Rex opened a box of shells and started pushing them into the gun, then pumped one into the chamber with a sharp slap of metal. "I've had this little baby a long time, and I was beginning to think I'd never have occasion to use it. But lo and behold, along *you* come, and—well, here's what I propose, my lad. Either you hand me the orb in such a condition that it doesn't hurt me, or I blow off one of your feet. Then you can be like your hero, the Stumpmeister, and scoot around in an electric wheelchair. How's that sound?"

"Why would you want to do that to me? I've never done anything to you, have I?" Josh wiped frigid sweat from his lip. "I only got this thing today, less than an hour ago. Your guys saw who gave it to me."

"Millie Carter?"

"Yeah. She ran up and handed it to me in the cemetery. I don't have any idea how it works. I swear I don't."

From the gun case Rex took two sets of ear protectors, large plastic earmuffs heavily lined with foam rubber, and tossed one each to Spit and Benoit. Then he took out a third set and put it on his own head, leaving his ears uncovered for the time being. "Tell me something, Josh. Is this the same orb that the Stumpmeister used to beat me at cards a couple of weeks ago?"

"I don't know. It might be."

"For the sake of discussion, let's assume it's the same one. It didn't hurt anyone that night, not even when Lewis tossed it to Millie. I was there, and so were you. We both saw it. Lewis tossed the crystal to Millie, and there was no fire, no sparks, no pain. But today, out at the cemetery, you tossed it to Mase there, and it burned him. When Spit got a hold of it, the fucking thing almost killed him. Why?"

"I think it has something to do with—" He halted, wondering how the hell he could put this.

"What?" Rex prodded him in the ribs with the muzzle of the Mossberg.

"I think it has to do with who it's meant for."

Rex's handsome brow knit as he considered this. "Are you saying that Millie meant for you to have it, and that it won't let anyone else near it?"

Josh nodded. He explained that Millie once gave him an orb and told him to give it to Lewis, and that the thing behaved itself while in his possession. It seemed to know the intentions of the one who had it.

"In other words, you're implying that it *likes* some people and not others." Rex's tan pinkened as he became angry, turning his face an unflattering salmon color.

"No, I'm not saying that. At least I don't *think* I'm saying that. It's not a matter of who it likes. It's a matter of who Millie wants to have it. I'm sure it likes you just fine, Mr. Caswell." The orb started to vibrate silently in his hand and grew menacingly warm, as if it had overheard the conversation and taken offense at something said.

"Why don't we give your theory a little test?"

Mason Benoit came forward, his hand in the air. "Rex, be careful, man. You won't believe what the damn thing can do."

Rex scowled. "You said it burned you! So why don't you have blisters all over hands? And the same goes for Spit! I don't see a mark on either one of you."

"It's not like regular fire," Benoit tried to explain. "It *feels* hot, and it burns like hell."

"And it'll suck all the breath out of you," Spit put in.

"And it causes your muscles to go all spastic, like what happens when someone gets electrocuted. Have you ever read about that, Rex? Where some dude picks up a live wire, and the juice starts running through him, and he can't put it down. It's like—"

"Fuck this! I don't want to hear any more from you idiots." Rex turned back to Josh. "Put that thing over here. I want to take a closer look.'' Josh held out the orb toward Rex, with it lying in his palm. Rex moved his face to within a foot of it, his eyes narrowed. He raised a finger to it. Josh detected a rise in the orb's temperature and a higher intensity in its vibration. The tip of Rex's finger made contact, which generated a warm throbbing sensation that Rex, too, felt, judging from the way his eyes widened. ''See that?'' he said to Benoit and Spit. ''I'm touching it. I feel some vibration and a little heat, but that's all. No fire, no sparks.''

''Maybe it likes you,'' offered Spit.

''How much do you know about its powers?'' Rex asked Josh.

''Not much. I know it makes you lucky at cards, and I know it can hurt people under some circumstances. I don't have any idea how it works or how to control it.''

Rex laid the muzzle of the Mossberg against Josh's cheek. ''You better not be lying to me, you little shit, or I'll do worse than blow your foot off.'' He plucked the orb out of Josh's palm with his free hand, using only a thumb and a forefinger, and held it suspended this way for a few seconds. Then he slowly wrapped his fingers around it and gripped it in his fist, a prize long sought and finally won.

''There it is, gentlemen—power!'' he announced. ''I can feel it coursing through me, warm and alive. You're looking at the next legend in the game of poker.'' He brought the orb close to his face, and shards of crimson light escaped between his fingers and danced across his cheeks. He closed his eyes, savoring the odd sensations flowing into his hand and arm. Josh drew back, tensing.

Suddenly, a flash and a thunderclap. Josh thought at first that the Mossberg had gone off accidentally, but the fury had come from the orb. Rex's hand became a ball of flame, from which spewed jets of tiny, dazzling-red sparks that exploded on contact with cement-brick walls, metal chairs, human flesh. Rex shrieked like an animal caught in a trap and convulsed onto the floor. Spit and Benoit flew to his side, screamed his name, asked what they should do. But Rex couldn't answer.

His eyes rotated upward, leaving circles of white. He foamed at the mouth and flailed, writhed and kicked. But he didn't let go of the orb.

Josh bounded out of the chair toward the door. His hand closed on the key and twisted it. He threw his body against the door, forcing it open, then plunged into the half-light of the warehouse. He scrambled through the debris of shipping crates to the outer door, only to find it securely locked. He saw Rex Caswell stagger into the doorway at the far end of the warehouse, having freed himself of the orb and clutching the Mossberg at the ready.

vi

As Millie pulled him ever deeper into her, Lewis's mental link to her strengthened. Just as he had no control over the muscles of his body, which at this moment drove his pubic bone against hers, he had no control over the images that streamed into his brain via the mind link with her, images gathered by her wandering psychic eye.

A dilapidated warehouse near the Henry Weinhard Brewery in northwest Portland. Josh running in panic, dodging mounds of refuse that reek of wet, rotting fiber. Encountering a locked door, whirling, looking for another way out. And in the distant dusk of the place, Rex Caswell, armed with shotgun, advancing, his face twisted into a killing grin . . .

vii

Lewis can feel the heat of rage as Caswell strides toward Josh, kicking aside empty crates and boxes, swearing vilely with every breath. Lewis senses, too, the burning in Rex's right hand, the one in which he'd gripped the orb only moments ago.

Clamor now from either side. Spit and Benoit on Rex's flanks, advancing with him toward the opposite end of the warehouse, their weapons drawn. The mingling smells of rage and panic. The fumes of surging adrenaline.

Josh also hears them and scutters along the rear wall, finds a door, and dashes into a cramped room that might have been an office long ago. Rusty file cabinets and ruined desks. Discarded IBM typewriters and wrecked chairs.

Sickly light pours through a painted-over window that someone has broken, probably a homeless person seeking shelter. But breaking the window did no good, because it has an expanded-metal screen on the inside. Josh sees that the wooden frame is rotting away. He knows that he can pry off the screen and escape through the window, if only he has time.

He casts around in the clutter, searching for an appropriate tool, hearing the approaching shouts of Caswell, Spit, and Benoit. He finds the amputated armrest of a typing chair, leaps to the window, and jams one end of the steel frame into the screen. He hauls back on the armrest with all his weight. Old wooden slats groan and squeak as they come loose.

Throwing aside the armrest, Josh attacks with his bare hands, mindless of splinters or cuts on his fingers. He rips the expanded-metal screen away. He launches a derelict IBM Selectric through the window, blowing out old panes and frames, then flings himself into the gray daylight. His chest slams against grainy asphalt. He staggers to his feet, only marginally aware of blood soaking through his shirt at the elbows. He wills his legs to move, his arms to pump, and dashes toward the mouth of the alley far away. Blood streams into his eye from a slice on his forehead.

Rex reaches the window, his eyes merely unthinking holes in his head. He sees Josh fleeing down the alley and raises the Mossberg. Earlier, he'd planned only to frighten the holy bejabbers out of the boy, to scare him into handing over the orb. But rage rules him now, and he squeezes the trigger. The barrel belches fire, and the roar cannonades down the alley, bouncing off old brick walls, reverberating into the next block, and the next, and the next. In a heartbeat, hot pellets rip into Josh

Nickerson's left leg, upending him and scattering bloody bits
of him against the side of a rusting Dumpster.

viii

"Nooooooooooooooo!" Lewis screamed as an orgasm tore
at his mind and body. He knew that what he'd seen was real,
that Josh Nickerson lay wounded and bleeding in a dirty alley.

"That's good, Lewis, good!" hissed Millie, humping him
greedily. *"Let your rage spill out, yes! Don't keep it in, Lewis!
Let it burn! Let it burn! Let it burn . . . !"*

He understood now that his anger was the fuel that Millie
needed to transform him. She'd shown him what happened to
Josh in order to fan that anger. She reveled in it and drank it
in. It was as necessary to her survival as human flesh and
blood.

Then it was over, as if they'd driven over a cliff together
and slammed into an icy river. Millie pushed him off and he
flopped onto the carpet, utterly sick and defeated. She spoke,
and her voice horrified him, for he hadn't heard that voice in
more than two decades.

"You really are on your own now, Lewis. Whatever happens to you—whatever you become—depends totally on
you."

Lewis raised himself on his elbows and became conscious
of his newly grown legs and feet. His left arm was straight
and strong, and he heard no ringing in his ears. He stared at
Millie, unbelieving.

She was changing. Growing taller. Lewis could hear the
stretching of bones, snapping and creaking like the skeleton
of an old wooden ship. He could hear the reformation of muscles and skin, a wet sound that evinced thoughts of blood clots
and tumors. Her head elongated while her scalp retracted her
dreadlocks like a million fishing lines on a million reels. Her
ears enlarged and her brow became pronounced. As her shoulders broadened, her chest flattened and hardened. Her hips

pulled in, narrowing and straightening. And out of her pelvic area grew a long, thick penis with a head that was almost blue, and beneath it a pair of testicles. Coarse hair appeared on the newly sinewy belly and legs. The feet lengthened and widened.

Lewis saw, too, that the symptoms of death disappeared as the body changed its sex. Bacterial pustules dried and flaked away. The flowered silk scarf fell to the floor, revealing that the wound beneath it had healed. The skin became lustrous and firm again. All signs of putrefaction disappeared, except the lingering smell.

A feature that didn't change was the eyes—the left one brown and the right one blue. Sizzling eyes, full of mocking and yet . . . loving. *The eyes of a brother?* This was no longer Millie Carter. This was Gamaliel Cartee, looking no older than Lewis remembered him from Vietnam.

Gamaliel picked up the tote that lay beside the sofa and zippered it open. Inside it were a wine-colored jogging suit, socks, shoes, and a light jacket of black nylon. Men's clothes, just the right size. He dressed as Lewis stared, as Lewis argued with himself over whether he'd suspected this from the very beginning. Millie was Gamaliel. Gamaliel was Millie.

And Lewis was their brother now.

"I don't know if we'll ever meet again," Gamaliel said, turning toward the door. "If we do, I hope it's many years from now. By then you'll understand."

"I understand now."

"I doubt that. The day will come, Lewis, when you discover how naive you've been all these years. You'll develop a totally new perspective about the real and the unreal, about good and bad."

"I have all the perspective I need. I know what I am, and I know what you are."

Gamaliel laughed. He reached into the tote and took out a set of car keys, which he tossed onto an end table. "The Jaguar is parked outside on Gander Circle. It's now yours. It's due for an oil change."

"Wait! Aren't there things you're supposed to tell me? Like

what my limitations are, hints on how to live among ordinary humans, all that sort of thing? You can't just walk out and leave me on my own.''

''Don't play games with me, Lewis. I know every trick in the book, believe me. As for the things you need to know, what can I say? I selected you because of your intelligence, your resourcefulness, your resilience, not to mention your proven capacity for killing. These qualities will serve you well in your new life. You're an inquisitive soul, and you'll soon find out all you need to know. You'll be good. *Very* good.''

''What about making another one of us—out of an ordinary human, I mean? How do I know when to do that? I'm not even sure I know *how* to do it.''

''Lewis, you're trying to keep me around because you'd like to take a crack at killing me. You'd do well to forget that. It can't be done, which you of all people should know. But to answer your question, I'll say that you'll know when the time is right to create another of us. There's no regular cycle for this kind of thing. When it's time to do it, you'll know, and your instincts will tell you how. Search for someone who's capable of intense, righteous anger. Someone like yourself. You'll be able to *smell* such a person, like I smelled you. War zones are good hunting grounds, because they're rich with anger and teeming with killers. I've spent many years in war zones, more than I'd like to count. In fact, I'm thinking seriously of going to Yugoslavia, where there's a great little war in the making.'' He pulled the door open, but hesitated a moment. ''Have a nice life, Lewis. I'm sorry we didn't get an opportunity to play some poker. Maybe next time.'' He stepped through the door and closed it behind him.

ix

''Tommy, the phone's for you!'' shouted Carlotta Iadanza through the service window between the bar and the kitchen of the Huntsman's Bar and Grill. Her husband was tending bar this afternoon, because the regular guy had called in sick with the flu. Tommy snatched the telephone from its cradle next to the cash register and wedged it between his cheek and shoulder, freeing his hands for the preparation of a very dry Beefeater martini.

"Speak!"

"Tommy, it's me, Lewis. I need a favor."

"Lewis! How the hell are you, troop? I've been worried."

"Sorry for not being in touch. I haven't been feeling too—"

"Hey, the VIP Center called yesterday. They're planning a memorial gathering for Dewey on Sunday in Waterfront Park. They're inviting the homeless folks down around the Skidmore District. I'm donating some food, as are some of the other restaurants in the area. Should be a nice event. I figured you'd be in interested in helping, so I signed you up. There's a meeting tonight—"

"Tommy, I can't talk about it right now. Like I said, I need a favor. A small one."

"No problem. All you need to do is ask. You know that."

"I need Rex Caswell's address. He's not listed in the phone book."

"Did you try the yellow pages under 'Hairball?' Or maybe 'Unredeemable Fuck-stick?' "

"I'm serious, Tom. I need to know where he lives."

X

Rex hauled the designer suitcase out of the darkroom into his photography studio on the third floor of his floating house. He placed it on the floor and opened it. For years he'd kept a packed suitcase ready, full of clothes, toiletries, spare cash, forged documents. He called it his "dash kit." A child pornographer could never know, after all, when his life might suddenly blow up in his face, requiring immediate departure to some remote and sunny clime that had no extradition agreement with the U.S. Every few months he recycled the clothing in the dash kit, just to keep it current. Going on the lam was no excuse for dressing like a jerk.

He checked the phony documents he'd paid dearly for several years back. Passport. California driver's license. Social Security card. Credit cards (just for show, not for use). Even phony pictures of a phony wife and kids. The documents said he was a management consultant named Roland Parker.

Everything was in order.

Except for Silhouette, that is. Silhouette was very much in disorder. She stood before him with a fist planted accusingly on a slim hip, a strand of blond hair dangling over one eye.

"I'm ready for you to tell me what's going on," she announced. "Enough of the bullshit, Rex."

"Sweetheart, I told you. Something's come up. I'm going on a little business trip, that's all."

"That's *not* all! Since when do you take the dash kit on a little business trip?"

Rex had no intention of telling her anything that remotely resembled the truth. Silhouette had become irrelevant to him. Soon he would drive his Mercedes to an airport in Hillsboro, a distant western suburb, where he would meet Mason Benoit and Spit Pittman. They would each hand him a briefcase containing a total of a million dollars, money he'd stashed with this day in mind. He would board a chartered jet that at this moment was en route from its home airfield in Northern California. He would fly to a rural airport in central Mexico and lie low in some quiet little hotel for a month or two, then make his way even farther south, maybe to Brazil. He would live off his Swiss bank account for as long as it took to fashion a new life.

Never again would he see Silhouette. Never again would he see Mason Benoit or Spit Pittman, who themselves would disappear, handsomely flush with "severance pay." Never again would he see Portland, Oregon.

"You're leaving for good, aren't you?" Silhouette said, her eyes filling. "Somebody's after you—the cops, the boyfriend of one of your models, or some pissed-off dad. And you're leaving. That's it, isn't it, Rex? You don't give a rusty fuck what happens to me.''

Rex sighed. What could he do? He'd shot an innocent kid. If the kid lived, he would certainly tell the cops who'd shot him. And this meant that Rex Caswell must disappear.

"Look, sweetheart," he began, "I don't know how long I'll be gone. It may be—"

"Forever."

"A long time. Things may get a little dicey for you. I'm going to leave you some money. Watch the mail for the next couple of days. You'll get a key to a luggage locker. I can't say where right now, but I'll put a note in with it, telling you where it is. Go to the locker and get the money.''

"How much, Rex? How much are you going to leave me?'' Suddenly she was sobbing uncontrollably, and Rex felt his own eyes start to smart.

"I'll leave you ten thousand in little bills. Pick it up and go south with it. Don't even look back, okay?''

Rex stared at an image he didn't believe, a reality too outrageous to be real, standing in the doorway behind her. Silhouette whirled in slow motion and shrieked.

xi

Lewis crossed the room on two strong legs and thrust his hand into Rex Caswell's throat. Rex fought savagely, and though he was bigger and more muscular, Lewis had no problem killing him. Lewis marveled at the way Rex's eyes bulged out of their sockets, full of horror at the sight of the old Stumpmeister in the body of a whole man, the pathetic cripple who ruled a gaggle of tatty old poker hounds at the Fanshawe. Rex's cheeks puffed up and turned beet red. His tongue protruded and turned purple. Lewis relished the sensation of piercing the flesh of Rex's throat with his fingers, finding the windpipe and ripping it out. The man of style went down like a discombobulated cyborg, geysering blood over an array of costly photographic equipment that he would no longer need.

Lewis caught Silhouette by the hair as she reached the second-floor landing and dragged her into the bedroom with its
wide-angle view of the Willamette River. A barge lumbered
downstream, pushed by a tug. Gulls circled and wheeled in
the rain. And Silhouette screamed as she'd never screamed in
her life.

"It's okay to scream—no one can hear you," Lewis said.
"This is the time for it."

She fell quiet suddenly and drew herself into a fetal ball on
the king-size bed, staring at him with mindless eyes. Lewis
slowly stripped naked and knelt next to her. The hunger had
begun to stir in earnest, and his cock was hardening. Silhouette
bleated like a sacrificial lamb, and he bent to her, his hunger
yawning and roaring.

xii

Afterward, he showered in the late Rex Caswell's private
bathroom, washing away both Silhouette's and Rex's blood.
From the wardrobe he selected something to wear, a conser-
vative double-breasted blazer and a pair of light wool trousers.
The clothes draped on him, having been tailored for a body-
builder, but this didn't matter.

While drying his hair with the late Rex Caswell's Euro Pro
hair dryer, he made a discovery in the mirror. His left eye had
turned brown, his right one blue. He recalled that Twyla had
once told him that he had "sensuous gray eyes," so the loss
was probably something to be lamented. Still, in return for a
good pair of legs, it was no loss at all.

He left the floating house with one of Rex's Burberry rain-
coats slung over his arm. Night was gathering in the east, and
the manager of the Sellwood Bay Club had turned on the overhead floods so that residents and their guests could come and
go without ending up in the drink. As Lewis strode through
the yellow cone of a floodlight, he experienced a feeling that

had become familiar during the past several weeks, an inkling of being followed. He heard, too, the rustling that accompanied the feeling, a sound that generated the image of a plague of locusts. He'd heard it on the dance floor at the White Eagle and in the foyer of the Legato Ristorante. He'd heard it in Goose Hollow, just before he and Millie encountered his aunt amid the horde of Billy Graham's Christians.

A hellish idea hit him, and he glanced down at his feet, now shod in custom-fitted calfskin that didn't quite fit. From the soles of the shoes his shadow sprawled in front of him over the planks of the dock—not black like the shadows cast by the handrail, but a deep and iridescent blue.

Thirty

i

JOSH NICKERSON WHEELED himself onto the deck that fronted the living room of his family's apartment, craving the few meager rays of sunshine that managed to dodge the scudding clouds. He leaned back in his wheelchair with his face to the sky, soaking up the light and heat, wishing that this simple delight could go on forever. But it wouldn't, he knew, because nothing went on forever. Not joy or sadness or grief or hope. Or least of all, life.

The morning smelled tartly of rain, for autumn was seriously under way, and the grounds of Sloan House were ankle-deep in the reds, yellows, and browns shed by the majestic New England elms that surrounded the place. Josh loved the fresh air, the smells, and the colors, even the cackling of the resident crows. He loved the *aloneness*.

In the three weeks since he'd come home from the hospital, he'd gotten scarcely five minutes to himself. His mother and sister had waited on him hand and foot, doting on him, feeling the constant need to "cheer him up" and take his mind off the fact that he'd suffered a seriously damaged leg. A day nurse had come in for the first two weeks. After that, his mother took a week of family medical leave to stay home with him. Finally Josh had managed to convince his mother and sister that he was well enough not to require constant attention. He wanted to read, enjoy some music, maybe even write. He wanted to be alone.

Thus, on November 17, 1992, Cheryl Nickerson went to work in the morning as on any other day. Kendra Nickerson went to school. And Josh went hunting for sunshine.

As always happened when he closed his eyes these days, he found himself looking into the faces of Nicki and Lewis, both of whom had disappeared from his life and left profound vacancies. Lewis had dropped out of sight on the day Josh was shot. Later, Josh had found out that Rex Caswell and his live-in squeeze had died horrible deaths mere hours after Josh had landed in the emergency room of Good Samaritan, where surgeons had labored heroically to save his mangled leg.

Intuition told him that Lewis was responsible for those deaths. He'd killed Rex for hurting Josh, and had then fled. As to why Lewis had killed Rex's girlfriend, Josh didn't know. The possibilities were too ugly, too weird, too much like what had happened to Ron Payne.

Jesse Burton had visited Josh daily during the two weeks he'd spent in the hospital, and had become close to the Nickerson family. Cheryl was glad for his interest in her son, particularly since Jesse had sons of his own and could "talk the lingo." Any friend of Lewis's was okay in her book.

Jesse hadn't shared with her all he knew about Lewis, and Josh was glad of this. Josh himself hadn't disclosed to anyone except Jesse the real reason that he'd ended up in Rex Caswell's warehouse almost six weeks ago. Rex had wanted a ball of red glass that could move on its own, burn people, and make you a winner at poker. Knowing how ridiculous the truth would have sounded, Josh had simply left out any mention of it. As soon as he regained consciousness in postop, he sent the police straight to Rex Caswell. The cops had found Rex and his girlfriend dead.

Within the past six weeks Jesse had flown back and forth between Chicago and Portland at least six times that Josh knew of, not only to visit him during his convalescence, but also to discuss with Paul Tran a strategy against the enemy, "Gamaliel's kind." Lewis would return, Jesse was certain. Lewis would come back to help put an end to the evil. How Jesse could be so sure of this, Josh couldn't guess. Unless Jesse, like himself, believed that no matter how radically Lewis might have changed externally—growing legs, shedding his battle scars, metamorphosing in God only knows how many other ways—he still possessed the soul of Lewis Kindred. He was still a good man in his heart, one who loved his friends and cared about the world. Lewis could never become a Millie Carter or a Gamaliel Cartee. Josh knew this with as much certainty as he knew that the sun would rise tomorrow.

ii

After picking up his luggage from the baggage carousel at Portland International Airport, Jesse Burton went to a pay phone and called his wife in Chicago, as he'd promised he would do. She needed to hear from him often these days, especially now that he'd begun spending so much time in Portland, pursuing a matter that he'd described to her in only the vaguest terms.

Helping an old Vietnam buddy find himself . . . Being there for a friend who'd given him his first lesson in decency . . . Doing for a friend what he would expect a friend to do for him . . .

Jesse knew that none of it sounded compelling to Shandelle. The fact that she put up with this strange behavior only strengthened his love for her. He vowed that when this was over, he would take her and the boys on a long vacation to a place with bright sandy beaches and bathtub-warm surf. Sitting in the sun with his family, he would try to explain why he'd needed to take a leave of absence both from his job and his home to spend his time and energies on people they'd never even met. He hoped he could make them understand without telling them the otherworldly details of the story, which he knew were beyond their understanding. As it was beyond his own.

He and Shandelle talked for ten minutes, saying the things they'd said on the way to O'Hare early this morning. He assured her that he loved her, that he wouldn't forget to take his blood-pressure pills. That he wouldn't smoke more than a pack a day. Yes, he would call every evening. No, he wouldn't forget his oldest son's birthday, which was only a week off. Oh—had she told him she loved him? Only three times since answering the phone.

He picked up a rental car and stowed his bags in the trunk. As he put his hand on the trunk lid to slam it down, he heard a strange thumping sound that seemed to come from inside a suitcase. Jesse's stomach started churning. *The cigar box!*

He tore open the suitcase and snatched up the faded old cigar box he'd gotten in Louisiana, with the ball bearing inside it. The marble-size ball of steel was in a frenzy, hurling itself against the inside of the box with force sufficient to raise welts on the outer surface of the stiff cardboard. The popping was loud enough to turn the heads of passersby. Suddenly the ball bearing burst through a corner of the box and bounced across the asphalt of the rental lot, careening off the tire of an Avis Grand Am and rolling to a halt at the base of the fence.

Jesse raced to a pay phone near the rental check-in office and called Paul Tran. He knew from the instant Paul answered that something was very wrong in the Tran household. He heard a sharp, staccato popping in the background, the source of which Jesse knew: a lacquered box with a glass marble inside.

"Paul, it's Jesse Burton! I'm calling from the airport. I just landed. My cigar box just—"

"Yes, Jesse, I know! The time has come, I think!" Jesse heard sounds of consternation on the other end, shouted words in Vietnamese. He didn't need to know the language to comprehend the terror in the voices of Paul Tran and his wife. "Jesse! You told me that the woman, Millie, gave an orb to Josh Nickerson, not so?"

Jesse confirmed this. It had happened at the cemetery on the day of Nicole's burial.

"Then it's Josh who's in danger! You must go to him now! Quickly! Do you have the key I gave you—the one that fits the front door of Sloan House?"

"I've got it. But I'm at the airport, Paul. It'll take me at least half an hour to get there, maybe more if there's traffic. Can't you—"

"No, I can't go, Jesse. I'm still too weak. I have doubts now that I'll ever be well again. You're the one who must act. Remember the things we've talked about. And remember what the *sorcière* told you: look beyond the known, and feel beyond yourself. Inhale the message that seeks you. . . ."

Jesse heard the words and mouthed them silently, but even now, after all this time and talk with Paul Tran, he doubted that he knew what they meant. He slammed down the phone and raced for the car, intending to set a record for the travel time between Portland International and Gander Ridge.

iii

Around noon the cloud cover disappeared but for an occasional charcoal-colored boulder that engulfed the sun for a half minute or so before passing on. Josh pulled off his sweater and rolled up his sleeves, wanting as much of the rare fall sunshine as he could get. He also rolled up the cuffs of his baggy pants, exposing the white cast on his left leg.

He took his Sony Discman from the saddlebag of his wheel-chair and booted a Depeche Mode CD. As he leaned back, he happened to see someone in the gazebo below, where he and Nicki had often sat together. A thrill of grief raced through him.

She was young, not over seventeen, and dark-complected. Her hair, so black that it was almost blue, cascaded in a fashionable thatch over her shoulders. She wore a long tan reefer coat over a sweater of nearly the same color, and white stirrup pants with high-top sneakers. Even from this distance Josh could see that she was beautiful.

The Nickersons' longtime neighbor, the young stockbroker, had moved away. Josh himself had seen the moving van on the very day he'd shot Millie. Weeks later, after coming home from the hospital, he'd overheard Kendra tell his mother about the new folks who'd moved into the vacant apartment, a woman with a stepdaughter. Melusinne and Camilla Cartier.

Could they be French? Josh had wondered. He'd since caught a glimpse of the stepmother as she watered the potted plants on the neighboring deck— a heavy, darkly complected woman. He wondered if the girl in the gazebo was the stepdaughter.

A cloud scudded over the sun. A crow cawed from its perch in a naked elm as midday darkened almost to dusk. The girl smiled at Josh, a shattering of white teeth. From this range he couldn't make out the color of her eyes. The crow glided toward the gazebo and flapped its glossy wings twice, three times to wheel and stall, to alight on the railing near the girl. It cackled again, then hopped to her outstretched arm, its wings spread wide to aid its balance. Josh watched breathlessly as she stroked the bird's head and blew gently into its face. The bird stood on her forearm as if mesmerized, listening to her whispered words and breathing her breath.

She slowly twisted one of the crow's wings, and Josh would have sworn that he heard the bones snap. Holding the poor

creature with both hands now, she twisted the other wing—
another snap. Then its right leg. Its left leg. And finally, grinning with feral amusement, she twisted its head completely
around and held the throbbing body up for him to see. A drop
of blood fell from the crow's beak onto her coat, but she didn't
seem to care.

If Josh had eaten lunch, he would have spit it up. He tore
the headphones off and wheeled the chair around, wanting to
be inside, wanting locked doors between himself and the creature in the gazebo. But maneuvering a wheelchair was
sometimes like rowing a boat, especially when squeezing
through doors—it often did the opposite of what you wanted.
After several attempts and a new scrape in the woodwork, he
got himself into the living room. But as he turned the chair to
slam the door behind him, a shape rose from below and
alighted on the rail of the deck.

It was the girl from the gazebo, having jumped to the sec-
ond-story deck as easily a normal girl might take the first step
on a stairway. She hopped down from the rail and strode toward him. Josh just managed to lock the doors before she
arrived. With his pulse hammering, he backed into the living
room, colliding with an end table. Through the panes of the
French doors he saw her raise a long finger to the lock, heard
the dead bolt click as if someone had turned a key. The door
swung open.

She stepped into the living room, elegant despite the crimson stain on her coat, smiling prettily. Josh saw that her eyes
were mismatched, brown and blue, as he'd known they must
be from the moment she'd broken the bird's wing.

"Hi, Josh. I'm your new neighbor, Camilla. I hope you
don't think I'm rude." She said the words lazily, sweetening
every syllable with Louisiana sugar.

"I know who you are."

"Of course, you do. I'll dispense with the pretense then. It's
only for the benefit of others anyway." The tan reefer coat
slid off her shoulders and dropped to the carpet. Her fingers

began playing around the bottom edge of her bulky sweater. "I'm sorry about your leg, I really am. Most unfortunate. Can you believe what a jerk Rex Caswell was? At least he got his comeuppance."

She pulled her tan sweater over her head, riling her hair and displaying the most perfect breasts that Josh had ever seen, small but pert, the nipples standing taut. She moved toward him, and Josh suddenly had a hard-on that threatened to burst his pants. Standing an arm's length from him, she unlaced her sneakers and slipped them off. Then she pushed her white stirrup pants down over her slim hips and stepped out of them, leaving only a pair of snow-white panties. She bent to him, kissed him, sending a pang through his young body. Moving her lips to his ear, she whispered, "I have gifts for you. I want you to take them. I want you to *use* them."

"I don't want anything from you."

"But you never got the opportunity to use the orb. Old Rex Caswell saw to that. Don't worry, though. The orb always gives you another chance, and another one after that, if need be."

She drew away from him slightly and knelt on the carpet, then tilted her head back. A lump appeared at the base of her throat and moved upward past her larynx, into her mouth. Her jaw unhinged like a snake's, and a dazzling arc of red peeked between her lips, its membranous rays flitting over walls. With her mouth open impossibly wide, she tilted her head forward again, staring brown and blue lasers at Josh. She disgorged an orb into the palm of her hand and held it out to him as her jaw reconnected."You've already fulfilled one of the requirements for membership. All you need to do now is to accept the orb and one other gift as well. This." She stood up again, and with her free hand pushed down her white panties.

Blood rushed into Josh's cheeks. He stared at her thatch of black hair, his body already taking up the rhythm of sex. He would have given in, but he remembered what Millie Carter had said only minutes before he'd shot her. She'd referred to

Josh as a "prospect." She'd meant for him to become one of her own kind, a maniac who kills and kills and kills. He remembered, too, that *this* was Millie. *This* was the piece of slime who'd killed Nicki.

He drove his fist into her abdomen, knocking her backward. She stared at him in shock, her sweet face a blank. Josh wished he could lunge out of the chair at her, catch her by the neck, and jam his thumbs into her windpipe.

"What do you think you're doing, you little wretch?" she growled. "You don't seriously believe that you can hold me off, do you?" She advanced on him, her eyes blazing brown and blue, her lips snarling. "I can get inside your head, if I want to. I can take control of your brain, your heart, even your prick. If I want you to fuck me, you'll *fuck* me!"

"Then why don't you do it? Why don't you take over my body and do whatever you want with it?" Josh worked the wheelchair backward, steering around the sofa toward the center of the room. "I'll tell you why. Because you need me to be *willing*. If you force me, it doesn't count, does it?"

"Believe me when I say this, Josh: I can make life so miserable for you that you'll come to me willingly. I'm fully capable of that, you know. I've done it before. Not a pretty thing to watch, but I always do whatever needs to be done. I can turn your world into a hell. By the time I'm finished, you'll beg for me!"

Josh tried to keep furniture between them, but it was useless. He'd nearly circumnavigated the living room, finding himself near the French doors again. He knew that even with two good legs he couldn't evade a creature who could leap to a second-floor deck from a standing position. "You're dead wrong!" he shouted at her. "I'll never want something like you. Just the sight of you makes me sick! I don't care what your body looks like—I know what you are inside. I know what you do to people!"

The doorbell rang, then rang again. Someone thumped heavily at the front door. *"Josh, are you okay? I hear voices in there! Josh, it's me, Jesse Burton! Open the door!"* The thumping resumed so furiously that Josh thought the hinges might break.

''Jesse, help me! It's Millie Carter. She's getting ready to—'' Suddenly the muscles in Josh's jaw froze as if someone had thrown a bucket of ice water in his face. He felt the tentacles of Millie's mind probing his own, latching onto the control buttons. He couldn't stop the takeover. Instantly he had a hard-on again, and Millie or Camilla or whatever she called herself attacked his clothes, tearing them off and flinging them aside. He could only watch, horrified.

Millie pulled him from the wheelchair and flopped him onto the carpet, then straddled him. She grabbed his cock and started to press it into her, but at that instant the living-room door blew open with a blizzard of splinters. Jesse had beaten it in with the heavy old-fashioned fired extinguisher that the landlady, Juliet Kindred, kept mounted in the corridor. The big man's face went slack when he saw the spectacle in the living room—a beautiful teenage girl, naked as the day she was born, meaning to have her way with the boy on the floor.

iv

Jesse looked beyond the known. He turned his heart both inward and outward in order to inhale the message that sought him.

And he saw the thing for what it was. Not a comely young girl with the face of an angel, but a vespertilian demon with hunkering wings and the eyes of a dragon. Fighting down terror, he launched himself at it, not knowing whether he could damage it or even slow it down, but needing to do something that might give Josh a chance. He struck the thing at full tilt, like the street fighter he'd been when he was young. They crashed through the French doors onto the deck with a shattering of glass and wood. The thing somersaulted over Jesse, grabbing clawfuls of his anorak. Jesse felt himself being hauled upward. He managed to clutch the thing by the throat as it hurled him over the rail, and because it hadn't steadied itself, Jesse took it with him.

v

"Let me make sure I have this right," the cop said, wrapping up. Josh sat in his wheelchair, looking peaked, wearing sweat gear dragged hastily out of a dresser drawer, because he couldn't stand the thought of putting on clothes that the monster had touched. An ambulance had taken Jesse Burton's body away. His mother had rushed home from her office and now sat close to him on a hassock, an arm wrapped protectively around him. "The dead man, this Mr. Jesse Burton, broke the door down to save you from a pervert who was trying to rape you. He wrestled the guy through these French doors here, out to the deck, and they both went over the side, landing on the flagstone patio downstairs. Is that right?"

Josh nodded.

"And you don't have any idea how the pervert got into the place?"

Another nod.

"And you can't explain why the pervert got away, while Mr. Burton died of a broken skull?"

Josh's eyes blurred with hot tears. "It doesn't seem right, does it?"

"No, it doesn't," agreed the cop, shaking his head as if he suspected that he'd heard only a fraction of the real story. "It doesn't seem right at all."

vi

At ten o'clock that evening Lewis Kindred walked into the Huntsman's Bar and Grill off the lobby of the Hotel Fanshawe, wearing a new pair of baggy Levi's, cowboy boots, a flowered western shirt, and a Stetson hat. Except for a few old barflies who sat in their regular places under the stuffed moose head at the far end of the bar, the place was deserted of customers. Not much business on Tuesday nights these days.

Tommy Iadanza was busy taking inventory of the liquor on the shelves in front of the great arching mirror. When he glanced up and saw Lewis, he dropped his clipboard and groped for the countertop, blanching. The bartender, a rotund two-hundred-fifty-pounder named Huett (the regulars called him Baby Huey), rushed to his boss's side and shouted something about a heart attack, but Tommy waved him off and told him everything was okay. Baby Huey didn't recognize Lewis.

Tommy regained control of himself and came over to where Lewis sat, his face slick with sweat. He looked his old friend up and down. "Talk to me," he croaked.

"How about we get a table, maybe a couple of brewskies?"

"No table, no brewskies. Just talk to me. You can start by explaining"—he leaned over the bar to get a load of Lewis's brand-new Justins—"the boots. Start with the boots and the feet, okay? Then tell me about the legs. And after that, tell me why you're wearing different-colored contacts."

Lewis sighed and started to talk. He didn't stop talking until he'd told Tommy everything.

vii

Minutes before midnight.

Tommy wheeled Josh Nickerson into the card room above the Huntsman's, where Lewis waited at the green baize table under a cone of lamplight, absently shuffling a deck a cards the way he'd done it since mortar fragments had ripped into his left arm more than twenty years ago—with one hand. When he saw Josh in the wheelchair, his casted leg resting on the extended footrest, Lewis's face tightened.

"I'll leave you two alone," said Tommy, parking the wheelchair close to Lewis. "If you need anything, pick up the house phone and I'll be here in a flash."

"Thanks, Tom. Remember, if anyone comes . . ."

"Yeah, right. I'll send her up. Or him. Whichever." Tommy ducked out, closing the door softly, as if this was a funeral parlor.

"So how's it going, Josh? Hey, sorry—I guess I know how it's going. What do you young dudes call it—a 'nasty hang'? I can't tell you how sorry I am that you got shot." He nodded at the cast.

"What happened to your eyes?" Josh asked, though his expression said that he knew perfectly well what had happened to them. The boy's face looked too weary with knowledge, and Lewis felt a pang. He was sorry Josh had to see him like this.

A long silence. "Jesse's dead," said Josh without looking up. "Or did you know that already?"

Lewis hadn't known, and new grief coursed through him. He asked how it had happened, and Josh told him. They were silent for what seemed a long time.

"Thanks for coming tonight, Josh," he said finally. "I needed you."

"I almost wasn't able to do it. Mom was pretty definite about not letting me out, and she didn't agree to it until Tommy told her who wanted to see me. You're the only reason she let me come." Studying his hands, he added, "We've all been pretty worried about you, Lew."

"Yeah, I can imagine. I guess I owe you some kind of explanation."

"I know why you left." He avoided Lewis's mismatched eyes. "Rex Caswell and his girlfriend, right?"

Lewis nodded. "I want you to understand something, though. I haven't—killed anybody since then. I won't say that I haven't wanted to, because the hunger has been strong. I killed Rex because of what he did to you and Dewey. As for the girl—" A deep breath. "I killed her because I needed to, because of what I've become. But I've fought the hunger."

"Where have you been all this time?"

"I went to Reno and played cards. Won a fortune, too, which I'm sure doesn't surprise you. As of two days ago, I'm banned from all card games in Reno. That's where I bought these clothes, by the way." He shook his head, as if to concede the insanity of it. "My problem now is that I don't know how much longer I can—"

The door opened, causing Josh to flinch, and in walked the being who this afternoon had called herself Camilla, wearing a wine-colored jogging suit that was much too large for her. When she spoke, her voice was deep and masculine, the voice of Gamaliel.

"Don't let me interrupt you, Lewis. You were saying something about not being sure how much longer you can hold back the hunger, I believe." She lowered herself into a chair, planted her elbows on the green baize. She made a "basket" with her delicate fingers, into which she laid her chin.

"You're wearing the wrong voice," Lewis said sarcastically. "Little girl should have little girl's voice. Big sergeant should have big sergeant's voice. Crimminy, Gamaliel, we can't take you anywhere."

"You're in rare form tonight, Lewis. What brought you back?"

"You."

"I'm flattered."

"Don't be. I'm here to kill you."

"May I inquire as to your motive?"

"I don't want you to get Josh. In fact, I don't want you to get anyone ever again. I don't want you to turn anyone else into whatever I am, and I don't want you to butcher any more innocent people. I think that about wraps it up."

"I see. But I'm curious. How did you know I had designs on your young friend here?"

"You're not the only one with a psychic eye. Mine probably isn't as finely honed as yours, but it still works. I've been keeping track of you because I knew that you would go after Josh the minute he was left alone."

"You nearly blew it, Lewis. I almost had him this afternoon."

"Like I said, my psychic eye isn't as good as yours, at least not yet. I'm glad that Jesse showed up when he did. That was no accident, you know. Jesse knew what he was doing."

"I'll confess he caught me by surprise. That's a very dangerous thing to do, as I guess he found out. Tell me: what made you so sure I would show up tonight?"

"I figured you would follow Josh, and I was right. What do you say to making him the stakes in a friendly game of poker?"

"Then you're here to play poker? I think I'm going to enjoy this." His grin looked all wrong on his young girl's face. "I'll play for any stakes you name. I'm not clear on one point, though—the part about your killing me."

Lewis ran his tongue over his dry lips and wondered how many of his thoughts were safe from Gamaliel. This charade couldn't possibly succeed if the creature could read his mind.

"It's very simple. We'll play draw poker for money. If I win, I kill you. If you win, you get Josh." When he heard this, Josh put a hand over his eyes, reminding Lewis of a little boy at a horror movie.

"It sounds like the sort of proposition no southern gentleman can resist."

"Cut for the deal?"

"No. Let's ask Josh to deal. Since he has so great a stake in the game, we ought to let him participate."

Lewis called Tommy on the house phone and requested the services of the house bank. Minutes later Tommy appeared with his chip bucket and receipt book. He sold ten thousand dollars' worth of chips each to Lewis and the stunning young woman who sat across from him. He presented an unopened pack of cards to Josh and quickly exited.

The players anted a thousand dollars apiece. Josh dealt smoothly, and the cards whooshed across the green baize, five each to Lewis and Gamaliel, faces down. Lewis watched them settle in front of him, and felt as if he was acting out a part in a script.

Even before he picked up his cards, Lewis knew what he'd been dealt—the same hand he'd seen on a dark night in Vietnam when he'd first played poker with Gamaliel. And again at this very table more than twenty years later when he'd meted out justice to Rex Caswell. It was the only hand that he could possibly draw, a necessary symmetry: the deuce of clubs, three of hearts, four of diamonds, five of hearts, and jack of spades. A potential double-ended straight. He needed a six or an ace, and the odds of getting either weren't good in an ordinary game of five-card draw.

But this was no ordinary game. Lewis had the red ball with him, which meant that he would win regardless of what he did. The red ball made him invincible. He *hoped.*

Gamaliel grinned slyly with his exquisite girl's mouth as he stacked his own hand in front of him, his shadow rustling on the table. "Don't look so smug, Lewis. The bauble can't help you now. Surely you haven't forgotten that I have one, too. The best you can hope for is that our orbs will cancel each other out." He winked. "If I were you, I'd play poker like I've never played it before."

He bet a thousand dollars, and Lewis saw him but didn't raise.

"What happened to your trademark smile, Lewis? And why aren't you raising?"

Lewis discarded his jack and drew the six of hearts, as he knew he would, the capper to a six-high straight. Gamaliel drew one card, glanced at it, and placed it squarely atop his neatly stacked hand.

"With cards like these, I see no need to prolong the agony," he said, his eyes glittering. He shoved his entire supply of chips into the center of the table. "I'll raise you all I have, Lewis. Now that you've lost your smile, I wonder if you've also lost your nerve."

Lewis's heartbeat thudded in his temples. If money had been the issue here, he would have unhesitatingly seen Gamaliel's bet and waited for the showdown. But money wasn't the issue. Josh Nickerson was. Lewis had no intention of surrendering the boy, regardless of how the game ended, but he wondered whether he was strong enough to fight off Gamaliel if he lost. Though he'd become like the beast in so many ways, he had no reason to think he was as strong.

In the motor pool in Vietnam, Gamaliel had drawn one card to complete a full house, jacks over nines. Thanks to the orb, Lewis's six-high straight had become four sixes and a stray five, a winner. The same scene had played itself out against Rex last month. Could the orb deliver a final victory now—against Gamaliel, who owned an orb of his own?

Sweat trickled into Lewis's right eye, the blue one, but he didn't blink. He could feel Josh's worried gaze, but he stared straight ahead into the innocent face of the girl before him, a face that masked a creature beyond human imagination.

"I'll see you and call," Lewis said.

The Gamaliel-girl nodded her pretty head and started turning over her cards one by one. *Ten of hearts, jack of hearts, queen of hearts . . .*

Lewis's pulse became jackhammer rapid. He became dizzy.

. . . king of hearts, ace of hearts. A royal flush. The strongest possible hand in poker. Lewis saw the corners of the girl's mouth widen into a grin. Another droplet of sweat flowed into his eye, blurring the room. He blinked at his own cards, which lay facedown. He fingered the top one and turned it over, saw that it was the nine of spades. The orb had transformed the hand into *something*—that much was evident. But not something that could beat a royal flush. *Nothing* beat a royal flush.

The door opened again, this time to admit a stocky, middle-aged man whose yellow hair was going rapidly gray, what he had left of it. He wore a rumpled business suit that had probably come from K mart and a clip-on tie. "Guy downstairs says there's a game up here," he said with a slow Midwest accent. "Mind if an out-of-towner sits in? Name's Legler. Dan

Legler, out of Grand Island, Nebraska, sheet-metal contracting. My company's bidding on some work up here in Portland, and—''

His eyes connected with Lewis's, and his face lit up.

''Wait a minute,'' he said, walking around the table. ''You look awfully familiar. Are you . . . ? Well, I'll be damned! It's the L.T.! Lieutenant Lewis Kindred, right? Can you believe it, after all these years?'' He clapped Lewis on the back and pumped his hand. ''You sure look different, but I'd recognize you anywhere, L.T. 'Course, I'm probably forty pounds heavier than I was then, and my hair's almost gone, so I shouldn't talk. How the hell are you?''

The door opened again, and through it came T. J. Skane, wearing the same tattered clothes he'd worn when Lewis had last seen him. Same tungsten-filings beard, sunglasses, and a baseball cap with the L.A. Raiders insignia. He grinned when he saw Legler, and threw his arms open wide. The men embraced like two long-lost friends, which they were, one of whom Lewis had watched burn to death; the other having ended up a legless, armless torso lying in the tall grass of the Ho Bo Woods.

And behind them came the osteopath from Beaverton, Dr. Scott Sanders, former medic of the Triple Deuce scout platoon, immaculate in his Brooks Brothers suit.

A reunion of the dead.

Or was it?

For a schizophrenic moment Lewis wondered whether *he* was the one who was dead, and these men were the living. Whether his consciousness had arisen from their remembrances of him. Why shouldn't this be so? Many cultures believed that immortality was possible only as long as the living remembered the dead.

The face of the Camilla-thing contorted in horror, glaring at Lewis as if to burn him with its hatred and condemn him to hell for contriving this trap. Jesse Burton had told Lewis that Gamaliel's kind feared only the dead. And for good reason, Lewis had thought. The dead knew the suffering that

Gamaliel and his species had inflicted on humanity.

Josh reached for Lewis and clutched his arm. "They're your friends from Vietnam, aren't they? They're the guys from the scout platoon. I recognize them from the picture on the wall— T. J., and Scottie and Leg—"

"They're the ones," Lewis said. "They're here to kill Gamaliel, I think."

The Camilla-thing jumped to its feet. "Do you really believe these miserable creatures can kill me?" Camilla began to change, not into the man-thing, Gamaliel, but into something for which human language lacks words. It had scales and razor teeth and vespertilian wings. It had dragon's eyes and tentacles equipped with claws. As its body shifted, it ripped the wine-colored jogging suit to tatters.

It thrust a six-jointed finger at Lewis, pointing, and shouted in a rumbling-lava voice to the gathered members of the scout platoon: "*He's* the one you should turn your anger on. If he'd been a competent commander, you'd all be alive today. You would have the bodies you're now enjoying for these few moments. You would have families, friends, and *lives*, if Lieutenant Lewis Kindred hadn't been so obsessed with killing me that he forgot about taking care of *you*!"

Lewis fought panic, because he knew that this was true. The dead of the scout platoon had come to help him, but Gamaliel had turned them against him with the truth.

"Know the truth," roared Gamaliel, laughing, "and the truth will set you free!"

The newly arrived veterans of the scout platoon began to change. Scottie Sanders developed a hump on his back that split the seams of his suit, and maggots wriggled out of his eyes. Danny Legler's face turned green and bulged with putrefactive gases, his silver-blond hair falling from his head in gobs. The skin of T. J. Skane's cheeks stretched tight as the flesh beneath it fizzled away, and his long hands twisted into claws. Lewis understood now that he, like Gamaliel, had much to fear from the dead. He'd become one of Gamaliel's kind, hadn't he?

Behind them, in the rectangle of the door, appeared Sergeant First Class Frank Markowski, beetle-browed and bristle-scalped, militarily correct except for the fact that a third of his skull was gone and a goodly portion of his brain had oozed all over his jungle fatigues. He grinned savagely with his bad teeth, a Pall Mall stuck straight to his lower lip. He pointed his M-60 machine gun at Lewis.

"I've waited a long fuckin' time for this!" he roared. "Thanks to this little puke, I didn't live to see my fuckin' grandkids born. I say, let's give him a taste of what we got because of him. Let's see how he likes being deader than a dinosaur dick."

Lewis expected a blizzard of 7.62-millimeter rounds in his face, and he would have welcomed an opportunity to die like a mortal man. But he couldn't let them hurt Josh. Josh deserved no piece of this hell.

He leaped to his feet, facing the advancing foursome of dead things. "Don't hurt *him*!" he pleaded over the roar of Gamaliel's laughter. "He never did anything to any of you. I'm the one who failed you, damn it! Don't you understand? If you need to kill someone, kill *me*!"

viii

For a blinding moment Josh was certain that these living nightmares would kill Lewis, and himself, too. But he felt a tug on a remote corner of his mind, a gentle probe. Light erupted behind his eyes, and his ears rang with the reverberations of Paul Tran's lacquered box.

ix

Paul Tran lay in the darkness of his bedroom, alone. He'd sent his wife away because he didn't want her to see what might happen to him tonight. He couldn't know whether he would survive the ordeal that he'd prepared so long to face.

He'd dredged up creatures from the darkest depths of human beings' minds, and he had no control over them. For all he knew, they might sense his telepathic connection and blast through it to this room. And then they might tear him to pieces.

He clutched the lacquered box to his chest, even though the marble inside it had abruptly ceased its thrumming. The time for warning was past. The time for battle had come.

The ceiling of the bedroom was like a movie screen, though in actuality the images moved in his mind's eye, unfettered by distance or physical barriers. The scene was the card room in the Hotel Fanshawe, where Lewis Kindred and Josh Nickerson faced a gathering of hell-things that at any moment might rip them limb from limb.

Earlier tonight, Tran had willed himself into a trance, using the regimen prescribed many years ago by an old Cao Dai priest. The trance had let him touch the minds of Lewis and Josh, and even the mind of Gamaliel. Using energies he'd honed through decades of meditation, he'd probed the layers that held the common memories of men long dead, and he'd roused them to life. Now he beheld the visions of Legler, Skane, and Sanders. And out of some deep mental well had crawled a thing named Markowski, a profane and meanhearted man who'd loathed Lewis Kindred in life and loathed him even more intensely now.

Had Lewis's guilty conscience roused the memory of Markowski and given it life, or had Gamaliel summoned him from Lewis's mind, needing an ally? Tran couldn't possibly know.

He *did* know, however, that Lewis and Josh were in mortal danger. The cause Tran had taken for himself so long ago was about to end in bloody fury. The scent of pending defeat was foul, and he damned his crippled body, made this way by the touch of the orb to his forehead.

He wished Jesse Burton was here. Jesse would've served as his arms and legs. Jesse would've joined minds with him, supplying him with precious psychic energy to fight the battle over the physical distance between the Hotel Fanshawe and this house. But Jesse wasn't here. Gamaliel had killed him, and Tran was alone.

He heard the door of the bedroom squeak, and thought at first that his wife had returned. He drew breath to rebuke her, but held back. A presence moved into the room with a crinkling of plastic, a masculine thing, hulking and black. Tran's skin prickled and his throat went dry.

"Who are you?" he asked. "What do you want?"

"Look beyond the known," answered a familiar voice. "Turn your heart both inward and outward. Inhale the message that seeks you."

A light snapped on, and beside the bed stood Jesse Burton, draped in a clear-plastic sheet of the kind used to cover bodies in morgues. His own autopsy had taken place already, and spatters of blood and other body fluids were visible on the plastic. He smiled sadly, and blood trickled down the side of his face from the wound on his head.

"Jesse, is it really you—or has my mind become as weak as my body?"

"Silly question coming from you, Paul. But let's not waste time. Lewis and Josh need you."

Tran sank against his pillow, depleted, his flesh sallow. "I fear I've done all I can for them. I have nothing left to give."

"That's not true. We can do more."

"*We?* You're dead, Jesse. And I'm to blame for bringing this calamity to you."

Jesse took his hand, hauled him up roughly. "Put on your clothes, man. You and I are going out on a combat mission. And bring this along." He took the lacquered box from him, opened it, and found the marble inside. It was no longer red glass. The marble had turned to silver.

"I don't understand. I—"

"Trust me, okay? We dead folks know some things you don't."

"But I'm a cripple, Jesse."

"Don't worry—I'll drive. I'll give you the strength to do what you need to do."

Tran pulled off his pajamas and began to dress, surprising himself that he could even move.

X

Out of the light came Nicole, her raven hair shining, her eyes glistening with excitement. She smiled at Josh and handed him something, a silver orb. The thing was too brilliant to look at directly, but once it settled into the palm of his hand, he knew that it was *power*. Prickling with the newly found energy, he reached out for Lewis, touched him, and Lewis's bleary eyes came alive.

Jesse Burton stepped into the room, tall and strong in faded jungle fatigues. Bandoliers of ammo crisscrossed his chest, and a peace symbol hung from his neck. He pointed his M-16 at the ceiling and fired a full clip on fully automatic, pulverizing acoustical tiles and causing a rain of plaster. Skane, Sanders, Legler, and Markowski instantly evaporated into membranous squiggles of light.

Its allies gone, the Gamaliel creature turned on Jesse, but Jesse caught it by its scaly throat before it could raise a claw against him. Tingling with the power of the silver orb, Josh and Lewis joined the fray, scrambling over the poker table. Josh ignored the pain in his shattered leg, wanting only to lay his killing hands on Gamaliel.

Together they fought the thing, Josh and Lewis and Jesse. And Nicole, too. Their ears rang with the rumbling of the lacquer box as they fought, as they tore out Gamaliel's eyes and heart, as they crushed his sinewy neck in their hands and beat in his skull with their fists. The Gamaliel creature was powerful, but his mortal enemies—the dead—were stronger. The thing disintegrated into gray flakes as it died, seeping through their fingers into a pile on the floor, and when it was over, a wind from somewhere blew the flakes away.

Josh fell against the card table, gasping, and Lewis lay hunched beside him, his face slick, his cheeks wet. They were alone, the two of them. Jesse and Nicole weren't here. Maybe never had been.

But someone else was: Paul Tran. He leaned against the doorjamb like a man drained of life or the will to live it, holding the empty lacquered box in his hand. Josh saw him first and called out to him, and Tran nodded, even smiled. But when Lewis looked up with his mismatched eyes, Tran lost his smile.

"Thank you," Lewis whispered hoarsely. "I'm sorry, Sergeant Hai. I'm sorry for doubting you, for suspecting—"

"You have nothing to be sorry for," Tran interrupted. "You're a good man. You've always done your best."

"I *was* a good man. Not anymore." Lewis waved his arm so that his shadow rustled on the carpet. "This is what I am now."

"No," said Tran, his voice pinching. "There's hope for you, Lewis, but you must act quickly. You know what you must do, don't you?"

Lewis bit his lower lip. "Yes, but I don't think—"

"*Do* it. Josh and I will help you."

Lewis and Tran carried Josh to his wheelchair and lowered him gently into it. Josh caught a fistful of Lewis's flowered western shirt and held tight, not letting him go. "First I want to see your cards, Lewis."

"Why? You saw Gamaliel's. Nothing beats a royal flush."

"But you had more than the red ball working for you. You had this." He held up the silver orb in his other hand, and its ghostly light danced against their faces. "Please, Lewis. Let me see them."

Lewis steered the chair around the table where his poker hand lay facedown, except for the nine of spades. The boy picked up a card and turned it over—the nine of diamonds. The next was the nine of hearts. Then came the nine of clubs.

Lewis sniffed. "Not a bad hand, considering. Too bad that four of a kind doesn't beat a royal flush." He managed a chuckle. "Ever see such bad luck in your life?"

"But there's one left," said Josh.

"A stray, that's all, worthless as a fifth wheel."

Josh turned it over, and when Lewis saw it, his breath went out of him. The card was a nine, but its suit was a new one, symbolized by a glistening red ball that contained swarms of alive-looking matter. What was this—the nine of *orbs*?

"I don't believe it," Lewis whispered, staring at it. "I've never seen . . ."

"It's a nine! You had five nines, Lewis! Don't you see what it means?"

"But it's impossible to have five of a kind. There are only four suits, for crying out loud."

Paul Tran's face tightened with urgency. "Now you understand, don't you? There's hope, Lewis, because the rules have changed. We've changed them—you and Jesse and I."

"You sent this," said Josh, holding up the silver orb. "You sent Nicki, too."

Tran smiled. "I sent symbols," he said. "Only symbols and memories. You and Lewis turned them into weapons."

Tommy Iadanza burst into the card room, his basset-hound eyes round with disbelief. He surveyed the ruined ceiling and clapped both hands to his head. "Who in the hell shot up the place, for Christ's sake? I've got guests in this hotel. . . . !" He saw the condition of Josh and Lewis, and forgot about the damage. "Lewis, there was an artist's sketch in the *Oregonian* a couple of weeks ago. You might've seen it—a guy who killed a girl in the Metro Plaza. He looked a hell of a lot like you. I strongly suggest that you get out of here before the cops arrive, or you're likely to end up in the Multnomah County lockup, booked on suspicion of murder."

xi

Lewis pushed Josh in his wheelchair along the pedestrian walkway of the Hawthorne Bridge, which was a lacework of dirty yellow lights. Paul Tran stumbled after them. Lewis halted at the midpoint and stared down at the bleak Willamette River, searching silently for something he couldn't name. Chilly rain fell, and a passing car whipped up spray that stung their necks. None of the three said anything for a long while.

"What happened back there?" Josh asked suddenly. "Where did the guys from your platoon come from?"

"I don't honestly know, Josh. If I were to guess, I'd say from inside our own heads. Paul might've had something to do with it." Tran leaned against the rail and kept silent. Lewis figured that he'd finally begun to mourn his dead Nicole.

"Like he empowered us, or something?" offered Josh. "Maybe cast a spell?"

"It could've been that. Or maybe he reached out to us with his mind and opened up mental pathways that neither us of knew were available to us. Maybe he gave us the ability to project our memories into the mind of someone else."

"Gamaliel, you mean. We projected out memories of dead people into Gamaliel's head, and we made them do what we wanted them to." Josh mulled this extraordinary notion a moment. Then: "But Gamaliel turned your own guys against you, Lewis."

"I think what he did, Josh, was turn me against myself. He preyed on my guilt. He knew I'd been a lousy platoon leader, and I'd gotten a bunch of good guys killed. He pointed this out to T. J. and Scottie and Leg, because he thought they were real. But what he really did was lay the guilt on me."

"So your mind changed those guys into—into something ugly? Is that what you're saying?"

"I changed them into things that wanted revenge against me, and I might've let them have it if Jesse hadn't come back."

"Jesse came back to you, and Nicki came back to me. They came back to us because we needed them."

"Yeah. If I were a betting man"—he winked, and Josh caught it—"I'd say that old Paul Tran here gave us the power to *call forth the dead* from our own minds."

"But what about Gamaliel? He was real, right? And Millie, and Camilla? They certainly didn't come out of our minds."

"Oh, they were real, all right. As real as you and I are. But the evil that they did is *human* evil, Josh—the darkest kind, yes, but no worse than the stuff we read about in the papers every day. There's no shortage of sicko butchers out there. Hell, I've been one myself."

Josh braced his forehead braced against the handrail. "Why are there bullet holes in the ceiling of that room? If Jesse wasn't actually there, how was he able to shoot up the place?"

"Guessing again, I'd say that either or both of us engaged in something called psychokinesis. Ever hear of it?"

"It's the ability to move stuff with your mind. You don't have to touch something physically."

"Right. To my knowledge, no one has ever demonstrated it in a laboratory, but it might explain the damage in the card room. If I were you, that's what I'd choose to believe, because the alternative is to believe in—"

"That's what I choose to believe," Josh said.

They contemplated the blackness of the river for a few moments, and the rain actually let up a little.

"It's good having two legs, Josh," Lewis said. "I'd forgotten *how* good But I can't afford them."

"What do you mean?"

"The price is too high. I don't have what it takes."

"But you're not like Gamaliel, Lewis. You're good inside. That must count for something."

"Maybe it does. But the fact is, I chose the orb, and I used it. I let Millie use me. And then I actually killed people, and''—He swallowed, shored himself up—''I'm standing here on two good legs. I feel—''

Paul Tran's voice cut through the traffic noise and the rain. ''Throw the orbs away—both of them! Do it now, while you're still able!''

Lewis glanced at him, this former enemy. The man he'd misunderstood so terribly for so long. Tran stared back at him, his hair slickened with rain, his clothes sopping. ''There's hope for you, Lewis. I can feel it. But you must throw the orb away. You, too, Josh. Throw the silver one after Lewis's.''

''But Nicki gave it to me,'' Josh protested. ''I can't just—''

''You *must*! Do it now—for Lewis's sake.''

Lewis moved to the railing, reached into the pocket of his jeans, and took out the orb Millie had given him, which in this light seemed nothing more than harmless glass. Josh took out the silver one given him by Nicole, and it, too, looked commonplace, less lustrous than it had looked back at the Fanshawe. Each held his orb for a moment, wondering, hoping. Each looked the other in the eyes, then looked to Tran for encouragement.

''For the last time,'' Lewis said, and he hauled his arm back. He hurled the thing into the night, and Josh did the same. Seconds later, light burst over the water as one of the orbs consumed the other, and sparks showered downward. Josh followed the sparks with his eyes until they winked out many stories below.

Lewis suddenly lurched against the rail of the bridge and sat down hard, as if someone had knocked his pins out from under him. His legs withered away, leaving the cuffs of his Levi's limp and empty. Even in the mist, his eyes shone an even gray, no longer mismatched.

They wept together there on the Hawthorne Bridge, the three of them huddled together in the rain, while passing cars and trucks bombarded them with spray. After a long while Tommy Iadanza arrived in his Taurus and parked next to the walkway, his emergency flashers blinking. "You guys look like you need a lift," he called to them.

"That would be nice," Lewis replied. "I don't have any money on me, but I can give you a nice pair of cowboy boots." He held up a black Justin and poured rainwater from it.

"Sold," said Tommy, and he got out to help them into the car.